THE GIRL IN GREEN

by the same author

NORWEGIAN BY NIGHT

THE GIRL IN GREEN

DEREK B. MILLER

FABER & FABER

For my wife

_____

First published in the UK in 2016
by Faber & Faber Limited
Bloomsbury House
74–77 Great Russell Street
London WC1B 3DA

First published in Australia and New Zealand in 2016
by Scribe, 18–20 Edward St
Brunswick, Victoria 3056

Printed in the UK by CPI Group (UK) Ltd, Croydon CR0 4YY

The right of Derek B. Miller to be identified as author of this
work has been asserted in accordance with Section 77 of the
Copyright, Designs and Patents Act 1988

A CIP record for this book
is available from the British Library

ISBN 978–0–571–31395–2

2 4 6 8 10 9 7 5 3 1

CONTENTS

Inspired by many actual events

PART I

AN
EARLY
SPRING

1991

1

Arwood Hobbes was bored. Not regular-bored. Not your casual, rainy-day, *Cat in the Hat*–style bored that arrives with the wet, leaving you with nothing to do. It wasn't post-fun or pre-excitement bored, either. It was, somehow, different. It felt rare and deliberate, entire and complete, industrial and inescapable. It was the kind of bored that had you backstroking in the green mist of eternity wondering about the big questions without searching for answers. And it wasn't in short supply, either, because it was being dispensed like candy on Halloween to Arwood and others like him at Checkpoint Zulu, at the rim of the Euphrates valley, in the heart of Iraq, by the world's largest contractor of boredom: the United States Army.

How long had he been bored? How long was he destined to be bored? Arwood couldn't even muster the motivation to care as he melted over his machine gun under the hot, hot sun that was pressing down on the sandy sand around him without a raindrop in sight and no one offering to cheer him up.

The M60 machine gun was the perfect height for leaning on. It was probably the perfect height for firing, too, but Arwood had no proof of that because he hadn't fired the gun since qualifying on it, and there was nothing to aim at because everything was far away, apart from a camel; and while he did point the gun at the camel for a while, it ultimately seemed a mean thing to do, so he stopped. That was eons ago. Nothing fun like that had happened since. Even the camel had gone away.

It wasn't that Arwood was unfamiliar with being bored and that his resistance was low. After all, Operation Desert Storm—now over—had really been just a month-long air campaign on exposed Iraqi troops, followed by a four-day ground war, which meant there wasn't a lot of ground war for him or his buddies, or much for people on the ground to actually do. For Arwood, the Gulf War primarily involved him doing a lot of nothing for three months, in the sand, jogging expectantly beside an APC with his gun for a few days, only to be told it was 'over'. But at least back then there had been a sense that something might happen. There was a sense of possibility.

Not anymore.

Possibility was but a popped balloon for Arwood.

And at the very moment they were all expected to go home, his company drew the shortest of short straws and they'd been deployed here to Checkpoint Zulu, 240 kilometres from the Kuwaiti border. He had no idea why. This time there was nothing to look forward to but peace. Endless, tedious, nondescript, fluffy-white peace.

You could eat a grenade, you really could.

It was into this stagnant vortex of quietude and for-nothingness that a form approached Arwood from across the desert.

Like everything else in Iraq, it came at him sideways.

Arwood didn't look. He sort of liked not knowing. Perhaps it was a guy wearing sandals who had a beard like Jesus. Or maybe it wasn't a man at all. Maybe it was the Ghost of Christmas Yet to Come, who was doing his rounds and was there to let Arwood know that—on account of global warming, acid rain, and El Niño, not to mention the global shortage of decent people and the high price of coal—Christmas was going to be cancelled.

Whatever it was was getting bigger, which probably meant it was getting closer. It probably wasn't something dangerous, though; it was approaching from this side of the ceasefire line. But it wasn't going to be anything good, either. It wasn't going to be one of

Charlie's Angels. It wasn't going to be Daisy Duke. It wasn't going to be Kelly LeBrock in her blue-and-white panties appearing out of red mist from a doorway. No, it was probably going to be orders.

A different mind, a different person, might have welcomed orders because it would have ushered in 'change'. Not Arwood. The only thing worse than boredom was labour, and he didn't want to wash anything, dig anything, move anything, stack anything, fill anything, load anything, unload anything, peel anything, or — and this was critical — smell anything awful. Given that he was twenty-two and a private, rather than, say, fifty and a nuclear physicist, all these things were on the shortlist of the possible.

No, he wasn't going to look up. He would cherish the uncertainty for as long as he could.

Which fate had decided would end right ... about ... now.

'Want a cigarette?' asked a man who was now man-sized and to his right.

The man stood next to Arwood's sandbags. Arwood considered them his sandbags, not so much because he was manning a machine gun behind them, as because he was the one who had filled them.

Arwood accepted the cigarette by opening his mouth. The man placed it in and lit it. Arwood inhaled, grateful only that it gave him a pretext to keep breathing.

'I'm Thomas Benton,' the man said.

'Uh-huh.'

'What's your name?'

'Arwood Hobbes.'

'Hobbes. Interesting name to take into a war zone.'

'Why?'

'No reason. Where are you from?'

'America.'

'Yes, I figured, given the uniform. Any place special?'

'Never felt like it.'

'I'm from a village in Cornwall,' Benton offered.

'I don't know where that is.'

'Cornwall is in England.'

'That's overseas, right?'

'Yes.'

Thomas Benton squatted down behind Arwood's sandbags because it was cool and shady there. Benton looked across the desert to the still town a kilometre and a half away.

'You're a journalist?'

'Yes. The *Times*.'

Arwood did not move from his resting position. 'When is this war gonna end?'

'What?'

'The war.'

'It did. The war is over. This is the peace. Now the lawyers are drafting the UN permanent-ceasefire resolution.'

'We're waiting for paperwork?'

'It's the Western way of war. Even Hitler filed his paperwork. Without it we become confused. What's your job?'

'I'm maintaining a vigilant perimeter.'

'Safwan,' Benton said, 'if you're curious, is way back there. That's where your general, Stormin' Norman, met the Iraqi high command. It is also where he made the mistake of letting them fly helicopters, which is what they are using to kill everyone connected to the uprisings down south and up north. It's a bloodbath.'

'I thought that was Safwan,' Arwood said, not bothering to motion to the town at the end of his machine gun.

'That's Samawah.'

'When do I get to go home?'

'The Americans are the ones sticking around the longest, though some of you shipped out on the seventeenth. It could be a while.'

Arwood finally moved his head by shaking it. 'It's not fair that we have to sit around here like the Breakfast Club.'

Benton shrugged and wiped his face with a red bandana. He was not smoking. He had eaten something in the morning that disagreed with him, and he'd opted not to push his luck further with a cigarette.

'It might not be calm for long. You should try and enjoy it.'

Arwood perked up. 'What do you mean?'

'Doesn't your commanding officer explain all this to you?'

'You mean Harvey?'

'I don't know his name.'

'Lieutenant Harvey Morgan. No, he doesn't explain anything. He's full of shit, and never makes sense because he keeps reading quotes from the government, and they speak in riddles. What do you mean it won't be calm for long?'

'The Iraqi civil war. It'll have to get here eventually. You see that green flag over there? On top of that onion-shaped water tower?' Benton pointed to a tower in the middle of the town.

'Yeah. If you watch it really, really closely for hours, it sometimes moves,' Arwood said.

'It's a Shiite flag. That means they've overthrown the Sunni government in the city. It's only a matter of time before Saddam sends troops here to change that back.'

'Uh-huh.'

'You're actually in the eye of a storm. You are the American soldier deepest in Iraqi territory. Did you know that?'

'Why are you here?' Arwood asked. 'At my post?'

'The view, mainly. It's as close as I can get without crossing the demarcation line. I'm embedded in your company. I've been reporting on what's been happening with your fellows.'

'Which is nothing.'

'Well, there was the mass surrender.'

'Yeah. That was fun.'

Arwood had enjoyed the mass surrender. Once the war reached

its tipping point, all the Iraqi soldiers gave up. A French journalist had reported that Saddam had forbidden his soldiers to wear white underwear lest they use it to surrender. Arwood had wondered about the mechanics of that. Usually you surrender in really dire circumstances, which is not when you want to be taking your pants off.

Arwood had become chatty with the POWs when they flowed to his location in late February. That was much farther south, and before they were deployed here. There was a certain affability to the Iraqi conscripts. Sure, they were the enemy and all that, but their accent was endearing, every one of them had a Groucho Marx moustache, and they were incredibly sincere about their desire to give up. There was very little not to like about them once they stopped shooting at you.

'There's nothing happening now, though,' Arwood said.

'Not here. But there is over there. And the world would like to know what it is. Or at least I'd like to think they would.'

'Is being English the same as being British?' Arwood asked.

'No. England is part of Britain. Which is also made up of Wales and—'

'So who banned all that music?'

It didn't connect until now, because Arwood had never met anyone British before, but word had gotten down to the troops that their allies — the British — were banning anti-war music back home, and so a good deal of time was spent ragging on them about it in their absence. On the BBC's blackout list were:

'We Gotta Get Out of This Place', by The Animals;
'Walk Like an Egyptian', by The Bangles;
'Killing Me Softly', by Roberta Flack;
'Two Tribes', by Frankie Goes to Hollywood;
'War', by Edwin Starr; and
'Everybody Wants to Rule the World', by Tears for Fears.

'That was you, right?' Arwood said.

'It was the BBC.'

'They really thought a bunch of straight dudes were gonna sing Roberta Flack in the desert?'

'What you have to understand about the BBC—'

'So you're sitting here with me because you want this civil war thing to get started, and you want a front-row seat?'

'Well, no. That's not fair,' Benton said. 'I do have questions, though. The kind that can only be answered over there,' he said, pointing to Samawah. 'Right now, no one knows anything. We're getting our news from radio broadcasts coming out of Iran and Syria. It's all ignorance, rumour, and frustration. I'd like to ask them some questions of my own.'

'Like what?'

'Like what? Really? Well, like … Did you plan this revolution? Are you getting support from Iran? Who is in charge? What are your aspirations? Do you want to see a whole and stable Iraq, or do you want a new state and to see it carved up along religious and ethnic lines? Or no state at all? Is this the return of the Islamic *umma*? Can you work with the Sunni after the way you were treated by Saddam? Are you prepared to cooperate with the West? Under what conditions? Are you coordinating with the Kurdish resistance up north? If so, how? Is there a unified command structure? Do you see yourself forming one? How well armed are you? What kind of training—'

'Yeah, OK, political stuff. I got it.'

'It's the future of the Middle East. In fact, it's the future of the post-Cold War order. In that town, in the ideas of those people, are the first clues about whether this brave new world of ours will maintain the colonially imposed and Cold War–sustained state system, or—'

'Do Arabs eat ice-cream?'

'That's the question burning a hole in your mind?'

'I have a follow-up.'

'Yes. They do.'

'What kind of ice-cream?'

'The usual stuff. Why?'

'I want one.'

'OK,' said Benton.

'And I've got an idea that I was thinking up while you were talking. You want to report on all that political stuff from that town, right?'

'I suppose I do, yes.'

'I want an ice-cream, and you said they probably have one there.'

'You think it's a good idea for me to go to the town and get you an ice-cream?'

'You sort of implied you might be going.'

Benton sat in the sand. He dug grooves in the earth with the heels of his boots. He'd been in the region since 28 February, the day President Bush declared this 'a victory for the United Nations, for all mankind, for the rule of law, and for what is right'. Benton's wife, Vanessa, had argued it was not a good day to leave her or their ten-year-old daughter, Charlotte, behind. Given that the war was over, she'd said, there was no good reason to be there, and it was dangerous. He'd said questions remained that no one was asking, because victory is always exciting and therefore wasn't when people probed for details. He'd said he'd be back in a few weeks. A visit into a rebel-held city — even for a few hours — could justify the cost.

Benton looked across the windless landscape to the listless Shiite flag. Something significant had already happened there, and something else was going to. He was sure of it. Saddam had forbidden journalists to enter the country, but so what? He was shy of his fortieth birthday and hadn't won any prizes. It was impressive to be at the *Times*, but he was among the rank and file, and he'd never distinguished himself. A visit to Samawah could change all that.

It was an interesting idea.

There was a downside to the plan, though, and being almost forty rather than in his early twenties, like Arwood, Benton still had some reverence for the wider systems of authority and power that made his journalism possible. You fall out with those, and you're out. He was talking to Arwood to manipulate the situation, yes, but he was still on the edge about whether to walk the literal mile.

'I was told not to wander off base, or I'd lose my press credentials,' he said.

Arwood field-stripped his spent cigarette and flicked the pieces into what should have been wind.

'If you follow the rules all the time, you don't really have any press credentials, do you?'

'Huh,' said Benton.

'It is my experience — and I learned this the hard way, believe me — that the trick to getting what you want without getting caught — and this is the important part — is not getting caught.'

'And how do you do that?' Benton asked.

'I just told you. Don't get caught.'

'That feels a bit circular.'

Arwood never took his eyes off the distant buildings and the absolute nothing that was happening over in the town. Now that he had the idea of an ice-cream firmly planted in his mind — which was seeping down into his very soul and filling it with strawberries — he could picture swarms of ten-year-olds suddenly bursting into the corner store and tearing open every remaining Popsicle, leaving nothing for him but sticky wrappers. It was a dark image.

'I have this theory that everything you truly need to know,' Arwood said, 'I mean, deep down and for the duration, can be learned from *Ferris Bueller's Day Off.* The fact that there was no sequel only proves that there was nothing left to say. To me, the army is Principal Ed Rooney, and you need to be Ferris.'

'If I go, you won't tell anyone?'

'I'm not paid to keep you in. I'm paid to keep them out.'

'They don't have Ben and Jerry's. Mostly Popsicles. Also they might not have any. There were economic sanctions after Kuwait was invaded, and there's been a war since. And it could melt by the time I'm back.'

'I'm prepared for you to take that risk.'

'Are you sure you'll be there when I return? I don't want to get shot as I approach the checkpoint. How's your eyesight?'

'Come back the way you came. I'll be here all day. Same bat time, same bat channel.'

'I don't have any money,' Benton said.

'No charge, dude.'

'No, for the ice-cream. I need to buy it. I'm not going to steal an ice-cream, am I?'

'I ... hadn't considered that,' said Arwood. 'You don't think he'll be friendly, and give you one?'

'He might, but it's presumptuous. I think it's inappropriate to ask, and if he gives me a gift it's customary practice that I return the gesture with a gift of my own.'

'It really is like a whole different place over here, isn't it?' Arwood was no longer leaning on the gun. He had perked up like a flower exposed to sunlight at the thought of an ice-cream. 'I don't have any money either. What kind of gift?'

'Something of the same value and significance as an ice-cream, otherwise he'll feel further in my debt and want to even things out, which is not what we want here,' Benton said.

'OK ...' Arwood bent down and pulled a comic book from his rucksack. 'How about this Amazing Spider-Man #312, Green Goblin versus the Hobgoblin? It's from 1989, and I paid a buck. It isn't current, but the trade is only for an ice-cream, so I think it's fair. There's got to be some kid over there who hasn't read it yet.'

'I don't know if they read comic books.'

'Jesus. How foreign are they?'

'Fine, give it to me,' said Benton, who stood up, dusted himself off, and put the comic book in his own rucksack, beside his camera and incidentals.

'So you're going?'

'It's half-twelve now …'

'Huh?'

'It's twelve-thirty now,' Benton translated, 'and I figure I can walk there in half an hour, spend about three hours or so interviewing, and be back by four o'clock, which is well before dark. You're sure you'll still be here?'

'I'm on until eighteen hundred.'

'I really don't want to get shot coming back.'

'I will not let anything happen to you. I promise.'

'All right then. *Audaces fortuna iuvat*, right?' said Benton.

'I don't know about that, but Ferris got Mia Sara.'

2

Benton drank from a bottle of water as he walked toward Samawah under the blue dome of heaven. His feet were hot. He wore cheap socks that were woven with nylon and polyester. He knew better, but had still done nothing about it when it came time to pack. They couldn't breathe as he stepped from rock to rock across the broken earth toward the squat city and its muted people. This always put him in a mood.

Closer, he found the small city unremarkable. He might have been in Jordan, or the West Bank, or Bahrain as he looked at the flat roofs and the canopy of satellite dishes made dirty from the sand and the winds and the absence of rain or the social pressure to clean them. Around the city was its litter — the discarded refrigerators and tyres, the bed frames and canvas bags. There was no topsoil. There was surely a proper reason for this, but Benton imagined that too many feet had walked here for too long in search of too much.

He approached a derelict oil truck in a wide and unused parking zone. Someone had painted, in giant white letters, 'We want Fredum. Bleads help Iraq peple.'

Benton put the empty bottle of water back into his satchel, intending to throw it in a bin later.

He checked his watch. *Dhuhr* prayer was around 11.30 a.m., and *Asr* prayer shouldn't be until around three-ish. He figured he had a workable window to get oriented and at least conduct a few discussions.

Towns have eyes in the Middle East. This one, however, felt blind — as though it were resting in the midday sun in preparation for a long stretch of work in the cooling night yet to come.

A boy appeared. He was thin, about twelve years old, and carrying a platter of glasses of tea over his shoulder like a French waiter. The boy wore sandals and had thick black hair. He was unhurried, and focussed on his task of delivering tea and lunch to the shopkeepers.

When the boy saw Benton, he stopped and fixed himself to the earth, paralysed. Eyes wide, he was motionless until an inner force shot into his limbs, making him jerk erratically. He twitched his head right and left and back to Benton, as though Benton might issue instructions that would end his indecision. Benton could hear the glasses rattle on the thin, silver platter as they amplified the boy's vibrations and started dancing to the arrhythmia of his heart. Soon enough, the cups could not keep up. One by one, the cups fell, smashing themselves on the hard earth, and the sweet water poured from the platter onto the boy's feet, scalding his exposed toes and forcing the boy to join in the dance he had inadvertently started.

Hopping in pain, the boy dropped the platter, and he turned and ran as fast as he could, back the way he had come.

Not loudly enough, not by a long shot, Benton called out, 'I'm not going to hurt you. I promise.'

But the promise never reached the boy's ears, and in a moment he was gone.

Alone again, Benton trudged toward the first buildings and into a narrow alley between them. It was shadier between the buildings, and cooler. He paused to scratch one foot with the other through his leather boots. It was unsatisfying. He'd have to take the boot off, and perhaps the sock as well.

Kneeling with his shoe untied, Benton heard a rumbling ahead of him, through the mouth of the light and narrow alley. It sounded like water. It was an impossible notion, but he half expected a tidal wave to come bursting into the passageway, a crest of salty white foam gushing around him to his waist, to flood his boots and cool his feet.

It was only when they were almost upon him that he understood the sound as a wave of human voices, foreign and excited.

His shoe tied, he stood and looked back, unconvinced by either choice of staying or going. The choice was made for him as he deliberated. They poured in as a flood to a *wadi*. They were silhouetted by the bright light of the Iraqi sun, and in that moment they overtook him and drowned him. Hands gripped him, and he shielded his face as people started pulling him, surrounding him, and pushing him out into the city. They called and yelled in Arabic. His bag was pulled from his shoulder, and he was no longer sure of anything at all.

He shouted for them to wait, but his voice failed him for the second time in Samawah. There were too many people, and too much emotion. When his head struck something hard, he fell to the ground.

Benton did not pass out. He was, however, bloodied and incapacitated. Two men were holding him up. They smelled bad. Their shirts were made of cotton and were sweaty. He couldn't see their faces. There was blood in his eyes. It came from his head. He raised a hand to find the source. He was pulled into a building and then pushed into a chair. There was a voice.

'American?'

Benton couldn't see who'd asked the question. The man was standing too close. The smell of all the people was overpowering. The sunlight was poking through the spaces around the man's face and through the shoulders of those around him.

'American?' the man said.

'I'm British,' Benton said.

'American?'

'British, for Christ's sake.'

'English?'

'Yes, yes. I can't breathe.'

The dark face in front of him yelled something in Arabic and then stood up, pushing the other people back. He shushed the people around him, bringing silence, order, and calm.

He handed Benton a cloth and a bottle of water.

'Thank you,' Benton said.

'Who are you?'

'I'm Thomas Benton. I'm a journalist with the *Times*. I'm here to understand what's happened and to learn what you're all going to do next. I'm … I'm hurt. I don't want to upset anyone or get anyone else hurt. Can we talk?'

There was mumbling and then Benton said, 'Do you speak English?'

'Yes, yes. Everyone speaks English. Everyone-everyone. You are not American? You are not here to help us?'

'No. I'm a journalist.'

In the quiet and uninterrupted moment that followed, Benton was able to look around and see where he was.

He wasn't in a cave dwelling or an Iraqi torture chamber. He wasn't even in a boxy apartment with barred windows and a dubbed Western television set playing in the background. He was in a pharmacy—a pharmacy that stocked L'Oréal hair products and Halls lozenges, and was having a twenty per cent–off sale on reading glasses if you used 1.50 magnification and didn't mind wearing orange.

The man who had been too close stood back and pulled a white plastic chair across the concrete floor. Sitting, he rubbed his face with a tissue and placed it in his jacket pocket.

'What is going to happen to Saddam?' the man said.

'I beg your pardon?' Benton said, wiping his own face with his red bandana.

'Saddam. We need to know what you are going to do with Saddam. What is our future?'

'I came here to ask you the same question.'

The man shook his head. No. This made no sense to him.

'You have an army. Big army. You drive Saddam out of Kuwait. OK. Now what? You take Saddam away?'

'Well … no.'

'Why not?'

'The international coalition was formed to restore Kuwait and secure the borders.'

'OK, OK, but the problem is Saddam. We fought a war with Iran, then Kuwait, then America. Always war because of Saddam. So … now it's time to get rid of Saddam, yes?'

'Isn't that what you're doing?' Benton asked. He felt a cut on his head. 'Why did someone hit me?'

'No, no. Sorry, your head hit the wall. People were very excited to get news. You are a journalist. So … you have news.'

'No. I'm here to get the news from you, and report it in Britain.'

'They don't need the news. We need the news. Are you going to get rid of Saddam?'

'It's our understanding,' Benton tried to explain, 'that you're having a revolution. That you're getting rid of Saddam. I'm here to understand your plans. You've already taken the city. There's a Shiite flag on the water tank. Are you being supported by Iran? Are you hoping—'

Another man, wearing the white coat of a pharmacist, interjected. Benton didn't understand what he said, but the crowd started to disperse, and the man he'd been speaking with nodded, stood up from his chair, tapped the arms of a few people, and then walked out.

The pharmacist looked at Benton's wound. 'I told them we were not being good hosts, that you need some help first, and that we can discuss this all over some food and tea. Clearly, you want to talk to us, and we want to talk to you. We should do it properly. Times are very delicate. Very delicate. I can tell you this, though: the answers to the questions you are asking don't exist yet. I was educated as a chemist. In chemistry, the answers are out there, waiting to be found. But in life, in politics, in war, the answers aren't there yet. Your whole profession has a very strange theory in the middle.'

'My head hurts,' said Benton, not only feeling a throbbing in his head but starting to hear it, too.

'I'll get you some aspirin, unless you're allergic. The Republican Guard took most of it. We have a few left. I'd like to put a bandage on you, too.'

'Yes. Fine. Thank you.'

The pharmacist shooed people out of the shop on his way to a small cabinet. He used a tiny key to unlock it, and removed a white plastic bottle.

'How are you?' Benton asked.

'How am I?' he said.

'Yes. How are you?'

'Worried. Very, very worried. But thank you for asking.'

The pharmacist was pressing down on the childproof cap when he stopped and looked at Benton. They could both hear it. It was as if the air were being sucked from the room and pushed back in, quickly and repeatedly.

'What is that?' Benton asked.

3

Arwood had always liked helicopters. When he was a little boy, he'd make them out of Lego with his uncle, who would come over sometimes when his father was 'out' and his mother was indisposed. It has always been one of his fondest and quietest memories from childhood.

When Arwood was ten, they moved on to models with glue and paint. Models worked for them as a shared activity, because it set them on a common task and didn't require much talk about why they were together instead of Arwood being with his parents. The less they talked, the more helicopters and other machines they would build. They liked to look up the specifications of the aircraft from a dated copy of *Jane's World Air Forces* that Uncle Maxwell had bought at a library sale.

Now he was twenty-two years old, and from this distance it actually looked like a model. It was about the same size. He felt a thrill at first as the massive gunship floated over the ridge and approached the city. The Mi-24 was a primary component of Iraq's order of battle, and had been used to devastating effect only three years earlier in the war against Iran. It was a Soviet-built brute of a vehicle, with all the charmless industrial hostility that the Cold War could create. It had twin cockpits, one above and behind the other, both encased in glass. To the sides were two massive wings with a twenty-one-foot wingspan. At the front was a 12.7mm Gatling gun with a payload of some 1,500 rounds of ammunition.

Under the wings were rocket launchers and mine-dispenser pods. And backing it up, at its six o'clock, was an Aérospatiale Gazelle helicopter, built in France. Together they formed a hunter-killer team.

Just like his models.

However, the angle of attack proved to Arwood that, unlike in Iran or in his basement, this team was not going to be used for war. It was going to kill people — regular, everyday, soft people.

Even at the pinnacle of his earlier boredom, Arwood hadn't been more than a quarter mile away from the base, and had had a radio. Looking back across the worthless space he'd been defending, he could see Lieutenant Harvey Morgan running down the line, fastening his helmet the way most of the enlisted men didn't, because — in the complex language of gestural soldier-speak — it meant *I'm a rule-following pussy* rather than someone who chewed cigars and shot gooks and Nazis.

'Look alive, dimwits,' he shouted.

It did not take long, however, for everyone to realise that the Iraqis weren't heading toward them. The helicopters took their positions over the city. And then, with an experienced and pitiless hand, they opened fire on the hospital.

The Mi-24 launched two rockets from under its left wing with perfect military precision, blowing in the sides of the hospital, and killing the injured and infirm and those who had taken the Hippocratic oath to help them. Their work done, the air team moved out toward the train tracks, with the intention of killing each and every man, woman, and child where a makeshift refugee camp had been set up and maintained by those fleeing other towns.

Arwood radioed his commanding officer and asked, 'What the fuck, Lieutenant?'

Off to his right, an Apache helicopter was in the air and taking a defensive position over Checkpoint Zulu.

Arwood cocked and trained his weapon. There was nothing to point at except north.

Behind him, Arwood's platoon ran the short distance to his position—the deepest legal position into Iraq—and, once there, started shouting ideas.

'Let's take it out!' was the first big idea.

It was Corporal Ben Ford. He was from Tampa, Florida, looked like a bulldog, and was almost as refined. However, he was not always wrong. 'Come on, man, let's waste the motherfuckers!'

Arwood took one last look down his sights to confirm that there was absolutely nothing whatsoever approaching the checkpoint, and then turned to see Ford appeal to the lieutenant, as though each of them were in the helicopter with a finger on the rocket launcher and the choice was theirs.

Whoever did have his finger on that trigger could have taken down the Mi-24 with a gentle squeeze. God only knows what that guy was thinking. The angels and devils must have been going nuts on his shoulders trying to separate their messages.

Arwood had heard that Iraqis and Iranians used to have helicopter dogfights. They were the only nations in history that did. It could be done. And how hard could it be? They hovered there like bottles on a cloud, waiting to be knocked down.

Lieutenant Harvey Morgan's West Point education was in full puff that evening, though. He did not order them to take out the Mi-24. He not only knew what his orders were, but somehow—against the philosophy, purpose, tradition, expectation, and standard operating procedures of the army—he even knew *why*. So the second big idea was to not take it out. Proof of the worthiness of this idea came from paperwork. He had loads of it. Arwood hated paperwork.

Morgan had a quote from the president. Arwood hated quotes from the president.

Morgan considered the words of the president definitive. Arwood considered the bullets blowing out the brains of children definitive.

Morgan considered the law to be the foundations of justice Arwood considered justice to be the foundations of the law.

Morgan considered Arwood's opinions to be irrelevant. So did Arwood; they did have that in common.

Morgan snapped the paper into shape, in a gesture smooth enough to demonstrate how much time he'd spent around the stuff.

A group of other guys gathered around. They wanted to hear this, too. One of them was an Arab-American soldier named Rob Husseini who'd been born in Maryland to Moroccan parents. He was twenty-three, and was the only one there who understood Arabic. The Arabic he understood best concerned food and events that take place in kitchens. The Arabic he understood least concerned law, justice, and war. The topics he understood least in any language were law, justice, and war.

While Rob didn't understand a great deal of what he heard from the refugees and POWs, he understood enough to make him the most miserable one there.

Morgan started reading aloud some of the official puff written by the State Department, which was boring until he reached this part: '... no prospect of US involvement in Iraq's internal conflict unless senior US political officials decide it threatens the coalition's military forces arrayed in defensive positions along a ceasefire line in Iraq south of the Euphrates River'.

'That,' said Morgan, as though he had proved something, 'was the State Department. And those forces are us.'

Arwood lit a cigarette. 'Those forces be we,' he said.

'What?'

'We be da force,' Arwood said.

Rob shook his head. 'Word is that the Iraqis are dropping leaflets from the helicopters, telling the Shiites that if they don't stop the rebellion they'll drop chemical weapons on them.'

Morgan ignored him. 'France says the rebellion is Iraq's problem to solve. Saudi Arabia said they won't touch this. Morocco. Egypt. Canada. The Brits. This is from the *Washington Post* yesterday,' he said, flipping to another piece of paper. '"There is no stomach in this administration, in the coalition, or in the region to undertake the kind of military involvement that would be necessary to aid the rebel groups in toppling the Saddam government. Such involvement in the internal affairs of another nation" — I'm quoting here, people — "would have enormous, enormous implications for what we are trying to do in the region overall and would, in addition, label the rebels 'lackeys of the United States', making their success more difficult." The guy then says, "We don't want our fingerprints on anyone involved in the rebellions," unquote. More or less.'

Morgan looked up. 'That's coming from Dick Cheney, our secretary of defense. If America gets involved, we undermine the integrity of the revolution.'

'Why?' said Rob Husseini.

'Why what?' said Harvey.

'Why would they hate us if we helped them?'

'Because Arabs always have conspiracy theories about the West being involved.'

'But we would be involved. And it wouldn't be a conspiracy. They're asking for help.'

'They don't really want it. They think they want it. What they really want, even more, is a reason to blame us. So we need to avoid giving them one.'

'Aren't we giving them one by not helping?'

'No. We're staying out of their business.'

'You're not making any sense, Lieutenant.'

'It's not me, it's Dick Cheney. The State Department believes that if we help these people now, they will hate us later.'

'Right.'

'And if we leave them alone to die, we'll be on better terms with them in the long run.'

'Got it.'

Arwood looked at Rob, who turned to watch the helicopters launch rockets at a tent community.

'This sucks,' said Rob. 'We should help these people, or get the fuck out of here.'

'I second that,' Ben said.

'I third that,' Arwood said.

'No one asked either of you. And you can't third something.'

'And yet,' Arwood said, 'it happened.'

A kid Arwood didn't know came up, saluted the lieutenant, and said, 'Refugees are coming in to Checkpoints Alfa and Eagle. And there are Iraqi ground forces coming from the north.'

'Refugees are coming here, too,' Arwood said, looking across the desert at people on the move, and at troops emerging from Ural troop transports. 'Looks like if we don't go to them, the civilians are gonna come to us.'

Seeing motion in the distance, he manned his weapon again. The rear sight of the M60 created a tall and narrow rectangle that was cut through the middle with a pin for a front sight. Through his sight, they came toward him as though framed by a doorway they would never enter.

Some ran. Some were walking wounded, and hobbled. Others couldn't walk at all, and were carried by those who would rather risk death than leave them behind.

Morgan used binoculars to scan the approaching refugees.

'We're to receive refugees and patch them up. We take POWs. We do not fire unless fired upon. And then we send them back when we get the pull-out order.'

They came for hours. Arwood had never seen people look like this. He had never seen terror on people's faces before.

Because he was one of the first people they saw, he was among the first ones they'd talk to. It was shocking to him how many of them spoke English. The whole country seemed to be bilingual.

One man carried a dead eighteen-month-old baby. Whoever had shot it in the chest had done so at such close range that there were powder burns on its T-shirt and nappy. It was limp, and looked like rubber.

The situation was chaotic. Their lines were being overrun by people — hundreds at first, and thousands later — who gathered around the remnants of the oil refinery inside the American perimeter. Young soldiers started handing out their own Meals, Ready-to-Eat, and people ate like they had never seen food.

Not all were refugees. Some were Iraqi conscripts and Republican Guard soldiers who'd surrendered. There were six of them behind Arwood, at a tent, and under guard. One was shirtless, wearing boots and beige standard-issue trousers. He was unshaven, and his head was pressed to the ground in either prayer or despondency or fatigue. Whatever it was, Arwood had no trouble interrupting him.

'Ben, watch this thing for me,' he said, and then walked away from the machine gun to tap the guy on his shoulder.

The Arab looked up, tears in his eyes.

'What the hell have you got to complain about?' Arwood said. 'Here you are, all safe and cozy, about to get some food and water, protected by all kinds of laws and nice guys looking out for your welfare. You should be the happiest sonofabitch in the Middle East. Meanwhile,' Arwood said, and then flicked his butt into the cloudless sky, 'I've been meaning to ask one of you fuckwits a question that's been on my mind: What the hell is wrong with you people? I mean, seriously. Who shoots a baby? Who does that? Did you do that? Was that your idea? Do you think there's a God that wants you to shoot a baby? What's going on over there? What's going on in your heads?'

'Saddam. He said the city is unclean. He is giving us 250 dinars to kill babies and women, and up to five thousand dinars for adult males. He said we can kill up to one hundred a day. That's the limit.' Then he said something in Arabic with the word 'Allah' in it, and that was when Arwood switched off.

'Ben,' he said, hopping up over the sandbags, back to his position. 'I've got to do something. I need you to cover for me. I could be a few hours.'

'What could you possibly need to do?' Ben said.

'There's a guy — an English guy. He went into town. He went there to take pictures before the attack. It was sort of my idea. I've got to go look for him.'

'Are you out of your mind?'

'Look, man, I'll zip over, pick him up, and zip out. It's Samawah. It's not like it's Moscow or anything.'

'You'll be AWOL.'

'Honour before orders.'

'You'd better haul arse.'

'Save Ferris.'

4

Less than two kilometres away to the north, Benton lay prone behind the pharmacy countertop with another random victim of the attack. The pharmacist was dead in the middle of the floor. A flying cinder block from a nearby explosion had cracked open his skull.

Benton and the other survivor stayed on the floor for hours. To call it cowering would be to demean their sincere effort to live. All they could do was hide and hope.

They did not talk. They did not share words of fear, anger, or remorse. They were two human beings controlled by circumstance, with nothing in common except everything.

Benton sweated profusely. The man handed him a bottle of water that had been lying next to them on the floor. Benton drank it all. He placed the cap back on top and set it aside.

There was no telling whether hiding on the pharmacy floor behind the service counter was a good idea or a bad one. Moment by moment, he told himself he should make a run for it. And yet, with each arriving moment he did not, because fear has an inertia of its own.

The windows had already been blown inward, so there was no proper separation between 'in here' and 'out there' anymore. It was a linguistic pretence sustained by convention. Either way, he could not hear the Republican Guard's assault anymore.

He heard distant shots and screams and yells, and the wailing grief of loved ones. Soldiers, Benton had believed, didn't do this.

Murderers did. It was odd, as he pressed his head to the floor, to think he didn't even have a vocabulary to name the people who might be his killers. *What are they, these people?*

During a lull in the shooting, Benton found the courage to unclench his muscles. He was surprised to find they were as stiff and sore as they'd become after long days trekking with camera equipment on assignment. The fear had made him exhausted. He lifted his head above the countertop and looked between the Halls Mentho-Lyptus drops and the reading glasses. There was smoke. There were dead in the street. There were people sitting dazed and walking slowly, and others running and crying. But there were no killers and no helicopters. They seemed to have moved off.

'Let's go,' he said to the man in the floor.

'Go where?' he replied in English.

'The American base is less than two kilometres away.'

'I have to find my family,' he said.

'Maybe they're already there. I'm sure people are running there.'

'Americans don't like Shiites.'

'You're a non-combatant protected by international law. They won't give a rat's arse whether you're a Shiite, a Sunni, or a Martian.'

'America hates Muslims. America kills Muslims.'

'I'm going. Come.'

'I must stay.'

'Why?'

'You don't understand. You're not from here.'

'I'm going.'

'Go with God.'

Determined, Benton abandoned his hiding place, stepped gingerly over the detritus on the floor of the shop, and cast himself into the harsh sunlight of the Iraqi revolution.

Samawah had 28,000 residents. It was not a large city. He was only half a kilometre into it, and he knew how to get out again. Route 8 cut through the town from the north, and then turned south-east toward Nasiriyah which, according to the pharmacist, was under the same kind of assault as Samawah. This was not going to be his road. In fact, any road that could accommodate a tank was a road he planned to avoid.

South of the al-Sharika road there was a wide-open stretch of land. Benton figured that the troops would be targetting large concentrations of people, and might therefore ignore stray individuals like himself, but that was a comforting speculation only. Also, if he was alone he might be able to yell loudly in English and identify himself, which might stop them from shooting him. In a crowd he'd be an object, not a person.

Benton slunk low, and made for a patch of palm trees near a smouldering truck riddled with heavy machine-gun fire. A young girl in a green dress was curled into a ball by the back wheel. He didn't want any more company between where he was and the covering fire of Arwood's M60, but the girl was in the spot he needed to get to, and few other choices remained. The truck was the first destination in a route from here to there.

Benton looked east. He could hear the Mi-24, but couldn't see it. Shots were being fired in the city. He knew there were ground forces going from door to door, killing every male over the age of twelve and many others, just for the experience of it, or the pay. But they seemed to be behind him or off in the distance. If he dropped the camera bag and kept only the few rolls of 35mm that he'd taken until now, he could easily jog the rest of the way.

Benton stripped the remaining film from the Pentax and tucked it into his front pocket. He paused before his sprint to check for new movement and—momentarily confident—started running.

There were concrete buildings to the east about three hundred metres away. It was not until the gunship rose above the walls that he had any idea of how well they masked the sounds of the rotors.

He ran faster.

When he reached the truck and the girl, he paused by the front wheel to pant. He hadn't covered much ground, but he was winded and scared. As the truck was already smouldering, he figured it wouldn't be a target, but the helicopter pilot was blowing families to pieces with an anti-tank Gatling gun, so perhaps there was a different logic at play.

The girl looked at him, and he at her. They regarded one another like strangers at the *souk*.

She was slender and very young. Her head was not covered, though it was possible that in the commotion her scarf had come loose. Her gently tanned skin was flawless and healthy, and her sandy hair was full and lush, the way that women's magazines promised it would be if you used their products. Her eyes were a very light brown.

Her accent was thick, and he didn't know whether it was English or Arabic she was speaking when she said, 'America?'

'Britain,' said Benton. 'Going to visit the Americans, though. Perhaps you should come.'

The helicopter was now starting to move in their direction. Whatever water Benton had consumed at the pharmacy had become sweat again. The need to decide whether to stay or run vanished when the helicopter sped toward them faster than the speed of choice. The pilot did not shoot. It may have been because he already had a destination that was fifty metres farther away. Also, his line of sight was blocked by the truck, and it was unlikely he saw Benton and the girl.

He stopped to hover ten metres off the deck—close enough for Benton to see the side of his helmet-covered head and his exposed chin.

The wind pressed down on them as from the wings of a dragon.

The pilot was taking aim at a tent village made of families driven from other homes by Saddam, or the rebellion, or Desert Storm itself.

History enveloped them like a sandstorm. It didn't matter which event was going to kill them, because now they were going to die. The reasons were immaterial.

The helicopter gunship opened up without remorse, or humanity, or mercy, or any heavenly virtue. Benton, from his angle, could see it all. He no longer had a camera. There was no documenting this. There was only submission. It was every war painting he had seen in the British Museum and the Metropolitan Museum of Art. It was the suffering of the saints. It was the inferno. It was the hell that is war, only this was not war. This — it was declared from marble steps — was peace: a world restored, the state system reaffirmed, and the hard faith in law again proclaimed for the benefit of all, except the dying and the dead.

'Come on,' he said, still not knowing how much English the girl spoke.

She refused to give him her hand; she resisted any movement at all. Which was why he grabbed it, and pulled her up and started running with her.

It was not a sprint. Neither of them was up to it. He felt as though his legs were dragging through a low surf, with the water pulling at his insteps, as in a nightmare. He gripped her hand too tightly — he could feel that, even then — because her delicate fingers were crushed together in his closed palm.

There was an American flag ahead. To reach it, they ran over the train tracks and down the slight hill, scurrying like field mice from an owl. As they advanced toward the American lines, Benton saw a lone soldier in US fatigues sprinting toward him. He couldn't be sure from this distance, but it looked like Arwood.

Benton had never seen Arwood run. He had, in fact, never seen Arwood's legs, which had been hidden behind the sandbags. And yet his personality came through his body's movements. He ran in a straight line directly toward Benton and the girl. He had no rifle. What he had was purpose.

To Benton's left was the helicopter. The smaller French Gazelle was nowhere to be seen. Past the hovering and murdering helicopter were the first buildings of the city, and the soldiers. They were coming. They flowed from the edge of a wall the way darkness runs like smoke from the edge of ruins at nightfall. They were jogging.

To Benton, it looked like they were late for something.

The girl was slower than him, even though she was younger. Fear can sap strength. He kept pulling her along, despite the soldiers coming ever closer. He ran toward Arwood as though this young man were pulling America behind him.

Arwood closed in on them, and once Benton and the girl reached him, he turned and kept running with them. For a few fleeting moments, Benton hoped that the Iraqi soldiers would ignore them and turn to richer targets, and that the three of them could make the American base without confrontation.

But those men did turn on them; those men who dressed like soldiers but acted like a gang or tribe were running an intercept course to keep the trio from reaching the American line.

'What are you doing here?' Benton shouted to Arwood over the gunfire, the helicopter rotors, and the voices. So many voices—fewer and fewer, and yet somehow louder because of it.

'I'm here to bring you back.'

'That's insane.'

'It's what you do, man.'

After only another minute, Arwood, Benton, and the girl slowed to a jog before stopping entirely. They had been surrounded. They were thirty metres from the ceasefire line. At least fifty US soldiers had their weapons trained on the Iraqis at that distance, but the Iraqis weren't facing the Americans. They were facing Arwood, Benton, and the girl. The man who moved into the centre of the row, with a smile on his face, was the colonel.

The colonel, like every other Baathist, sported a thick black moustache. He was tanned, not only because of his race but because he'd been spending some time outside doing the killing himself. Benton figured that to be this highly ranked and yet on a foot patrol meant he was ambitious and ruthless.

And yet, those eyes. Like so many Arab men, his eyes were soft and brown like a doe's. They were clear and gentle. One could be lulled into a sense of safety by such eyes. Unfortunately for the world as a whole, this man's serenity was a product of his own inner acceptance of his actions; it was not an implied promise to act decently in the world itself.

When the entire complement of soldiers came to rest, Arwood whipped out his Beretta 9mm, chambered a round, and pointed it directly at the forehead of the colonel. He held the weapon like a gangland killer. With a developed diplomatic style that would not change for the rest of his life, he said, 'Apparently we didn't kill enough of you fuckin' douchebags during round one.'

The colonel smiled at Arwood. He smiled because he was no mere foot soldier facing the Americans. He smiled because he was a colonel, and he knew that the ceasefire was in place and the Americans had no intention of shooting the Iraqis unless they were fired on themselves. He understood the deeper structures at play, and that all of them were on his side.

'Looks like you're lost,' he said. 'And yet you have found something that belongs to me.' He turned to look at the girl, who was still holding Benton's hand. Strangely, though, she did not look back at him. Instead, she was looking at Arwood as though he were an older brother or a close cousin—someone she could identify with and had learned to trust. And Arwood looked at her. Her body had straightened. She was on the balls of her feet, and she bounced gently.

Benton looked between her and Arwood, and he knew that a kind of promise had passed between them. Arwood saw her not as a foreigner, or an Arab, or a Shiite, or a family member of a rebellious tribe, but as a young girl, a girl in junior high school he might have known in Portland, Maine, or Harrisburg, Pennsylvania, or St. Louis, Missouri. She was a cute girl—a girl too young for him, obviously, but cute all the same—who might have smiled at him in the hallway while holding her maths books to her barely developed chest and then looked down quickly because she found him cute, too, but he was an upper-class man and so, later that day, she'd tell her friends about the guy she'd seen and had her first crush on. Whether or not any of this was true for her, Benton couldn't say. It was Arwood's mind—such as it was—that was easier to read. There was no denying, however, that these two young people somehow *felt* each other. For that moment, they may have been the only people in all of Iraq who looked into each other's eyes across a divide and found themselves in the same place.

Arwood looked away from the girl and back to the colonel. How he had such a presence of mind to talk like this, Benton would never know. Clearly, even then, Arwood had what people would later call 'authority issues'.

'Oh, you mean her? Naw, man. She's my cousin. She's an American. Cindy-Lou Who from Whoville. Wandered off after the movie was finished. Mum and Dad asked me to come and get her. Got to bring her home now. So get the fuck out of my way before I splatter your brains and follow the red-brick road all the way home.'

The other soldiers looked confused. Based on his experience in Iraq, Benton was reasonably sure that at least some of them understood enough English to follow what Arwood was saying, but his language was so vernacular there may have been no understanding his meaning. They didn't look as though they wanted this kind of trouble. Whatever else their nefarious plans for the day, facing down the sharp edge of Desert Storm was not on their to-do list. If Lieutenant Harvey Morgan hadn't called out at just that moment, there was a chance Arwood's gambit might have worked. The Iraqis might have let Arwood — being crazy — walk off with the girl in green. But he did intervene, and the Iraqis didn't let them go.

'Stand down, private!' Morgan yelled. He was walking briskly toward their position. Behind him, like a phalanx, was the second cavalry, and they were ready to pounce. If Morgan had simply raised a finger, every Iraqi would have been obliterated, and every American would have been delighted to have done it. Rob Husseini probably would have been the first to fire. But Morgan did not give that order, because the paperwork on the subject was clear.

The girl bounced on her toes. She no longer held Benton's hand. Rather than stand down, Arwood stood closer to the colonel in the form of pressing his automatic to his forehead and physically pushing him back toward the American position. But that smile never left the colonel's face.

'See how easy it is to obey the man with the gun?' Arwood said. Then he turned to the girl. 'Come on, cuz. Mum and Dad are waiting for us at Checkpoint Zulu. We're gonna have a big homecoming — cake, candy, Roman candles, the works.'

Looking at Arwood, and only at Arwood, she started to walk. The colonel stepped to the side, Arwood's automatic still against his forehead, Morgan still telling Arwood to stand down, and the US infantry still ready to pounce. They circled and changed positions. Arwood walked backward and the girl walked beside him, facing forward toward Checkpoint Zulu and the M60 machine gun Arwood had left behind. With his free hand, he took hers. And for a short eternity they were walking toward freedom. Then the colonel withdrew a Soviet-made 9mm Makarov from his belt, and shot the girl in the back. The girl fell to her knees. She did not look down to her body and her heart. She looked at Arwood. His eyes were the last of this world she would know.

When it was over, as she lay dead at his feet, still looking up at him, Arwood did regain a place in the moment. Unlike earlier, when he had stood posturing with the weapon in one hand like a gangster in an American movie, now he put two hands on his weapon and raised it in the proper assault position, as he'd been trained to do.

Half a second—more or less. That's all Arwood needed to murder the colonel. But Benton took that time away from him: he placed his hand over Arwood's outstretched arms and said, 'We have to go.'

5

It was a short walk back to the safety of Checkpoint Zulu. Lieutenant Harvey Morgan took Arwood by the upper arm as though he were a schoolboy who'd been busted with contraband, and walked him back to the ceasefire line. Though it had been for only a few minutes, Arwood Hobbes had technically abandoned his post, abandoned his weapon, been absent without leave from the base, crossed the ceasefire line in violation of an international agreement and American policy, and then topped it off by pulling a weapon on a military officer from a country with whom the United States—and the entire UN coalition—had a ceasefire agreement.

The ceasefire, Lieutenant Morgan reminded Arwood, was between Iraq and everyone else, not among the people in Iraq; that was their problem. Harvey, though he was only twenty-six, next launched a barrage of loosely affiliated words he'd collected over the past six months, sourced from the highest and lowest levels of political discussion:

They were held together with spit.

Arwood wasn't listening, and wouldn't have given a damn in any case. He was walking back to base without his mind, body, or soul.

Benton trailed behind them, escorted by other soldiers who didn't talk to him.

'None of this matters anyway,' Morgan concluded. 'Short of dropping chemical weapons, no one's gonna do anything. I mean, really, what are we supposed to do? Occupy Baghdad? Teach these people how to run a town meeting like we're in fuckin' Vermont?'

The moment they crossed the straight and imaginary line that separated one part of Iraq from another, Lieutenant Harvey Morgan stopped, waited for Thomas Benton to approach, and then poked him in the chest, saying, 'You're out of here. Tomorrow morning, you fuck directly off. I want you off this observation post.' Then, as he took Arwood's arm again, he shouted over his shoulder, 'I hope it was worth it.'

Arwood was taken to the mess hall. Lieutenant Harvey Morgan had decided to make an example of him, knowing that tensions were running high among his men and that this needed to be stopped. Lashing Arwood, in his view, would ensure that even the dumbest of his company would understand the consequences of doing anything remotely similar to what Arwood had done. And this example needed to be made because the events beyond the perimeter were continuing. The helicopters were still shooting. People were still dying. Men were still being lined up and executed in front of their children to make sure the rebels (if there were any rebels) 'got the message,' which they did.

Lieutenant Morgan's rant may have begun as a walk-and-talk lecture, but it did not end as one.

'You are in the worst kind of shit you can possibly imagine,' Harvey yelled in front of everyone. 'You can't even spell the kind of trouble you are in right now. I'm going to have to go home tonight and re-read the entire Uniform Code of Military Justice just to understand what the hell just happened here. Are you getting this, Hobbes?'

'Yes, sir.'

Arwood wasn't paying attention. Lieutenant Morgan was speaking to the gallery. Arwood was merely a prop, and he knew it. He didn't care. He was still looking at the girl who was looking at him.

Besides, this man wasn't going to take out a pistol and shoot him. This man wasn't going to stare him down with a Makarov pistol on his belt, and mock him. This man wasn't going to shoot a girl in the back. This man, whatever his faults, was not preternaturally evil, and there was nothing he could do to make himself matter in a moment like this compared to what Arwood had just experienced.

Or so Arwood thought until Lieutenant Morgan proved him wrong by saying this: 'And for what? For what? You did all that for what? For some fucking Arab bitch.'

What struck Arwood in his gut, as a wordless pain that he could not articulate until much later, was a sudden understanding that the only thing worse than evil was deciding that evil didn't matter.

And for that reason, and that reason alone, Arwood Hobbes stood up in front of fifty other soldiers, without hesitation or regret, and beat the living shit out of Lieutenant Harvey Morgan.

Arwood Hobbes was collected by the military police. Thomas Benton was sent to Harvey Morgan's commanding officer, Major Alan Wilcox, and Wilcox told Benton calmly that he was to now consider himself *persona non grata* at Checkpoint Zulu. His credentials would be pulled, and he was to go away. Wilcox was a midwesterner, and did not raise his voice or use hysterical language or gestures. He communicated his decisions to Benton, and Benton said that he understood.

'One thing, Major.'

'What?'

'If you court-martial Arwood Hobbes, I'll make sure it's covered in the press. I know people at the *Boston Globe*, the *Baltimore Sun*, and the *Washington Post*—people who cover the Pentagon and the White House. They will ask questions publicly and on the record about why Arwood Hobbes is being prosecuted.'

'The army does not have to answer those questions,' Wilcox said. 'We have procedures. I don't know how it works in Britain, Mr Benton, but in the US those questions will be ignored for reasons of due process.'

'No, Major. They won't be answered. But they won't be ignored. Because it won't be the answers that'll hurt the Bush administration—it'll be the questions.'

Later, when Lieutenant Harvey Morgan was sent to the infirmary for general care, stitches, and a cast, he was advised—very quietly and without any hysterical language or gestures—that it would be best for him not to file a report of the incident. The problem, Major Wilcox explained, was that a few days earlier, on the twenty-sixth, General Schwarzkopf had made a major political gaffe by telling David Frost on international news that the US had been 'suckered' into letting the Iraqis fly helicopters in the ceasefire agreement, and that in retrospect he thought the Iraqis had planned to use them against the rebellion the whole time. Now the White House was in full defensive mode over his comments, because every Iraqi civilian death suddenly seemed like America's fault as a result of Stormin' Norman having been hoodwinked by a bunch of carpet salesmen. This was tarnishing America's victory, and was seriously annoying the White House.

The simple fact was that there was no way to even describe, let alone explain, Hobbes's actions without using the word 'helicopter.' And that was the word the White House didn't want to hear from the press anymore.

Lieutenant Harvey Morgan was purple and tender. He was also angry. 'Let me get this straight. I'm supposed to take a public beating from Arwood fucking Hobbes just so the president doesn't get embarrassed in a press conference?'

'It is my experience that most promotions in the military are the result of making your commanding officers look good, or else keeping them from looking bad,' Major Wilcox told Lieutenant Harvey Morgan.

'Is that true?'

'So far as I know, and I'm a major.'

'What am I supposed to do with him?'

'Something will come up,' said Major Wilcox.

Something did come up, and it didn't take long. Benton left as instructed, and opted for the first transport plane leaving the next morning for the north. Two days later he was in Erbil, Iraq. From there he turned around and followed everyone into the mountains when the Kurdish counterattacks against Saddam failed. Benton was now embedded again, but this time with the civilians.

He was there almost a week, reporting, meeting people, and sending back stories, before — to his surprise — Arwood arrived. It was not a coincidence: it was poetic justice. The refugee crisis in Turkey was so dire that the UN passed a resolution calling it a 'threat to international peace and security', which opened the floodgates for thousands of American special forces and other troops to assist in the largest humanitarian relief effort since World War II without needing the permission of Iraq to do it. Major Wilcox told Lieutenant Harvey Morgan that this was exactly the sort of place Arwood should go. 'If he wants to help the Arabs so much, then here's his chance.'

It didn't bother either of them that the Kurds weren't Arabs.

Benton first saw him sitting on a rocky outcropping, his feet dangling like a child's, in an area popular with reporters and staff at the UN High Commissioner for Refugees. Arwood acknowledged him, but at first said little. A press tent had been set up in a flat area at around 1,300 metres in altitude. It contained refreshments and desks, offered familiarity and free information, and so became a natural congregation and propaganda point.

Arwood didn't look well. He was thinner to the point of being malnourished. He carried no weapon, and, while still in uniform, seemed disconnected and aloof from the few other troops in the area. It seemed as though he wasn't reporting to anyone, and no one had any particular job for him to do.

Benton collected him, then led him into the tent and opened a can of cold Coke.

'Drink,' Benton said, and Arwood did.

'I didn't expect to see you here,' he said to Arwood.

'Major Wilcox heard you were up here, filing stories. He thought it was fitting we be together. Harvey put me on the plane himself.'

'You didn't come find me when you got here. Why not?'

'I haven't been doing much of anything.'

'Do you have an assignment, a mission, a CO?'

'Harvey said they're dropping aid to the refugees. I could catch it.'

'What I mean is, who are you reporting to?'

'No one. He told me to come up here, and that I couldn't come back until they called me, which would be when my company ships off home.'

'I've never heard of such a thing, Arwood.'

'I'm starting to think we don't hear about the weirdest stuff on this planet.'

'I'm in touch with some of the aid agencies here. The Red Cross is here. The Turkish Red Crescent. The High Commissioner for Refugees. I want you to come with me. Get some food and rest. Tomorrow I'm doing an interview. I guess some of the first pallets are going to be dropped—frozen chickens, other sundries. We have equipment to lug around, and some questions for the staff. I'm sure you could be very helpful.'

'Can I ask you something?' Arwood said.

'Of course.'

'Did you know her name?'

'Who?'

'The girl in green. I guess you knew her, right?'

'We'd been crouching behind the same truck. We ran together. I never learned her name.'

'So we'll never be able to tell her family what happened?'

'Arwood,' Benton said, 'I don't think you appreciate the enormity of the catastrophe that's happening here. Tens of thousands, maybe hundreds of thousands, are dead. There are mass graves. Starvation. Exposure. The state of Iraq is ripping itself apart. America thinks the Shiites are backed by Iran, and they're letting them die. And Turkey doesn't want support flowing to the Kurds, lest they create a new Gaza Strip here. Everyone's hoping for a palace coup in Iraq, and it isn't happening. Saddam is trying to hold power by any means necessary that won't draw in the coalition again. It's hell on earth, Arwood.'

'Yeah, but—'

'But what?'

'Well … a person's a person, no matter how small, right?'

'Drink your Coke, Arwood. You need to get some rest.'

Arwood sipped his Coke, but did not respond to Benton. Instead he muttered softly to himself, 'I thought that was the whole point.'

6

Märta Ström was a project officer for the UN High Commissioner for Refugees, based in Dohuk. She was Swedish, thirty-four years old, and had been working in humanitarian affairs since graduating with her master's degree from Uppsala University when she was twenty-five. She was scheduled to meet a reporter from the *Times*, and was killing the time before it happened by leaning against a rock with a cigarette and marvelling at the worst humanitarian disaster since World War II.

The British were calling it Operation Safe Haven, and the Americans were calling it Operation Provide Comfort. Märta refused to call it anything but a nightmare. The temperature at altitude was below freezing. The refugees couldn't get farther into Turkey, couldn't return home, had no military protection other than the lightly armed Pershmerga fighters, and the situation was volatile. The death count was untallied. Thousands. Thousands and thousands — a tremendous number of them children. They weren't warm enough. They weren't fed enough. Many had been separated from their families. She had watched a three-year-old boy die of starvation. She couldn't save him. She decided she'd never have children.

She could have a cigarette, though. Cigarettes were especially satisfying when the smoke mixed with the cool air. They were best with a stiff drink. There was none of that around, unfortunately.

There was an airdrop coming in soon. She'd been tasked with speaking to the press about it. It was not her preferred job.

47

The guy she was to meet—Thomas Something-or-other—was
to photograph it and ask her about the general situation. Saddam
had been fully victorious by around the fifth, and was now calling
the airdrops the 'ostentatious dropping of crumbs' by the West.
Whether he was the devil or not, it was hard not to agree with him
on that point.

Two white men, both clean, approached her from over a small
ridge. One was in his forties and the other in his early twenties, or
possibly a teenager. She took the older one for the journalist, but
couldn't make sense of the younger. He wore a T-shirt that said, *If I
were an Iraqi POW I'd be home by now*. She decided she didn't like him
before he'd even stopped moving.

The adult one readjusted his shoulder bag and then extended his
hand. 'I'm Thomas Benton. You're Ms Ström?'

Märta tossed the cigarette away and shook his hand. He was all
business, and his handshake was firm. He didn't smile at her, and she
didn't smile back.

The younger man just stood there, and she decided not only to
dislike him but to ignore him entirely.

'This is Arwood Hobbes,' said the Brit, slightly complicating her
plan.

'OK,' she said.

Arwood Hobbes said nothing.

Märta checked her watch. They had a few minutes, assuming the
airdrop was on time.

'We could set up over there,' Benton said, pointing to a flat area
not far from where an armoured personnel carrier was parked. It
was American, and occupied by two men—one black, one white.

'You want to photograph the truck?' she asked.

'No. I want to stand on a flat surface as we talk and I take pictures.
It seems a reasonable place. Is that all right?'

'Yes. Of course,' Märta said.

As they walked, Benton did not ask questions or make small talk, and Arwood also said nothing. She realised that Benton hadn't explained who Arwood was or what he was doing there. She opted not to ask.

'Just arrive in Iraq?' she said, perhaps a little too loudly. There were many refugees seated and sprawled across the mountain. No one was moving. Everyone was talking. She'd adopted a louder register of speech from the moment she'd arrived three days ago.

'No. I've been here over six weeks. I was in the south.' He didn't elaborate.

He had a handsome enough face, but it wasn't especially memorable. He reminded her of a man from a postwar photograph from the 1950s: not the dashing one in the middle with his arms around his buddies; one of the others … toward the back.

'I know some of the other journalists who were out here,' she said. 'Robert Fisk. Martin Woolacott. Jonathan Randal. Nora Boustany. You know them?'

'Yes,' Benton said.

He was taciturn, but not sullen. That, she found interesting. For a war correspondent, he didn't present as someone pleased with himself, someone for whom the world's suffering was the backdrop against which to display his own ego. Instead he seemed resigned, attentive, quiet. Though she walked behind him, he turned to check on her, and when he did, he carried an expression of someone trying to fit together two mismatched ends of a home appliance.

Benton explained what he planned to do: supplies were coming in by air, and he wanted a shot of it happening and from as close as possible. Airdrops made for dramatic imagery, and that's what was needed to attract media attention and hence gain public support. With that, or so the theory went, came political support.

'That's fine,' she replied.

'Which way are they coming?' he asked her.

'From the north-west,' she said. 'The US Air Force is going to do the drop.'

Benton's questions were factual and unpolitical. Märta recited the UNHCR's party line of alleviating the suffering of people caught up in armed conflict and ensuring respect for international humanitarian law. It was nothing he couldn't have learned by phone. Still, she hoped the conversation might produce some sense of urgency, because that was why she'd agreed to the interview in the first place. Looking around her, though, she knew this man would either be moved by what he was seeing or he wouldn't be. Her words would do nothing to change that.

'I did meet a captain and his two lackeys from the air force,' she said, looking up at the sky for the first plane. 'One of them had the nerve to explain that the plan was to drop the food further and further into Iraq so the people would have to start chasing it like squirrels after nuts. I told them that would be illegal, and that forcing people back into a country they fled is called *refoulement*. I then tried to explain where it was best to position the supplies so that they wouldn't be snatched up by mobs. I said there needed to be a gender-based optic on this so that women wouldn't be muscled out of needed provisions by determined men. I said that order can feed more people than chaos.'

'What did they say?' Benton asked.

'No much.'

'Why not?'

'They were too busy staring at my tits.'

Benton nodded.

'Here they come,' she said.

As she had anticipated, the air force started pushing pallets out of the transport planes from much too close and much too low. The parachutes opened, but the pallets of frozen chickens did not land well. The air force should have used sling-load helicopters, but they didn't because there was no doctrine to tell them to do so, and pushing pallets out of planes was faster, cheaper, and more dramatic.

Some of the pallets were cushioned in their landing by the soft bodies of the Kurds, who were crushed under them and died.

As the seals broke on others, the chickens bounced free and chased the uncrushed, who scattered like free-range bowling pins.

'Now, this is special,' Märta said aloud.

'I think,' Benton said, 'that maybe we should find some shelter.'

Exposed to the aerial bombing, they ran to the only shelter that made any sense — the US Army's armoured personnel carrier — and banged on the window.

'Open up and let us in,' she said to the black military officer driving it. This was not UNHCR protocol.

'No,' replied the man.

'We are going to be crushed to death by frozen chickens.'

'I am under orders not to allow any non-military personnel into the vehicle. Now step back, please.'

'What's the problem?' Benton asked Märta rather calmly, considering the circumstances.

'You should be crouching down under the truck,' she said to Benton, who was not crouching down. Neither was Arwood Hobbes, who stood with his hands behind his back as though admiring a rainbow.

'I've done enough of that lately,' he said.

'He won't let us in. Orders,' she said.

'Maybe you should go over his head,' Benton suggested casually.

'You know what? That's an excellent idea,' Märta said.

She knocked on the window again. 'You — name and rank?'

The officer considered this for a moment, and then — though there was no requirement to do so — decided to answer. 'Herb Reston. US Special Forces. Sergeant, first class.'

'Where are you from, Sergeant?'

'What?'

There were explosions. The chickens were rolling into unexploded ordnance in a zoned-off area, and shrapnel was flying everywhere — that, and chicken parts, or what Märta hoped were chicken parts.

'Where are you from? That cannot possibly be classified.'

Herb was obviously thinking about his reply, and whether a reply was sanctioned or not sanctioned, and what the consequences might be of offering one.

'Kankakee, Illinois,' he finally said.

'Is that a big town or a small town?'

'Small town,' said the large black man to the small blonde woman.

'Reston. Army. Kankakee, Illinois. Here's the thing, Herbert. If I survive this, I'll be going to Silopi, Turkey, in three days. There are three telephones there being used day in and day out by the people at CNN to file stories. When I get there, I'm going to dial 001-800-555-1212 and ask for directory assistance for Kankakee, Illinois, and I'm going to use my calling card to call your mother. I'm going to tell your mother that you refused to allow a woman into the safety of your vehicle during a life-and-death moment and — sorry for the assumption, Herbert, but I'm going to guess from your black, boyish, and sincere face that your mother is a God-fearing woman, and I'm going to describe your actions as very unchristian. And then I'll start to cry. And while I've never met your mother, I'm going to bet my life that my crying is going to make her very sympathetic to me and very angry at you, possibly for a very long time. So I'm going to count to three, and you have to make a choice about whether you want to please the army or please your mother and possibly God. One … two …'

On the count of two — as when he was five and his mother laid down the law — Herb opened the door, as much to his own surprise as that of his French passenger, who'd been riding shotgun as part of a NATO observation team.

When the back door of the APC opened, Märta, Benton, and Hobbes all climbed inside.

With the door closed, it was rather quiet.

Two of the chickens bounced harmlessly on the hood of the APC, and another rolled hard against the left front wheel, to no effect.

Arwood Hobbes was the first to speak.

'What do you think is the terminal velocity of a falling frozen chicken? It's got to be, like, a hundred miles an hour, don't you think?'

The man in the passenger seat turned around. He was in the French military. His English was heavily accented, almost to the point of affectation.

'Shouldn't you be with your unit?' the man said.

'That's where I was going, but then I chickened out.'

The man did not reply.

'Chickened out,' Arwood repeated, assuming he hadn't been heard.

The French officer made a sound by puffing a bit of air through his dry lips.

'Come on, Tigger, you know I hate that sound,' Herb said.

The man called Tigger then shook his head and mumbled something more audible and in French. Only Märta understood him and smiled.

'You speak French?' he asked her.

'I'm based in Geneva.'

'Maybe we can speak later. There are too many Americans here.'

'Why are you called Tigger?' Märta asked.

'That's my fault,' Herb interjected.

'I don't understand,' Märta said.

'I was being ironic and said he was "fun, fun, fun," because, you know, he's not, and somehow Winnie the Pooh came up, and Tigger, and I started calling him Tigger because Tigger's fun, fun, fun, and he said he knows that song, and the best thing about Tigger is that he's the only one, and I agreed it's a good thing there's only one of him and ... I don't know. We've been stuck inside this truck for a long time. And now, you know, chickens.'

Herb looked up in the sky to see if any more pallets were on their way down. It looked like the C-130 aeroplanes were moving off now, their job done. 'I just don't understand,' he said. 'Who would do something like this?'

'Clearly,' said the French officer, 'it is the air force. This is what I have come to expect from the air force. I expect it because dropping things on people is what the air force does. Drop aid to the refugees. Drop aid on the refugees. One little preposition to separate them, and no doctrine in place to draw the distinction. One little word, and *voilà*. Crêpe à la Kurd.'

'Maybe Perdue done it,' Arwood said.

No one responded.

'Maybe Perdue done it,' Arwood repeated.

Herb shook his head.

'That's the motto,' explained Arwood, 'of the Perdue chicken company. They make prepared chicken dishes so you don't have to. Because ... Perdue done it.'

'It wasn't Perdue,' Herb said.

Arwood was prepared for this possibility. 'How about Colonel Sanders?'

Herb Reston was not laughing, though he was likely the only one in the APC who knew who Colonel Sanders was. 'What is wrong with you?' Herb asked. 'You got PTSD or something?'

'Well, there's a phrase. Post-traumatic stress disorder. I wouldn't call it post-traumatic, no,' he said, as three men about twenty metres away grabbed a chicken from a woman who was standing with two small children, and then pushed her to the ground as she tried to resist. 'I admit I've been wondering for the last few days about why I can't sleep, and when I do, I dream of strangling dinosaurs with piano wire. I don't think it's because of something I did. I think it's something I didn't do. I think I have pre-traumatic stress disorder. I think I'm stressed out from not being able to do the right thing. And then, to top it off, the army has decided that my inaction wasn't inactive enough, and by not doing even less I was doing too much. And so I'm getting bad paper when I'm done. I'm not convinced my brain is working on the same frequency as the world around me. I mean, look out the window. How can I be the only one who finds this hilarious?' he asked. He did not laugh, though.

Arwood's voice no longer sounded sarcastic. It sounded farther off, as though he were speaking from the far end of an accident. Then he snorted. '*Refoulement*,' he said.

Märta looked to Benton as Arwood's keeper. As Arwood spoke, though, Thomas Benton turned away and said nothing.

The day wasn't over.

7

It was a child. That much was certain. Maybe eight or nine years old, judging by the size of the empty shoes.

Everyone had thought it was over. Arwood, Benton, Märta, Herb, and the Frenchman whom Herb called Tigger had all stepped out of the armoured personnel carrier once the aerial bombardment of frozen chickens was over, and the mobs and riots had subsided. After an hour, the explosions had stopped, the panic had relented, and the chorus of normal human misery had resumed its dull lament.

From the APC they'd walked to a small ridge that overlooked a wide and flat area. Only a few people were wandering around there. Most of the fighting had stopped. The women had all lost in their melees with the men to collect food, and the medics were already attending to the wounded, beaten, and stabbed.

The child had been below them in the wide-open gully. There was a ridge above it where people had started to gather. It was hard to know why that child might have been there. That didn't matter much now, because whatever he'd stepped on had blown him into a thousand mismatching pieces. What did matter was the other child—the one still in the minefield, metres away from the empty shoes, and paralysed with fear.

All eyes were on the boy. The American soldiers, who'd arrived the day before, were all shouting to the boy not to move, as they too were not moving.

The American soldiers yelled in English.

It was unlikely that the nine-year-old boy understood English.

And even if the boy didn't move, what then?

Nothing about this was productive, and it was Märta who sized up the situation and exerted some leadership.

'You,' said Märta to a man near her, who looked slightly better dressed than some. 'Do you speak English?'

'Yes, OK, OK,' said the man in penny loafers and grey trousers.

'You speak what he speaks?' she asked, pointing to the boy.

The man shouted something in Kurdish, which Märta didn't speak. The boy turned around at the sound of the man's voice, which Märta took as an affirmation in response to her question, and immediately told the man to tell the boy not to move. From here on he became Märta's voice, and, like every other Westerner trying to change the world through a translator, Märta had no idea what he was actually saying.

While Märta tried to calm the child down by proxy, Tigger calmly explained to Herb that all this was the fault of the Americans.

'Oh, really?'

'Ah, yes. All your compatriots think they are in the Dutch countryside in World War II. They are giving out Hershey bars again. Patting the children on the heads.'

'So we're being friendly to the locals — what of it?'

'They aren't Dutch. They're Kurdish,' explained Tigger. 'They've been taught not to receive a gift without giving one back. So, having nothing, they are scouring the countryside for objects to give back to your soldiers — hand grenades, cluster munitions, anything of equal value to a Hershey bar. Your people have no idea where they are, what they're doing, or what the consequences of their actions might be. None. And now this kid is out there, and I have no idea what we're going to do. I suspect he will die and we will have to watch. As we always watch. Helpless, from the sidelines.'

'I'll get him,' said Arwood, who had been listening to their conversation.

'Don't be ridiculous,' Tigger said.

'No, really. I'll do it,' he said, and without further ado he slipped from the ridge and walked casually past Märta and her penny-loafer-wearing translator, directly into the minefield.

'Wait!' Märta said after a pause that lasted too long.

Arwood walked into the contaminated area, his footsteps clear and sharp in the dirt.

Benton silently approached Märta, who was still on the ridge. To Märta, Benton seemed more concerned than surprised. Whatever was happening here was the product of something else. Benton and Arwood had come from the south, near Samawah, where the fighting was hot. Something had set Arwood off on this trajectory that she didn't understand, but perhaps—from the expression on his face—Benton did.

Arwood walked casually toward the child. His smile was as tender and wholesome as a Tennessee sunrise. When he reached the little boy, Arwood dropped to one knee as though he were taking orders or issuing a small prayer, though both were the furthest from the truth. He looked into the blue eyes of the little boy and said, 'Arwood.' He patted himself on the chest. 'Arwood,' he said again.

A piece of shrapnel from the explosion that had killed the other child had lacerated the boy's soft face with a laser-straight cut from his chin up past his left eye. It was deep and bleeding, and would obviously scar, but his eye was unharmed and the blood loss was modest.

The boy was in shock.

Benton watched from the top of the ridge where, by then, a hundred people had gathered. Herb and Tigger had stopped arguing, and Märta and her translator had stopped talking. The spectacle of Arwood Hobbes crouching in the minefield with the boy had united the refugees and the international staff in a common moment that everyone could understand and no one could explain.

'Arwood,' said Arwood, patting himself gently on the chest again.

The boy stared at Arwood. He was traumatised. There was no predicting how he would react. He could just as easily have sprinted off across the minefield. But he didn't. Without a sound, as though released from a cage, the child leap into Arwood's arms and held him as though Arwood were the winged Buraq who would fly them both away on a night journey to a fabled place where they could find whatever had been lost.

When the boy was firmly engulfed in Arwood's arms, the ubiquitous silence broke. To Benton, it was as though all the languages of the coalition were being spoken at once, pulling the moment apart by trying to fix it. The hundred people on that ridge had swelled and swelled again. To a million refugees. To all twelve thousand American forces from all four branches. To two thousand French, one thousand Italians, one thousand Dutch, one thousand Turks, four thousand Brits, others from Australia, Belgium, Canada, Germany, Luxembourg, Portugal, and Spain. Their boots all muddy, they were yelling a thousand thoughts in a thousand tongues.

Arwood wasn't paying attention to any of this. He didn't have a plan or a motive or a strategy. He was present only in the moment, and responding to its imperatives. He took one step and then another. Arwood carried the child — as thin as a shadow, and vivid as a dream — in his arms by placing each foot that hadn't blown up earlier on the same spot so it wouldn't blow up later. Step by step, unhurried, he walked with the boy back to the ridge and up its slender path, past Tigger and Herb, and close enough to Märta and Benton so they could look into the child's eyes as he was carried past.

Arwood handed the child to the people crying most before disappearing into the wailing crowd that surrounded him with hands, arms, and love.

Hours later, after dusk fell and the mob had dispersed, Märta went looking for Benton. She found him sitting alone on a rock with a can of Fanta. She said, 'Want to join me in Wonderland?'

Benton looked at her. 'I don't know what that's supposed to mean.'

'It's a recreation tent. I want to talk to you about what happened this afternoon with your friend. I haven't been able to focus.'

'It was quite a day.'

'You seem to be taking it well.'

'You don't know me.'

Soldiers weren't welcome at Wonderland. It was a recreation space of five large tents arranged into one covered area where the international staff of different non-military agencies would decompress at night after what counted for a day was done. It earned its name from being the place where everyone could wonder out loud what the hell they were doing there.

The military lived behind walls. They dug in like Romans. In the Forward Operating Bases, or FOBs, the military served home cooking that agreed with their soldiers' tastes and tummies, played hard rock and hip-hop, and built a colony as hermetically sealed and dissociated as a Marriott hotel on Mars. The command renamed every local road, destination, and object so it was memorable and pronounceable to kids with high school educations. In making life easy, because war is hard, they created a universe so artificial that you could be stationed in Iraq for years and never learn a thing.

The humanitarian staff lived in tents on the ground among the people. Listening to the same sounds, they heard the same conversations. There were no walls, no guards, no weapons. They were safe, not because they had defences, but because they'd been invited.

That night, Wonderland glowed yellow from the inside. A Honda generator hummed its syncopated beat, and some thirty people were hanging around on the floor and chairs. A few were reclining on an expensive red Roche Bobois sofa that seemed to have dropped from the sky, because no one could account for how it had got there.

The majority opinion was that it had belonged to Saddam. The dissenting minority opinion was that Saddam didn't have good enough taste to explain the sofa. The first group was anxious without an explanation, no matter how preposterous. The second group was simply happy not to be wrong. The sofa faced a 19-inch cathode ray-tube television. There was nothing to watch on Iraqi television but the dictator himself, and no one — not even the most media hungry of the student volunteers who might speak Arabic — wanted to watch Saddam. Luckily, though, some enterprising German kid had had the foresight to bring a VCR with him to Kurdistan, as well as the necessary RCA cables to plug it into the back of whatever television set might be found. So, at night, Wonderland lit up like *Cinema Paradiso*.

The German kid's name was Dominik. He came from Kaiserslautern at the edge of the Palatinate Forest. Being near Ramstein Air Base, it sometimes felt overrun by NATO military personnel, all of whom insisted on speaking English. For this reason, it had been an excellent place to get hooked up with English-language videos during the Cold War.

The video library at Wonderland in April 1991 consisted of

Cheers, Season 3;
Magnum, P.I., Seasons 4 and 5;
Golden Girls, Season 2;
Seinfeld, Season 1;
Gremlins;
Ghostbusters; and
Platoon.

There was some debate about what to watch.

The universal was *Seinfeld*. Everyone liked *Seinfeld*.

When Märta had invited Benton to Wonderland she had had designs only on a conversation. She had wanted to see him alone after the minefield incident. She needed to talk, or maybe listen, because she needed to understand. Arwood was nowhere to be found, and he didn't seem like someone who could explain himself when asked. She needed an analysis. She needed to know whether whatever Arwood had might be contagious.

Märta had first worked with United Nations Volunteers at the age of twenty-six, starting in Lebanon in 1983. She was offered a job in the system, but the infighting between the Department for Peacekeeping Operations and the UN Development Programme was so vociferous, so intractable, and so counterproductive that she decided on UNHCR instead. UNDP's development work seemed ideological and immune to historical reason. Peacekeeping was a military activity that insisted on universal best practices, even when no practice was universally best. But humanitarian affairs was goal-oriented, legally grounded, morally valid, and logistically adaptable. She was more at home in that sector, but she still hated the way the UN worked, and knew it wouldn't last forever.

Though she was an improper fit, she was eventually able to blend with the other professionals. Being smart, though, she was still able to see the experience for what it was: there were a lot of cowboys taking a lot of risks without good reasons. It was a man's world, and as a Swedish woman she knew it would be an uphill battle to gain the respect of a field staff that attracted a lot of people with military backgrounds looking to make the lateral move to civilian life. It all encouraged recklessness as a means of moving up.

The problem was that risk—like speed—was relative, and in the humanitarian sector there was no marker to use, because everyone else was climbing without a rope along with you.

Arwood was her first clear reality check in a long time. He really scared her. He was the first person she'd seen who was heading toward disaster so obviously that she could measure her own distance from it. Without something to stop her progress, though—some wisdom, some insight, some tool—she was terrified she'd start walking into minefields, too. Not from bravery, but because of a slow acculturation to risk.

The TV was on. A girl with a twinkle in her eye was spreading a blanket over the twentysomethings on the floor. Eyes were closing, and hands were on the move.

'The kitchen's in the back,' Märta said, walking past the adolescents.

She found a bottle of Jack Daniel's in the refrigerator with a masking-tape label that said, LIQUID COURAGE. It wasn't hers, and she didn't care. There was no ice, though the bottle was cold. She motioned to Benton to follow her to a dark corner of the tent where two black folding chairs faced a table that was too short to use, but they used it anyway and were lucky to have it.

'Not exactly *La Rotonde*,' she said, 'but it's what we have,' pouring them each a three-finger portion. She raised the white plastic cup to toast.

'Skål,' she said.

'Skål,' Benton answered.

They each drank half a cup.

The introductory music to *Magnum, P.I.* played—bum-Bum-BUM *BUM!*—and someone accompanied the music with a groan that lasted long enough to inspire clapping, followed by laughter that rang itself out. Magnum's deep voice emerged as the remaining sound as he explained how to become a world-class private investigator.

'You wanted to talk?' Benton asked, seated. He was unsure what was happening. He was more concerned about Arwood, but Arwood was missing. No one had seen him after he'd disappeared into the Kurdish crowd. It was when Märta took the drink away from her lips that he noticed her hands were shaky. Her voice, though, was not, and her countenance was grave.

'Your friend scared the shit out of me today.'

'I'm sure you've seen worse.'

'The thing about this line of work,' she said, 'and I'm sure it's similar to yours, is that I know I can leave whenever I want. As much as I sympathise with these people, their problems are not my problems. But with your friend? I think that could happen to me.'

'Arwood's going through some things.'

'Like minefields.'

'That's not what I meant.'

'I'm sorry,' she said. She sipped her drink again. 'What did you mean?'

'It's been an especially hard month for Arwood. He's very young and very inexperienced. I don't think he understood until a few weeks ago what people do to each other on this planet, and how easily and often they do it.'

'How well do you know him?'

'In some ways, I feel like I know him very well. We've been through hell together recently. I haven't known him long, though. I'm not sure that matters.'

'Did something happen during the war?'

'No — afterward. Arwood was stationed with an army unit monitoring the ceasefire. He was in Third Squadron, Second Cavalry Regiment, in a place called Checkpoint Zulu near Samawah. There's nothing there. He was a machine gunner stationed at the northernmost point of the post. It was a terrible place,' Benton said, turning to look at the young people watching Magnum emerge in his swimsuit, moustache, and Rolex from the Hawaiian waters.

Märta poured them each another drink. She leaned back afterward and lit a cigarette.

'Anyway ... I was there, too, with a couple of other journalists. We weren't doing anything useful. We all wanted to get closer to the civil war itself and report on it, but we couldn't. Saddam had kicked us all out, and we couldn't legally get in. I was feeling headstrong about being manhandled all the time, and wanted to see something else. It was ironic, because the Americans rather cleverly gave us journalists what we all wanted: access. They embedded us in their military units. As a result, we saw the war up close and intimately, but from a one-sided, one perspective angle. The Pentagon outsmarted us. We'd been completely coopted, but it was so exciting that no one noticed.

'Eventually I figured this out. I decided to cross the ceasefire line where Arwood was stationed. I wanted to go into Samawah and see what was happening. Interview some people. Take some pictures. See the war from another side. Get that other perspective. I made him think it was his idea, because he was an earnest kid. I honestly didn't think anything was going to happen. While I was there, the Republican Guard came and killed everybody. Arwood came to get me. Which he also didn't have to do. But it wasn't smooth.'

'What happened?'

'I don't want to go into it. Not just yet. I just ...' Benton trailed off and then sipped his bourbon again. 'I think ... what happened today with Arwood ... that was completely my fault. He wouldn't have been banished up here if it hadn't been for me, and he wouldn't have suffered whatever he's going through were it not for me. Also, it was useless. I dropped the film because it was slowing me down. I can't file the story for half a dozen reasons, including legal ones. So the fact is, Arwood walked through the minefield because I put him there.'

'It can't be that linear,' Märta said.

'It really is.'

Märta finished her drink and said nothing.

'I'm starting to think,' he eventually continued, 'that maybe we leave parts of ourselves behind in certain situations — some essential piece of ourselves that we have to cut off, otherwise there's no way out. The future becomes a kind of journey to discover what you might actually have left behind and what you're supposed to do about it. It's more than trauma. It's like a phantom limb, but with a piece of your soul.'

Märta watched Benton. She studied his face. She'd known dozens of war journalists and photographers. It was stunning how impressed they were with themselves. A few deserved it, but most were parachute journalists who would drop in, take some pictures, and rush out onto *Oprah* so they could tell the world about their bravery and close calls, and how committed they all were to the ideal of a free press to support an informed democracy. She liked to say to them, 'You realise that when you're gone, I'm still here, right? Me and the rest of the girls?' And they'd laugh, as though she were speaking through strawberry lip balm.

Benton exuded none of this. He seemed sincerely miserable. It was refreshing. Maybe it awakened something in her Swedish soul.

'Why do you do this?' she asked.

'Do what — this job?' he asked.

'Yeah.'

'It's a kind of momentum, isn't it? It's a job. A set of skilled tasks you eventually know how to do, which means you don't know how to do other things, so eventually there you are. When the paper calls and sends me on assignment, this is the kind of assignment they send me on. They don't ask me to do other things like … I don't know … photograph food for the *Lifestyles* section. In fact, I think I might like working on a cookbook.'

Märta smiled. 'Really?'

'Well, sure. It's honest and direct work that requires some creativity and technical skill. You get to see the benefits of your effort immediately. I imagine the people who work on that sort of thing are rather easygoing, and enjoy it. It's useful, but there isn't too much riding on it, really. I wouldn't mind being in that atmosphere. Besides, after taking pictures of gourmet food, you get to eat it. That must be nice.'

'Actually, you can't. A lot of the food is chemically treated. Much of what you see in magazines is entirely inedible. My boyfriend imports food into Sweden. I've been to photography sessions.'

'That's disappointing,' he said.

They did not return to the topic of Arwood that night. What she wanted was proof that she wouldn't become like Arwood. Instead she learned that she wasn't alone with her fears. That recognition created an intimacy she needed. Looking at Benton, she realised that she wanted the world to contract for an hour rather than expand, and for her senses to be directed to something specific rather than to be scattered across the terrain of Kurdistan.

She put her hand on his. It covered his wedding ring. She felt it press against her palm.

He looked down at her hand. He looked surprised, but he did not resist. Instead, he laid his free hand on top of hers. Neither smiled.

Before morning they were lovers.

The crisis ended with a whimper. The Kurds wouldn't get off the mountains until they could be sure of their safety. But Dohuk was below the 36th parallel, which was the demarcation line of the ceasefire in the north. US Lieutenant Colonel Abigail manoeuvred his companies closer to Dohuk to intimidate the Iraqis so they'd pull out and the Kurds could move back in.

General Jay Garner put two American battalions close by. Two different strike scenarios were drawn up. The Marine Expeditionary

Unit, backed by other coalition forces, was going to secure the high ground to the north and east of Dohuk. The idea was that the MEU's marine helicopter squadron would fly one marine rifle company to the high ground south of Dohuk, a second company would secure the road to the south-west, and a third, mounted in armoured amphibious vehicles, would pass through the second company and secure a blocking position ten kilometres south of Dohuk on the highway to Mosul. If that worked, and Dohuk was taken without a fight, 45 Commando and the Dutch marines were planning to pass through Abizaid's battalion, enter Dohuk, and secure the town proper, as they had at Zakho. That isn't what happened, though. The US National Security Council screwed it up, calling it all to a halt because they didn't understand the situation, and this signalled weakness to Saddam. He got on television and said that Iraq would fight to defend Dohuk. This meant that no one was going home and that the northern disaster was going to press on and on and on, because there was nowhere to resettle the refugees.

Washington tried to blame their field commanders, but that is what people in Washington do, because Washington is the kind of town that attracts the kind of people who do that. As usual, it was the people in the field who sorted it out, while all the members of the National Security Council went on to better jobs later.

The press never covered the real story, and the army flowered it over in diplo-speak. What happened was that an American lieutenant colonel named Dick Naab had a long talk with an Iraqi colonel named Nashwan, who explained that Saddam had already issued orders to hold the town and had said so on the national TV, so it would be an insult if they now surrendered it and Saddam had to back down. It was Naab who came up with the idea of having the Iraqis 'invite' non-combat forces into Dohuk to start the repatriation.

Nashwan, being pragmatic, saw the logic of the manoeuvre by recognising that it was in Saddam's interests to make the coalition forces go away, which they wouldn't do until the refugees were resettled, having said as much on television in their own countries. So Nashwan took this proposition back to Baghdad, Saddam gave it a think, decided it was a good idea, and the invitation was offered.

All that was left to do was move hundreds of thousands of destitute people from the mountains, which is what was done in one of the most remarkable and unsung humanitarian operations of the twentieth century. The end of Operation Provide Comfort was not mentioned in any newspaper in the United States or Britain.

Märta went back to Sweden, and slept for three weeks. For the next several months she followed Benton's bylines in the newspaper, but after a year she stopped. She and Erik were engaged, and soon married. What she had had with Benton she considered private, contained, and over: a *tryst*.

She thought the word meant the same as the French *triste* — 'sad'. It was strange to learn, on looking the words up, that they were only distantly related.

PART II

THE LONG, COLD, HARD, AND DARK OF IT

22 YEARS LATER

8

The cragged land holds tightly to the last heat of the day. Thomas Benton's collar flaps gently in the late-summer shamal wind. He sits on the bleachers by the Domiz refugee camp, overlooking a pitted and littered playing field as the world fades to a pastel pink under an expanding indigo sky. Iraqi, Kurdish, and Syrian children are kicking and chasing an oblong American football up and down the remains of a once-tended soccer pitch. A well-meaning man from a US aid agency shouts instructions to them about what they are doing wrong.

A skinny boy without shoes is covered in dust. Or perhaps he is made of dust. If he is, he is dissolving before Benton's eyes, because behind him is a thick and heavy cloud choking everything slower than himself. By his speed and direction, this means most of the Eastern world. Blacked out, he is a Semitic stick figure of eyes, teeth, and feet. This boy—this genie, this pillar of fire—has somehow gained a measure of control over the foreign ball, and with tremendous timing and balance shoots from the far edge of the pitch. As the ball passes between the two broken and bent tubes that were once the posts, the children—on both teams—all cheer. The applause is as youthful and sincere as it is startling and welcome.

Benton watches the children as he opens a Kit Kat chocolate bar he bought from a cold store, and pops open a Fanta bottle scarred opaque from reuse. He is sixty-three years old. It is a poor dinner for an old belly, but its virtue lies in familiarity. He learned long ago that being a successful world traveller means little more than having the ability to eat anything without suffering adverse consequences.

A man whom Benton hasn't noticed before is sitting on a lower bench. As the ball passes through the posts, he leaps from the edge of his seat and cheers. He is an Arab. He wears shabby trousers and a blue blazer. His black hair is dirty and poorly cut. From the fit of his jacket, it seems he is wearing donated clothing. That, or he is vanishing.

He turns to Benton — the only other person in the bleachers — and smiles. It is not a smile of happiness but of pride, and in this precious moment it runs deeper than an empty well. He looks to Benton because he needs to know if anyone saw what he saw.

To Benton, it is a familiar look in the Middle East. Answering the man's unspoken plea, he speaks first. 'That your boy?'

'That is my son. He is better than Beckham. Better than Ronaldo.' His accent is Arabic, and his English is inflected with British intonations rather than American ones.

'He's got talent,' Benton says through a weak smile.

'I would like to see Beckham chase around a ball shaped like that.'

'So would I.'

'Fifty-two aid agencies here. Not one brings a real football for the children. Imagine that.'

'I don't have to,' Benton says.

'Where you from?' the man says.

'England,' Benton says. 'A town in Cornwall. You've never heard of it. Fowey.'

'Is it near Penzance?'

'Further east. Halfway to Plymouth. What do you know about Penzance?'

'I saw the musical with the pirates,' the man says. 'West End. In 1996. It was May. That was very nice.'

'Ninety-six was a better year.'

The man puts up his hand. He can't talk about that.

'Why were you in London?' Benton asks.

'I did my master's degree in education at the University of London. When I got back to Damascus, I was made principal of the elementary school where I worked. I liked the theatre. It was too expensive for a foreign student, but there were half-price tickets in Leicester Square the day of the performance, if you weren't too picky about what was left. I was often very lucky back then.'

'You're Syrian?'

'I'm nothing,' he says, the smile gone. He glances back to his son and makes sure he is still there. 'There is no Syria. There are no Syrians. For the first time in three thousand years. I am a ghost. I live in a tent. There is no work here. Nothing for the kids to do all day. I had to pull him out of school. Now he's a year behind, when he was once ahead. I teach him by myself in a tent with no books, no maps, no Internet. I have nothing but my son. But he is worse off. He has only me.'

Benton knows he shouldn't ask the next question but does, because it is the only question to ask.

'Your wife?'

'My wife? My wife was eight-months pregnant when a government sniper shot her and my unborn daughter. It went through my daughter's brain and out the back of my thirty-four-year-old wife, a woman whose kindness and gentleness of heart contained more poetry than will ever come from Ali Ahmad Said. They died from the same Russian bullet, provided as a gift by Vladimir Putin. When I got to the hospital, I saw eight other men like me—because that day eight other women were shot the same way. You see, the government snipers were playing a game. They shot pregnant women that day, ones that were near term. And they shot them in the same part of their bodies—through the baby. For target practice. For a laugh. Maybe for a bet. Assad wanted to teach us that we were powerless.

He wanted us to know he was in charge. The big man. I haven't told my son. At home, I was still checking under his bed for monsters at night. He was too old for this, I thought. Why at eleven? But now I know he was right to ask me to check. How do I tell a boy who is so sensitive and gentle that his mother has been murdered and that his baby sister will never breathe life? How do you explain to a child that the only place there aren't any monsters is under the bed? I can't explain it to myself.

'My son is waiting for her to come here and meet us. He is excited about the baby coming with her. Every time I try to work up the courage to tell him the truth, I vomit. I don't even have tears. My body cannot accept the truth. It tries to reject it. Coughs it up like an illness that will destroy me. I sob without tears. The air leaves me. Have you ever in your life seen anything like this?' the man asks.

His eyes plead for an answer.

'Yes,' Benton says.

'I don't believe you.'

'I wouldn't lie to you.'

'You've been to Syria? You came from there?'

'I saw it here. In '91. In Iraq.'

'Kuwait? Desert Storm?'

'No. After. The civil war.'

'Ah,' he says. 'The Shaaban Intifada. You saw it.'

'In Samawah. I saw it all.'

'Why did you see it?'

'Because I couldn't close my eyes.'

The man nods. 'Yes,' he says. 'That's right.' He turns back to watch the boys as he talks.

Benton says nothing. The boys have regrouped and are chasing the ball back toward the other end of the dirty pitch. Benton removes a bright red bandana from the inside pocket of his jacket, wipes his face, and returns it there.

'You know what *shaaban* means?' the man says.

'No.'

'It means "separation". Iraq was splitting apart. He was a weak tyrant after a bad war. Iraq erupted. No plan. No vision. No weapons. Everyone competing. Everyone running away, but not toward. You see the difference? They all hated Saddam, but what did they love? No one knows. Iran making trouble. Like now. But it erupted. Like now,' he says, tilting his head to the west, toward Syria, though possibly toward all of it. 'But then Saddam killed everyone. Everyone-everyone. So fast. No mercy. One hundred thousand. Two hundred thousand. No one knows. He did this in two months. Imagine. No one remembers. Hundreds of thousands. No one remembers.' The man continues to stare ahead. 'How can the world swallow up a hundred thousand people without a trace? I am terrified by this world.'

'I remember,' Benton mutters.

'You speak Arabic?' he asks.

'No,' Benton says.

'A very beautiful language. Filled with nuance and poetry. Many games. Many, many wonderful games. Puns and jokes and allusions. But also contradictions. You see, *shaaban* is the same word as the eighth month of the Islamic calendar. There is a story that on the fifteenth day of the month of Shaaban, the doors of mercy and forgiveness are thrown open, and those who sincerely repent for their sins are accepted by God. I am not a religious man, but I find this very beautiful. It seems wrong to me that this word should be shared by such events. That the word should be shared by God's forgiveness and also such cruelty. It is wrong. They should not be shared. I can't help but see this. This is my education. And so it is my curse.'

The man turns away from Benton and watches the children, who see nothing but the ball.

'Tell me why you're here. You are important? A Big Man?' the man says.

'I'm not important. I'm an old journalist. I'm a dinosaur. They want me gone.'

'You're a journalist. You can tell the story.'

'They're letting me run out a budget line that I asked for so they can fire me when I come up empty. I asked to come here for spurious reasons, and I think they know that. They had to let me because of my seniority, but I've cashed in all my chips. I've given them the excuse they need. This is my last trip.'

'Where is your wife?'

'In the bed of another man.'

'Go back to England, my friend. Make peace with your wife. Forgive her. Forget the work, the newspaper, all of this. It is all dust. We are all dust. Your family is all that matters. Save them, if you can. It is the only way to honour the dead.'

'I have a debt to pay before I go back.'

'Here? In this place?'

'It's an old debt. A friend of mine saw something, and he said he wants to set it right.'

'What did he see?'

'I don't know. A coincidence. An echo. A midday moon in a blue sky.'

'I don't understand.'

'Neither do I. There was a news broadcast,' Benton says to the man on the bleachers, 'about an attack not far from here. They had footage somehow. It was broadcast all over the world. It happens sometimes that there is footage of an incident, it catches the world's attention, and it goes around. Anyway, the man I mentioned ... he saw someone in it who looked very familiar and yet who could not have been there, because she was already dead. She died long ago. In March 1991.'

'Ah,' the man says, not sounding surprised. 'He saw a ghost.'

'I don't believe in ghosts,' Benton says.

The man shakes his head. 'That doesn't matter. People see things that do not exist all the time. They see hope. They see love. They see trust. They see a future. These things do not exist for many of the people who see them. Ghosts are no different. You see? Whether they exist or not, we see them. Your friend, he saw a ghost.'

'This girl is in a video. She's not a ghost. I've seen it.'

'So you have seen this girl, too.'

'Yes. It can't be her. She's someone else. The resemblance, though, is uncanny.'

'So you have seen proof, like your friend, but deny it.'

'It is proof that there is a girl who was caught in an event who looks like someone I once knew, if briefly. It is not proof of a ghost.'

'Proof. There is nothing more theoretical than proof. The pagans asked the Prophet Muhammad for proof — he split the moon in two, but that was not enough for them. In the West, you stare at the bodies of our dead in fifty thousand photos, all at the hands of Assad. Tens of thousands. You have the photos. High-level Syrians smuggled them to you. They have been forensically analysed. The videos are everywhere. And yet some of you debate whether you have proof — and if you have the proof, what does it mean and what should you do? We have all the proof we need. It is the making sense of it — that's the problem. Deciding what to do about it — that's the problem. You came here to find this person? This girl? To help her? To help your friend?'

'I don't know why I'm here.'

'Ah. Then you're here to suffer. You are in good company.'

They watch the boys run for a few more moments. Benton then makes to leave, but as he does, the man says, 'You think we're going to die here? Me and my son?'

'I think,' Benton says, 'that whatever comes next isn't life.'

'That's right,' says the man, turning away again. He nods to himself as he watches the boys. 'That's right,' he whispers.

Benton checks his watch. Night falls quickly here. He stands up, dusts off his clothing, and puts the empty bottle and Kit Kat wrapper into his satchel. He'll toss it in a rubbish bin when he finds one.

'Keep your son safe,' Benton says as he leaves.

'Remember us,' the man says. 'Me and my boy, and my wife. My daughter's name was to be Adar. Adar. Remember her for me in Cornwall. Remember her for me so that the earth does not swallow us up and we die twice.'

9

Only three days before, Benton was sitting in his living room, drinking beer from a glass, watching a re-run of *The Good Life* with Richard Briers. The actor had died in February, and somehow it felt like a national loss. Tom and Barbara had come around for a bath and drink after their chimney 'cleaned itself', leaving them covered in soot. Benton was enjoying the cold drink and the warmth of the show. Vanessa had gone. He'd kicked her out three weeks earlier, on finding her in their bed with another man. Their daughter, Charlotte—a scholar in palaeontology at the University of Bristol—had since been trying to solve their marriage as though it were an evolutionary riddle. Her technique was to study each of her parents' morphologies to find common traits, in order to try to prove that they were, by nature, members of the same family. Benton tolerated it, knowing she couldn't help but arrange dead things into orderly systems.

She was not actually helping, though. He had decided he needed a break from her calls, and so gave himself a seventy-two-hour respite from answering them. So when the phone rang as Tom and Barbara headed upstairs to bathe together, he let it ring.

The ringing, however, became persistent, and while persistent was in character, Charlotte was never deliberately rude. After fifteen and finally twenty rings, he had to answer it or unplug it. As he didn't have his reading glasses, it made unplugging that damn little plastic thing on the base of the phone all but impossible; and so, with little choice, he opted for his daughter's lecture and answered it.

He turned down the volume on the television, but didn't turn it off as he took the call.

'Hello?' he said.

'Did you see her?' said a voice that was not Charlotte's. It was a man's voice.

'Who is this?'

'Come on, Ferris. Who do you think it is?'

'Arwood?'

'Did you see her?'

'Who?'

'It was live on Al Jazeera five hours ago, then it was picked up by everyone. It's on the Web. BBC, CNN, MSNBC. It'll be on *The Daily Show* if anyone at the White House says something stupid enough about it. They're playing it over and over on the news. The clip is too good not to show. You haven't seen her?'

'No,' Benton said. 'What are you talking about?'

'No need to wait for the loop. Al Jazeera has it on the website. It's on YouTube, too. You know what that is, right?'

'Arwood … Christ. I mean, it's been—'

'Benton, listen, OK? The video. I need you to see her.'

Benton rubbed his eyes with his free hand. 'I don't know what you're talking about. I haven't read the papers.'

'The papers. That's quaint.'

'You know what I mean. How did you get this number?'

'You live in the same place and have the same job. Go watch the video. I'll call back in ten minutes.'

'What am I looking for?'

'I'd hate to ruin it. Type in "mortar attack, Kurdistan, green dress, today". You can't miss her.'

'Who?'

'Ten minutes.'

Benton sat at his workstation PC, which was old and slow and black. He turned on the speakers, expanded the image until it filled the screen, and sat back to see what had summoned forth the voice of Arwood Hobbes from the silence of twenty-two years.

He was right: it was easy to find.

More often than not, when the topic and locale are the Middle East, the screen becomes beige. It is a world of earth tones and browns, harsh lighting and harsher angles. When the story turns to the troops—to the Americans, the Brits, to the Iraqi regiments, or the irregulars—they move like matching and replaceable figurines in their dull clothes and camouflage. When the story turns to civilian life, though, their distinctiveness and humanity bursts to the fore in a tapestry of colour.

Because of this, the girl in green shone like an emerald against this pallid earth.

A newswoman stood close to the camera. It was a bust shot. Behind her was a line of refugee women and their children. Three-quarters of all the people streaming out of Syria and heading for Iraq were women and children. More than half those fleeing the country were children. Al Jazeera was making a point of it, to its credit.

The date was 20 September 2013.

The refugees had formed an orderly queue. The camera frame did not extend to the front of the line, so Benton could not see what they were collecting. It might have been water or cooking oil. It was a liquid, anyway. They all had buckets, or empty water bottles, or cooking pots—anything that could hold whatever they'd be given. The girl, though … she stole the scene from the camera, in part because she never tried to. It was the way she stood apart from everything around her. Even the most alienated people on earth seemed removed from her.

The eye had no choice but to welcome her in and become transfixed.

She did not wear a headscarf. Her hair was not black. It was sandy blonde — her complexion that of an Australian surfer. She stood on the balls of her feet like a child, and bounced as though she were cold and waiting for a bus on Oxford Circus. She bounced to a rhythm that was produced by a force deeper than her own heart. Her posture was unselfconscious. She stood as though unseen and unseeable. In this way, she captured the attention of the world for almost twenty whole seconds while performing the most fundamental of civilised acts: she waited her turn.

That was when the mortar landed.

Someone less familiar with acts of war might have missed it, but Benton's eye was attuned. The presenter was standing in the right third of the screen. The girl in green was in the left third in the upper quadrant, and the mortar came down in almost the dead centre of the viewing frame.

A mortar explosion is no larger than an IED, or an unexploded cluster bomb, or an anti-personnel landmine. But unlike the others, the mortar comes from above, and if the angle is right and the frames-per-second of the video are fast enough, you can see it drop. The Zapruder film that caught Kennedy's assassination in 1963 ran at 18.3 frames per second. An iPhone runs at thirty frames per second. This one was at least that fast, and made it possible for Benton to see the thin black line drop from the sky.

A falling mortar sounds like a small dropping bomb, which is what it is: the sound falling and the pitch dropping, like an ambulance pulling away and out of sight. We whistle the sound as children. SS … ssss … ssssss … boom. This is because Western children imagine themselves above the bomb.

From below, it sounds very different. The air compresses. The bomb becomes louder and the pitch higher until the moment of detonation. BOOM. If you have heard it before and survived, you are primed to hear it again, at any provocation, for the rest of your life. And Benton was primed to hear it.

There was a small flash before the audible explosion caused by the mortar landing on dirt. The dust kicked up into the blue sky, and smoke filled the screen. The girl—whatever might have happened to her—was obstructed by the debris. The film ran for forty-eight seconds.

He watched it again.

And again.

And again.

He learned the exact moment in the film when he could see her face most clearly. He paused it there. He leaned in to the screen. He stared at her. He stared at her until the phone rang again.

Benton answered on the second ring. He didn't say anything.

'Are you looking at her?' the voice said.

'Yes,' Benton said.

'Miraculous, isn't it?' Arwood said.

'It's an uncanny resemblance.'

'Is that what we're calling it?'

'She died in your arms.'

'Yes, she did.'

'It was twenty-two years ago. She was fourteen or fifteen. She'd be thirty-seven years old now if she were still alive, which she isn't, because she died in your arms, and no one knows that better than you do.'

'The dead don't age.'

'This isn't the same girl. You know that.'

'They're saying the Kurds did it. The attack. It's turning public opinion away from them. Plus Barzani's been killing people, and the Kurds are infighting, and maybe this is the moment to pull back on some support.'

'Who's saying that?'

'The news reports. You're in the news business. You don't know this?'

'I'm off today.'

'You don't watch the news?'

'I'm more relaxed when I don't.'

'They're saying the Kurds are attacking the Syrian refugees coming into Kurdistan. This is their proof.'

'That doesn't make sense. The Kurds have no motive for that. It's also not their MO.'

'There's a flight to Baghdad from Heathrow in twelve hours. You transit through Vienna. I've already bought you a ticket—business class. Pick it up at the counter. I assume your office can arrange the visa.'

'Arwood, it wasn't her. It was an unfortunate girl who looks like the girl from '91.'

'It was even the same dress.'

'A lot of girls wear green.'

'Personally, I think it was al-Qaeda,' Arwood said. 'I think they did it to pin it on the Kurds, undermine support, turn northern Iraq into a soft target. It would be helpful if a journalist were to cover it.'

'Arwood, listen,' Benton said, sitting back from his computer. 'Even if I boarded that flight, we couldn't be there for three or four days, at best. I have to get to London, to Vienna, to Baghdad, transfer planes, make my way to the camp, and together we have to get to the site. She either died in the attack itself, was wounded and died later, was wounded and was carried off by others, or suffered one of the other horrible fates that befall children and young women over there.'

'Come on, Ferris. Where's that fighting British spirit?'

'This story won't even exist in twenty-four hours, and by the time we answer the question of who actually did it, a thousand other distractions and stories will have taken over. The fact of Kurdish responsibility will have worked its way into the popular imagination, and there's no backpeddling in a culture with no interest in the past. We'd risk our lives in Iraq for a Twitter feed.'

'Here's an idea,' said Arwood. 'How about we set things right because we want to? Forget the big picture. You come over, cover the story, we visit the site, we go home. And for what it's worth, I think she's alive.'

'You want us to go there? To Iraq?'

'Benton, we never left. Don't you realise that? Gulf War, Operations Provide Comfort, Northern and Southern Watch, Iraqi Freedom, and New Dawn. There has not been a day since '91 we haven't been in Iraq. Not a day. So, yeah, Iraq. That's where the party is. Also, I think you owe me. I think you were planning to go into Samawah, and you got me to think it was my idea. Right?'

Benton did not answer quickly enough, though he had had plenty of time to think about it. Arwood took this for the answer it was.

'The thing is, Benton, I now understand that going in was the right thing to do anyway. You had to go. It just didn't turn out well. You still owe me, though. So how 'bout you be a stand-up guy, get over here, file an interesting story for your newspaper, and just maybe we set things right and save that girl's life? I mean, why not? You busy?'

'Iraq feels very far away from where I'm sitting,' Benton said.

'You're a war reporter with thirty years on the road. This is nothing more than another flight and another drive in the desert—nothing you haven't done a hundred times before. I've followed your career. How about you retire with a bang?'

'All right,' Benton said. 'I'll come, but not because I believe it's the same girl or that she's alive.' And as an afterthought, he added, 'Where are you?'

'I'm already here, man. I'm in Dohuk. I'm already here.'

10

Benton walks back from the football pitch to the prefabricated container that has been set up by the International Refugee Support Group as a satellite office in this section of the camp. For a few steps, he accompanies the long line of women in their evening procession to the nearby town where they collect water, night after night.

The refugee camp was outfitted for fifteen thousand people. It is now home to more than fifty thousand. By day, the bright blue-and-white tents undulate and glimmer in the intense and cloudless sky south-west of Dohuk. Beige and brown stone buildings squat low and solid on dirt roads. It is remarkably flat here. The sky is enormous. Children are everywhere.

Following a small path between tents, he passes women who are busy cooking, cleaning, stacking, carrying, organising, and talking through events with other women, building local strategies to survive. The men, though — who knows what the men are doing all day? Complaining, mostly. Arguing in the way that fish in a bowl might debate the future of the seas. They cannot accept being helpless. Deals are being struck. Lies are being told. Hope is placed on a hook as thin as breath, and in their desperation men bite for it. Still, the camp is calm. Neat, if not clean. Beneath it, in the talk and whispers and the meetings, a new future is being negotiated, but Benton knows the outside world is deaf to it.

Benton finds the IRSG container easily enough. It is where Arwood said to meet. It has a flimsy steel door on hinges, two windows on the side, and two wooden steps leading up as in a trailer without wheels in a park. The IRSG logo is stencilled in orange on the door.

There is no obvious reason to do so, but Benton knocks. He hears a chair immediately scrape across the plastic floorboards, and then heavy feet advance to the door.

The latch turns, and the door opens. A hand is extended from a man with a familiar smile but different eyes.

'Twenty years,' Arwood Hobbes says.

'Twenty-two,' Thomas Benton says.

'Still punctual,' Arwood says.

'I've been told I'm incapable of change.'

'Come on in.'

Benton releases Arwood's grip and steps into the office. It is a spartan place, with a sheet-metal desk and a black office chair, and facing the desk are two folding chairs for visitors. A round meeting table sits in the middle, surrounded by bright-orange plastic chairs. There is a public relations calendar set onto the wall, but it is too small to adorn it. Below, a bright-orange power cable runs along the edge of the back wall with three outlets, and each one contains an extension. An expensive uninterrupted power-supply unit, which could power the computer and peripherals for hours if the electricity went off, runs under the desk.

On the wall to his right, across from the desk, is a UN High Commissioner for Refugees map of the region, a map of the camp, and various printouts from the UN Mine Action Service with indications of unexploded and abandoned ordnance. Arrows and circles have been drawn all over them. On the far wall, across from the entrance, are a few posters from the NGO itself. Discreetly, someone has also pinned up a Dilbert cartoon strip with Catbert shouting, 'It's not in the *budget!*'

'Nescafé?' Arwood asks, starting a white kettle with an orange button.

'Sure.'

'A lifetime, right?' Arwood says, opening two brown tubes containing instant coffee mix, and looking in the drawers for some creamer and sugar.

'At least the one.'

Arwood puts his feet up on the desk like a colonial magistrate bored with the natives. 'Look at you, all here in Iraq and shit. Was it something I said?'

'How've you been?'

'It's like Joe Walsh said, "I can't complain, but sometimes I still do."'

'Not even a hint?'

'No wife, if that's what you mean,' he says. 'Had a three-year relationship with a nice girl named Rebecca when I was in my thirties. That's long over. No kids. I never really settled into a normal life. I did join the Columbia Record and Tape Club. You know, where they send you a selection every month and you need to say no to it if you don't want to pay? I never said no. Never paid them either, come to think of it. That was kind of normal, kind of Everyman Americana. Then I joined Alcoholics Anonymous, where you need to say no to drinking when people give you drinks. Never said no to that either. I liked the meetings, though. I liked to introduce myself by saying it'd been eighteen minutes since my last drink. The tight-arses got pissed off, but other people laughed, and the girls wanted to be near me just to smell my breath. Happy times.'

'You look OK,' Benton says.

The kettle pops sooner than Benton would have suspected, and he takes that to mean the water was already hot. Arwood must have been a few cups into his stay here already.

'Time will tell,' Arwood says, then smiles. Benton smiles, too.

Arwood was twenty-two when they last met. He's in his mid-forties now. His face remains boyish, but he carries the years in his eyes. He is still lean. His body is taut. It is not the body of someone who drinks and smokes all day.

'So how is it we're getting to use this space?' Benton finally says.

'I know the programme manager. She's an old friend of mine. We have a free run of it. These are our digs until we make the flatlands out in Ninawa tomorrow.'

'Who is it?'

'Not telling. Not yet. It's my only good surprise.'

Arwood hands Benton a coffee. Across his left knuckles is the word LESS.

'Tattoo.'

'Oh, this? Yeah. My first was 'Death Before Dishonour' — put that on my shoulder when I joined the army in 1989. But then, you know, I came back from Desert Storm not dead, and all dishonourabilised.' Arwood makes two fists, and puts them next to one another for Benton to admire. His knuckles are cracked from the dry air. They say MORE and LESS.

'You like them? I think they make a good matching set.'

The tattoos are in a serif typeface. They have faded, as though the concepts themselves have been overused.

Benton uses a white plastic teaspoon to take sugar from a kilo sack, and stirs it into his mug. 'I've seen GOOD and EVIL,' he says, 'and LOVE and HATE. Never those.'

'Yeah, well … I know what these mean,' Arwood says.

The Nescafé is hot, and tastes the same as it does everywhere else, which is its virtue.

'So there was this other guy in the tattoo parlour at the time,' Arwood continues. 'Same deal. Across the knuckles. Guess what his said? YOUR NEXT. Can you believe it? What an arsehole. Didn't even spell it right.'

Night falls beyond the shatter-resistant windows like a carnival shutting down. It is best not to be out at night. Teenagers have nothing to do here. These are the world's newest street-corner societies. This is when it gets dangerous: when something new is being formed.

Arwood takes a cigarette from a soft pack. He taps it a few times on the table, and lights it as though it should have been lit already.

'I've got a car and driver,' he says, leaning the plastic chair back so it is now on two legs. 'A local kid named Jamal. Works for the IRSG. They're gonna loan him to us for the one ride — there and back. I figure we top him up a hundred bucks, and make it worth his while. It's a week's wage around here, if you're lucky. There are only one or two stops to make.'

'The girl,' Benton says. 'You know exactly where it happened?'

'The mortar attack? Yeah.'

'They weren't specific in the news reports. It was between small villages.'

'The coordinates were in the sitrep from the UN,' Arwood says, pushing two stapled pieces of white paper across the desk. The top reads, 'UN STRICTLY CONFIDENTIAL (File reference: 0009/22-14, Security Information Sensitivity, Classification and Handling) 1600 hrs EST 22 September 2013 DSS-IRAQ Daily Situation Report, Events and information pertaining to UN staff safety and security over the last 24 hours in Iraq ...'

'Where'd you get this?' Benton asks.

'The NGO. It's not really confidential. Everyone on the mailing list gets one.'

Benton skims the note and slides it back.

'I used it to get more details, and asked around a bit, and I now have very accurate GPS coordinates. I'm off by metres.'

'Made an impression here?' Benton asks.

'No. People know about it because it's on the news, but the internationals aren't interested. Most people here don't think the Kurds did it, but they're so factionalised and unpredictable one never knows. The locals are numb to this stuff. It was one of a dozen attacks this week alone. Only reason it comes up in conversation at all is because it came with art. All eyes are on the Syrian side. Assad's as much of a fuckin' psycho as Saddam ever was. Everyone at the camp here is mostly concerned with what's walking or being dragged across the border. No one understands why we're bothering to go look. I tried to be convincing but I wasn't, so you'll need to come up with an explanation. I can't think of one. And the truth sounds nuts.'

'The truth is nuts. It's comforting to know it sounds that way.'

'What little we know is that everyone hauled arse after the attack. Left the bodies behind. The zone's hot. No one's been back since. Al-Nusra and ISIL are in the area now. They hate each other. You know these guys? ISIL is al-Qaeda, but apparently even al-Qaeda hates them, because they aren't following orders and seem to have their own plans. This story is definitely going to develop.'

There are two empty chairs by the table. Benton imagines the girl in green sitting in one of them, flipping through a fashion magazine while sipping a Coke Light from a clear straw as the scent of the fragrant pages wafts upward, casting a spell of glamour and luxury and permanence. He can't decide which of the two girls he's seeing. He doesn't believe they were the same girl. But he doesn't know enough about them to tell them apart.

Charlotte, his daughter, was fourteen once, too. That's what she did, sitting at the kitchen table in Fowey, at breakfast, as Benton tried to lay down the law about soft drinks. Vanessa was no help. The women ignored him. Why wouldn't they? Coke Light makes you thinner.

'Kurds didn't do it,' Arwood says.

'Video says they did. The world believes the video.'

'Cameras lie.'

'I thought the line was, "The camera never lies,"' Benton says.

'That's the line, but it's not true. Cameras lie because they're held by people.'

'You've changed,' Benton says.

'It's the mileage.'

'Whose office is this?' Benton asks.

'I don't want to tell you yet,' Arwood says. 'There's not gonna be a lot of fun on this trip. A little. But not much.'

'I'm a little past surprises.'

'Then you're in the wrong place.'

'Tell me. Please.'

'I'll give you a hint: FFCs.'

'What?'

'Flying frozen chickens.'

'That's your hint?'

'You don't remember Perdue's Revenge?'

'Do I remember frozen chickens falling from the sky? Yes.'

'So ...What's your guess?'

'Why are you punishing me?'

'Let me make this more simple. Do you remember getting laid that night?'

'You were gone. How do you know what happened that night?'

'As it happens,' Arwood says, 'all those refugees outside who look like props are actually people with eyes and opinions. So ... think blondes.'

'You don't mean—'

'Märta Ström. Or however she pronounces it.'

'Märta's here?'

'She could walk in any minute. She knows you're here. I talked to that Spanish assistant of hers. In fact, she was supposed to be here when you arrived. But she's not. If I were you, I'd read something into it.'

'What did she say when you said I'd be here?'

'That's your first question?'

'No. Of course not. Is she well?'

'Yeah. She seems fine-ish. This lifestyle isn't the best for Nordic skin—all the sun and all. At least she doesn't have vitamin D deficiency.'

'You two have stayed in touch all these years?'

'No. I know people in the region, though. She's got a helluva reputation for being hardcore. Unlike you, she has not taken her foot off the throttle. Could have been director at any number of places, but she still prefers the field. I got in touch through channels. Turns out, she remembers us. I think we made an impression.'

'She probably remembers you for walking through a minefield.'

'Yeah, I don't do that anymore. Not literally, anyway.'

'Did she seem ... pleased to hear from you?'

'I don't know. She's got a better poker face than the Russians.'

'She was reserved on the outside. Maybe she's still like that.'

'It's because she's blonde,' Arwood says. 'I think it's the eyebrows. Harder to track blonde eyebrows in low-light situations. The proof is that you never have to wonder what the Greeks are feeling. Or the Italians. Or the Spanish. Or the Arabs—'

'I get the idea.'

'Japanese. Jews. Jamaicans—'

'Thank you, Arwood.'

'Anyone south of the Rio Grande—'

'I'm going to take one of your cigarettes,' Benton says.

'Happy, sad, angry, and blank. That's what blondes give you,' Arwood says.

'I didn't know about the dishonourable discharge,' Benton says.

'They call it other-than-honourable, which is nice, because it lets people guess.'

'What happened?'

'You saw what happened.'

'Nothing else?'

'You know what I did to Harvey.'

'They were extraordinary circumstances. If that was the result, then they overreacted.'

'It's the army, Benton. They overreact for a living.'

There are no cars at night. No tyres on roads, no teenagers driving too fast, or taxis refusing to let people merge. There is only the hum of the generators. Above, the stars are orderly, and separated by vast distances.

One sound catches Benton's attention—a stringed instrument. The player is skilled, and the song is sad. It is coming from a place nearby, out in the night.

'It's a buzuq,' says Arwood quietly, guessing Benton's question. 'Looks like a mandolin with a long neck. He's not half bad, this guy. He's been playing out there for almost a week. Families sometimes go and listen to him.'

'What's the plan tomorrow?' Benton asks.

Arwood reaches down into a drab-green rucksack and takes out a neon-green document holder and an iPad. He places both on the table. He removes a foldout map of Iraq, Syria, and Turkey that already has highlighted routes, destinations, and sticky notes on it.

'When did you do all this?'

'Mostly after I saw the news. Same day I called you. As soon as I saw her, I knew we were coming. I started calling in favours and moving money around. Isn't it amazing how much the people in this part of the world remember? When they say they'll never forget something, they don't. And kids … they grow up so fast. I feel like I've got clarity again. Don't you think so, too?'

'Kids grow up fast, yes. I have no clarity, no,' Benton says.

Arwood points to the border between Syria and Iraq. 'There's a pontoon bridge that went up in August last year between Syria and Iraq at Peshkhabour. Way up north. Looks like a road over the Tigris.

They're streaming in from Aleppo, Efrin, Hasakah, and Qamishli.' Arwood points to the Syrian cities and villages. 'The video we saw was taken here,' he says, pointing to a spot east-south-east of the bridge. 'It was a humanitarian food convoy. They were dropping off some provisions for a mobile medical unit handing out water and rations to the refugees walking in. There was a lot of food there. Food's a commodity here.'

Benton looks at Arwood, and tries to read his face.

'You're still holding to this fantasy that she's alive?'

'It's a big maybe, I admit, but I think she's there. Waiting for us.'

'Maybe? That's what's anchoring our strategy?'

'No. My hunch is what's anchoring it. My gut. My feeling that we've got nothing better to do, so let's go find out.'

'It was three days ago, Arwood. There are rumours stretching all the way to Lebanon about children being abducted and their organs being harvested for international buyers. They abduct ten-year-olds and strap bombs to their chests, telling them that they'll be fine and that only the other people will get hurt. The idea that she's still there and needs us to rescue her is ... well, it's lunacy.'

Arwood reaches into a bag under the table and takes out a bottle of Johnnie Walker Red and places it next to the Marlboro Lights. He takes two plastic cups and then pours them both generous portions. He's clearly done with Nescafé.

'Listen to me, Thomas,' Arwood says, with an intimacy that pushes away the years. 'I believe that we were called back here. This one single attack. I've checked the numbers, Benton. I've become quite good at numbers over the years. The chances of its being filmed at all, of its being shown, of me seeing it and both of us seeing her ... chances that low require a poetic kind of maths. The State Department documented over 6,700 separate terrorist attacks worldwide in 2012 alone. Those 6,700 attacks killed over 11,000 people. More than 21,000 injured. Almost 1,300 taken hostage or kidnapped. These aren't war statistics, man,' Arwood says. 'These are peace statistics. Mission accomplished, and all that.'

Benton sips his blended whiskey, and says nothing.

'I'm not even including state-driven slaughter in Syria or the DRC, or Sudan, or Pick-a-stan. And in this year of tears? 2013? Gonna be even worse by the time we're done. But the camera eye caught this one. And we saw it. And we alone know what it means. And to ignore that is to turn your back on this big old goofy world and all its mysteries. So you're coming with me. Because somewhere in that soft belly is that gonzo journalist who once walked into a Shiite stronghold for a story and an ice-cream cone. So let's go into the desert and find what we find, including the girl. That's my speech. You want a better one, you call Bill Murray.'

Outside, the stars shine, the men talk, and the buzuq sings a song for which there will never be any words.

11

The interior walls of the prefabricated office are the off-white of a 1970s space station. When the door opens, the whiteness falls away into dead space. The illusion is so complete that Benton is startled not to be pushed into the cosmos.

Instead of an astronaut stepping in, though, it is a time traveller. She is still blonde and still attractive, both for the qualities she has and those that remind him of the woman he once knew. She is fuller than when Benton last saw her, which is not unpleasing, and her eyes have turned from a glassy blue to a fine lead crystal.

Benton glances at her eyebrows. 'Hello, Märta,' he says.

'Hello, Thomas.'

Märta settles into one of the visitor chairs in front of her own desk. She looks at Thomas Benton. He has darkened with time. His face is fractured: it has become more delicate, like old pottery.

She smiles.

He smiles at her.

Neither says a word.

'Oh, come on, people,' Arwood says. 'The line is, "Of all the refugee camps in all the towns in all the world, he walks into mine." It's sitting there like a penny.'

'I forgot you were a movie buff,' Märta says.

'Where have you been?' Arwood asks her, deciding that Benton has passed on his own chance to speak. 'I thought you'd have been here hours ago.'

'I've had a very bad day.'

'Compared to what?' Arwood asks.

'Every other day for the past few months,' she says.

Even Arwood has no reply to that.

'What happened?' Benton asks.

Benton's voice is as soft as she remembered it. It is familiar, but changed. It is lower. It is older. Which is to be expected.

'This is as bad as I've ever seen it. The Syrian government is performing summary executions in al-Bayda and Baniyas. They're aerial-bombing civilian populations. They're razing entire neighborhoods. Everyone's focussed on the chemical-weapons attacks, but they weren't even the worst atrocities. Aleppo is a nightmare. They're targetting doctors — did you know this? Targetted assassinations of medical personnel, so they can't help the wounded. They're using unprecedented kinds of cluster munitions, supplied by the Russians. They're—'

'We know,' Benton says quietly.

'It bears repeating, though, doesn't it? The World Food Programme is demanding access to get food into areas where the Assad regime is actually besieging and starving to death the local population as a means of warfare. They're collecting people — thousands — and murdering them, documenting it, and lying to the families about their fates. The *Guardian* is reporting on ten-year-olds having their teeth pulled out with pliers. And then Assad says, on US national television, no less, "No government in the world kills its people unless it's led by a crazy person." They seem to suffer no cognitive dissonance when they say this.'

'We know,' Benton says.

'And meanwhile, these people calling themselves ISIS, or ISIL, or whatever it is—'

'Märta. We really do know.'

'Do we really?'

This wasn't the first conversation Benton wanted to have.

'A few months ago,' he says, trying to regain ground, 'one of my colleagues got sick, and they asked me to go to Syria. I had to report on the beheading of a Syrian soldier. I was metres away from it. I was invited. I was there with an Al Jazeera journalist who had witnessed four of them that same day. Maybe he was one of the soldiers you described. Maybe it was an innocent boy. I don't know. What I know is that the crowds were cheering around us, women ululating, children clapping, as a man murdered another man with a small knife and then carved his head off. I couldn't sleep for days. The journalist from Al Jazeera — I called him. He's not the same. We really do know—'

'I had to help one of them today,' she says, interrupting him. 'This morning. Our medical team saved one of their regional commanders.'

'What do you mean?' Arwood asks.

'A commander of ISIL. It was near the Syrian border, but on the Iraqi side, where we have a mobile surgical unit. They limped across. His name is Abu Malik al-Almani.'

'Always Abu,' Arwood says, sipping some booze. 'Abu Abu Abu.'

'What happened?' Benton says.

'A lot of the fighting is in the Syrian north-west. But they come back to Iraq for supplies and recruits, and to stir things up here, too. They know we have medical units on this side of the border but not in Syria, because we're not allowed in, so they bring people to us and other NGOs when they're shot up.'

'Why don't you turn them away?' Arwood asks.

'Well … three reasons. We're obligated by international humanitarian law to treat all non-combatants equally. Their wounded qualify. Also, we can't have access to non-combatants unless we're allowed access by the belligerents. Humanitarian space is negotiated and maintained through relationships with people like this—people who hold territory. And the third reason is that if we don't treat them, they'll kill us.'

'It's nice when things line up, isn't it?' Arwood says.

'The word from some of the refugees here,' Märta says, ignoring Arwood, 'is that al-Almani's group went into a village near the border, gathered up over a hundred women who they said weren't dressed appropriately, and murdered them in front of their families. There was some local resistance, and this one—Abu Malik—'

'Abu Abu Abu,' Arwood says.

'—we patched him up,' Märta continues. 'Before he left, he thanked me. I had to shake his hand. He extended it, and his men outside were armed and fresh from killing people. I had no choice. I've been in situations like that before, in Afghanistan with the Taliban. But this was worse. This girl of yours, the one you're both so keen to find — we suspect that her group was coming from a village east of the one that was slaughtered. They must have gotten word of what happened, and decided to risk the walk to Iraq. She survived that, only to die in the mortar attack on this side. So, yeah, sorry I'm late.'

'She's not dead,' Arwood says, kicking back the last of the Johnnie Walker. 'I don't know why everyone keeps saying that. What's that thing with the cat in the box and the nuclear vial of quantum stuff? If that fucking cat isn't actually dead, our girl's not dead.'

'I don't know,' Benton says, 'whether everyone should be drinking a little more or a little less.'

'This trip of yours,' Märta asks, 'it's going to be quick, right? Because—and I'm sorry to say it like this—but this quixotic adventure is not a high priority for me. I'm very happy to see you both and help, but I don't want Jamal out on an unnecessary run for too long. He's my only dedicated driver, and I can't allocate resources because the *Times* wants a story and Arwood Hobbes needs to satisfy his curiosity. This is a favour for old times' sake.'

'It's a milk run,' Arwood says, standing up, brushing down his jeans, and slurping the last of the whiskey from his cup. 'I'm going back to my tent,' he says. 'It's been nice seeing ya, doll face.'

'No one talks like that anymore, Arwood,' she replies.

'No one does a lot of great stuff anymore.'

The door closes behind him, and Märta and Benton are alone.

It becomes blessedly quiet. For a long moment, they sit and enjoy it.

It is the first time they have been near each other since 1991.

'You look reasonably well, considering,' Märta says, sipping her whiskey from a plastic cup.

'Considering how nervous you make me?'

'I was going to say, "considering you're over sixty now."'

'Gentle.'

'Would it make you feel any better to know I'm glad to see you?'

'I suspect it would.'

'I am glad to see you, Thomas Benton.'

'You're looking—'

'No need to say. You've heard about my day, and I haven't showered yet.'

Benton takes the cue. 'Right,' he says, uncrossing his legs and making ready to go. 'I have some packing to do, and Arwood has quite a day planned for us. For some reason, he has us on a strict timeline, and I'm still behind on the details. If I didn't say so already, thank you for letting us use the office and providing so much help. It is kind of you. You obviously don't owe us a thing. I'd invite you for dinner when we get back if there were any place to go.' Benton stands and brushes his jacket.

'Are you still married?'

'What?'

'Married. You still have the ring. Women usually take it off afterward, but not always men. Are you still married?'

'Why?'

'Because I know a good place to eat. Right now. If you're hungry and have no other plans. And there's a shower there.'

'Oh,' Benton says, sitting down again.

'You're shocked.'

'No, no. I'm just … a little less Swedish than you are.'

'Or more British, anyway.'

'That, too.'

'What's her name? Your wife?'

'Vanessa. As it so happens, we're separated.'

'She's there and you're here, that sort of thing?'

'No. More officially than that.'

'Here's the thing, Thomas. I'm fifty-six years old. Erik and I split long ago. I very rarely take on new lovers, but I seldom say no to old ones. Surely that's one of the reasons you're here, right?'

'Um—'

Märta, for the first time, looks perplexed, which was not on Arwood's list of facial expressions.

'Or … isn't it?'

'Can I answer that later?'

'Why are you separated?'

'I found her sleeping with another man. Which, in a roundabout way, was probably my fault.'

'Why?'

'I think it has something to do with my personality.'

'When was the last time you cheated on your wife?'

'Well … as it happens, it was with you. So, twenty-two years ago.'

'You haven't been with another woman in twenty-two years, and that woman was me?'

'I like to space out my infidelities.'

'Thomas?'

'Yes?'

'Get in the car.'

12

There is a private security guard posted outside the seven foot-high wall surrounding Märta's house in Dohuk. The yellow headlights wake the guard, who had been dozing. In an effort to prove he's been alert the whole time, he springs from his plastic chair and unlocks the padlock on the sheet-metal gate with elaborate Moorish designs across the top. Smiling, he waves them inside.

Märta parks the Land Cruiser on a short and well-paved driveway, and they enter a two-storey house with a flat roof and barred windows that looks the same as every other such house extending from Algeria to Tehran.

Inside, the floors are tiled and the furniture simple, aside from a bright-red Victorian wingback in the living room.

Benton holds his duffel bag and briefcase. He feels like a schoolboy about to be seduced by a friend's mother. He would stockpile this feeling if he could.

'This isn't so bad,' Benton says, his voice echoing off the walls.

'We're paying three thousand dollars a month for it in a country where the average annual income is six thousand, but that's the industry these days.'

'Is it always like this?' he asks, not knowing what else to say.

'The insane prices? Yeah, pretty much.'

'I meant your accommodations.'

'No. It varies. In Iran, during the Bam earthquake of 2003 — you remember that? I had to stay with Médecins Sans Frontières until we were able to set up a temporary base camp of our own. That was tent and cots. Thirty thousand dead. IRSG was doing family reunification. That was especially grisly.'

'What are you doing here?'

'In Dohuk? You didn't even check the website?'

'This has all come out of nowhere for me. I was watching television when Arwood called. I haven't heard from him this whole time.'

'We're working on child protection and health. We do a little crossover work on community services. It's a good portfolio for us, and I'm glad to be in a stable place. Except when I head to the field and visit the mobile units, like today. Then it's worse. In Iran, everyone was dead. So much grief. Sometimes, though, you bring a child back to its family and the world glows. Without those moments, it can be too harsh. Our turnover rate is high. That's the life, though. You following things in the region?'

'I still cover international. Less fieldwork than before.'

'What's your take on what's happening now?'

'No one ever asks me.'

'Tell me.'

'I think the state system is being rejected like a bad transplant. They haven't developed an independent political philosophy to support it, and they can't go around quoting Rousseau and Locke as convincing authorities against the Koran. So now it's a choice between secular authoritarianism and Islam. And not the nice kind. I'm not hopeful.'

'The bedroom's upstairs on the right. The bathroom's on the left, if you want to shower. I think I left the hot-water heater on. If the red light is glowing, you'll have plenty. If not, you might want to use a cloth instead. It's frigid. I'll shower down here.'

The red light, happily, is on, and Benton takes off his clothes carefully to avoid looking in the mirror. The hot water splays down into the peach-coloured bathtub with a water pressure that would be the envy of Kensington. A thin layer of dust forms a perimeter around the spreading water until Benton steps inside and disrupts the flow. As the water pulses down on his face and chest, Benton closes his eyes and imagines he is standing right there.

Downstairs, Märta showers quickly and wraps herself in a terrycloth robe as though she were stepping from a Swedish or Finnish sauna. She plugs in her laptop, then her iPhone in the kitchen, and takes a long drink of water from a plastic bottle with a blue top. She runs her fingers over the countertop and sees the dust that's collected there. She has discussed this before with the girl. Yes, dust storms produce dust — no denying it. But the point of the young lady's job is to come by afterward and clean it away. Even where jobs are in poor supply, there always seems to be a reason not to do them.

Down the road, the Lebanese have set up a rather impressive supermarket, with many products flown in from the UK, the US, and Egypt. What she can't buy there comes from the *souk*, which has a far better selection of fresh fruit and vegetables than Stockholm.

The fridge is well stocked. She has a chilled Montrose rosé from Provence. It's better than the screwtop suggests. She brings two glasses upstairs.

Benton hasn't yet finished with the shower as she turns down the bed and places the glasses and bottle on the nightstand. Like a college girl, she has draped a thin purple scarf over the lamp to create a warmer mood. Wiser than in her youth, she uses a low-wattage bulb to reduce the fire hazard.

The master bedroom has glass doors that open onto the roof of the first level. Dohuk is surrounded by the Zagros Mountains. From the roof, she has an unobstructed view of the chiselled edges of the jagged hills, and can watch the snow line descend as the nights shorten.

Like everyone else who has a rooftop in Dohuk, she has a plastic dining set so she can benefit from the breezes in summer and the warm tiles and clay on cool nights. She waits there for Benton. She imagines him drying off and sprucing himself up in her poorly lit bathroom, trying to look like James Bond. It makes her smile.

She opens her robe to feel the breeze. No one can see her from here. She wants to feel the day slip off. She can still feel that monster's hand in hers as they shook. He looked her in the eye. He tried smiling. It is not only the fresh air that cleanses her. If this were Sweden, if she were on a rooftop in Stockholm, she would not feel so self-conscious about being undressed. In being herself she can rebel against the noose that is slowly drawing around her.

It's a shame that much of what once made her Swedish is gone now. But one characteristic she has unapologetically retained is her absolute faith in the fundamental pleasure of a good drink. If she were empress of the Northern Vales, she'd instruct the sages to rewrite the calendars so that time would be measured in liquid—by 'half a bottle ago,' or 'when the vintage has matured'. Poetry would soar again, and music would fill the halls. It might subvert punctuality. But what really matters—birth, love, death—doesn't abide by the clock anyway.

Märta pours herself a glass, and lets the wind blow her robe.

'Am I intruding?' asks Benton, stepping onto the rooftop, too, wearing flip-flops too small for his British size-9 feet. She has a few extras for guests, but the Asians don't stock shoe sizes big enough for Western men.

His clothes are ridiculous. His sweatshirt is from the 1980s. The stitching on the shoulders droops off the shoulders, making him look like a giant tea cozy. It is also short. The elastic waistband is comically high. It is the pallid grey of an ancient university sweatshirt abandoned for years in a drawer; it looks as though it has internalised the very darkness.

It says, in big block letters, PREPARE TO BE FALSIFIED.

His dark-blue sweatpants are baggy. They are cottonesque and cleanish.

His hair, such as it is, is tussled and wavy. He may have tried using a hair dryer. Perhaps for the first time. As an act of triage, he has brushed his hair back in the hope it will make a difference. In its own way, it has.

'No, not intruding,' she says, closing her robe. 'I was expecting you. Or something like you.'

'I'm older,' Benton says.

'Your clothes, however, are timeless.'

'My daughter got the jumper for me. She's a palaeontologist now, if you can believe it. She specialises in a 300 million-year-old shell called a brachiopod. She rattles on about the wonders of phylogenetic systematics and the pleasures of cladistics. She belongs to the Willie Henning fan club.'

'I don't know what any of that means.'

'It's a method of classifying organisms in the natural sciences on the basis of shared characteristics called synapomorphies. It's quite a new approach to the science of classification, and it's the most accepted now, as it's explicit in its hypothesising, and it's empirical in its methods. Which, given the state of knowledge today, you'd think would disqualify it. Charlotte was studying earth sciences at uni, and was attracted to this as if it were a church.'

'It sounds complicated.'

'The science is, but the logic is admirably simple. Charlotte says that one of the most satisfying parts of her job is knowing for a fact that she is building and contributing to the fundamental wealth of human knowledge. I, on the other hand, am absolutely confident that I am not.'

'You're envious.'

'Envious, yes. Jealous, no. She's earned her peace of mind.'

'It's a cute jumper, all the same,' Märta says.

'I'm told,' Benton says, looking down to his top, 'that it is very funny if you're a scientist.'

'You mean on account of what it says?'

'Ouch.'

'There's a glass and bottle just inside near the bed. Bring them out, will you?'

Benton does as he's told. There is a small box on the rooftop, and Märta opens it and then hands Benton a pristine terrycloth and motions that he should clean off the lawn chair before sitting on it. He does this and then takes a seat, folding the cloth and placing it beside himself on the next chair. Märta does the same. He pours himself a glass and tops up hers.

'Skål,' she says.

'Skål,' he replies.

After a sip, he stretches out his legs and takes a deep breath.

'Dohuk isn't a bad duty station,' she says. 'The shopping is adequate, they're tolerant of foreigners. Violent crime is low. It's more of a wrong-place, wrong-time problem. Unless, of course, you've come here looking for trouble. Have you?'

She leaves the notion hanging for a moment. Benton's countenance is hard to read.

'I found you,' he says, spinning the glass by its stem.

'What are you doing here, honestly? Did you even know I was here? I was sure you did until I saw those clothes.'

'I didn't, if you can believe it. Arwood knew you were here, but he didn't tell me. I really am here about that girl in the video and because of how strongly Arwood feels about it. Which doesn't mean I'm not very happy to see you. It's comforting to know that people from your past are still out there. Still here on the planet with you. Part of getting older, I guess. We're only missing Herb Reston now, and that Frenchman. I forget what everyone called him — something from *Winnie-the-Pooh*.'

'Tigger.'

'That was it.'

'They're here, too.'

'Of course they are.'

'No, really, they are.'

'What are you talking about?'

'It's not as though they were wandering down the street and I bumped into them. I hired them and brought them here. I hired Tigger first — ages ago. I was at UNHCR when we all met. I worked next for the Red Cross. I asked Tigger to come with me to the IRSG when I took a management position. The support group said I could pick my senior team. Tigger was in French intelligence, got out, did some political analysis as a policy wonk for a while, then wanted to get back into fieldwork. Like me, he found the development people too ideological, and so came over to humanitarian field operations, which is more pragmatic. Tigger and Herb eventually became good friends. I think of them heckling the world stage like those Muppets in the box seats. What were they called?'

'Statler and Waldorf. How are they?' Benton asks.

'Grown up. Both are married. Both have children. Now we're back in Iraq, after the Americans and everyone else has left. They're four weeks on, two weeks off, for six months, and then they return home with a healthy pay packet.'

'How long have you been here?' Benton asks.

'Thomas,' Märta says, ignoring his question, 'if you're wearing those clothes, then you really didn't fly here to see me. In which case, what are you doing? You really need to tell me. It can't be for this story you're talking about. This mortar attack. It's a fly in the ointment around here. There's no way the *Times* would follow up one crime in ten thousand.'

'Do you remember,' he says, 'when we met in that tent in the mountains—'

'Wonderland.'

'Yes. I told you that something happened in the south before we met, but I didn't want to go into it. What happened was that a girl died in Arwood's arms. It was a girl in a green dress, one who bore a striking resemblance to the girl in the mortar video he's hoping to find. The first girl's death was pointless and cruel. It was also invisible. No one saw it. The girl in the video, though—her death, which was also pointless and cruel, was nevertheless seen by the entire world. The first one happened in front of us. The second one happened in front of us all. We didn't go back for the girl in '91. We left her body behind. We had no choice, but this time we do. I think Arwood is here for the girl in the video because he's fixated, and he's broken, and he needs to either bury this girl or return her body to her family, if that's even possible. That may seem a mad reason for coming to this part of the world. Personally, I don't think it is. I've seen people do a lot more to achieve a lot less. As for me, I'm here for Arwood, because he saved my life, and I ruined his.'

'So you're here out of loyalty?'

'As I said,' Benton says, 'I'm old-fashioned.'

'Do you trust Arwood?'

'I believe he wants to solve this for reasons I understand. So ... yes. We'll drive to the spot, confirm her death, see if there's some way to learn her identity—papers, brand of clothing, anything—return her to her family, if we can, and write a story so people know that the images they saw on television didn't end in a dramatic puff of smoke like all the CNN coverage did back in '91 and now all the drone attacks do, too. I want to clear the smoke—maybe for the first time in my pathetic career. As for the details, I won't know until tomorrow, when he briefs me on the mission.'

'There's a mission?'

'It's a turn of phrase.' Benton smiles and then sips his rosé, wishing it were Talisker.

'It's getting cold,' Märta says.

The mountains have retreated into the night. There are no lights
on the high ground. Nothing is separating them from the sky except
the absence of stars.

'Inside, then?' he asks.

'Are you feeling guilty?'

'About Vanessa?'

'Yes.'

'I'm enjoying being with you.'

'When you said "separated" …'

'The morning after I caught her with the other man, I told her I
wanted a divorce.'

'Do you?'

'No.'

'Why did you say it?'

'It was the cruellest thing I could think of at the time, and I'm
something of a coward.'

'Do you think staying with me tonight will punish her?'

'I think I want to see what's under your robe.'

When they finish, Märta does not immediately disappear into the
bathroom. She pulls up the blanket and lies back into her pillow. Her
left leg touches his right. She has angled her body away from his to
make room for her full relaxation.

Benton does not interrupt her solitude. He studies the angles of
the walls again instead. He measures their thickness by their colour,
their temperature by their finish. They are clean, but remind him of
too many collapsed buildings, too many twisted steel rods reaching
from too many structures in so many cities, like stripped ribs open
to the air, the people and families they once protected exposed, and
everything vital open to the scavengers.

13

Arwood wakes, stretches his arms, and — to check his sobriety — keeps his eyes closed as he brings a cigarette to his lips with his left hand and lights it with a Zippo from his right. It is actually harder than standing by the side of the road and trying to touch your nose with your finger, because the Zippo can set your nose on fire, whereas the cop isn't allowed to.

The other nice thing about starting the day with a cigarette is that, whatever else happens later, at least the first move was yours.

It's going to be a good day. Arwood can feel it. Today is the day he's been dreaming about and anticipating for a long, long time. He always knew he'd be back here to finish his business. He'd known ever since his father kicked him out of the house after he got back from Desert Storm.

'What the hell are you doing with yourself?' his father had said to Arwood, who, by late June 1991, had been back from the Gulf for a month. Arwood was deep into a new video game called *Civilization*. It mainly involved taking over the world by destroying everyone else's. He played it in his boxer shorts and dog tags while chain smoking.

'I'm trying to civilise the world, Dad, the old-fashioned way. Why, what are you doing?' he'd said in the blue light of the cathode ray.

His father had come with an agenda and a message, and was in no mood for Arwood's flippant attitude, which the US Army had — implicitly, if not contractually — promised to change when his son enlisted. Instead, they sent him back early, emotionally damaged, and even more obnoxious, because now he wasn't afraid of anything and had no respect for authority, including his father's.

'It's time for you to get out and see the light of day, and maybe even look for work. You're a man, for Christ's sake.'

'I had a job, Dad. I was a soldier. I was paid for it,' Arwood said, not taking his eyes from the glowing monitor. 'I was kicked out, but my need to conquer foreign lands is not yet sated. Ya see, all those little orange people, there to my north-east, are getting a little grabby with the mineral wealth in my sphere of influence, so I've decided to genocide their arses and let that be a lesson to all the other civilisations, especially the purple ones in the south. I don't like their attitude either, but maybe they'll learn to step down once they see the bloodbath I'm inflicting on their orange kinsmen. The thing about this game — and you only know it after you've played it for a really, really, really long time — is that I'm not sure the other civilisations are capable of learning what I'm trying to teach them. How fucked up would it be if I'm spending all this time killing people to send a message they are actually not capable of understanding, because they don't have those algorithms in their brains? I don't have it worked out, but I think I'm on to something.'

'Watch your language.'

Arwood turns to his father for the first time.

'Are you serious?'

'You have three days to get your act together, and either get a job or get out. Your mother and I aren't carrying you. You were lazy in high school, so you joined the army. You did the minimum there by specialising in that damn gun rather than something that could have made use of the high IQ that God gave you. And then, when you actually did your service, you dishonoured yourself, your country, and your family. So, yeah, I'm serious.'

'I did my job and then some.'

'The US Army doesn't think so.'

'They don't think at all.'

'You fire that weapon at anybody?'

'No.'

'Then you didn't do a fuckin' thing.'

Arwood takes a pull on his cigarette, blows it out, has a languorous scratch where it feels best, and then sits up just in time to let the ash fall onto the sleeping bag rather than into his left eye.

Up, alert, and exfoliated, his only regret is that he's alone.

The reason he is alone with the cigarette this morning is that he couldn't find a girl to ride pillion last night. After Benton and Märta pulled away, Arwood started looking for company himself. No point in being single, surrounded by the mountains and dust, and not trying to get laid. The fact is, other than complaining and getting drunk, it's really the only sport in town.

He'd been working on a girl named Ann. They met at the cafeteria. Ann was in her late twenties and old enough, so his thinking went, to appreciate the value of an older man who wanted to make her intensely happy very briefly.

Sadly, Ann was a talker. And while he often liked loquacious women with strong opinions, it did in the end come down to what they said rather than how they said it, and what Ann said was annoying.

As best as he can figure it, the reason he woke alone to a cigarette was that the conversation had turned insipid, and Arwood has never been good at recovering from the dizziness caused by thin arguments.

Arwood liked to imagine logic as being like a taco shell. Sure, logic is fragile, but the shape is stable and supportive if you're delicate with it and use it correctly. What you can't do is ignore its structure, overstuffing the bottom and squeezing it from the top.

Ann worked for a non-governmental organisation called—no

shit—Happy Planet®. She was a project officer. For almost twenty minutes last night, Arwood had tried to care. He tried to care about her master's degree in conflict resolution, and about her internship with the United Nations Volunteers, and how the UNV had helped her 'almost' get a job with the UN, and how that failure had led her to Happy Planet®, where, presumably, she would make the planet happier, though Arwood wasn't sure the planet itself was unhappy. What he couldn't get past was how every statement she made about the world was in the form of a question, while everything that should have been a question was presented as a statement.

'You see,' she'd explained to Arwood, who knew that feigning attention to her pet philosophies was the surest path to wearing her thighs as a hat, 'I wrote my thesis on participatory action research? So I'm here to teach people how to transform conflict by empowering them through narrative, so they can better resolve conflict rather than revert to war? It's … well … I guess it falls under conflict transformation, technically, but I think that term is overstretched these days—it's been unpacked too much, if you see what I mean—and I'd rather go back to the more solid work in conflict resolution that takes more seriously the postmodern, post-Foucauldian, and postcolonial assumptions about the status of knowledge. Because, you know, we don't just want to transform conflict, we want to resolve it, but without imposing the solution or anything? I'm especially interested in this new school of thought in development studies, which says that the only solution to our misapplication of power in these instances—given the subaltern status of the participants—is to not even be there.'

He had wanted the sex. He really had. He had wanted to receive muffled feedback through a pillow as he massaged her milky-white arse and slapped it red. But he didn't want it *that much*. Arwood Hobbes was forty-five years old. Having started when he was sixteen, it meant he'd been having sex for almost thirty years. And while sex after thirty years is still totally great, it most often doesn't feel quite as good—not in the long run, not for the memories, not for the big smile—as setting someone straight. This is why he really had no choice but to tell Ann, sincerely and from the heart, that 'technically speaking, war is a conflict-resolution mechanism'.

Ann split, and Arwood slept alone, but the Great Taco of Logic remained intact, and in a postmodern world that is no small thing.

Up, out, and ready for the day, Arwood doesn't knock on Märta's office door, and instead steps brightly into the prefab to see whether Benton is there yet. It's seven-thirty. He finds both Märta and Benton inside at the conference table.

Märta speaks first, and catches him off guard with a phrase no one's ever said to him before: 'Oh good, you're here.' She continues, saying, 'I'm taking you both to see Louise Ballan, who's the head of the International Committee of the Red Cross sub-delegation here. She's Swiss, from Nyon. Very bright. A little intense. Big hair. Try not to stare at it. We're going to see her. She knows a lot, and it never hurts to have a friend with a helicopter. And as for you,' Märta says, pointing to Arwood, 'the only words you speak to Louise are "Good morning," "Thank you," and "Goodbye."'

'I want to be on the road by eight-fifteen,' Arwood says. He isn't smiling. 'There's a timeline. We don't have time for lectures.'

Märta walks across the room to a pile of equipment on a folding table. She talks as her hands pick up Motorola headsets, and she starts placing batteries and checking the signals.

'All my people,' she says, 'are registered with the UN. They all have DSS call signs, VHF radios, timetables for radio checks, and maps showing where to call in when on the road. We're connected to the Dohuk radio room. You,' she says, handing a Motorola headset to Arwood, 'are Romeo Charlie Niner Two, and you,' she says to Benton, 'are Romeo Charlie Niner Three. Ahmed Haddad is the

one on the radio. He's Egyptian, a little on the heavy side. He's
well tapped in up here, and he's on the ball. He's young, and he eats
too many potato chips, but don't let that throw you. I will let him
know you're with us. I'm calling you' — turning to Arwood — 'a
consultant. And you,' she says to Benton, 'are a visiting journalist,
which happens to be true. You're in the system. Please use it. It'll
keep you safe, and remember that your actions are a reflection on me
and the International Refugee Support Group.'

Arwood watches Märta click the batteries into place. 'Why don't
you just use the charging bases for the walkie-talkies?' he asks.

'Because Motorola batteries tend to overheat when you charge
them inside the handsets rather than outside, which shortens their
life cycles, and anyone who's worked in the field knows that. I know
what I'm doing, Arwood, and you two don't. Here,' she says, handing
a map to each of them. 'These maps have all the roads in northern
Iraq. We don't officially call this place Kurdistan, though everyone
does. Each checkpoint is in blue. I'm logging your journey with DSS,
and I'm putting a time estimate on it. Ahmed knows exactly how
long it is supposed to take to get from one point to the next, and
he stays in touch with local authorities, so he even knows if there's
traffic. If you do not radio in your location within twenty minutes
of each check, he'll call you. And if you don't answer, he'll call me,
and then he'll notify the police and we'll have to come look for you.
If you veer off your planned journey, you will force everyone to start
looking for you, which would divert needed resources from any real
emergency. So don't. Are we clear? What's your call sign, Arwood?'

'OU812.'

'Thomas?'

'RC 92 and RC 93. We'll stick to the filed route and abide by
procedures.'

'Is it true,' Arwood asks, 'that the French call these "talkie-
walkies", not "walkie-talkies"?'

'Yes,' Märta says.

'Isn't that being contrarian? I mean, "walk" and "talk" aren't even French words.'

'The radio room,' Märta continues, 'can be contacted on the handset and also by phone. Here's the number.' She points to the tops of the maps. 'Right now, in front of me, you enter that number into your cell phones. Both of you. Then assign a speed dial to it.'

Arwood and Benton do as they're told, while Märta hands Benton an extra phone. 'It isn't protocol, but please take this extra one. It's my personal phone and has an Iraqi SIM card. I charged it last night. I'll use the IRSG's phone. If you lose yours, or it's taken from you, you have a backup. Trust the system, trust Ahmed, and strap this phone to the inside of your leg.

'Now, we need to meet Louise and Ahmed before you leave, so they can put a face to a name in case you two get into trouble.'

Benton follows behind Märta and Arwood as they drive through the camp and onto the road that takes them to Dohuk, where the ICRC sub-delegation has its office. Benton looks at the children who are barefoot, in flip-flops, or in Chinese knock-offs of Crocs. A two-year-old is screaming and wriggling in her mother's arms, and the woman has a vacant expression. She and Benton look at each other.

When Charlotte was two and a half, she became obsessed with hair clips. She needed to touch them, collect them, put them in the box, take them out of the box, lose them, find them, put them in her hair, take them out of her hair so she could see them, have them in and out of her hair at the same time so she could wear them, and see them and hold them at the same time, and she needed to sleep in them, but she couldn't sleep in them because they had sharp edges and could hurt, so she wasn't allowed to until, finally, he and Vanessa relented after a scream so angry, so long, and so high-pitched that the wavelengths were converted into light and she glowed with the hellfire of a thousand suns at the cosmic injustice of her parents' arbitrary authority, but alas, she couldn't sleep in peace because the sharp edges of the hair clips hurt her head.

He can't imagine Charlotte as that child. He should be able to, but it is not possible. Not really.

Louise's Red Cross office isn't in a prefab. It has its own two-storey beige building, and there is a large placard outside with its name in French — *Comité International de la Croix-Rouge*. There is an Arab guard sitting on a white plastic chair out front. He is unarmed. On his matching table is another of the ubiquitous Motorola handsets.

Märta waves to him as the Toyota passes through the doors and into the parking lot, where it joins half a dozen other Japanese vehicles with the same colours but different markings.

The foyer is clean. There are posters of the ICRC working in different countries. Others contain quotes from the Geneva Conventions. Benton sees Arwood studying the posters as they walk to Louise's office. One reads: 'Prisoners of war must be allowed to use tobacco. (Convention III, Art. 26)' He smiles and points, and tries to get Benton's attention, but Benton ignores him.

The doors are all marked with the names and titles of the staff. Märta leads them to the left, past an HP printer and a Xerox machine, past a line of maps showing the region, then Iraq, and then the Middle East in its entirety.

There is a plaque on the wall commemorating their dead from the 2003 bombings in Baghdad that closed their offices in the capital and in Basra — the town where the uprisings started in 1991.

At a desk, in front of a PC, is a young Muslim woman in a fashionable headscarf and Cartier glasses. She is slender. She has elegant cheekbones, thin wrists, long fingers, and perfect fingernails. There is an effortless grace to the way she moves. Headscarves make it a little harder to pin down a woman's age, because hair is more of a cue than we often realise, but Benton puts her at about twenty-seven.

Compared to the young British women he works with in London, she seems exceptionally composed.

She smiles warmly when they arrive. Märta embraces her, and they kiss on each cheek.

'Farah, this is Thomas Benton and Arwood Hobbes. Benton is a journalist with the *Times*, and Arwood is a consultant with me. Louise said we could come by for a short chat. They're headed west to al-Qanat near the border.'

Farrah extends her hand, and Benton shakes it. It is like holding the wing of a bird. She smiles diplomatically and says, 'Very nice to meet you.'

She does the same to Arwood, who shakes as well and — blessedly — says nothing.

'Farrah is from Erbil. She knows this region better than anyone else I know,' Märta says.

'The situation near al-Qanat and al-Rabiaa is not good,' she says, directing her comments to Benton. 'The Ninawa province has certainly not been the worst, not compared to al-Anbar, but there are reports of ISIL groups clashing more and more with the Kurdish Pershmerga and the Shiites. Also, some of the Sunni tribes find ISIL too brutal, so they are turning on them, too. But not all. Deals are being struck. Also, the Kurdish PKK is moving south from Turkey and linking up with other groups. The situation is very fluid. It is best not to go there if you can avoid it.'

'We're going. So if we can get on with this—' Arwood says.

Farrah smiles again. It is then Benton realises that her grace is not a form of polished diplomacy, but a highly refined survival skill.

Märta raps gently on Louise's door and swings it open enough so that they make eye contact. Benton can see them both from his angle. Louise ushers them in. She's on a call, and the speakerphone is on. She's taking notes on a legal pad with her free hands. 'I'm on with AirOps,' she whispers. 'Give me a second.'

A dry, humourless, and distinctly Russian voice that channels the collective charm of the former Politburo comes through old speakers on the phone. Disembodied, it says, 'We had three stretcher cases yesterday without stretchers. This created problem for loading and off-loading of wounded and other messy people. Technically this isn't our concern, but the Iraqi Red Crescent — which is not always the most cooperative national society, not that this is news — is using ambulances for collecting patients, and they don't have stretchers for stretcher cases. They only have the one used in the ambulance. This results in blood leaking onto the floor of my aircraft, which is bad for the aircraft. It also smells very bad and irritates me, and makes everything tacky, including my instruments, and I don't like it. I now think if we are carrying bleeding wounded we need a new solution for protecting against blood spillage into, and from, the aircraft. So I'm telling you — my boss.'

'Thanks, Spaz. I'll tell the head of mission, and I'll see what we can do about the sheeting. You're helping save lives, Spaz. We're all grateful.'

'Yeah … OK,' he says, and unceremoniously hangs up.

Louise hangs up by pushing an orange button. She opens her palms. 'Busy morning. You know how it is.'

'His name is Spaz?' Arwood asks.

'We don't know his real name.'

'Is that good?'

'It's working so far, which is pretty much the definition of success around here.'

'Louise Ballan,' Märta interjects, 'this is Thomas Benton from the *Times*, and Arwood Hobbes, who is temporarily with me. They're headed up north for the day. I wanted you to all meet and see if there's anything that wasn't in the UN sitrep this morning.' Turning to the men, she says, 'After I left the UNHCR in 1995, I was with the ICRC myself. They have a network of their own, and they don't share information. So this conversation is not to be repeated.'

Louise is in her early forties. She is slender and big-chested, wears heavy and dated glasses, and her hair is the greatest mass of black, tangled curls Benton has ever seen. She sees him looking at it and smiles.

'Hypnotic, isn't it?'

'I didn't mean to stare.'

'Everyone stares. It's hypnotic.'

Benton smiles, and reaches out his hand to shake hers.

Arwood does the same, and says nothing.

'Where are you going?' Louise asks, sitting down again and ignoring Arwood.

Märta is about to speak, but it's Arwood who answers. 'A few kilometres south-east of the Yaaroubiyeh border crossing in al-Qanat. There was an attack three days ago,' he says. 'We're going to the spot — as soon as we're done here. We're going to find the girl. You know the one.' He checks his watch.

'I would recommend against it,' Louise says, starting to shuffle some papers around on her desk. 'There's word that ISIL is targetting Iraqi police and security forces, not only to weaken them but to scare people off from joining them. That area is overlapped by half a dozen unfriendly power players, including the Kurds, Jabhat al-Nusra, and ISIL, at the very least. We have refugees passing through, but we're trying to divert them to better routes or else send them south into Jordan instead, though conditions there are getting very bad. And the Kurds are … unpredictable at this point.'

'Thanks. We're going anyway,' Arwood says, and then, to Benton's embarrassment, makes for the door.

Louise and her hair nod. 'Hobbes, huh?'

Arwood stops. 'That's my name.'

'Any relation?'

'What difference would it make?'

'OK.' Then she looks at Benton. 'You do know, I assume, that dozens of journalists have been kidnapped by the Syrian government and the Islamist insurgents alike, right? That no one is talking about it on the theory that not publicising it will undercut the motive to do it? Also, the attack you're talking about, the mortar attack—the claim of responsibility by that Kurdish group is unconfirmed. Most people don't think it was the Kurds. I don't think it was. I wouldn't go near the Syrian border now if I were an English journalist travelling with an American.'

'We heard,' says Benton. 'And, perhaps unfortunately, many European governments are regularly paying ransoms to get their journalists back, which means a market has already been created and prices set. In any event, we won't be there long. In and out over the next few hours is the idea. We're going to check the site, take some pictures, and come right back.'

'We've got to get on the road,' Arwood says, clearly growing impatient. 'Thanks for the information.' Arwood, this time, walks out.

'Can I ask you a question?' Louise asks, looking at Benton.

'Of course.'

'This was one attack in a thousand. Over eight thousand Iraqis have been killed this year. It's a blip on the radar. Why is the *Times* covering it?'

'Because it was on global TV and you remember it,' he says. 'It's not a good reason for something to be a story, but it is a common one.'

'I was told through the grapevine that the *Times* is trying to turn a profit for the first time in two hundred years. This doesn't seem like the way to do it.'

'It's a big old goofy world,' Benton says.

'It sure is,' Louise says.

Märta lingers when Benton has gone.

Louise is not smiling.

'None of that sounds right, Märta.'

'I know.'

'The American. Is he CIA?'

'CIA?' she says, sitting down. 'No. No way. He doesn't fit the profile.'

'He's smarter than he looks. He seems very at ease in a conflict zone. He's in shape. He's focussed. He's punctual. He could be Directorate of Operations or a contractor. There's a whole universe I don't even understand.'

'No,' says Märta. 'People from the Directorate of Operations, despite thinking they're all mysterious, are actually pretty easy to spot. They're political moderates, college-educated, have weak religious affiliations, are patriotic but not zealous, are able to work in formal administrative systems and follow instructions, and are not especially materialistic—though boys will be boys, with their cars and TVs. They're all square pegs in square holes, and they love their jobs and hate their bosses. Arwood doesn't fit. He has a bad discharge from the army, and the CIA has grown very competitive and selective since September 11. I don't see him being able to have a boss or a job. Also, my experience is that the CIA, despite crossing almost every conceivable moral line, still respects the boundaries with humanitarian organisations and journalists.'

'We don't know that,' Louise says. 'Maybe they just haven't been caught yet.'

'I don't think,' Märta says, 'that Arwood is working his way up a bureaucratic organisation.'

'They hire assassins, too. And he sort of does fit that profile. Your reputation would go to hell if he's any way connected to that world, and the International Refugee Support Group would lose access to thousands of non-combatants who rely on you. And since we all look the same to most of these people, a lot of other organisations, including the Red Cross, would suffer, too. So you're gambling with the whole system here to help two strange characters follow a non-story and look for a dead girl among eight thousand others. It doesn't add up. Why are you doing this?'

'I don't know, Louise. Maybe it's because their irrational belief that one girl and one story still matter is somehow infectious. It's like a first kiss. I can barely remember feeling that way.'

'It's not our job to feel that way.'

'No. But I still like it.'

14

He introduces himself to Benton and Arwood as 'Jamal'. No last name. No family. No affiliations. He shakes hands with a limp and weak touch common to the region, and which Arwood has always taken as a measure of the gesture's unimportance. Jamal leans against his early-1990s Toyota Corolla as Benton and Arwood get in.

The car has heavily worn grey vinyl seats. Like every Toyota in Iraq, it is white. Jamal starts the car and puts the vehicle into third gear far too soon, based on a theory—shared by all—that it will improve petrol mileage and reduce engine wear. As they chug their way out of camp, a box of tissues slides across the black dashboard, threatening to fall, but it never does. Jamal does not glance at it even once.

No one speaks. Jamal has been told the destination.

When they are on Route 2 and reach their cruising speed, Arwood breaks the silence. 'I love a good road trip!' he says from the backseat as he slaps Jamal on the shoulder and hands him a CD. 'Put this in, man, will you?'

'No CD. Only a tape deck,' says Jamal, without looking at or taking the CD. They left camp in the direction of Dohuk and haven't yet run into the customary early-morning traffic. The haze blends with the pollution in the morning light, obscuring the horizon. There is a musty smell in the air. Benton is seated up front with Jamal, and Arwood is in the back, moving around without a seatbelt, like a lanky teenager on the way to the beach.

'Really? A tape deck?' Arwood says.

'It's a Sony.'

'Sony. Nice.'

Arwood tosses the disk out the window. 'So much for Tattoo You.'

The ride to Zakho takes only an hour. They pass vistas of dry beige grass and unfinished stone walls erected by men to mark out their property. They look like ruins of the past, but are meant to be the future.

Here and there, the ground drops from sight, and wadis open in the earth, full of tall grasses and short trees.

After twenty minutes on the road, they come across their first roadblock. Worryingly, Benton sees Arwood's hand disappear inside his satchel and remain there as Jamal rolls down the window.

'What's going on, Jamal?' Benton asks.

Jamal says, 'No problem, no problem,' which Benton considers little more than a verbal tic in postcolonial societies. He's as clueless as he was a moment ago.

There are two oil drums to the right of the road, and a makeshift pole with a white flag on the end of it. The right end has a counterweight made of scrap metal, and the guard—a beardless boy—is holding a Chinese-made AK-47 with its distinctive plastic stock.

He is not pointing it at them.

The boy says something in Arabic to Jamal. Jamal answers. The boy speaks again.

As they talk, Arwood asks Benton, 'You pick up any Arabic along the way?'

'Words and phrases,' Benton says. 'I can link them up a bit. You?'

'I can say, "Open the door or I'll open your head."'

'I see.'

'I can also say, "The international telephone exchange is presently busy; please hold on and await your turn."'

'That's awfully specific.'

'I was in Israel in 1993. I had a thing for this Italian violinist who was studying there. She was so gorgeous it was maddening. She wore these ripped jeans I can still see. When she left for Rome, I called her all the time. They had a recording on international lines from public phones as you waited for a line to open. They repeated the same thing in Hebrew, Arabic, English, and French, and that's what it said. For some reason, they put the telephone centre inside a student bomb shelter. Do you know what the acoustics of bomb shelters are like?'

'Yes, I do.'

'All those languages trying to rise above each other to get their messages across to people who weren't there. It was obviously a metaphor for something, but I could never figure out what.'

'That was only two years after we met. What were you doing there?'

'Making contacts.'

Benton turns away from Arwood when Jamal uses the word 'Habibi', at which point Arwood says, 'Now's a good time to scooch. Down. Scooch down. Now. Like this.'

Arwood scooches way down like someone regretting his decision to get on a roller coaster. Benton does the same, but doesn't know why.

'Why are we doing this?'

Jamal starts to pull the car away from the checkpoint.

'The guy outside wanted money. Jamal said he'd give him his love instead, and then pulled off. So ... we're either about to be shot at or we're not. It's a coin toss, really. So ... scooch.'

'There's nothing behind us but sheet metal. Shouldn't we bend over?'

'I'd rather get shot in the head and have it pass through my arse than get shot in the arse and have it pass through my head. Wouldn't you?'

'I've never thought about it.'

'Could be the last decision you ever make.'

'Jamal,' Benton says, 'are we going to be shot at?'

'No problem, no problem.'

'See?' Arwood says.

'Jamal!' Benton says again.

'It's OK. I know his family. His name is Muhammad. He studies engineering. He's trying to make some money. He didn't realise it was me. Roadblocks are popular because of the refugees. The Syrians come with their money, so we take it away. He shouldn't be doing this, but he wants *away*.'

'Away. Sure. Who doesn't.'

'No, no. Not "away". A *Wii*. Nintendo. Wii II, actually. Very expensive in Iraq. Have to find someone coming through Dubai. Make special arrangement. I think it's a mistake, though. More games on the old one, and the new one isn't back-compatible.'

'It's true,' Arwood says, sitting up again. 'I would totally get the older one if I lived here.'

'Very hard to find a job here. Very hard. Nothing to do. So people shake up the refugees.'

'Shake down,' Benton says. 'They shake down the refugees.'

'OK.'

'That's not a nice thing to do,' Benton says.

Jamal shrugs. 'We run to them, they do it to us, they run back to us, and we do it to them. Everyone knows. They know how much is fair to charge. You overcharge, you fight. You charge fair amount, everyone is OK. Everyone knows everything here.'

'So we're not going to get shot?' Benton asks.

'No problem.'

Jamal is driving at sixty kilometres an hour. The road is well paved. Every time Jamal comes up on a car going slower, he honks and flashes his lights. None of the other drivers are bothered by this.

'You know the Middle East?' Jamal asks. Benton notices that this is the first time Jamal has asked a question that isn't directly about the route itself.

'Who, me?' Arwood says, looking out the window, and taking in the cool and dusty morning air.

'Yes.'

Arwood laughs as he scans the Iraqiness of the passing countryside. 'Dude, I've been to more places than Johnny Cash, and I've seen more weird stuff than Han Solo. Especially in the Middle East. You know Johnny Cash?'

'He is a soldier, like you?'

'What makes you think I'm a soldier?'

Jamal takes his hands off the steering wheel, and makes circles around his own face with his index finger. 'Your eyes.'

Arwood ignores this. 'He was a country-music singer. Played guitar. Dead now.'

'Drugs?'

'No, man. He got old.'

Jamal doesn't say anything.

'What about you, Jamal?' Benton asks. 'How did you luck into this job with us?'

'Märta told me you wanted a driver. Märta is a very important person. She is very respected here. Speaks Arabic. She said you needed a driver. Said I could trust you.'

'Who, me?' Arwood says.

'No. Not you,' Jamal says, motioning to Benton. 'Him.'

The land changes. What was brown becomes green. The mountains now exert their presence. The rising sun has infused the air with the full weight of day. The road starts to climb, and the engine strains as Jamal puts the car into overdrive rather than downshift as he should.

Arwood has grown impassive. Benton looks at his right hand

dangling down as he rests his elbows on the two front seats. MORE, it says.

More what?

Benton looks at the hills. The line across the top of them, in the distance, is so crisp they seem to have been shaved flat by a scythe. Well-tended fields line the road. Farmers do not look up as the car passes. Horses with low backs and tyres used around their heads as harnesses pull makeshift wagons in disrepair. Every colour is faded. Every building is squat and forlorn.

Something is missing, though. Something that has always been here when he has been here. Something that has always accompanied him.

What is it?

'Something's different,' Benton says aloud.

Arwood's fingers are tapping his bag. He looks anxious. Busy. Something in four/four time. A rock beat, perhaps.

'What?' he says.

'Something's different,' Benton says again.

'What do you mean?' Arwood asks, the wind blowing his hair, but cooling nothing. 'Different from what?'

'I've been to places like this many times. Something feels different.'

'We're alone,' Arwood says. 'There's no international presence. No UN peacekeeping operation, no US Army, it's all local now, except for the aid agencies.'

'Maybe that's it.'

'Got any tunes?' Arwood shouts to Jamal. 'What do you feed that Sony?'

Jamal opens his glove compartment. There are a few Maxells and TDKs slipping around. 'You know Hossam Habib?' he asks.

'No.'

'You know Tamer Hosny?'

'No.'

'You know Yasmine Hamdan?'

'No.'

'You know Nancy Ajram?'

'No.'

'You know Mohamed Mounir?'

'No.'

'Seriously?'

'I want some Western tunes. Got any Stones?'

'I only have this,' Jamal says, taking out a gold-coloured ninety-minute tape, and handing it to Arwood. It's a TDK MA90 Metal Bias.

Arwood whistles. 'Damn. I haven't seen one of these since, like, 1988 or something. Whatever's on this was loved. How'd you get it?'

'Passenger left it here. Long time ago. Been here since they made the car.'

'Don't clean out that glove box too often, do you?'

Jamal shrugs. 'If there's no tomorrow, why get rid of yesterday?'

'That's deep. What's on it? The label came off.'

'Something loud. Something with birds.'

'Yardbirds?'

'No.'

'Flock of Seagulls?'

'No.'

'The Eagles?'

'No. Something about crows.'

'Sheryl Crow?'

'No.'

'Counting Crows?'

'No.'

'Put it on.'

The Sony tape player starts, and for the first few seconds, before the music begins, it feels like the tape deck is actually sucking the ambient sound from air, making everything more silent. And then 'Remedy' by Black Crowes starts playing, and Arwood Hobbes goes bananas.

'Fuck, yeah! We are listening to this until this trip is over. This song is from '92. I was listening to this over and over in Montana when I got back from Desert Storm. I fuckin' love this album. Cosmic voodoo, I'm telling you.'

'There's no coincidence, Arwood. Nothing's coincided with anything else.'

'Yeah, well, that's because I haven't told you everything. There's a coincidence. And now we've got a soundtrack for it from the same year.'

'What haven't you told me?'

'Everything will be illuminated, my warm-beer-drinking friend.'

'Our beer is as cold as everyone else's. I'm tired of that line.'

Benton looks at his UN-provided map, and sees that they are coming up on a roundabout designated Echo 23. He checks his watch, and then picks up the Motorola handset.

'Romeo Charlie Niner Two, to Echo Base, over.'

The response is immediate.

'This is Echo Base, you are loud and readable, over.'

'Echo Base, we have reached Echo 23, over.'

'Romeo Charlie Niner Two, you are thirty minutes late on your ETA to Echo 23. Do you have anything to report? Over.'

Jamal looks back at Benton and shakes his head. 'Please,' he says. 'It's no problem. I'll take care of it. He should have known my car. Muhammad doesn't stop internationals. He didn't know you were here. Don't make trouble.'

Benton hesitates and then says, 'Negative, Echo Base. Only some minor traffic. Over.'

'Roger, Romeo Charlie Niner Two. Continue to Echo-22. ETA is twenty-five minutes from present location, over.'

'WILCO Echo base, over and out.' Benton places the radio on the floor, because when he leaves it on the dashboard it has a tendency to slide around, making that grinding vinyl-on-vinyl sound that he finds annoying. He glances at Arwood, who is staring at his fancy watch, which has a GPS inside it. Before, he thought Arwood was simply in a rush to get to the girl. But his continued glances suggest something more to Benton than wanting to hurry.

'Arwood, you said something about a timeline before. Did you mean that literally?'

There is a road sign up ahead in English and Arabic with the name of a village off to the right that leads on to the foothills. It is no town Benton has ever heard of.

'Jamal, turn into that village up there,' Arwood says. 'On the right. Don't miss the turn.'

'I thought we were going to Zakho, and then on to the site of the attack?'

'We are. I want to pull in here for a minute first. You want a Fanta and a Kit Kat?' he asks Benton. 'I want a Fanta and a Kit Kat. A trip to Iraq isn't complete without a Fanta.'

'I'm fine for now,' Benton says. 'We have plenty of water.'

'Oh, come on. Jamal? Fanta?'

'We're very close to Zakho. It's safer there. There's a shopping mall if you need anything.'

'Pull in here first. Now, Jamal.'

Jamal makes the turn, but does not look pleased. 'This is not a good town. It's a Sunni village. Close ties to the old regime. We do not have good relations with them.'

'They'll love me. There's an intersection with a café on the corner. It has plastic yellow chairs. You park and wait for me there. I won't be long.'

Jamal pulls into town.

Two men are squatting on the side of the road with their feet flat to the ground, in the way of Asians. Their arms rest on their knees, and their sandals are as dirty as their hands. One of them is smoking a cigarette.

The men watch the car proceed down the road toward the centre of the village.

'This is not a good idea,' Jamal says.

'What are we doing here?' Benton asks Arwood.

'We're going to have a Fanta. Now stay in the car.'

Arwood opens the door and hops out before the car comes to a complete stop or Benton can even reply.

Arwood has taken his rucksack and whatever was inside it.

'Arwood?' Benton says through the window.

But Arwood isn't listening. He is looking at his watch as he hurries away.

With Arwood gone, Jamal stops the music. The car's engine is running. They are waiting. Neither of the men knows why.

15

When Benton started his work as a war reporter, he thought it would be daring, exciting, and even rebellious work. He immediately learned he was wrong. Like every other reporter in 1982 who was interested in war, he was sent off to the Falklands. The British prime minister, Margaret Thatcher, had an iron grip on the reporting, though, and the only authorised vessel for journalists was the HMS *Stanley*. When they were finally let off the ship, the journalists were led around by the Royal Marines like the sheep that populated the place, and were told where to film and not to film. Benton was thirty-one years old in 1982 — old enough to object, but too naïve to know where to direct the objection. He made the mistake of lecturing a lieutenant colonel about Roger Fenton and the Crimean War, explaining that, as a reporter for the *Times*, he couldn't possibly follow in the same footsteps.

The Royal Marines had no idea what he was talking about, and they were not bothered by their ignorance. The lieutenant colonel held up a finger, pointed with it, and said, 'That's where you can shoot.' Benton refused. The Royal Marines — who knew exactly where to lodge their objections about Benton — complained to the *Times*. And Benton was sent off to Lebanon, which was very far away from the Falklands and the Royal Marines. It was a busy time to be in Lebanon.

Benton knew that Vanessa didn't understand the mental displacement that comes with being both here and there at the same time — how 'here' and 'there' become meaningless concepts. Of course, you can be in Lebanon and Cornwall at the same time, because you can be mentally present in more than one story. The only difference between here and there, really, is that 'here' we are subject to the forces of gravity.

She took him for addle-brained, and once called him a modern-day Walter Mitty. In some ways, she wasn't wrong. He was distracted. He was forgetful. Even as a father to little Charlotte, he was seldom present in her life. What Vanessa got wrong, though, was that he was not a modern version of Walter Mitty dreaming of being a war journalist; he was a war journalist dreaming of being Walter Mitty.

Between 1982 and 1991, he covered Grenada, Honduras, the Iran–Iraq war, the American invasion of Panama, and then Desert Storm and the aftermath.

During that time, their daughter, Charlotte, grew into a ten-year-old. He remembered looking at her when he came back after the Shaaban Intifada. He didn't see her as a child anymore. He saw her as a kind of automaton. He looked at her in the doorway of their home, and looked through her skin to her skeleton: the jaw, the teeth set inside it; the shape of her skull, and what it would look like if she died now rather than later. It occurred to him that her life was continuing, right then, due to the successful firing of the smallest of electrical impulses telling her heart to pump again … and again … and again. How long could that last? How much faith and love can you invest in the hope that a little impulse will fire again … and again … and again?

We say 'God bless you' when a person sneezes, because our forebears thought that, for a moment, the heart stops and the blessings of God, called forth by someone who cares, would start it up again.

God bless you.

God bless you.

God bless you.

Could he say that between every beat of her heart?

He couldn't see her as a child anymore—only as something that was, eventually, going to break.

Little Charlotte stood in the doorway without the resources to make sense of the expression on her father's face, wondering if she'd done something wrong. She was young enough to think that right and wrong were in play.

God bless you.

He kissed her on the forehead, pretended to smile, and went upstairs for twenty years.

Vanessa was harder to isolate. She wasn't a child. She wasn't a developing life force that could be moulded or conditioned. She was a grown woman with a mind that she asserted into their lives and into his own. She could interrupt his inner conversations. She knew how. What he couldn't fathom was why she bothered.

Eventually, the nothing he offered them accumulated. It gained as particles to a cloud, and as a cloud to a mass that developed its own gravity. It pulled Vanessa into it. Eventually, she rebelled, and decided she wanted more. So she took it.

Good for her. Bad for them.

In the Toyota, Benton looks at his watch as he and Jamal wait for Arwood to return. Charlotte is probably at the university lab now. Then she'll be having dinner with her boyfriend, Guy Waters.

Guy Waters. The man who will keep Charlotte safe and dry forever in a land of crystal blue so that she can grow old and die, starting now.

'It's been a long time,' Jamal says. 'Too long to buy a Fanta and Kit Kats.'

'How long's it been?' Benton says.

'Seventeen minutes.'

'That's a long time.'

'How did he know the chairs would be yellow?'

'What do you mean?'

'Your friend. He said the chairs at the café would be yellow. Most café chairs are white. Only some are yellow. How did he know they'd be yellow? Has he been here before?'

'I don't know.'

'Have you?'

'No.'

'We are here for a reason that I don't know. Do you know the reason?'

'No,' Benton says.

'How well do you know him?'

'I'm increasingly not sure.'

'Something's not right. That man — over there, in the blue shirt. He's writing down my licence plate.'

'Are we in danger?'

'Yes. Yes, we are in danger. This is how it happens. There are rules. You break the rules, you are in danger. We are breaking a rule.'

'What rule?'

'There are places you go and don't go, depending on who you are. Your family, your religion, your tribe. You cross those lines, everyone knows. They know very quickly. Nothing travels faster than a whisper in Iraq. That is why the winds all have names.'

'You're not responsible for the stupidity of your passengers.'

Jamal shakes his head. 'You're not from here. You don't understand.'

'Should I go out and get him?'

'I don't know.'

'I'll go to the shop. If he's in there, I'll get him.'

'Yeah, OK. OK. But don't stay there. And don't go anywhere else. Come right back. I'll have to tell Märta. She's going to be very angry.'

'I'll take care of Märta, don't worry. She knows Arwood can be impulsive.'

'This car is all I have. I have a family. They need me to keep this job. Domiz is safe. I don't want to go to Baghdad.'

'I'm going, and then I'll come right back.'

But Benton hasn't gone farther than two metres from the car before Arwood himself comes around the corner. He is clutching a white plastic bag with some bottles in it. They smack against each other violently as he makes for the car.

He opens the door to the Toyota, and gets into the front seat rather than the back one.

'Go.'

'Where the hell have you been?' Benton asks.

'Get the fuck in, and let's go.'

Jamal doesn't ask anything. He starts the car in second gear, and drives too fast on the uneven road that is split and cracked from the hard rains of last season and the season before. Jamal looks in the mirror every two seconds.

'This is a big problem. Very big problem.'

Arwood is breathing hard. He is tapping his foot like a junkie at a bus stop.

'Arwood,' Benton says as gently as possible, 'I would like you to tell me what just happened.'

Jamal turns right onto Route 2.

Arwood takes an object from his pocket. His hands are moving too quickly for Benton to see what it is. It's metal. It looks like brass.

Jamal shifts into fourth gear as the road evens out. He is passing other vehicles. He is flashing his lights and honking.

'I never thought we'd see him again, Benton. I really didn't. I went home afterward, and drank Jim Beam and played video games before my dad kicked me out. I bought a motorcycle. Got as far as Montana, and then started looking for work. Never occurred to me that the sonofabitch who shot her was still alive, living this parallel life in Iraq. I was an American kid. The world wasn't all globalised back then. Everything seemed so far away. Not anymore, though. I got so sick of watching all of it. Anyway, maybe if he'd been a private or corporal it would have been harder. But a lieutenant colonel, on the ground, in Samawah on 29 March 1991? How many of those could there have been? Turns out, the answer is one. So if you know the right people, and pay a little money, all of a sudden you've got a name and an address and a timeline. He got kicked out of Baghdad when the Americans did that de-Baathification shit, and went to stay with a cousin in the north near Dohuk and south of Zakho. Which, coincidentally — like I said — is the road we needed to travel to get to the girl. So, actually, some things are coinciding. We are at the nexus of some major cosmic voodoo.'

'What have you done, Arwood?'

'Something I was supposed to do a long time ago.'

'Arwood, what have you done?'

'What have I done? What I should have done twenty years ago. What you stopped me from doing. I put a bullet in the motherfucker. Now all that's left is saving the girl. And then everything will be fine. Everything will be the way it was supposed to be.'

16

Jamal's hands clutch the black wheel at the ten o'clock and two o'clock positions. He drives with the intensity of prayer. Before reaching Zakho, he turns left off Route 2 onto a road toward Dayrabun that takes them toward the Syrian border. It is a two-lane road. On the outskirts, they run into refugees again.

They have been silent in the car since Arwood's admission. It seems to Benton that Jamal's strategy is to get the day over with as soon as possible and try to forget it ever happened. Benton doesn't have a strategy yet.

Arwood is the first to break the lull. 'They have to pay mules for passage across the border,' he says. 'They walk with their children for up to eight to ten hours through the dark. Once across, they get robbed. Then they continue on foot, hoping to reach one of the camps. I don't even want to imagine what's going to happen in the camps when ISIL overruns them.'

They drive slowly against the flow of the river. Benton looks at the colours worn by the refugees. They looked brighter on television.

He could be home now. He should be home now. He should be with Vanessa. He should invite Charlotte and Guy for dinner. Investigate her life, not this. Ask her questions about her ancient shells that once lined the coasts of forgotten continents that let you walk from Damascus to Fowey.

'Do you still have the gun?' Benton asks, after about twenty more minutes of silence.

Arwood smiles. 'Guns aren't helpful out here. You need friends. I've got friends.' He looks at his Suunto GPS watch, and again at his map. He points to a dirt road leading south-west. 'There,' he says to Jamal, then pointing. 'That's the path. Go there.'

'That's ISIL.'

'We're in Kurdistan,' Arwood says. 'ISIL is in al-Anbar in the western desert. They're south of here. Not up north.'

Jamal shakes his head. 'That was then. Now is now. After the Sunni tribes unified with the Anbar Awakening, ISIL went to other places. With the Syrian war they have moved back to al-Anbar, but are also in many other places. Here and there. It's a big mess. A very big mess.'

Benton cannot read Arwood's mood. He seems remarkably steady. The foot tapping ended once it was clear they weren't being followed. He seems too steady for someone who has just committed premeditated and carefully orchestrated murder—unless that's something he was already comfortable with. Either way, Arwood is beyond Benton's understanding now.

Arwood says to Jamal, 'Listen, kid. It's like *Chinatown*. You see *Chinatown*? We just need to "find the girl". The rest is noise. We're looking for a spot south of Dayrabun near the foothills. Whoever's there is there. Whoever's not is not. That's the fact of the desert. In fifteen minutes, we'll know.'

'Which means that whatever happens is what happens,' Benton says.

Arwood turns around and looks at Benton. 'The girl's alive.'

'The girl is dead,' Benton says loudly, asserting himself. 'She's just as dead as the girl the colonel shot in '91. As dead as all the people we saw die in Samawah. Now as dead as the man you killed, however evil he might have been. We need to get back to Domiz, regroup, and then leave this country before anyone knows we were here, or else we're going to an Iraqi prison, and we're going to die there. No one will come for us—no one. Because we will not only have burned our bridges with Märta, but we'll have put all her work in jeopardy. No one is going to walk across a minefield for us, Arwood.'

Arwood looks out the front window. He is unfazed by Benton's scolding.

The land has levelled off again. It is bush and rock. It is the cradle of Western civilisation, and nothing grows here. Not a crop. Not an idea.

'Is this why your people are so brutal?' Arwood asks Jamal. 'Because of the land? The land isn't merciful, so you figure your people shouldn't be either?'

Jamal does not turn his head, but anger swells in him—anger he was planning to bury and keep hidden until this was over, but Arwood has pushed his button. 'World War II,' Jamal says loudly. 'You kill sixty million people. You kill more people than anyone ever. With bombs and tanks and gas. Then you make Hello Kitty. Think it was always like that. You think you are so special, but you are the worst.'

'Hello Kitty is Japanese. You can't lay that shit on us.'

'My Little Pony. That's American.'

'Shut up and drive.'

'Ms Märta teaches us many things. Things they never teach us in school here.'

'What else does she say?' Benton asks.

'She says America has a big mouth and small ears.'

'That's not right,' Arwood interjects. 'We talk softly and carry a big stick. We have a big stick, not a big mouth.'

'No, no. Big mouth. Small ears.'

'It's a Swedish expression,' Benton explains. 'She's translating from the Swedish. Jamal's right.'

'You know what? Who cares? Because what makes us better than you,' Arwood says to Jamal, 'is that we can imagine a better future. All you can imagine is a better past.'

'Fuck you,' says Jamal.

'Whatever. When this is over, I'm going home to green grass and high tides forever. You're stuck here,' Arwood says.

The horizon is so flat that it curves with the edge of the earth. Objects in the distance do not become closer; they grow as though the passage of time itself swells their mass. They drive for more than an hour. Jamal turns off the main road, and then off the secondary road. He follows tyre tracks in the dirt made by some vehicle with massive wheels, and therefore heavier than the Toyota. If the truck did not detonate an anti-vehicle mine, the small white car probably won't either.

They pass two men walking. They hold hands in a way Western men do not. Together they watch the car drive by. No one waves or smiles.

The land is shattered. The few green strands of grass that do push out and survive are too far apart to form a field or even a bed. What lives is sharp and determined, faceless and eternal. The earth is spent. Whatever it was, whatever civilisations once crossed it and blessed it with art and ideas and possibility, it will never be again. It is barren now. They drive across it in order to leave it behind.

The Japanese engine and the wind fill their ears. They are out of conversation, and beyond emotion.

In time, they come onto the carcass of the convoy. There are three vehicles. One is a small tanker truck, which has exploded and is on its side, its wheels facing south like a hippo with rigor mortis. The other two are cargo trucks. Both remain standing.

The area is utterly motionless.

'Up there,' Benton says. 'What are those?'

Arwood looks at his GPS watch again to confirm they are in the right place.

'They're Ural 375s. Russian army. Iraq uses them. Those two are 6×6s. I don't know about the tanker. Get closer,' he says to Jamal.

'I don't like it here.'

'We won't be here long,' he says, pointing ahead. 'Park by the one on the far left.'

Jamal parks the Toyota parallel to the first Ural. The canvas tarp covering its back sits like ragged wool over a mammoth. It is mostly intact. There are rips, possibly from shrapnel. It is dark inside.

Arwood is the first out of the car. 'Start looking,' is all he says as he walks away.

Benton steps out from the car. The sun is high and the air is warm. It is good to stretch. He grinds his foot into the earth to hear the sound.

The bones of the Ural don't look to have been picked over by the vultures and nomads yet — otherwise the ground around it would have been littered with jetsam. It is not a good sign that even the local thieves haven't come for the spoils.

Below the trucks are the bodies. Their flesh is covered in yellow dirt. Their blood is dried and blackened. They are scattered about.

'We're here,' Arwood says. 'Find the girl.'

'There's nothing alive here, Arwood,' Benton says. 'Nothing has been alive here for days.'

Benton watches Arwood and Jamal walk briskly and separately, from body to body, trying to identify the dead and see whether the girl is among them. Benton feels no need to rush the confirmation. There is a certain reward in delaying the moment a little longer, though he knows they have to go.

Dusty, tired, and sunburned, Benton takes his camera from his satchel and starts clicking. Since getting on the plane at Heathrow, Benton has been able to convince himself that he was only coming for Arwood. That it was the placement of the mortar that gripped him. Now that he is here, and Jamal and Arwood are counting bodies, he has to accept that this was not the reason. It was the girl. It really was. Not to rescue her, of course—days have passed since the attack. But in coming here, he could at least acknowledge her death. He could return her body to her family, or at least bury her remains. He could offer her some dignity. In doing this, he could live on better terms with himself, which is a skill he's been losing. This might be a strange place to find it, but, as Arwood said, it's also where he lost it.

Benton raises a high-resolution digital SLR camera to his eye and shoots some more. The *Times* will want its money's worth, which it cannot possibly get, so to play out the game he needs to get as close as possible.

He sets the camera on automatic so it can make its own decisions. If he doesn't like the results, a kid in the photography department will clean it up in Photoshop. The days of the purists are over. Benton doesn't care. The camera frames are too small to capture reality anyway.

But he needs to snap some photos, so he does: here's one for aesthetic value; here's one for romantic associations; here's another with a familiar colonial motif; here's a tragic one of Meals Ready to Eat that children confuse with cluster munitions; and here's a melancholy flower growing beside a corpse.

'This is bullshit,' he mumbles to himself.

'What are you doing, Benton?' Arwood shouts.

'Huh?'

'Let's hurry this up,' Arwood shouts again.

'Yeah. OK.'

'Over there,' Arwood says. 'That one. Go look at that one.'

Arwood is pointing at a body about twenty metres away. It is in a foetal position, its back to them. It is away from the others. She must have been one of the walking wounded and made it that far.

Benton turns off the camera and places it back into his satchel as he walks to her body. He kneels to the ground when he reaches her. When he does, he knows.

She is smaller than he remembers; smaller than she looked on television. He wants to touch her shoulder, as he would wake Charlotte on school days, but he does not. She is not his daughter. It is the four-day-old corpse of a stranger. The connection is an illusion, and whatever feelings her appearance reignited, the fact is that this girl is another person, another victim, of a war that lives on as a continuum across generations.

And yet, his sadness for her is also real, and for a moment he allows himself to feel it, if only because its wellspring is humanity's only hope.

You should have been taken to the mghassilchi — the body washer — he thinks. By tradition, she would have been cared for by her co-religionists, and she would have been tended to before her body was laid to rest in the earth, with the expectation that her soul would travel to God, where it belonged. Instead, Thomas Benton sits beside her, dry and dirty, and soon to leave.

'They should all be washed,' he yells, as Arwood pushes over another corpse with his foot to check its face.

'Yeah, OK,' he says. 'You do that.'

'What's happened to you?'

'What's happened to me?' Arwood yells. 'This. And more of this. And a lot more of this. Meanwhile, I'm still the only one I know doing anything about it. Are you going to leave that one and keep looking, please?'

'Arwood,' he says too softly, 'it's her.'

Benton walks to the front of her body and looks into her face. She is in a foetal position — knees up, her hands against her belly. She is soaked in dried blood. She was shot in the stomach, walked this far, dropped in pain, and stayed in pain until she was dead.

Gently, and carefully, Benton brushes the hair back from her face. It was cut into bangs not so long ago. She and her stylist would have discussed the length. Being a girl, she probably had strong opinions. It is unlikely she would have considered the results perfect, if she was anything like Charlotte in her own teenage years.

He studies her face. It is familiar, but not as familiar as he thought it would be. The distance and the angle and the distortion of the camera must all have made her look more like the girl from 1991 than was actually the case. She looks different enough, in fact, that he is surprised he was mystified at all. Surely, death has changed her. And time. And the sun. And the neglect. It doesn't matter — whatever connection he felt with her through the television screen is gone. She is another dead girl.

From his bag, he takes a small bottle of water and opens it. He first cleans the earth from his hands. Then he pours some onto his red bandana. He washes her face with the towel, brushing her eyelashes, tracing her cheeks, dabbing the tip of her nose. Her eyes are closed, but there is no peace on her face. Not even in death.

If only it would rain.

'I'm so sorry for you,' Benton says to the girl. 'And I am so sorry that more people are not.'

Arwood hasn't heard Benton, and has continued his search. Benton is not certain how long he's been alone before he hears Jamal's voice calling him: 'Mr Thomas?'

He looks up at Jamal. The poor boy must have turned manic after the morning's events, let alone now, after seeing more than two dozen dead on the ground, abandoned here to dogs.

He is smiling, almost laughing, as he calls out to Benton.

Mad as a hatter.

'Jamal, calm down. We'll head back now. I'll take a few more photos, and then off we go. But if you don't collect yourself, I won't want you driving. Most deaths in the field are actually caused by traffic accidents—'

'She's alive! The girl—she's in the truck. Mr Arwood found her.' Then he says something in Arabic that might be a prayer, but could just as well be hip-hop lyrics.

'Who's alive?'

'The girl.'

'The girl is dead. She's right here, Jamal. Open your eyes.'

'That girl there,' says Jamal. 'She has a blue dress. The girl in the green dress is OK. She has been living off the rations in the humanitarian truck, just like Mr Arwood said. He is a crazy man, a very crazy man, but he was right. The one in the green dress—she is alive.'

17

Benton stands at the back of the Ural 375 and watches the young girl in the green dress dangle her feet off the back like the teenager she is. Arwood has given her an apple. She has bitten off a piece that's a little too big for her mouth, and she's trying to get an angle on the thing with contorted jaw movements in an effort to work it down to something manageable. Arwood sits next to her. He's rifling through his rucksack. He eventually finds what he's looking for, and removes a juice box — the sort with the little plastic straw glued to the side. In English, it reads, 'Juice Drink' and 'Contains juice.' Without a word, he removes the straw, places it through the little silver button on the top, and hands it to her as though to a little sister before the movie starts.

She takes it without looking at him.

Jamal is around the front of the truck, for some reason.

Arwood looks at Benton and smiles. 'I told you so,' he says.

'You most certainly did, and I have never been more wrong. Is anyone else hiding here? Have we looked about?'

'There aren't a lot of places to look. There's food and water in here, and the canvas kept her cool enough. If we can get her back to Märta, I think she'll be fine.'

'You've had quite the day, Arwood Hobbes. We aren't finished talking about it, not by a long shot, but this goes on the balance sheet. It surely does.'

'Let's go home to the refugee camp, where we belong.'

'All right,' Benton says, taking a quick look around. 'What's her condition?'

'She's very happy to see me.'

'She trusted you? When you looked in the truck?'

'Why wouldn't she?'

'You're a piece of work, I'll hand you that. Look, do you think she might answer a question for me before we leave? I might be able to salvage my job if she does. I can't say I'd given it any thought until now, but given events—'

'What do you want to know?' Arwood calls Jamal over to translate.

'I'd just like to know what happened,' Benton says, taking a recorder from his own jacket.

Her eating is voracious. While she doesn't appear starved, there was clearly no fresh food in the truck, and all she's been eating is dried rations and MREs.

'Jamal, ask her what happened here.'

Jamal hops down from the truck and dusts his hands off on his jeans. When he translates, he sounds young and kind, like someone's son.

The girl talks with her mouth full of apple. Jamal nods, and asks clarifying questions that Benton doesn't understand.

The girl points toward a small gully back by the tracks they followed here. She points at her own clothes.

Jamal frowns. He points at his own clothes, and repeats the word she used.

She nods, and points at two of the dead people.

Then Jamal says, 'We have to go. We have to go right now. Right this second. Very dangerous. Very, very dangerous here. Big mess. We have to go. Right now.'

Arwood hops down and extends his hand to the girl. She takes it, and walks with him, hand in hand, to the car.

'What did she say?' Benton asks, jogging alongside Jamal. 'Why are we running? No one's here. No one's been here for days.'

'ISIL.'

'I thought we had this discussion.'

'No, no. You don't understand. The girl was near the back of the line. She had the best view on everything. She says it wasn't Kurds. It was men wearing black, like ISIL. She saw them carry the mortar, but didn't know what it was. After the mortar landed, she hid in the truck. She saw two men come out after all the other people ran away. She said they shot the survivors. Everyone. Everyone. And then, when they were finished, they went to the video camera the news people were using, and took something from it. It is over there,' he says, pointing to the spot where the camera once stood on its tripod. 'After they took this disk, they went to the tanker truck and put a big black flag on it. This means it is theirs. They will come for it when they want. Anyone caught near it, or taking from the truck, dies. Maybe they come in a month, in a week, in a minute. We don't want to be here. We must go right now.'

'Why hasn't she run away?'

Jamal doesn't translate because he knows the answer for himself: 'Something about cousins. I don't understand. Look, she's fourteen years old!'

'The video camera they picked up, is it still there?' Benton asks. 'You said they took a disk, not the camera.'

'Who cares? Your head is more useful than a camera. Have to go.' They reach the car, and Jamal gets in and starts the engine.

'I'll be right back,' Benton says, seeing that Arwood and the girl haven't reached the car yet.

'You crazy man! Get over here.'

'I'll be right back,' Benton says over his shoulder.

There, eighty metres from the Ural, sits the video camera. It's a familiar high-end consumer model with HD video. It is obviously broken, and the lens is cracked.

Panting, he collects the camera, which burns the tips of his fingers with the heat of the midday sun. Gingerly, he unscrews the fastening bolt that connects it to the tripod, and drops the dead weight to the ground.

Arwood has thrown open the back door, and Benton flops himself onto the hot grey vinyl and pulls the door closed.

'Go,' he says, leaning his head back for a rest, but the vinyl only scorches his neck. He is too tired to move it away. He settles into the burn. 'We're done,' Benton says.

The girl sits between the two men. The camera is a grey stone that lies across his lap. Jamal is running the Toyota in third, as usual, and Benton hears the underpowered engine thump like a dated outboard.

Jamal is not making a sound. Neither is the radio. There is only the breeze through the window and the breath of one extra passenger who has finally stopped eating.

Benton musters the gumption to cock his head left. Arwood, on the far side of the car, is looking very pleased with himself. His eyes are closed. His sunglasses are off. He is enjoying a moment that shouldn't be happening.

The girl is quiet. Benton doesn't want to stare, but he has no choice. She is the spitting image of the girl in green. They look at each other and—against all reason—he can't help but wonder if she recognises him.

By the truck, he wants to say. *We were crouched together, hiding from the helicopter. We ran into the Americans, and you met Arwood, who tried to save you. I had more hair. Do you remember me?*

'How are we for petrol?' Benton asks Jamal instead.

'We're good.'

Jamal makes contact with the main road heading east and speeds up.

They are all quiet in the car. There is little traffic, as people rest during the hottest times of the day. They will open their shops again later; for now, they are home with their families. The speed cools the car. Benton finally peels his neck from the seat, and drinks an entire bottle of water. Sated, he turns to the girl and decides to be sensible.

'Do you speak English?'

The girl shakes her head.

'My name is Benton,' he says to her, touching his chest. 'What is your name?'

'Adar,' she says. 'Adar.'

18

Märta stopped smoking ages ago. These days she doesn't smoke, unless she's socialising, drinking, worrying, fundraising, or needs a cigarette.

She needs a cigarette now. She does not have one. And so she holds her Bic fountain pen as though it is the cigarette that she ought to have. She is sitting on an orange chair at a white table, listening to a briefing provided by a Swiss-based research organisation concerning affairs in eastern Syria that might affect operations in northern Iraq. It is early evening, and she is already tired.

The researcher is young—late twenties. She has blonde hair and eyes that speak of her excitement at being part of something darker than herself, as though proximity to horror somehow might strengthen her own character. In most cases, though, it's the opposite. It unravels us. But Märta isn't about to explain this to her.

The girl began her presentation, some thirty minutes ago, by quoting Thierry Lefebvre's 1927 article 'Le vilayet de Mossoul', telling everyone that 'Ninawa is no longer Iraq and not yet Kurdistan'. This remains true, Märta thinks, but, as a piece of analysis, sort of leaves you hanging. The girl then seemed to prove Märta's point—and not her own—by focussing the rest of her talk on change and the future, rather than on continuity and the past, which was the West's first error over here.

The Swiss researcher holds a laser pointer, and the red dot dances over the bullet points in PowerPoint. There are twelve other people in the room, each from a different aid agency or governmental mission. Märta wants to feel more magnanimous about the young woman's efforts to explain the Kurdish versus Sunni versus Shiite dynamics in Ninawa, but she feels the girl is misunderstanding what she's otherwise accurately describing. She speaks in a cluster of words that have no organising principle:

followed by 'solutions' such as:

Märta's national staff once explained to her — after she insisted that their annual report be translated into Arabic for the first time — that almost none of these words have homologues in Arabic. In fact, the ideas themselves are so foreign and often irrelevant that Arabic speakers, in speaking to one another, simply insert the English term into their conversation. This happens directly in front of senior Western diplomats, who are oblivious to its significance.

The analysis being once again *hors sujet,* she checks her watch, and realises that Benton should have radioed in by now.

By *before,* actually.

She calls Benton's phone. It rings and activates the voicemail.

Why do men build the very systems they refuse to use? Why don't they follow instructions? You look them dead in the eye; you snap your fingers to ensure brain activity; you tell them what you're going to tell them, you tell them, then you tell them what you've told them, but still nothing.

She calls Benton's phone again. It rings and activates the voicemail.

They do this with their health, too. They think they'll be fine. They aren't. Then they crumble like a dry sandcastle.

Benton's phone rings. He answers it.

'Hello?'

Märta stands, waves an excuse to the rest of the room, and then ducks out into the hallway before letting Benton have it: 'Where the hell have you been? Why aren't you following instructions? It's late. The radio room can't make contact, and you haven't called in. If you're not on your way back, you better turn that car around—'

'We found her. She's alive. She's sitting next to us.'

Märta places her hand against her cheek. 'The little girl? The teenager?'

'The girl in green. The one from the video. The reason Arwood made all this happen. She's in the Toyota with us. She's fine. She's a little malnourished, I think, and she seems to like and trust Arwood, which might suggest shock and trauma, but otherwise she's fine.'

'How?'

'She's been living off the rations that were in the convoy. We're coming back.'

'Have you been listening to the radio-room instructions?'

In his silence, Märta finds meaning. She can visualise the look on his face. It is the look that men get after women use such phrases as 'Did you call about that appointment? Did you remember to mail that? Did you unload the dishwasher like I asked?'

Every moment waiting for a man to answer such questions is a moment wasted.

'If you had been listening, like you were supposed to, you'd know you need to take the northern route through Zakho and stay there tonight at a DSS-registered and -qualifying hotel if it's after five-thirty. There's a list in the folder I gave you. Where are you?'

'Travelling south, the way we came. Too late to turn north now. Hold on. There's something happening up ahead,' Benton says. His voice sounds far away from the phone. 'Lots of traffic suddenly.'

'There are roadblocks being set up,' she explains, 'which is what you would have known if you'd been maintaining your radio contact. Apparently the police are looking for someone. I don't know the details. You want to stay away from any traffic jams, any official roadblocks, and anything that could constitute a target.'

'What do you mean, a target?'

'Benton, just tell me what you see.'

She can hear Jamal shouting something, but his distance from the telephone, coupled with his Arabic accent and high voice, keep her from distinguishing a word. All she can hear is Arwood yelling, in response, 'Turn around. I don't care. Turn us around!'

His instructions are the last words she hears before the explosion.

19

Dr Charlotte Benton sits at a private work desk in the Department of Earth Sciences at the University of Bristol. It is mid-afternoon and quiet. The window to the lab is open. Her room is filled with fresh air and suffused with solitude. Her fellowship at the institution has provided her with an assigned workspace, where she stores her papers, reference books, instant coffee, and fossil collection of Silurian-era brachiopods. She takes a moment to send her father her third text message of the day, in an effort to spark a conversation with him. He hasn't responded so far.

To the uninitiated, Silurian-era brachiopods look like modern brachiopods, which most people would call shells — the kind you find in *spaghetti vongole*. To be fair, it's close to the truth; they haven't evolved much in four hundred million years, because they were so wickedly perfect even back then. But these are very old, and they are hers, and so they are special.

Many of her fellow graduate students in palaeontology went on to study dinosaurs. Charlotte likes dinosaurs, too, but the trouble with dinosaurs is that *everyone* likes them. So there's a lot of competition for research grants and university positions. The big problem is that there aren't enough dinosaur bones around. Movies aside, you don't grab a spade and a paintbrush and uncover a T. *rex* in your backyard, and then rope it off and call the media.

With a greater supply of dinosaur scholars than a demand for them in the market, and way more demand for the bones than a ready supply, her buddies are now looking at a professional life filled with longing, searching, hoping, and fundraising. 'You need to be sensible,' she'd told Todd Jenkins, a fellow graduate student. He was choosing his dissertation topic, and not wisely in her view. 'Dinosaurs are not a path to stability and contentment in palaeontology. In your heart, you know this.'

Poor Todd. Now he's divorced, because his wife wouldn't move to Nevada to chase early Jurassic bones.

But Silurian-era brachiopods? Totally different story. There are thousands and thousands of them within easy reach. All she needs to do is chip away some shale, and there they are: satisfaction by the bucketful. Also, the world was a supercontinent four hundred million years ago. It was called Pangaea. This was the late Paleaozoic era and early Mesozoic. Charlotte's brachiopods were clustered together in what are now very scenic places near wonderful beaches with great coffee, many of them on the Mediterranean and in the Levant. To be an evolutionary biologist with an interest in plate tectonics, and to have specialised in brachiopods, is to be a happy human.

At this moment, aside from mild hunger pains, the only thing standing in her way to complete contentment is the fact that her father is trying to divorce her mother because she slept with someone else, and that now he's being a baby by refusing to pick up the phone and talk to her.

Messages have been left and words have been spoken into an old Panasonic answering machine—though, apparently, not enough of them. She sends another text. This afternoon, while taking a break from compiling a bibliography, she has committed herself to talking sense into her father and trying to reinvigorate her parents' marriage. Her mother has been dismissive but not resistant, so attention is now on her father.

Charlotte is thirty-three years old. She knows she cannot manage her parents' marriage. To some extent, she accepts this. But the circumstance itself doesn't require their separation. There is a possibility here of reconciliation, a chance to live a unified life as they have in the past, if they can both overcome their pride and their vanity, and their apathy, and their unwillingness to compromise. She doesn't see her actions as meddling or naïve; she sincerely believes that rational people can be talked into what's good for them if they can be made to see their situation clearly. And that means she's obliged to try.

And there is also the fact that it's never too late to come from a broken home. So she'd rather not.

Charlotte removes a brachiopod from under an old-fashioned lab microscope, where she had been using a tiny probe to clear out sand and debris to mask four hundred million years of inner morphology. She blows on it, better exposing the growth lines of the inner brachial valve.

How old were you? she wonders aloud.

It's not necessary to work this way, but she has recently argued in print that both students and scholars benefit from tactile experience, because — as recent cognitive work has found — it adds to memory retention, and the more ways scholars can experience the old shells, the greater their capacity to make creative associations, thereby advancing the field. Plus, touching shells is fun. And happy people are productive people.

'Just imagine,' she told her students at Bristol, 'holding in the palm of your own hand a tiny shell that has survived intact for four hundred million years. Imagine the near impossibility of two organisms — you, on the one hand, and it, on the other — coming into contact and creating inspiration after all that time. It is as unfathomably unlikely as our existence itself, and almost as wonderful. It is no wonder that Stephen Jay Gould called his book *Wonderful Life*. That was exactly right.'

Charlotte sends her father another text message, and waits.

It is ridiculous for him to avoid her.

'What do you think?' she asks the shell. 'Should we call him?'

Charlotte calls the *Times* and asks for her father. She has the number in her mobile. The call is passed through to the editorial department. Someone named Dick answers, and she wonders, again, why anyone would call himself that.

'He is in Iraq,' Dick says.

What Charlotte did not tell her students was that, of the few people in the world who know the feeling of holding a 400-million-year-old shell in the palm of their hands, even fewer know the feeling of breaking one.

'Well … shit,' she says.

'No, it's OK,' Dick says flatly. 'He'll be back in a few days. He's at the Domiz refugee camp. Near Dohuk, in the north.'

'Why?'

'You've probably seen that video of the girl in that mortar attack. He's … I guess he's investigating it, or something. I don't have the file. I'm sorry.'

'This was something urgent?'

'Who are you?'

'I'm his daughter—Dr Charlotte Benton.'

'Oh. Well, I wouldn't call it that. Word at the water cooler is that he asked for it. Personally, I don't see any open questions of actual importance to our readers. It's not like any British nationals were in the attack, or anything. But, well, there he is. Should be easy to reach. It's a UN camp, so it has excellent Internet access.'

'Thank you,' she says to Dick, and they end the call.

'Bastard fled the scene,' Charlotte says to the broken shell. 'In all your years, have you ever?'

The Domiz refugee camp has its own page on the Internet, and is easy to find. One of the first things she learns is that Eddie Izzard has been there to help draw attention to the needs of children, which was rather good of him. Thankfully, he had been wearing a black UNICEF T-shirt and sporty trousers, rather than his traditional garb as an executive transvestite. Which was probably a good call. Otherwise, the camp looks utterly miserable, and for a moment she is less angry at her father.

Charlotte calls the UN office there, and is connected to someone with a heavy Arabic accent. He clicks some keys and shuffles paper. He says her father is registered in with Safety and Security, under a call sign reserved for the International Refugee Support Group — the IRSG. He provides her with a local number at the camp. He cannot connect her. She'll have to call herself.

Charlotte calls using an Internet telephony service. If she used her department line, her grant money would be gone after three minutes.

It does not ring for long before a young man's cheerful voice answers. He sounds European. She can't place the accent.

'Hello,' he begins. 'This is Miguel, IRSG. How may I help you?'

'Yes, hello. My name is Charlotte Benton. I'm looking for my father, Thomas Benton. I was told he might be with your organisation right now.'

Miguel begins to answer her. Or to speak, anyway, because the words flow from him like notes from a tightly wound music box.

Charlotte does not know when or how to interrupt Miguel. The conversation turns rapidly from her father, to the NGO, to the camp, to his own motivations for joining the NGO and going there. Maybe she missed a transition, because now Miguel is saying, '... political awakening, for me, was definitely the bombing in Madrid on 11 March 2004. I was eighteen, and until then I had no real interest in politics. It was always something far away from me. Maybe a little dirty. A little cold. I am not sure. So it was both shocking and yet not a surprise to me when my own government blamed the Basque separatists. Not that ETA had not done terrible things in the past, but they did not do this. What my government showed us was that they would use the blood of our citizens to advance their own agendas, rather than seek the truth and act in our best interest. The time of Franco was not so long over. I was so angry. It motivated me into political science, and then into practitioner work, and eventually into humanitarian relief operations. You know?'

Charlotte looks down at her broken shell. For a moment, it becomes a broken heart.

Mi corazón roto.

'So… do you know where my father is?' she asks.

He is in the area, Miguel explains, but he has left the camp. A driver of theirs named Jamal is taking him and Mr Hobbes to the location of an attack that happened a few days ago.

'Who?' she asks.

'Hobbes,' he says. 'Like the philosopher from Oxford who wrote *Leviathan* and introduced the idea of the social contract. But this man does not seem to be a philosopher.'

'Oh,' she says.

'You never seem to meet people with the names of philosophers, do you?' he asks. 'You never hear, for example, "Would Mr and Mrs Kierkegaard please proceed to Gate 43." I wonder why not.'

'No,' she agrees. 'You never do.'

'I've been to many places. I have never met anyone named Kant, or Machiavelli, or Spinoza, or Wittgenstein, or Aquinas. Have you?'

No, she hasn't. But she has met a Marx or two.

'That is true,' says Miguel thoughtfully.

Miguel explains that he does not know where her father is at this very moment, but perhaps the radio room knows. Would she like him to check? No, that's fine, she says. So long as someone knows. She does have one question, though: 'Why can't I reach him? He has a telephone.'

'Don't know.'

'Could you ask him to call me, please?'

'Yes, of course. Perhaps later,' Miguel says, rather unexpectedly, 'you could call me on video. I could put you on the iPad. I have an Iraqi SIM card for receiving calls. I could walk you around the camp. Give you a tour. There's a little button in the corner that lets me look at you while you look at the refugee camp.'

'That's a little creepy.'

'Oh, no! We do it for the donors and the fundraising. Many cannot make the trip here, so I have invented something wonderful that permits us to walk around the camp and meet people, eye to eye, and see things as they do, and I can introduce you. It is a little unusual, yes, you will see, but they see your face, and people are happy to know that someone from far away cares about them. Also, many people here know me, and when they see me with the device, they know something very interesting is happening. You should walk with me. Perhaps your father will have returned by then, and we can see him. If not, it is a stroll in the deserts of Babylon. We should do this together. Unless you have something else planned?'

It occurs to Charlotte that what she is doing with her shells could ostensibly wait a little longer. Maybe a lot longer.

'That's certainly—'

'Unique and special, yes? Oh, I'm sorry, I interrupted you. Please, continue.'

'I was going to say "different from what I'd planned on doing today", but your description is also apt.'

'So it is a date, then? Good. It is now about five-thirty in the evening here in Iraq. And we are two hours past GMT. So perhaps, when your day is done in a few hours, you will join me for an evening walk—what they call in Italian a *passeggiata*. Do you have a word for this in Great Britain?'

The term 'pub crawl' comes to mind, but Charlotte decides to keep it to herself.

'I ... ah ... sure.'

'Wonderful,' says Miguel, with what sounds like genuine enthusiasm. 'I look forward to talking to you again and showing you our world. Meanwhile I will follow up with Märta to see where he is, and together we will find him. He will be so happy to see you here. Perhaps the battery on his phone has run down, and he doesn't have a car charger. It happens all the time. But with the VHF handset, we'll be able to find him. And then we can bring all these worlds together, like back when the continents were one. Do you know about this? Our continental drift?'

'Yes,' she says. 'Yes, I do.'

20

Benton drops his phone out of the car window when the bomb detonates seven car-lengths ahead of them at an official roadblock with a heavy police presence. They are in the right lane, moving slowly in the direction of Mosul on Route 1. To their right is rocky desert. To their left is rocky desert with shrubbery. Sand has collected on the side of the road. Up ahead are black smoke and people shooting.

'What part of "turn around" don't you understand?' Arwood says.

'We'll get stuck in the sand. This isn't a 4×4.'

'I'll take my chances. Turn around. And downshift, would you? What it is with you fucking Arabs and fourth gear?'

Benton grabs the front headrest with both hands, and slides forward in his seat as two men wearing black headscarves walk up the midline of the road.

'Jamal, try,' says Benton. 'If they're looking for foreigners, they'll kidnap or kill us when they get here. If we try to get away, it'll be the same, but we might get away.'

'OK, OK, I'm going.'

'We should let Adar out of the car,' Arwood says. 'They might not care about her.'

He says this too late. Jamal has already turned the wheel to the right and has pressed the accelerator.

'Downshift! Into first,' Arwood yells.

'The wheels will spin. The wheels are bald.'

'Do you have a gun?' Benton asks Arwood as the black-scarved men start to jog toward them.

'There are a dozen arseholes out there with assault rifles. I'm not Jason Bourne. That's not the only play left.'

The car skids into the sand and onto rock. The lower gear pulls them over the first hill, as Arwood said it would, but the wheels slip. There's no purchase. The angle is too severe.

'Put it in third, like on ice,' says Benton. 'Like on ice.'

'Ice? There is no ice. What ice?' Jamal yells.

The men with the rifles and black headscarves come closer, looking into cars, slapping people, looking at wallets and family names. Some people are yanked from cars. They all look the same—hands up, shoulders up, helpless. There is the sound of occasional gunfire at the front of the line.

Benton hears Arwood say into the phone '… no matter what you do', but his own heart is racing too fast and pounding in his chest too loudly, and it blocks his ears from anything that doesn't send signals to the most primitive part of his brain—the part that knows to run from beasts and hide in shadows. He cannot focus on what Arwood is saying.

With his remaining time, Benton lifts the video camera and spins it around until he finds what he's looking for: a second SD memory card from a side slot.

'They are coming. They see us,' Jamal shouts.

The car is stuck. They're spinning their wheels.

The chip is hard to remove. Benton tries pulling it, and it doesn't give. He looks for a button, but doesn't find one. He needs some pliers.

'Push it,' Arwood says, seeing Benton's trouble.

'I want to pull it, not push it.'

'Pushing it does pull it. Trust me.'

Benton pushes the thin edge of the chip, and when he releases the pressure, it clicks and rises a bit higher than it was. He removes it and shoves it into his shoe.

Adar has assumed a foetal position, and is holding her hands against her ears as the car lurches forward, then back, then forward again as Jamal tries to rock them over some kind of scar in the earth.

The men outside are ten metres away. They're interested in the Toyota now. Their car is the only one that has tried to get away. The men are pointing and yelling at them. Benton doesn't understand. They wear tan clothing. They have beards but no moustaches, and on their heads are black scarves.

'Whatever you're going to say,' Benton says to Arwood, 'you'd better say it now. Because we're in big trouble.'

The shots are not loud; they are pops absorbed by the sand. The invisible bullets blow out the wheels of their car. The radiator is pierced, and scorching water sprays over their windscreen.

The men yank open the doors. They shout at the passengers. Their eyes are doey-brown and have a faraway look, as though they are going through a routine that holds no surprises for them. There is nothing immediate in their eyes — nothing present or soulful or reachable.

No, not nihilists, thinks Benton as he is dragged from the car and thrown to the ground. *These people are filled with purpose.*

The only other time Benton has been dragged from a car was in Lebanon in 1982. There was no al-Qaeda in those days. In Beirut there were complex but learnable codes of conduct that made the landscape more stable and traversable. The leadership was better maintained, though the number of factions was staggering. He was released when they learned he was a journalist. Back then, no one wanted bad press.

He often thought that his feelings of safety in Beirut had been irrational until, during a visit to Bangkok in the late 1980s, Benton fell into a casual conversation with an Israeli eyeglass designer named Ari who was in Thailand for scuba diving. He'd served in Lebanon, and agreed with Benton. 'When I was there, I knew why people were angry, so I could avoid the violence. When I visit my cousins in Los Angeles … who knows?'

Two men pull Benton into the hardscrabble earth by the side of the road. Looking up, he can see that Jamal's hands are resting on his head, his fingers locked together. His shoulders ride high, and his head is slumped, as though this might protect his brainstem from a 7.62 millimetre bullet.

Adar is pushed forward and onto her knees. One of the men is pointing to the ground. He wants them all to kneel.

Arwood does not kneel and instead makes his move, but not with a gun. 'If you kill them,' he shouts, 'they won't pay for us. It's all or nothing. If you want your money, if you want to get rich and stop taking these shit jobs, you will stop pushing them. No one pays for bodies.'

The mercenaries—the terrorists, the killers, the evil-doers, their captors, their executioners; there is no lexicon yet for such men—all look at each other. It is the first pause they have taken in their actions; the first indication that something unexpected or unusual is happening.

'Jamal, translate for me,' Arwood says. 'Tell them what I said.'

Without lowering his hands or turning around, Jamal says something. Maybe it's a good translation. Maybe it's not a translation at all.

The two men who are deciding whether to kill them are not the only gunmen here. There is a team at work. Civilians are starting to run away from their cars, and sometimes the killers let them. Sometimes they shoot one in the back.

As Benton is pushed farther away from the road, he has a better angle on what's going on farther ahead.

He sees smoke rising from the black shell of a burning car. Like zombies, the killers do not run in pursuit. They are unhurried in their movements and gestures. Bullets are fast enough for their purposes.

To his left, on the next hill closer to the bombsite, are three men kneeling on the ground with their hands over their heads, as Jamal is doing. One turns to look at Benton. His eyes are wide with fear. His lips are open, as if to share a thought.

Benton watches as the man is shot. The blood adds to the colour of the land.

The executioners are unceremonial. One is filming the murders on a smartphone of some kind. The other shoots the second man in the back twice; he falls forward. The same shooter turns the rifle on the third, who is also on his knees. He, too, is shot twice. His shoulder blades clench together as the scapula tries to protect his spine from further trauma. He tries to stand. He plants one foot and rises. He manages a second step. It is a bold instinct to survive. The gunman, for a moment, lets him—for a moment.

Adar sees this, too. It is too close not to see, too loud not to hear. She cries in terror and makes to stand up, but the man behind her forces her to the ground again. Her knees hit the dirt beside Jamal.

Benton looks at Adar in the sand, and sees Charlotte.

His heart is pounding. He does not want to see this. He does not want to see this little girl get shot again.

And then, as ever, Arwood.

Arwood drops his shoulders, straightens his shirt, and turns to face the terrorists with one hand up, making the universal motion for two bills being rubbed together. 'We're journalists. Beloved, expensive, handsome, and rich European journalists, whose governments like to pay ransom, just so you guys never have to be without needed funds for killing people. If you shoot us, there will be no money—only bombs landing on your head. My video camera is in the car. Go look. Jamal, tell him.'

Jamal says something in Arabic.

There is more shooting in the distance. Some of the remaining police cower behind cars and ineffectually shoot back. They are not soldiers, and many of them are young and new to the job. Unlike their assailants, they aren't cold-blooded murderers, either. Most are regular people who need jobs or want to help Iraq, or else they are Shiites who are proud that their tribe is finally in charge of the government backed by the Americans.

As Arwood spouts more bullshit, Benton decides that his chances of dying in the next five minutes are very high. As Arwood said in the car, the only real choice left is how to face it. And since no one really knows, Benton decides it really comes down to only one issue.

'Onto your feet, young lady,' he says to her delicately, as he reaches down and puts his right hand under Adar's arm, raising her up and supporting her weight.

What are these people?

Benton decides they are Stooges. So inspired, he dubs the larger one Larry and his shorter companion Moe. It is Moe who presses his rifle against Benton's chest.

Benton remains standing, holding Adar too tightly. He is hurting her. He doesn't know how to hold her more gently.

And yet they are on their feet, and the issue is resolved.

Waiting to be shot, Benton has an epiphany, and learns that the opposite of brave is not cowardly, but resigned.

This is a feeling clearly not shared by Arwood Hobbes.

'That man, right there?' Arwood yells to Larry and Moe. 'That's Ferris Bueller. You know who that is? You caught a big fish—well done. It's time to start placing calls. Luckily for you, I have the number.'

This, of all things, is what Jamal adopts as a good idea and chooses to translate. Benton hears him say something-in-Arabic, something-in-Arabic, something-in-Arabic, something-else-in-Arabic, Ferris Bueller, something-in-Arabic, and then *baksheesh*.

Larry and Moe look at each other. Arwood is smiling, and holding his hands wide open in the manner of P.T. Barnum.

After Arwood shot the colonel, Benton thought Arwood might be a sociopath. Now he wonders if he might be genuinely insane. Twenty-two years is a long time not to know what someone else has been doing.

'So are we good here, or what?' Arwood asks.

Märta dials, dials again, and then dials again. There's nothing. Or Benton isn't answering it. There was definitely an explosion, though. She is new to the use of crowd-sourced real-time intelligence using humanitarian mapping software, but one of the interns has installed Ushahidi, and she's looking for SMS messages or tweets about any incident on the road that Benton is travelling. There is nothing yet, anyway. People might still be burning.

Märta feels claustrophobic, and needs both air and a cigarette. Taking her purse, she leaves the briefing and walks quickly to her Land Cruiser.

Dusk has arrived. The sun burns orange and heavy on the horizon. The sun does not fall here; it is pushed away by the night. Nothing yields power in Iraq, not even the day.

The wind picks up with nightfall, as the air cools faster than the land. She drives along the uneven road between the undulating tents and past children in shabby clothing, as the men smoke and the women gather up their water jugs for the long walk.

On her mobile, she calls Ahmed in the radio room. He answers, and she drills him.

'What's going on north-west of Mosul?'

'I'm sending the sitrep memo around soon. There were roadblocks and—'

'I know that part. Skip ahead. What's going on? What blew up?'

'It's unclear. There's been an attack of some kind on one of the roadblocks. The police say there was an explosion and some gunfire. Everyone except your team is either back already or has been diverted to Zakho. I have one UNICEF team inside city limits there, and I expect them to be at the hotel in a few minutes, just before curfew. I will give their names to the police, but I think they are very busy now. They will be of no help right now.'

'Yeah, OK. Thanks, Ahmed.'

'Do any of them have a smartphone?' he asks as an afterthought. 'I could do a Find My Phone. We usually leave those activated here.'

'Benton has an iPhone, but it's my personal one, and I don't think I have that setting on. I'm not very technical.'

'There's nothing else I can do.'

'Keep me abreast of developments out there. I was speaking with Thomas when we got cut off. I think it's when the blast occurred. I think they were there, and close enough to have been hit by it, or at least seriously startled. I think we have a problem. I'm going to be at Louise's office.'

'This is very bad. I have to tell UN security.'

'Yes, it is.'

Shukran she says, and hangs up.

By the time the call is over, she's inside the foyer at the ICRC's sub-delegation office. Farrah is gone for the night. Like most national staff, she lives in Dohuk, and they want her back before nightfall, too.

The lights to the facility are all off, and the space feels hollow and abandoned, except for Louise's single bulb. She works late, and typically sleeps on the sofa. She's unmarried, and this isn't a family duty station. Märta has long suspected that Louise might be slightly OCD. It made her an excellent lawyer before she joined the movement, and she's a good case manager, but she lacks a certain social flexibility—she's a stickler for rules, which is going to be a problem, given what Märta plans to say next.

Louise frowns as Märta comes in. 'Shouldn't you be at home? Basking in the warm glow of Netflix?'

'My idiots are missing.'

'The ones from this morning?'

'And the driver, yes. And now there's a girl with them.'

Louise pushes back from the desk. She says nothing.

'You want to say "I told you so,"' Märta says, plopping onto the sofa across from Louise's desk. 'I'll say it for you.'

'Are you worried? Communication failures happen all the time.'

'Handset is getting nothing, and Benton's phone went dead during a bomb blast. I don't know how close they were. I can't send anyone to get them.'

'Herb and Tigger would go.'

'I'll bet they would, which is why I won't ask. I don't run a private military company.'

'I can't get involved, for obvious reasons, but I can pass on some numbers. The private military companies are a part of life now,' Louise says, removing a piece of maple sugar candy from a green cardboard box. 'Want a piece?'

'Too sweet.'

'You eat that salty licorice.'

'Salty.'

'Did you give him a backup phone?' Louise asks.

'Who?'

'The older gentleman.'

'Yes, I did.'

'Are you having an affair with him?'

'Yes.'

'How long has it been going on?'

'Two nights, twenty-two years apart.'

'I don't have a label for that,' Louise says.

'Neither do I.'

'What are you doing, Märta?'

'I'm doing what I'm always doing here. I'm trying to protect civilians while doing no harm.'

'You may have to rethink your methods.'

21

They are hostages and alive, off-road, and heading south in another white Toyota Land Cruiser.

Moe had put the hood on Benton's head before pushing him into the back seat. He could hear Adar's cries, Jamal's heavy breathing, and Arwood's bullshit, too, until something struck his remaining words out and Arwood finally stopped talking.

Larry must be driving, because Benton heard the diesel engine start while Moe was still beside him. Unless there are more than two of them now. Time will tell.

There is no good direction to travel in, but south is worst, because south of Ninawa province is al-Anbar and the great western desert where ISIL is retrenching. There are no mapped roads that pass through it. The highway from Mosul to Baghdad is far to the east. As far as Benton knows, nothing passes directly through the desert itself, but he doesn't know much: a map is only a map, and not every road is documented on it.

They drive for more than twenty minutes. They are safer inside the car. They can be shot anywhere, so it's unlikely to happen where it will make a mess.

The breeze from the open window presses against Benton's hood, filling his nostrils with the fabric, and for a moment he can't breathe. His neck cramps as he turns away. It is only when he lowers his head in defeat that the fabric bunches and he can breathe again through a small gap near the neck.

Benton's inner thigh starts to vibrate.

His world is black, so he cannot see whether anyone else has noticed. The phone's silent vibrations are muffled between the vinyl seat and his leg. He'd forgotten it was there. His captors didn't search him after taking his primary phone and satchel away, because most men frisk others poorly.

Benton lifts his hips to keep the phone from vibrating against anything other than himself. There are wind gusts and engine rumble, tyre buzz, and scree kicking up into the chassis. They harmonise a dull white noise that fills the cabin and insulates the sound.

The sun is almost down. He can feel that. Desert voices belong to women. It would be nice to hear Märta's voice, if only he could answer the phone.

Hello? he'd say.

Thomas? Where are you?

Held hostage. I should have listened to you.

Would you like to come back?

Yes, please.

This is the conversation he wants to have. It is not her voice, though, he is hearing. It is Vanessa's.

Moe is sitting in the far-back seats. He says something to Larry, the driver, that Benton doesn't understand. It must be something he doesn't mind Adar or Jamal hearing. The vehicle turns. No one else says a word.

The driver slows, and later slows further. The light changes. They are behind a hill now, or in a garage, or the sun has set entirely. The temperature drops.

Märta — assuming it was Märta — has stopped calling. She tried three times.

Could it have been Charlotte? She's been trying to reach him. She's been wanting to tell him he's a cretin for turning on her mother after ignoring them both. She wants to explain to him — he supposes—that he has no right to disappear at a time like this, to place something distant and historical and abstract like peace in the Middle East over something proximate and tangible and immediate like herself and her mother. She will be eloquent in her juxtapositions and her line of reasoning. She will be linear and faithful to logical progression, and she will substantiate her claims on accepted norms of social behaviour among adults, which she learned about from someone other than her father.

It couldn't have been Charlotte, though. This isn't his phone. It is Märta's phone. She has called it three times, and he hasn't answered. Now he has to trust that she knows what to do with silence.

The Land Cruiser stops after hours on the road and off it. The route has been too complex to memorise, and the sun has set, so Benton is completely without his bearings. All he knows, for certain, is they have gone up. Way up. When the door is opened, cold air rushes in, along with the new danger. It is almost welcome.

Moe yells at his hostages to get out, and slaps their heads, giving them a direction to walk. Adar has stopped her crying. There are no city sounds. There's no traffic or village life. They are someplace desolate. Unwitnessed.

A third man comes out to meet them. His footfalls are crisp. He shuffles as he walks. He mumbles quietly to the other men. He sounds surprised. He is asking questions.

Benton names him Curly.

The longer Curly speaks, the angrier he gets at Larry and Moe. Whatever he says, he is saying in front of Jamal and Adar, who surely understand what's being said. Which either means it doesn't matter because it's incidental, or he's going to kill them all anyway, so it's also incidental.

Nothing can be deduced here. Even Sherlock Holmes would be lost.

Moe grabs Benton's arms and cuffs them behind his back, using a zip cuff.

Benton gently pushes his wrists outward as far as possible while Curly tightens them; too tight, but they would have been tighter if Benton hadn't pressed back.

Moe pushes and slaps them as they walk blindly. After twenty steps from the car, Benton's feet land on something different from the packed earth. It is smooth and manmade. The pressure on his ears increases. There is an echo. It is even colder. It smells like a musty cellar suffering from water damage.

It's into this chamber that Arwood decides to speak. Again.

'I said before that there's money to be made off us. But I forgot to tell you this. If you don't make a deal for our release, you'll be the ones paying the price. My people are watching. I strongly suggest you make a low ransom demand, take your money, and get this done. Because if you don't, you're dead men walking.'

At least four distinct voices laugh. So there are four Stooges, who speak English well enough to chuckle at Arwood.

Which introduces Shemp as the fourth stooge. And this means that Benton is running out of Stooges faster than they are.

When Benton's hood is removed, he sees nothing. His eyelids are sticky, and his vision blurry. The glaring bare bulb on the ceiling is little help. When he does manage to focus, he makes out a square room about five metres by five metres, with slits on the wall in front of him near the ceiling, like in a World War II pillbox. To his right is a door of drab-green sheet metal and rust. It is closed. To his left, there is another that seems more robust and may lead outside. There are two dirty mattresses on the floor behind him, and nothing else.

When his eyes focus, he sees that Arwood's hood has been removed as well, his arms bound behind him. Jamal and Adar are there, too, standing in the corner as though they can avoid their circumstance by giving it a wide berth.

He turns, and sees that the door to the outside is closed as well. They are all boxed in together.

'Everyone OK?' Benton asks.

Jamal nods, and Adar is immobile and hangs her head. Her face has vanished into the darkness of her hair, which shields her.

'We're going to need a plan,' Benton says.

'Oh, I have a plan,' Arwood says. 'I wasn't bluffing. We're being watched. I've got people.'

22

It has been said that the US Army was designed by geniuses to be run by idiots. When Arwood returned to the United States in June 1991 as Operation Provide Comfort wound to a close with a whimper, he wondered what they had been geniuses at doing.

He avoided a court-martial somehow, and the mandatory 'bad conduct' or dishonourable discharge that comes with it. Instead, he was given an 'other than honourable' discharge. At first, he had no idea what that meant, and didn't care. His buddies called it 'bad paper', and after that they weren't his buddies anymore. Apparently, bad paper is contagious, and it doesn't matter how you contracted it.

He went home to his parents' house, because he had no apartment or job. It was a nondescript white ranch house with three small bedrooms. At first, this was exactly the atmosphere he needed. It was a staid purgatory that demanded nothing of him, gave nothing in return, and offered no judgement, because there was no one around who cared enough to be judgemental. Not until his father chewed him out.

After that, Arwood decided to call Veterans Affairs and see if he could get some help from them. He wasn't suicidal or anything, but he wanted to know what they could do to help him out, because he was lower than he'd ever been, felt more alone than he knew was possible, and the furthest into the future he could imagine was reaching for the door handle that led outside.

It was kind of interesting speaking with the Department of Veterans Affairs, because Arwood learned that the US government considers eligibility for psychological counselling to be a reward for not really needing it. By excluding veterans with less-than-honourable discharges, they were excluding those who had acted the worst in a war — probably for psychological reasons — and, rather than helping them out, instead set them loose on the general population, resulting in pretty predictable violence, wife-beating, alcoholism, criminality, family disintegration, long-term unemployment, welfare, emergency medical costs, unpaid medical bills, loan defaults, drug use, federal and state drug-enforcement costs, state legal fees for prosecuting criminals, prison costs, and appeal processes, not to mention all the traumatised children they beat the crap out of.

But Arwood was told that he wasn't *necessarily* excluded. His was an in-between case — being other than honourable — that may or may not have been disqualifying, based on the standards set under Title 38 Code of Federal Regulations (C.F.R.) §3.12. Now, as it was explained to Arwood one afternoon by phone in 1991, as he wiped potato-chip crumbs from his AC/DC T-shirt, he still might retain eligibility for VA health-care benefits for service-incurred or service-aggravated disabilities, unless he was subject to one of the statutory bars to benefits set forth in Title 38 United States Code §5303(a), Authority: Section 2 of Public Law 95-126 (Oct. 8, 1977).

'Uh-huh,' he'd said.

He might be eligible for pending verification status. 'You have to put in a request for an administrative decision regarding the character of service for VA health-care purposes, and that must be made to the local VA regional office or VARO. Do you know where your VARO is?'

'Um —'

'This request may be submitted using a VA Form 7131, Exchange of Beneficiary Information and Request for Administrative and

Adjudicative Action. In making determinations of health-care eligibility, the same criteria will be used as are now applicable to determinations of service connection when there is no character-of-discharge bar.

'Sir? Are you there?'

With his savings from the army, Arwood bought a very used red-white-and-blue Yamaha FJ 1100 motorcycle, and disappeared into America at $0.98 a gallon. He realised, in looking at his Rand McNally map, that he'd actually seen less of the country than he'd seen of Iraq, and he'd only seen four towns in Iraq. His goal was simply to put as many miles as possible between himself, his father, and anyone who might understand that phone call.

Arwood Hobbes tried working regular jobs—supermarkets, photo labs, record stores. But regular jobs for regular people had in common the element of routine. Routine, he found, could be a great way to hold things together if you're already a together kind of guy, but Arwood was in pieces, and he wanted to do something that might put himself right again. Holding the line was not going to make that happen.

He arrived in the Midwest, only in the sense that you can't get anywhere without passing through it, and he had to stop for money for petrol. Amid the flatness, he found hand-written signs for yard sales and flea markets, all of them selling guns.

Arwood wasn't a gun nut. He didn't have any happy childhood memories of hunting with his grandpa or learning to track with his daddy. He had never heard lectures on nature and conservation, or on Teddy Roosevelt. Guns were mechanical things he'd been trained to take apart, put back together, and use. They were fun to play with at the outset, but, after basic training and jogging in the desert, what Arwood had come to appreciate about guns was that—more than anything else—they were heavy.

What he did like, though, was sales.

Supply and demand made sense to him. It was a simple seesaw, a singular philosophy with one fulcrum on an unalterable axis—much like talk radio.

Still, though, Arwood was dissatisfied. It wasn't the money he wanted; it was a higher calling, a purpose. He was still pissed off, and he had no way to get over it.

In Montana, at one well-attended and well-stocked gun show in the autumn of 1991, Arwood met a large, bearded man named Nick Harwood. Nick ran a booth selling military-surplus items—lots of wool, backpacks, bayonets, gloves, and camping gear. Arwood had been standing next to him, selling re-loads and second-rate small-game rifles at someone else's table for $8.50 an hour plus lunch, minus questions.

He and Nick started talking. Like a lot of other guys who look like they could unscrew your head and pour your guts into a bucket, Nick was actually soft-spoken, pleasant, and slightly defeated.

Nick lived out of an RV that pulled a trailer full of what he called 'stuff'. He'd buy stuff where there was a lot of it, and then sell the stuff where there was less of it. If he was lucky, petrol prices stayed low, and the people who had it weren't too far from the people who needed it. Lately, though, he'd gotten into a new line, mainly because he had a slipped disk, and driving the RV was literally a pain in his arse he didn't need anymore. That was what he was into now, he said: 'brokering.'

'Like with stocks and stuff?' Arwood asked.

'Same logic, but different stuff. A broker is someone who sits anywhere he wants, and instead of dragging stuff around from place to place with a bad back, he brings supply and demand together for a price, or else a cut. The nice thing is, you never need to take possession of the stuff, or actually move stuff around. You're the connection guy. You can bring anything you have access to to anyone you want to have it—if you've got access to the goods, know the right people, and have the chops to make the deal happen.'

'What's the hard part?' Arwood asked.

'The hard part?' Nick laughed. 'The hard part is matching up the supply with the demand, and gaining the trust of both sides so they think you're the man to be the bridge for them. The more mainstream the goods, the greater the competition. The more unusual or niche or dangerous, the less competition. Most people don't want to take big risks.'

'What if minefields don't bother me?'

'Anything that bothers other people and doesn't bother you is an asset in this life.'

'This is interesting,' Arwood said. 'How do I start?'

'You'll need a phone.'

Arwood shook his head as though he were being told he'd need a third hand for his second penis. 'I live on the road. Where am I gonna get a phone?'

'You'll need to stick around someplace, or work the pay phones. I think you should stick around someplace. I'll tell you what,' Nick said, sizing Arwood up and having nothing better to do than take a chance, 'I've got a little place outside Bozeman. It's a cabin, but it's got electricity and a phone line. You want to give it a go, the place is yours for $150 a month.'

'What's in it for you?'

'$150 a month.'

'That's a pretty strong argument.'

'You think that's the kind of life you want?'

Arwood said it was. It really, really was.

Arwood realised quickly that weapons were his game and that the US wasn't his market. As it happened, 1991 was a stellar year to become an arms broker. The Berlin Wall was down, the Warsaw Pact was defunct, all of eastern Europe was begging to join NATO and the EU, and the only thing of marketable value left behind in the former Soviet Union was military hardware. No one was getting paid, the military had nothing to do, and everyone needed jobs because communism wasn't so much being replaced by capitalism as by reality.

That was supply taken care of.

Transportation wasn't too hard to arrange, either. There were plenty of surplus Soviet air platforms lying around in the newly independent states of the former USSR, and no one had any work for them. If you offered to pay the pilots and some bribes, the planes went wherever you wanted them to.

That left only demand.

But these were the salad years. Everyone was buying. By the late 1990s, Arwood knew his way around the planet. Planes and a bank account in Geneva were all he needed once he cracked the nut on domestic transport problems in conflict zones, which usually involved hiring the same charter companies the humanitarian organisations used, and simply filling them on their return runs.

It all came together.

And yet, all through this period, what Arwood Hobbes really wanted was to close the chapter on a piece of old and unfinished business. What he needed was intelligence information, and that was finally what he'd received a few weeks before arriving in Dohuk—before the mortar attack—from a Kurd named Jindar Zafar.

The Leopard Room, beneath the Hotel d'Angleterre in Geneva, is a short stroll eastward from the Mandarin on Quai du Mont-Blanc, past the spot where Lake Geneva draws to its south-western tip and the Rhône River is born under the Pont de la Machine—as though it were named for making the river rather than for pumping its water into the public fountains. Like the Thames or the Seine, the Rhône is trimmed by concrete as it runs through the city, but, like

Geneva itself, the river has less drama and less majesty. It performs its functions and lives its life as quietly as possible. With its understated and dour birth between the Alps to the south and the hamlet-rich Jura Mountains to the north, one would never suspect that the freshwater river eventually bursts into the spirit-filled Catholic world of the Riviera, swells the grapes on the *Côtes du Rhône*, dances down to the estuaries near Marseille, and then — as quickly as it came — vanishes from Europe altogether, leaving only the taste of its sweet water to lap the wide shores of North Africa.

Geneva was undeniably beautiful. The problem was the Calvinist mood. It was serene here to the point of sterility. In Arwood's view, the collective goal of Swiss life was to get from birth to death without incident. If that wasn't your own philosophy, the city would never be more than a distraction from the life you actually wanted to live.

Arwood liked the Leopard Room for business, because it looked colonial and felt smarmy. It was three steps underground, and despite its being only a stone's throw from the lake, you'd never know it was there. It was dark, filled with earth tones and woods. It was as good a place as any to draw green and purple lines on maps, soiled only gently from gin and tonics and the rank egoism of a self-serving philosophy. It really was a top-quality place to sell weapons.

Arwood had been drinking a bourbon on the rocks, wearing a black T-shirt and Levi's. He was leafing through a blue-cloth book by Norman Angell written in 1910 that explained how future war in Europe would be futile because it would be economically irrational.

Arwood laughed so hard, he spilled his Maker's Mark. He was wiping it off his leather jacket when his associate entered and took a seat beside him to the right of the piano.

Jindar Zafar wore an exquisite blue Super 140 suit from Corneliani and a yellow tie by Lanvin. His shoes were J.M. Weston. His watch was IWC. Zafar was in his early fifties, and looked to Arwood as though he knew exactly how much longer his prime would last. He joined Arwood at a table near the back, filled with books used as furniture, topped now by Norman Angell.

'So, Mr Jindar Zafar. Still lookin' like dat.'

'Mr Hobbes.'

'Want a drink?'

'I don't think I'll be here that long.'

'You could have had two already if you'd applied yourself.'

'I'm a Muslim, Mr Hobbes. We don't drink. You wouldn't understand.'

'Really,' Arwood said, tossing the soiled napkin onto the table and calling a waiter to remove it. 'I was sitting in Manama waiting for this arms dealer I know, and while there I learned about how the Saudis drive across that new fancy bridge of theirs and get thousand-dollar hotel rooms at the Meridian, where they have bottles of the finest booze in the world brought up to them by the youngest of Russian hookers. I'm talking fourteen years old. You find them in business class on Emirates — maybe you've seen them. After the Saudis and their guests are done, they drive back across the bridge and tell the West we're corrupt and morally adrift. So what else do you plan to teach me about how you mystical and wise Orientals live your lives that I can't possibly understand?'

'I choose not to drink to honour my religion.'

'Well, that's entirely different, isn't it? Meanwhile, without a beverage, you look like a gangster waiting to get shot. So settle into the chair. You're embarrassing me.'

'Do you have what I want?' Zafar asked.

A young man with the physique of a distance runner sat himself down at the piano in the corner of the room. His jacket probably fitted the last guy who wore it, but there was no telling. He started playing 'Smoke Gets in Your Eyes'. No one in the room seemed pleased to hear it.

Arwood had to lean in to be heard. 'Do I have what you want? The interesting part is whether you have what I want. People selling information don't always have the information. So let's start with you. Where's the fucking colonel, and when's he gonna be there?'

Jindar Zafar straightened his jacket, sat back, and crossed his legs. 'Up north. In a village on the road to Zakho. He has a cousin. After Saddam was killed, he took to hiding there. It's in Kurdistan.'

'Why was he killing people in the south, if he's from the north?'

'He is Sunni. They are Shiite. He is well connected to the network from Tikrit. It is usually easier to kill people farther from home.'

'Uh-huh. I need GPS coordinates and a time window. There's a lot to coordinate.'

'Are you really this driven to kill a man because of a grudge over twenty years old? You'll take that risk, pay this cost, for something so distant?'

Arwood removed a photograph from his bag and slid it across the table. It was a picture of himself in Iraq in 1991, taken during the long quiet of the air war and before he was stationed at Checkpoint Zulu. He looked young and handsome. He was in the middle of a hearty laugh beside another young man who looked the same. They were both laughing, because a third man in the middle—his face obscured from view, his black fingers in relief against the white fabric—was holding up a T-shirt that read, I HATE SAND.

'You see this?' Arwood said. 'That's Alan Vicars on the right, and John Griffiths behind the shirt. We were friends once. This is a special picture that I carry around, because it is the last time I remember laughing at something that was meant to be funny.

'The colonel killed a little girl the next day, and she died in my arms. I don't even know who else he slaughtered, but I know about her, and that's all that needs to matter. Since then, in my life—' Arwood put the picture back into his jacket pocket and stopped explaining himself.

'Without a real cause, without something urgent and visible, you risk being seen as a madman.'

'You don't know what happened down there in 1991.'

'I do know what happened,' said Jindar Zafar. 'It happened up north, too. Among my people. You know this. You went there next. Saddam did it to everyone. But if people act on old grudges every day, the world will be bathed in blood. There must be a way to move on. Forgetting, or letting go, or forgiving, is sometimes necessary.'

'Maybe next time.'

'My advice?' Zafar said. 'If there is a sign, if there is a cause that others can understand, then go. If not, take that as a sign, too. The people you are asking to help you in Dohuk and Mosel — they are your friends. You have been good to these people. They will help you. But there is no reason to ask for favours and put people at risk without some greater purpose.'

Arwood was unmoved.

'Here is the information you want,' Jindar finally said, pushing a plain envelope across the table. 'It is all here. The time and place are very clear. The village has a café. There are yellow chairs. His is the fourth door on the left. There is a blue tile to the left of the door, with the Arabic number for five on it. Can you read Arabic?'

'I know the numbers.'

'If you are late—'

Arwood finished off the bourbon, which by now had lost its bite and only tasted sweet. He could drink it all night.

'If the intelligence is bad, I'll find you.'

'How would you do that, Mr Hobbes?'

Arwood laughed. 'You fancy dressers always miss the obvious. How would I find you? I'd wait for you at your fuckin' tailor's, that's how.'

23

'Who makes these?' Arwood asks, regarding the black hood on the floor. He's sitting on the mattress and playing with it on the end of his foot.

'What?' Benton replies.

'Who makes them?' he repeats. 'I've never seen one for sale in London, New York, Milan, or Cape Town. I've never looked in a shop window and seen one over the head of a mannequin. No Christmas sales at Bloomingdale's. No pop-up ads on the Internet.'

'I don't know, Arwood.'

'These are not repurposed items. They're useless for anything other than covering or carrying heads. How do supply and demand find each other? And for real … how much do they cost?'

'I don't know.'

'Has anyone considered that if we simply raided the factories that make these and grabbed hold of their mailing lists, we'd probably have the entire global terrorist network by the balls? Even knowing where the orders have been placed, and for how many, would wrap up the entire intelligence game. Am I the only one who has this figured out?'

Adar starts to cry again. Benton looks at the fourteen-year-old child who is traumatised, isolated, and under continued stress. If she even survives this, he knows, she'll never be the same, or whatever she might have otherwise been.

'Is something wrong?' Benton asks Jamal, in the hope it is something specific.

'She knows one of them,' says Jamal, who is still standing in the corner as though he's ready to go at any time.

'One of them was in the convoy attack?' Arwood asks.

'No. One of them is from Shaddad. South of al-Hasakah. West of here and near her village. It is Sunni. She says the village has a dark history. They have been treated very badly by the Shiites. Very bad. She does not know his name, but she knows his family. She says she has heard that the father was murdered by the *Shabiha*. This is Assad's secret militia. His death squads. They are Alawite tribe. They are Shiite. They hate the Sunni. Adar is Sunni. So she runs away to Iraq to hide.'

Arwood pulls up his knees and leans back against the wall. 'If he's all disgruntled, he should be off killing government troops with the rebels. Not blowing up civilians in traffic or murdering cops. This doesn't help us.'

'No, no,' Jamal says. 'That's not what happened. She said he came from a good family. Everyone knows their family. Mother is very nice. Boys are nice. But he became very angry. And then he met someone who explained that these people are heretics. They are infidels, and they are the reason the Muslim people are weak. She says that the boy is like all the others. No one wants to be weak anymore. They are tired of being weak. They want to return to a time when they were strong and united. They cannot stand the humiliation anymore. The West does not understand our humiliation.'

'The fourteen-year-old said all this?'

'No, I say all this.'

'You're not much of a translator,' Arwood says.

'I am a driver.'

'And you think,' Arwood says, 'that if these people felt proud and respected, they'd stop packing ice-cream trucks with explosives to kill as many children as possible? They need jobs and a hug?'

'I'm saying there are reasons.'

'There are always reasons, Jamal, but not justifications. Listen, I've been watching these douchebags for years. These guys aren't choosing between a job in auto mechanics and beheading infidels. Yeah, they're discontented, and maybe they've got a good reason, too. Fair enough. The thing is, there are a lot of hard-luck cases in the world, and a lot of places on the losing side of history. But not all those places celebrate mass murder because they're angry. See, little Johnny Hardluck might feel bad one day and say to his mummy, "Mummy, I feel so bad I'm going to cut somebody's head off." That could happen in Pittsburgh. We have psychos, too. But how Mummy responds is kind of what makes one place different from another. So if his mummy says, "That's a good idea, Johnny, you slice them up real good, and if you die, we'll be extra proud of you," then we know what kind of people we're dealing with. Around here, you kill a hundred children with an exploding ice-cream truck, and your family gets a pension and its own website. That doesn't happen in Pittsburgh. That is not a minor distinction. When we act badly, we at least feel really bad about it, and try to find ways to avoid it later. These people do exactly the opposite. That's why we're better than them. Got it?'

'They are being manipulated by the elites,' Jamal says.

Arwood gently bangs the back of his head against the concrete cell. This is not the first time he's had this conversation. But usually, when he does have these conversations, he's trying to get laid. At least this time he can speak his mind.

'Jamal, you can only manipulate ideas that make sense to people already. If an imam gets on his soapbox and tells all the Sunnis to go out and kill all the New York Yankee fans, they wouldn't make much headway. Because it wouldn't make any kind of sense. Go kill the Shiites? That makes sense. Unfortunately, everything happening down the mountain, and even up here, makes sense to people, whether they like it or not. And these assholes? In there? They aren't gonna stop. You see, it's all explained by Loggins's Law. You know Loggins and Messina? No? Doesn't matter. It's like this, Jamal: we will never get along with anyone—not now, not later, not ever—if their mamas don't dance, and their daddies don't rock and roll. Because it's mind over matter, my friend. And you cannot change people's minds about what matters.'

Jamal does not translate any of this for Adar.

'You should both rest,' Benton says, taking a position on the mattress similar to Arwood's. 'You'll need your strength. And if they offer you food and water, don't be proud or stubborn. Take it. You, too,' he says, looking at Arwood.

'Yeah, yeah.'

Jamal and Adar don't move.

'What's the name of his family?' Arwood asks.

Jamal asks Adar, but she bows her head and says nothing.

Benton leans his head back against the wall, and the paint flakes behind him, dropping little pieces down his trousers. The air is dry. It is tinged with a scent of cooking oil and a familiar spice he can't name. Benton cannot hear, but still feels, some manner of village life outside. Over some hills. Gently, as on a breeze, he closes his eyes, and he drifts over the mountain they climbed, turn upon turn upon turn.

Charlotte once explained to her father how everything in life was connected. She could tell him which aspects of an organism were connected by evolution to others—either closely or distantly, but unified from common origins. It didn't really matter to her how far apart they had become over time; the shared evolutionary characteristics remained. 'We're not on a ladder of evolution with missing rungs,' she'd explain. 'It's more like a big bush.' When she came home from university and stayed with them in Fowey, she'd try to share her enthusiasm for her studies. She'd read essays aloud from

Stephen J. Gould with wonderful names like 'Bully for Brontosaurus' and 'George Canning's Left Buttock and the Origin of Species' and 'A Darwinian Gentleman at Marx's Funeral.' She said the twigs on the branch were expanding and splitting and growing. Some twigs stopped, while others pressed ever outward. In the end, the bush of life is populated by what lives farthest out. 'We are not at the top of the ladder,' she explained. 'We are only the farthest from the centre, on our own fragile and particular twig.'

'Which,' said Benton, trying to get his head around it, 'means that everything still alive after all this time is also a successful twig.'

'Right. Isn't that wonderful? It means we're all connected, and always will be.'

He had said 'Yes,' because she obviously thought it was, which was nice.

'We really are out here on our own,' Benton says, aloud.

'We'd better not be, because if we are, we're royally—'

Then the Stooges come in.

Curly is the first through the door. He speaks English, but his accent is thick and he slurs his speech.

'Where you from?' he says, looking at Benton.

'England,' he says.

'America?'

'No. England. Perhaps you've heard of it.'

'What is your name?' he says.

Arwood jumps right in and answers for all of them. He is even helpful enough to spell them out. Benton hopes the man doesn't have the inclination or skills to type them into Google.

'What are you doing in Ninawa?' he asks Arwood.

'I'm here for my health. The climate is good for my allergies. He's a journalist. He's covering the film festival.'

Curly ignores Arwood, and takes hold of Jamal and Adar. He

pushes them through the rusty green door into the adjacent room as Shemp follows them out, walking backwards, training his rifle on Arwood and Benton, whose hands are still bound.

'Don't you fucking hurt them!' Arwood yells.

Shemp is expressionless as he closes the door. The bolt slides into place from the other side, and a padlock is reinstalled.

Despite his hands being tied behind him, Arwood hops up like a karate instructor and rushes to the door. He places his ear against it and listens.

'Curly and Shemp locked it,' Benton says, sitting down again, this time with his hands behind him. 'We're locked in.'

'That's what you've named them?' Arwood asks as he wanders around the room, looking closely at it.

'I don't know their real names. I have to call them something to keep them straight in my mind. It's important to remain sorted in these circumstances.'

'Yeah, that's true,' Arwood says, scanning every aspect of the room. 'Stooges, though. That's pretty good. I didn't think of that.

'So, listen,' Arwood says as he walks slowly along the wall, looking for … something. 'Did you get laid last night?'

'That's not an appropriate conversation, and it hardly seems significant, given the circumstances.'

'You mean for a hostage situation?'

Benton tips his head and concedes that Arwood may have a point. 'What are you looking for?'

'Usual stuff. A nail, a sharp edge, wire cutters, machine gun, talkie-walkie. Anything useful.'

'I thought you had a plan.'

'Wire cutters won't hurt my plan.' Not finding any, though, Arwood flops down again onto the other mattress. 'Was it any good?' he asks.

'You honestly think I'm going to tell you?'

'The weird thing about my plan is how much it depends on whether or not Märta woke up feeling like she'd stick her neck out for you in a pinch. It's not much of a nail to hang this plan on, I admit, but I still need to know. So how was it?'

'You're a troglodyte.'

'We're in a cave.'

Benton is unresponsive.

'Look, I don't need any of the fluid and sticky details, I simply need to know what level of risk Märta is prepared to take to get you back. So was it not nice, nice, very nice, or complex?'

'It was nice and complex,' Benton says.

'We stand a chance, then.'

They both face outward into the empty room, which is as large as a two-car garage. There is nothing to look at except the burning bulb and the two machine-gun slits about six feet up the eight-foot wall.

'I'm terrified for those kids. I don't want them to die,' Benton says.

'The Three Stooges were all Jewish,' Arwood says. 'In fact, all four of the Three Stooges were Jews. That's the problem with your labelling scheme. I don't think these guys are Jewish. I suppose we could ask.'

'Probably not,' Benton says.

'I dated a Jewish girl once,' Arwood says. 'Rebecca Caplan. For three whole years.'

'What happened?'

'She came to her senses, obviously.'

'Obviously.'

'The thing about Jews—'

'Arwood, please.'

'No, seriously. The thing about Jews is that they know everyone else who's Jewish. It's a thing with them — people you wouldn't have known were Jewish. Like the Stooges. Or Lou Reed.'

'That's fascinating, Arwood,' Benton says.

'Amy Winehouse.'

'Did anyone see you kill the colonel?'

'Julianna Margulies — you know who she is? *The Good Wife*? I like that show. Mark Knopfler from Dire Straits. Rebecca would point out Jews like it was a version of punch buggy. Jew. Not a Jew. Like that. Everyone knows Einstein and Kafka and Barbra Streisand, but not necessarily Scarlett Johansson or Harrison Ford.'

'It could be why the security forces set up the roadblock. Because they were looking for you.'

'Jack Black. You see *High Fidelity*? That was a great movie. I've heard it's a book now, too.'

'And then ISIL attacked the security forces,' Benton says. 'But they did it quickly. So was it a target of opportunity, or a coincidence?'

'Captain Kirk and Mr Spock were both Jewish. Shatner and Nimoy. So was Chekhov, as a matter of fact.'

'You're not answering my questions.' Benton's shoulders are beginning to ache. He lowers his head to stretch, as on long-haul flights.

'OK, you want to talk about this? Fine. I was in the car thinking about what these knuckleheads are up to,' Arwood says, 'and all I can think is that none of this was planned. An attack was probably planned. Killing people was planned. Blowing up the cops, the whole thing. Was it because of me? Who the hell knows? All you need to do to get the emergency services to show up around here is blow something up real good. And if it was a roadblock set up for me, and the Stooges took advantage, what of it? They were obviously planning to do it at some point anyway. But not this part. Capturing us could not have been planned. We didn't even know we were gonna be there, so they sure as shit didn't. They've now got themselves some hostages they don't know what to do with. And I think Abu

Shemp got pretty annoyed when the rest of the barber quartet came back with us. I think we're off-book. I think orders are not being upheld. I think this is improv, and we can affect the dynamic. That's what I think.'

'Abu Shemp?'

'Fuck 'em.'

'I was actually reaching a pretty similar conclusion,' Benton says.

'Which means the situation can be influenced.'

'It also means,' Benton says, 'that it can be scrubbed.'

'I don't know what that means.'

'It means they could kill us all, and pretend their error never happened.'

'They could let us go, too,' Arwood says.

'Letting us go has a downside. Killing us doesn't. They're killers, and killers kill people to solve their problems.'

'I see your point,' Arwood says. 'This might be a good time to call back Märta. She called you at least three times.'

'How do you know that?'

'Vibrations through the seat. If Abu Larry—'

'Abu Larry was driving. Abu Curly was in the back.'

'I don't want to play who's on first. I'm just saying that if he'd been sitting next to us, we'd all be dead.'

'I guess we're very lucky people, then.'

'The luckiest,' Arwood says.

'You'll need to get my phone.'

'Isn't it down your pants?'

'No, it's down my trousers. My pants are what I wear under my trousers. You people are making a mess of this language, you know that?'

'Let's hope there's a signal in here.'

That is when they hear two gunshots from inside the next room.

24

The Mayflower Chinese restaurant in Bristol does not deliver to the university, for reasons Dr Charlotte Benton cannot explain. It's on Haymarket Walk, which is too far for a pickup, and that's why Guy has offered to bring it to her. The restaurant's takeaway menu is only available from 6.00 p.m. on weekdays and Saturdays, which is a bit later than Charlotte would prefer, and for this reason Guy is hyper-vigilant about placing the order the moment the clock strikes, so he can deliver it to her at the palaeontology lab before her blood sugar drops.

Guy rides a 1959 Lambretta scooter. It's turquoise and white. It is, somehow, hipper than he is. She isn't sure how to address this. She's hoping the hipness might rub off and the problem will go away by itself, though she isn't optimistic.

He shows up wearing a retro helmet, with the straps hanging unfastened by his ears. He smiles as though he's cooked the food himself. He wants her to be happy.

'Thank you so much,' she says as he takes the roast duck with pineapple and sweet-and-sour wontons from the paper bag.

Charlotte is no longer a fan of Westernised Chinese food, but its reassuring sameness evokes nostalgia, and nicely counterbalances the evening's goal of locating her father, who is giving her no reassurance these days. Guy is understanding and accommodating. He smiles as he removes the chopsticks from the bag, and places the folded napkin beside her.

He understands she needs to work alone, so he readies to leave.

'You don't mind terribly, do you?' she asks, and of course he shakes his head and helmet. He'll go to the movies, he explains. It starts at ten, so he'll be back late.

'What are you working on?' he asks.

'Revisions to the paper for *Cladistics* about methodological challenges in theorising phylogeny by inference to morphological data. It's a big topic. I feel like I have to ground the argument in empirical data that lends itself to alternative interpretive possibilities to illustrate the problematic, otherwise it's all a bit abstract.'

'Right.'

'I might add some pictures.'

'Super.'

It isn't that she didn't want to have dinner with Guy. It is more that she considers her parents' problems to be a private matter, and while she loves Guy and appreciates his support, she doesn't want his opinion just at the moment, especially in the middle of the process. Better to exclude him from the drama altogether, and report in when there is something to understand.

Charlotte knows her mother has cheated on her father, and yet she is on her mother's side. The injustice of this needs to be set right. And finding and talking to her father is the way to begin. The fact that he fled to Iraq at the moment he should have met with her mother to reconcile with her needs to be addressed. And preferably alone.

As she watches Guy and his hipster helmet slip from the lab into the hall, she considers that maybe the reason she is not marrying him is that it would mean he'd always be around.

Once she hears the old Italian scooter start up and zip away, she double-clicks on Miguel's icon and listens to the computer connect her to the camp in Iraq.

Miguel is alone at Märta's desk in the prefab office. Hers is the fastest computer the NGO has, and she doesn't mind him using it. Curfew has fallen, and he's decided to spend the night on the sofa, which he's allowed to do after radio check. From a care package prepared by his mother the last time he went home, he has made himself a cold plate of food with chorizo, Serrano ham, manchego cheese, fresh pita bread from the camp, and olive oil from Greece. He arrays the food on the plate, and lets it breathe.

Pity there is no Corte Inglés supermarket here, but, compared to the people outside, he knows he is lucky to have this, and would never think to complain.

The computer starts to ring. There is a call. It is Dr Charlotte Benton. It is wonderful timing, though he has bad news. At least he will not have to dine alone.

'Hello? Charlotte? That is you, yes?'

'Hello, Miguel. I'm eating. I'm sorry. My schedule—'

'Oh, I was hoping for this. We can now eat together and become friends.'

As Miguel slices a tomato and rubs it on a piece of pita, and applies olive oil and a thin slice of manchego, he sees that Charlotte is thin, with angular features and wide brown eyes. She looks intelligent and calm and—to him—older than her youthful face suggests. Hers is less a striking beauty than a maternal warmth—the kind of face that warms you with its approval and acceptance. Her glasses are round and too big for her face, like those of the librarians he used to lust for in his youth.

'Ms Charlotte, I have some unfortunate news. Your father is not here in the camp now. So we cannot see him. Ms Märta has not given me news yet. So I fear we must put off our walk together until tomorrow morning.'

'Ah. OK.'

'You look sad, Ms Charlotte.'

'You think so?'

'In your eyes. Is it because of your father? You should not be worried.'

'No, no. I'm not worried.'

'No, you are not. The sadness is deeper. Am I intruding? This is indiscreet. I am sorry. Is it because of your father?'

'My parents, actually.'

'Your relations with them are not good?'

'My relations are fine. But they're going through a hard time with each other. I'm concerned for them.'

'I am very sorry to hear that. Why is your father here, so far away, if there is trouble at home? Should he not be there with you and your mother to help?'

'Yes, I think he should.'

'This is why you are looking for him. You are angry at him for his absence.'

'No, I'm not. Well ... yes. Actually, I am.'

'*Claro*. I will help you. Oh my God, what are you eating?'

'Oh, this?' she says, holding it higher in her chopsticks. 'It's a fried wonton.'

'Is it good to put that into your body?'

'Probably not. But it's comforting.'

'I think we must find your father quickly, before you do further harm to yourself.'

Charlotte looks at the wonton, and decides there is no way to bite it gracefully. It will crumble onto her shirt. Or, if she treats it like sushi and takes the whole thing in, she could be chewing it for days in front of Miguel.

Discreetly, she places it back, and takes a tiny piece of duck instead.

'Why are your parents having the troubles? Has your father taken a lover, and your mother has now learned of it, and the passions are raging?'

'I don't think we should be talking about this.'

'No. Of course not. These things are very private and painful. Is it true? Am I right?' Miguel asks.

'No. Actually, it is my mother who had the affair and, in my view, my father who drove her to it.'

'And to protect his ego and his honour, you think he has run off to Iraq so he might suffer by his own hand and recover his manhood?'

'Well ... no. I think he ran off because of his denial and cowardice and unwillingness to face my mother.'

'You are angry at him for not staying to fight for your mother. For not staying to declare his love, and demand she come back to him because of the many years they have shared their lives together. Yes?'

'Yes, actually. That's it.'

'And yet—' Miguel adds.

'And yet what?'

'It sounds almost too selfless. Too detached. Too ... how do you say? When something floats above and looks down, but does not emotionally touch?'

'Aloof.'

'That is not a pretty-enough word for such a melancholy and damaged state of being, but OK. *Aloof*. Have you no feelings about this yourself? How has he driven her to this?'

'Aren't you in the middle of a massive refugee crisis in a war-torn country with terrorists?' Charlotte asks.

'It's dinnertime. Everyone's eating. How did he drive her to this?'

'It was his absence. He was never there.'

'So he was never there for you, either.'

Charlotte does not reply to this. She looks over at her meal, and no longer feels hungry. Miguel is right. Nothing about it can be good for her.

'What do you do for a living, Ms Charlotte?'

'It's Doctor, actually. I'm a palaeontologist. I try to understand how things are related to each other.'

'So you do professionally what has been impossible for you to do personally.'

'Look, Miguel, I hadn't quite formulated my thoughts yet. I don't even discuss this with my boyfriend.'

'Ah, you have a boyfriend. Of course, why wouldn't you? What is his name?'

'Guy.'

'Guy?'

'Yes. Guy.'

'This is a name?'

'Yes.'

'I thought it was an English word for "just anyone".'

'It also means that.'

'I see. You would rather settle for the embrace of just anyone rather than risk losing someone specific the way you have lost your father. I understand.'

'Um—'

'There is more to your father's visit here, Dr Charlotte, than perhaps you know. And perhaps, in a way, it will soothe you. Perhaps he was running from the most important aspects of his life, but he has real business here. Ms Märta has told me he is here for the girl in green. Do you know about her?'

'The girl in green?'

'You have seen her, I am sure. The mortar attack in northern Iraq. It is on the news. It was on many stations. My mother, in Barcelona, she says it has played many times. The mortar came down and killed many people, and they show the video on the news. Your father thinks the girl who stood so alone in her green dress may still be alive. He has come, with Mr Arwood, to find her. They left for Ninawa this morning. In fact, I scheduled this call because I thought they would be back before curfew, but they are not. Let us meet again in a few hours. We will know more then. And there are some people I would like you to meet. Do you like children?'

'Sure, Miguel. But before all that, why would my father try to rescue a girl in Iraq? He's a journalist.'

'Perhaps,' Miguel says, 'because it is his way of rescuing you.'

'Honestly, Miguel, I really am not sure whether you have a remarkable insight into the human experience, or whether your certainty in yourself is what makes your arguments so compelling,' she says.

'My mother once said to me, "Miguel, the world is a noisy place. There is little point in mumbling."'

'Of course.'

'Later, after we eat, I will affix the iPad to the walking stick, and then off we will go together in search of your father, who must now return to your mother so you will not be sad anymore and have to eat the fried wontons and marry a man who is like every other man. OK?'

At home, Märta leans over the countertop separating the dining area from the kitchen. Her legs are crossed at the ankles, and she is sipping a beer. Tigger arrived moments ago, and is sitting on the sofa with his legs crossed and an outstretched arm. Herb is on a bright-red chair across from the sofa that both he and Tigger refer to as 'the thinking chair,' a term taken from a children's television show they both watched with their kids, called *Blue's Clues*.

'Let's call the meeting to order,' Märta says.

'I have a question,' Tigger says, raising his hand.

'Already?'

'What the hell were you doing, letting them go out there in one of our vehicles—'

'—with Jamal driving?' Herb interjects.

'I was getting to that. Yes, what Herb said.'

'I made a mistake,' Märta concedes.

Tigger and Herb glance at each other. Herb points to Tigger, who nods, agreeing to speak for them both. 'Our question is built on the assumption that you made a mistake. We sincerely want to know what you were thinking.'

'I agreed to let Arwood use the office for old times' sake, and because I didn't see any harm in it at first. And I think he played me. He told me Benton was coming, and I wanted to see him. And then it escalated.'

'How?' Tigger says.

'By seeing Thomas.'

'Did you sleep with Thomas Benton last night?' Tigger asks.

'Yes,' Märta says.

'How was it?'

'Nice.'

'So you gave him a car and Jamal, and sent him to a dangerous area because of schoolgirl feelings?'

'I agreed before I slept with him.'

'Which does not disprove my theory, but … why?' Herb says, leaning forward in the thinking chair.

'I felt this sense of possibility I haven't felt in a long time. They wanted to fix something that everyone else had written off for lost. It was … well, it was like the minefield and that boy, remember?'

'Of course we remember,' Tigger says. 'But there is a difference between watching someone walk into a minefield and sending someone—'

'—specifically, Jamal,' Herb says.

'—in one of our cars. You should have run this by us.'

'You're right, and I was wrong. Is there anything else?'

'No,' says Tigger. 'Herbert and I have been looking into matters for the past two hours. Let's all get started.'

'I guess the first question is, do we know they survived the explosion?' Märta says.

'We don't,' Herb says, 'but we think probably they did. Ahmed, in the radio room, talked to the chief of police in Mosel. The Iraqi police are out in force over there now. They killed four of the attackers, captured one, and if there was anyone else, they're gone. One of the cops found our car a little ways off the road. There were bullet holes in the wheels, but no blood and no bodies. So they are out there. Somewhere.'

Herb is in his late forties, and has maintained a soldier's physique. Unlike Tigger, who is long and sinewy, Herb is muscular, big, and athletic. He speaks with a soft and deep voice that Märta has grown to find comforting.

'My read is that they tried to escape in the car, got shot at, got out, and that's when they disappeared,' Herb says.

'There are only two ways to disappear in the desert,' Tigger says, reaching over to the coffee table for a Diet Coke. 'Voluntarily and involuntarily.'

Märta drinks her beer with her left hand tucked under her right armpit. She has let her hair down. It falls to her shoulders. She is barefoot. 'We should build out the scenarios,' she says.

'If they got away on their own, they would have called by now,' Herb says.

'Yeah. We should be thinking they're captured and being held.'

'Agreed,' Tigger says. 'Anyone hungry?'

'I don't eat after seven,' Herb says. 'And how can you be thinking of food?'

'I'm always thinking of food. It's the irony of thin people.'

Märta reaches behind the counter, extracts a bag of mixed cocktail nuts, and pours them into a small ceramic bowl. She reaches forward and hands them to Tigger, who immediately targets the cashews.

'What groups?' Märta asks.

'They could be criminals looking for money. They could be jihadists,' Tigger says. 'They could be jihadists looking for money. We should hope they are financially motivated. Otherwise, I don't know.'

'Something that's worked for us before in Pakistan with jihadists,' Märta says, 'was contacting some of the Muslim world's more respected scholars of jihad, and having them talk to the kidnappers, to let them know that the notion of Islamic struggle, even at the most extreme, does not apply to the humanitarian organisations. It hasn't always worked, but it has worked. The International Committee of the Red Cross and the local Red Crescent can be helpful here, too. The ICRC has a mandate to serve as a neutral intermediary, and they can extend their good offices and serve as mediators when the time comes. Maybe Louise can back us up. But this isn't the Taliban. Say they were captured by al-Nusra, al-Qaeda, or ISIL. What does that look like?' she asks.

Herb looks at the bowl of snacks, and sits further back in his red chair. 'We're not sure whether Nusra and ISIL have broken with al-Qaeda yet. There's so much internecine fighting that looking for a pattern is to overlook the actual pattern that it's all a mess. They're posting their murders and massacres on YouTube. Everyone's jockeying for position.'

Märta sits on a stool by the counter, her blue skirt cutting across her shin. She is still holding the beer, but is no longer drinking it.

'Why post that stuff?' she says. 'Why put on display that you're murderers? Aren't they repelling people with their violence?'

'On the contrary,' Tigger says. 'It shows strength and conviction. Maybe not to us, but to many others. Sometimes it is hard to accept that people are fundamentally different, but the simple proof is that foreigners are confusing. The reason it's working, since you asked me, is that in the West we take military action, and then wrap a communications strategy around it to win hearts and minds. The jihadists have a communications strategy, and they wrap a military strategy around it to show they are serious about what they say. You see the difference? Our ways of warfare are not asymmetrical. They are opposite. We are entering a new era of warfare with the non-Western world, with non-Western rules and non-Western methods. We are unprepared.'

'We don't need Big Theory, Tigger,' Herb says.

'I disagree. It would have been good to have a better theory before invading Iraq in the first place. Of course, this is all a pantomime, because we all knew this in 1991, which is why we didn't take Baghdad in the first place.'

'Louise thinks Arwood might be CIA,' Märta interjects.

'Do you?' Tigger asks.

'No.'

'Why not?' Herb asks.

'Yeah. Why not?' Tigger asks.

'I talked to Louise about this already. The CIA is a formal administrative system. I don't think he fits.'

'Whether he's CIA or not, I don't trust him. He's got bad paper,' Herb says.

'What does that mean?' Märta asks.

'It means he's got a dishonourable discharge, or something close enough to it. He was kicked out of the army after Desert Storm. It means that for one reason or another his country thinks he's a disgrace, and I'm not about to question that judgement until I've got a good reason to. I know the army. I gave my career to the army. It gets the benefit of the doubt over Arwood Hobbes.'

'Benton trusts him, and I trust Benton,' Märta says.

'I don't see why,' Herb says. 'I also don't understand their relationship. None of us have been in touch with either one of them, and I haven't been keeping tabs on 'em. You said this morning that

Benton hasn't been in touch with Hobbes, so I don't think even he really knows what he's getting into. All we really know for a fact is that Benton's been working a steady job at the newspaper since Margaret Thatcher. Otherwise, I think you're too close to this with your ... you know—'

'Vagina?'

'I was going to say "lover," but OK. Vaginas don't scare me. I realise sex doesn't mean a thing to you sophisticated French and Scandinavian types, but my experience tells me differently. Be that as it may, I want to be on record here about one important thing: I'm here because Jamal is missing. The boy's one of ours, and that's what I'm here to help with. The others put themselves in harm's way for whatever reason, and those reasons sound dubious. So that's on them. Meanwhile, Jamal didn't ask for this, and he has a family we know, and he shouldn't have been out there. And, quite frankly, I'm a little sick and tired of national staff being treated like they're disposable or second-class citizens in their own countries that we invaded. And when I say second-class, you know what I'm really saying.'

'That's not fair, Herb.'

'It is fair, Märta. We pay them less. They have less job security. They aren't covered by the same insurance. They usually take bigger risks, they are far more exposed than we are—because everyone knows who they are and what villages they come from—and when we all go home because the situation's become too hot, we leave the natives behind to fend for themselves. After all, this isn't colonisation, it's cooperation! Meanwhile, do you have any idea how many translators and staff hired by the US military we left behind after we pulled out of Iraq and Afghanistan? Tens of thousands. We dragged our feet, didn't process their visas, didn't care for their families. We use people up, and leave them for dead, which many of them become. It is dishonourable and short-sighted, and I don't like it.'

'We're not the US military, Herb. And that's not what's happening here,' Märta says.

'NGOs do more or less the same thing. Unfinished projects, unkept promises, unbalanced pay scales, disrespect for local knowledge and experience — it's close enough to the same thing. And, no, we're not doing that with Jamal, because I'm not going to let it happen. And if anything comes down to the wire, he's my priority.'

'I'll notify the British and American embassies of Benton's and Hobbes's status,' Tigger says. 'And I suggest I call Clip Maxwell at Firefly Consulting. We need to set up a crisis-management group. And then, my friends, we need to sleep. Tomorrow will be a very full day.'

25

Arwood jolts to his feet when he hears the gunshots. Benton rolls onto his knees and presses his head to the mattress, inhaling its body odour and mould, before taking hold of a knee and pushing himself upward to stand.

Arwood is already at the door by the time Benton is ready. He has pressed his ear against it. Arwood's face is placid in the harsh light of the solitary bulb.

'What do you hear?' Benton says.

'Shh.'

Benton watches Arwood reposition his ear to the left, lower on the door. His face is unchanged.

'If they killed those kids—' Benton mumbles.

Arwood moves quickly from the door to Benton, turns himself around, and, with his hands still bound in plastic cuffs, grabs hold of Benton's belt, unbuckles it, unsnaps and unzips his trousers, and thrusts his hands down them to collect the phone.

'They kill children all the time,' Arwood says, ripping the phone from the Velcro. 'Oh, shit. It's an iPhone, isn't it?'

'I don't know. I didn't look. I guess. Why?'

'No buttons—that's what's wrong with it. Ever tried working one of these with your hands tied behind your back?' Arwood slips the phone into his back pocket for now, needing his hands to do up Benton. 'User-centred design, my arse.'

Arwood reassembles Benton's trousers. As he does, Benton

notices that Arwood has altered his first tattoo from when he enlisted. It now reads *Death Before Dishonorabilishness.*

Finished, Arwood takes the phone out of his pocket and presses the Home button. He turns so Benton can see it. 'Is it on? Is it lighting up?'

'No.'

Arwood rotates it in his hands and finds the power button. He depresses it and places his thumb over the speaker, muffling the chime.

'Arwood, what do you do for a living?'

'I solve problems. Is it on?'

Benton looks down. 'Whose problems? And, yes, it is.'

'Is it charged? Icon's in the upper right.'

'Yes, it is.'

'We've got a signal?'

'No. Whose problems, and how do you solve them?'

'You know that saying, "Give a man a fish, feed him for a day; teach him to fish, feed him for life"? That's all very sweet until people come to take his fish away and make him a slave. Meanwhile, you give a man a gun, he can get as many fish as he wants. And keep them. We're on the GSM phone network in Iraq. There should be a signal.'

'It could be the concrete walls,' Benton says. 'I'm still wondering why those slats are positioned so high.'

'We're in a bunker or military fortification of some kind. Something old. We need to find a signal in here. I'm going to walk and you're going to follow me, checking the bars. Here we go.'

Arwood stoops to raise the phone higher, and Benton stoops to see it. Together they shuffle across the room like two old men with their hands behind their backs as they scan for a signal.

'No one would give me a job when I got back,' Arwood says as they walk. 'With my discharge papers, I couldn't get a job at Denny's

or Dairy Queen. Bad paper leaves you worse off than if you were
a felon. People don't forgive a bad discharge. They feel like you
personally let them down, no matter where you went or what you
actually did, or the fact that you served and they didn't, and that
their pain doesn't mean shit. It's like being convicted of treason and
then being freed rather than facing the firing squad. There are no
second chances, no do-overs, and no cleaning that record, no halfway
houses, no rehab. Some people deserve that. Some don't. Mainly, I
worked flea markets and gun shows across the Midwest.'

'But you now have professional-level knowledge of geography
and international affairs. You hadn't heard of the BBC when I met
you in '91.'

'I found business better in the Middle East than in the Midwest.
Travel really is broadening. Besides, I was never stupid. I just didn't
know anything.'

Arwood stops by the long wall across from the mattresses and
looks up at the slits in the bunker walls. 'Do you really think it's
possible,' he says, 'to spill every kind of blood, experience every kind
of human emotion, and weep every kind of tear on a piece of land
for over six thousand years, and actually leave nothing behind in the
soil? A psychic scar of some kind? I don't believe that. I mean, forget
the Bible. This place has been populated since the Sumerians. That's
six thousand years. You ask me, this land has to be haunted. It has to
be. It's a ghost factory.'

'Arwood,' Benton says, standing himself upright. 'If you came
here to murder that man, why did you bring me with you? Or Jamal?
Why couldn't you have done this nasty business yourself, and left us
out of it?'

Arwood turns and faces Benton. He looks surprisingly young
and sincere.

'I had the intel on the colonel. But the guy I bought it from said
something that made me think. So I sat on it. And then the mortar

attack happened, and it all came together. That girl is the reason I'm here. But the parallels are impossible to ignore. Even you have to see them. Last time, the colonel lived, and she died. This time, he died, and she's going to live. Last time, we didn't take Baghdad. This time, we did. Last time, we were battling the government; this time, it's the insurgents. It's all inside out, but exactly the same. Don't you see?'

'So you came here to murder him.'

'I came here to confront him. Then he pulled out that same Makarov and pointed it at me, so I blew him away. And you know what? The Klingons are wrong. It's actually much more satisfying to get revenge while you're in the mood for it. That's what happened, and I don't regret it. It is scary and freakish to kill another person, but I swear to God there are times when the pros outweigh the cons. So why are you here? No one put a gun against your thick head.'

'I felt I owed you. You came to get me in Samawah.'

Arwood shakes his head. 'You don't owe me anything. I'm the one who convinced you to go look around. I put you there.'

'No, you were right. I needed to do my job. You reminded me of that.'

'I was twenty-two years old. What the hell did I know?'

'You can be right without understanding why. Kids are like that all the time.'

'I don't believe that's why you're here,' Arwood says. 'You must have been looking for any excuse to get out of England, and I gave you one. You said in the car that things are rocky with your wife. So is that it? You're running as far away from yourself as possible? If that's the case, then I've got bad news for you. Buckaroo Banzai was right: no matter where you go, there you are. And so here we are. Again. Back at Checkpoint Zulu.'

'I think,' Benton says, 'that the reason my wife cheated on me is that she was unable to reach me any other way. And I think this was the case because I lost something significant after what happened to us here in '91. Though it may seem cowardly, the reason I'm here is to try to recover what I lost so that I might have a different relationship with my wife and daughter when I get back, if I ever do.'

Arwood is quiet for a moment before saying, 'That actually makes sense.'

'Well, thank you.'

'Did you tell your wife this?'

'No.'

'Dude—'

'It's a process,' Benton says.

Arwood, with nothing else to say on the matter, spins around and raises his arms to his waist. 'Do you see my watch?'

'Yes,' he says.

'Read our coordinates to me. My hunch is that we're near Kursi in the Sinjar Mountains. You felt how we drove south-west, how it was flat, and then we started bouncing along going up again? How the road got all twisty, like we were in the Alps? My ears even popped. Only reason for roads to twist like that is mountains. There aren't many mountains down here — not on the way to al-Anbar. I think we're west of Tal Afar. This is not a high-rent district.'

'Just … stop moving around. The numbers are very small.'

'In your own time. No reason to rush.'

'OK. It's N36° 23' 15.88", E41°47'32.87"'

'Repeat them.'

Benton does.

'Remember them.'

'I can't possibly,' Benton says.

'If they take the watch, or we're split up, or I'm killed—'

'It's too many numbers. I'm not a computer. I'm thirsty, I'm tired, I'm in pain, I'm sixty-three years old—'

'It's only eight numbers, not sixteen. You think of a building you know, you place each number in a room.'

'Jamal and Adar might be dead. I'm not in the mood to play memory palace.'

'Fine. Remember the longitude. They'll see it's near the road, and can start looking there. That's the second set of numbers. Forty-one is when Pearl Harbor was bombed. Picture it. Forty-seven was the year the National Security Act was signed by Truman, creating the CIA and the air force. Picture it. Thirty-two … um. That's tougher. Oh, '32 is when Babe Ruth played his last season. Made that called shot against Root. Shut Chicago up for probably the first and last time. We're talking baseball here, not cricket.'

'That didn't happen. I saw a documentary. He was pointing to the dugout. They were heckling him, and he was responding that he only had two strikes. It's myth. Folklore.'

'I saw that video with my own eyes.'

'Yes, Arwood, but you don't know what it meant. Like the shots behind the wall.'

'Stay focussed. Nineteen eighty-seven. I think *Ferris Bueller's Day Off* was '86, unfortunately. Did you see *The Princess Bride*? That was '87.'

'No.'

'Mandy Patinkin? Robin Wright? Wallace Shawn? André the Giant?'

'No.'

'You have no memory of Mandy Patinkin as Inigo Montoya saying, "My name is Inigo Montoya, you killed my father, prepare to die"?'

'No.'

'Your life is empty. What about *Robocop*? That was '87, too.'

'No.'

'*Dirty Dancing*?'

Benton is silent.

'Come on.'

'I might have seen it.'

'Cute little Jewish girl in the Catskill Mountains seduced by the gentile help, and their beatnik ways at the summer resort?'

'I hadn't really—'

'So: Pearl Harbor, air force, Babe Ruth, *Dirty Dancing*. All-American numbers. See? More coincidence. Makes it easier to remember.'

'You used your American brain to make sense of the numbers, Arwood. That's why they are now American numbers. I'm wondering if you're really OK.'

'We need to send those numbers.'

Benton has had enough. There is no way of sending those numbers. No way to type them into the phone. No way to catch a signal and ride it to safety on a moonbeam.

He steps backward to the wall, leans back against it, and eases himself to the floor. Once down, he rolls onto his side and massages his left shoulder by kneading it into the mattress, which is thin enough to be a hard surface.

Hands would be better—a woman's hands. Vanessa's and Märta's hands are different. Vanessa's are longer, softer, gentler, but she lacks strength in them. He confuses this sometimes with a mental state, as though her fingers lack will. Märta is all purpose. She's structured and orderly in her touch. She works it like a job. It's less sensual, less tender, but more productive. He needs both of them right now.

'Don't quit,' Arwood says.

'I need a second.'

'Does this thing have voice recognition?' Arwood says, wiggling the phone behind his back for emphasis.

'I have no idea, Arwood.'

Arwood presses the Home button to wake it up, then presses it again and holds it down. This activates Siri, Apple's chipper, artificially intelligent software.

'Call Märta,' Arwood says loudly, despite the phone being behind his back.

'*Kan du upprepa det?*'

'What the hell was that?' Arwood says.

'Swedish. It's her phone.'

'I don't speak Swedish.'

'The telephone does,' Benton says. Unable to take the smell anymore, he rolls off the mattress and rubs his shoulder against the floor instead.

Arwood mumbles something pejorative about the Stockholm syndrome before concluding, 'You're gonna have to use your nose.'

'What?'

'Your nose. Get on your knees. You can see the Contacts icon, or address book, or whatever it is. Tap it with the end of your nose, then scroll—'

'Scroll?'

'Like a seal pushing a ball. You scroll to Märta's name, and try calling it with your nose.'

'I don't think that—'

'I'm not fucking around, Benton. This is what needs to be done, unless you can type with your dick.'

Benton rises to his knees, using the same technique as before, though it requires even more effort now.

'We don't have a signal, and I'm too tired.'

'Someone's coming,' says Arwood, who drops to the mattress and slips the phone under it as quickly as a teenage boy hides a magazine.

Benton and Arwood hear a padlock being removed from the other side of the inner door and a deadbolt sliding into the open position. The light overhead is turned off, and the room becomes black. The door is opened slightly. A hand tosses an object into the room, and closes the door again quickly. The locks are reapplied.

Above them is the pink of dusk spreading across the ceiling. Below, not far from the door, is a piece of cloth. It appears black—a product coughed up from the void.

'Is that it, or is there something under it?' Benton asks. 'A grenade?'

'I didn't hear anything fall. But if I'm wrong, we'll know in a second.'

The fabric has collapsed onto itself and rests, its message as uncertain as its origin. To Benton, it looks organic and as natural in its free-flowing shape as an octopus. It seems to attract the light into its black folds.

Benton is the first to say what they both see: 'It's wet. Toward the right.'

'I see it.'

'It's blood.'

'We can't be sure.'

'Of course we can be sure. We can see it, feel it, taste it, smell it. You want to confirm it's blood and not tea, then go ahead.'

'Fine, Benton. It's blood.'

'It's the green dress.'

'What do you mean?'

'It's the girl's green dress, Arwood. The girl's dress is bloody. It's Adar's bloody dress.'

Arwood walks over and moves it around gently with his foot. The colour is impossible to make out in this light, but the arms of the dress, and the way the sleeves flare, and the straight edge of the colour under the neck — they are the same.

Arwood kneels down and smells it. He puts his tongue in it.

'For the love of God, Arwood.'

He spits it out. 'It's blood.'

'So they shot her. And then they proved it.'

'It doesn't mean shit.'

'Are you mad? You're looking at the evidence right in front of you.'

'I'm looking at her bloodied dress. I accept it's hers. And I accept it's blood. But whose blood? Who knows? Do you know? I'm staring right at it, and I don't know. And neither do you. You just explained the same thing to me with baseball!'

'This is different.'

'It's exactly the same,' Arwood says. 'We're looking at something, and we don't know what it means. Welcome to Iraq!'

'You're denying the obvious, because you can't accept it. The kids are dead, and we're next. Maybe you were right. There is some mystical force at work, but not to save her. We're destined to kill this girl over and over and over again.'

'No,' Arwood says. 'The dress tells us nothing. The answer is in the hand that put it there. Why? Think about it. I'll tell you why. To terrorise us. Know how I know that? Because they're fucking terrorists, Benton. Dogs bark, cats meow. These guys do this. If they wanted us to know — really know — she was dead, they'd have walked her into this room, shot her in the head right in front of us, and dragged her body out. They didn't. At the moment, all we know is that she's other-than-here, there's a bloody dress, and these fuckwits are into mind games. That last one — being into mind games — that's a new and important piece of survival information. All of which tipped their hand, not ours. And what about Jamal? Where's his ... what was he wearing, anyway?'

'I don't remember. Clothing.'

'Well ... you see my point.'

'This is just swell,' Benton says.

'Let's get out of these cuffs.'

'How do we do that?' Benton says.

'Well ... I'm thinking we bite through them. I'm thinking you bite through mine.'

'Why? Why not you bite through mine?'

'Because you're too technologically illiterate to work the damn telephone, that's why. And if needed, there's a tiny chance I might put up a good fight. You can't. So my net assessment is that my hands are more useful than your hands. I'll stand. Make it easier for you. Get comfy.'

'I'll be glad when this war is over,' Benton says.

'Haven't you read the papers, Thomas? The war is over. This is the peace.'

26

Charlotte has decided to take the call with Miguel from home, as Guy has gone to see a summer blockbuster that involves superheroes and supervillains engaged in superfighting. He won't be back for hours.

Though it is not her routine, Charlotte showers, brushes her teeth, puts on a summer dress of yellows, reds, and oranges, and puts her hair up. When she is done, she has little choice but to ask her reflection in the bathroom mirror a candid question: 'What are you doing? Yes, you. You think this is a date? You tell anyone about this, and so help me,' she says, flicking off the light and leaving her hair down.

On her way down to the computer, she puts it up again.

Sitting on a chipped Danish chair, she launches the computer application and places the call to Miguel. She could have waited for Miguel to ring at the proper time, but then she would have been a girl waiting by the virtual phone — not even an actual one — and that wouldn't do. But calling him, she thinks as it rings, suggests a certain eagerness, doesn't it?

Not when you're calling about a lost father, you dimwit, she says to herself.

Charlotte hasn't really been out of Bristol — out of the lab itself, come to think of it — in ages. Aside from the odd visit to her mother in Fowey, she hasn't even been to London in over half a year. That would have been unthinkable in her twenties — nothing she could have admitted to. And yet, now, it's not the same. Routine has set in, and she rather likes it. She's learned, as an adult, that it can be spiritually rejuvenating to exhale London and let it go, like freeing a trapped ghost so it might return to haunt its own terrain. One can actually feel free of London, though its gravitational force and imperial control are always present.

Iraq, though. Can one even get there from here?

As the computer rings, Charlotte suddenly feels exposed, and wants her neck covered. She yanks out the hair band and lets her hair fall, just as Miguel answers.

'Hello? Is that Charlotte? *Buenas noches!*'

'Good evening, Miguel.'

'You let your hair down. That's very nice.'

'Ah … no. I usually wear it down. It's … natural.'

'I can see, though, how your hair gently curves toward your neck as it drops down, and then waves itself out again like a flamenco skirt, because only recently it was tied in the back. But no matter. I see you are not eating the fried tom-toms. That is good.'

'Wontons.'

Miguel's image is a bit wobbly, and behind him there is a map of Iraq with a UN logo and the letters UNHCR, which mean nothing to her.

It strikes her as odd that someone living in a war zone, among tens of thousands of displaced people, can be so cheerful. Before she can interrupt herself, she asks, 'Why are you so happy?'

'I think this will be a very nice walk, don't you?'

'That's not what I mean. You're away from friends and family. A girlfriend, maybe. Everyone around you is miserable. You look like you just landed a research grant.'

'That is the pinnacle of happiness? A research grant?'

Isn't it?

'One can't really find happiness in places like this,' he continues.

'You need to take it with you, and hand it out to those who need it.'

'That's sweet, but by that logic, you eventually run out.'

'I hadn't noticed. Maybe my analogy is wrong.'

The screen changes as the iPad Miguel is using switches to the forward-facing camera. Miguel and Iraq are gone, and instead there is a view of a small office that reminds Charlotte of the kind she's seen at construction sites where the workmen walk up a few wooden steps into a lorry while removing their hardhats and reaching for a cup of bad coffee. There is a round table and some plastic chairs, an orange extension cord, and more maps on the far wall. Between those maps, though, is a mirror. And as Miguel moves closer to the wall, the contraption he has built comes more clearly into view.

She can see him from the waist up now. He is slender and earnest, and has floppy hair. There is an earnestness and boyishness to him. There is no way he is over thirty. In his right hand he holds a broom handle, and at the top of the handle is the bottom part of a dustpan on which he has rested the iPad and secured it with electrical tape. The iPad cover itself is baby blue, like the colour of the UN logo. He is smiling and waving.

She waves back.

She feels like an idiot waving back, and does not understand how it has come to pass that Miguel gets to set the terms of their goofiness.

'Do you watch the television show *Game of Thrones?*' he asks.

'No.'

'OK, good. Because many people who watch that television show — and some of the donors do, unfortunately — are unnerved by what comes next,' Miguel says, swivelling the iPad around on the handle to reveal Charlotte's disembodied head impaled on a stick in Iraq.

'In the history of the world,' Miguel says, 'this is the one view of yourself you never get to see. But with the benefit of modern technology, now you can! Meanwhile, introductions are necessary. Dr Charlotte,' he says, 'may I introduce you to Head of Charlotte. You may be in London—'

'Bristol.'

'OK, but Head of Charlotte is here in Iraq with me. You are now in two places at once. Time and distance have been overcome. To the people here, you are here. Isn't that fascinating?'

If Miguel were not Spanish and were from, say, Hull, she would classify this as serial-killer behaviour. And yet, for some reason, she doesn't.

'OK, let's get moving,' he says.

Miguel has the camera facing the outside world now. Charlotte sits in her kitchen in her sundress facing a laptop, her hair smelling of chamomile, as she watches a world emerge before her as through an alien portal. That world fills her, and her lungs seem to breathe in the exotic air of a land that she has only heard about in passing, and yet that now feels immediate and populated by real people who can see her and know she is there.

She cannot see it, but she knows that Miguel's hand holds Head of Charlotte steady as he walks. In her kitchen, and there in Iraq, Charlotte and her doppelgänger bounce to the rhythm of the Spaniard's gait over the uneven and ancient earth. It is dark there, darker than in Bristol, but fires burn, and streetlights shine down through hard yellow dust onto the dark-skinned children running in brightly coloured clothes, all faded by the sun and tattered from overuse.

The land is covered with tiny stones and a thick dust that will never be washed away, because there is nowhere for it to go.

Miguel's voice accompanies Head of Charlotte. He explains the layout of the camp, who is there, who has come, who is going, who is 'at risk', who is there to help, what might 'build resilience' there, and what is undermining their efforts. From habit, he speaks about what is needed and what might be yet to come if that need is not met.

She stares at the brown and filthy tents with the faded UNHCR logos that are identical to the one she saw earlier on the map. Boys wear T-shirts with Western company logos and names of sports teams. Many of the children are barefoot.

They pass some women who smile at her and Miguel. Some of their heads are covered; many are not. Some children look lower-class, peasantlike, and poor, the way Gypsy beggars on European streets seem born into the clothes they wear. Others look shiny and clean and bright-eyed and incongruous, as though they have come from middle-class lives almost like her own, only to wake up one day to find themselves living in a tent as their country tries to kill them, with their earlier everyday dreams of dolls or soccer balls or boys or video games dismissed as fantasies of former privilege that they will never experience again.

These people have never been so close, have never been so real to her, as they are right now.

'Come, I want you to meet Ayman,' Miguel says, in a voice he might use when pointing out Barcelona's hippest shoe stores. 'Ayman is six, and his English is wonderful. He is the best student in the MRE class.'

'The what?'

'Mine risk education. These are the educational activities aimed at reducing the risk of injury from mines and unexploded ordnance by raising awareness and promoting behavioural change through public-information campaigns, education, and training, and liaison with communities.'

Miguel says this in the singsong and faraway lilt of aeroplane cabin crews running through safety procedures. It is entirely possible he didn't hear his own answer — it is that automatic.

'Here, come in,' he says, turning a corner when they arrive at a tent that, to Charlotte, is indistinguishable from any other. Miguel knocks on the pole that holds it up. A woman in a purple scarf nods to Miguel and smiles. She also smiles to Head of Charlotte, and does not seem surprised by the contraption.

Inside the tent is a boy—Ayman—who is waving to her from the floor where he was, until she interrupted him, colouring something with his stubby crayons. With the new audience, and his friend Miguel there to see him, Ayman reaches into a pile of comic books, and takes a colouring book that he holds up to Head of Charlotte.

At first she doesn't understand what she's seeing. The image is clear enough, but it is an image so unexpected it's hard to understand. The colouring book doesn't depict Superman or Spider-Man, but shows pictures of landmines and bombs, and of children standing near minefields, with big Xs over certain pictures where the children are chasing balls past barbed-wire fences, where they will die. Ayman has coloured in the children and the balls and the mines the same way he has coloured in his favourite football heroes. He has drawn circles around the children who will live, because they have done things the right way; he has left uncoloured the children who have done things wrongly, because they cannot be helped, and their lives will exist from this point forward only in outline.

'Ayman and his mother escaped from Syria after their town was attacked by one of the jihadist groups,' Miguel says. 'The government arrested Ayman's father and said he was an insurgent, but he was not. He worked at an electronics store—stereos and televisions, and things like that. They have not seen him since. His big brother is also missing, and he has been very sad. But the MRE class is very nice for him, because he plays with other children who have also lost people, so he no longer feels alone, and it has helped him make new friends here and take an interest in art. He has made this wonderful picture of what his village looked like before the massacre. It is here someplace. Ayman, where is the one with the tall blue building I like so much?'

Charlotte smiles at Ayman, who turns away from her to rummage through a stack of papers marked by crayon scratchings. While his back is turned, she moves away from the computer camera for a moment and cries.

By the time she looks back, Miguel has taken Head of Charlotte outside again into an even darker environment. To speak with her, he has turned the camera around so they now face each other.

'I'm sorry,' he says. 'I did not mean to upset you. I did not even think it might. I suppose I have lost my common sense with such things. You must understand, it is very good that Ayman is learning these things. They will help him be safe and save other children. People have been putting information like this in cartoon form since World War I. I think the colouring book is new, but the logic is the same.'

'How long do they have to stay there?'

'Things are getting worse, not better. The war in Syria is not ending. Iraq is weak and getting weaker. These new insurgent groups have not touched us here in Kurdistan yet, but it is perhaps a matter of time. We are vulnerable here. There are no defences. The people will stay while it is the safest place to be. Then they will leave. It is the way of survival.'

'Where is my father, Miguel? Have you found him? We haven't talked about this yet.'

'Listen, Dr Charlotte. Something has happened. I only learned of it an hour ago. I'm sorry to have kept it from you, but I wanted you to understand where we are. Your father ... he is missing.'

27

By midnight, they are asleep. Märta wanted to keep working, prepping, building out possible models, positioning assets, calling in favours, but Tigger and Herb insisted that the greatest resource would be a full night's sleep, their strength for the next day, and a clear head with which to make sound judgements.

Overruled, she went to bed. But she can't sleep.

As she lies there, she talks to herself in Swedish. It is how she prefers to mumble. There is no one here to talk to in Swedish. She works in English, and has more professional competence in it because so much of her vocabulary is specific to her profession: explosive remnants of war; unexploded ordnance; protection of civilians; international humanitarian law; small arms and light weapons; antipersonnel landmines; child soldiers; gender-based violence; development; humanitarian action; international humanitarian law; signatories; ratification; internally displaced persons; results-based management; impact indicators; logical frameworks; camp design; evacuation.

At home, they call it 'charity work.'

God, she says, remonstrating with herself for the insomnia. It's one-thirty in the morning. She's worrying like a wife whose husband is a POW. Her ex used to worry about her, though she told him not to and that she was very safe in most of her jobs, and at least as safe as any beat cop in the others. Now the tables have turned, and she has to play the woman.

Why did she agree to let Jamal drive?

There used to be helicopters at night. When the Americans were here, they controlled the airspace. They would have shows of force. The distinct sound of Apaches could be heard overhead at all hours. But it is not only the nights that are quieter. The workday is different, too. There are no civil-military coordination meetings. No arguments about CIMIC, and the differences between coordination and cooperation. No armour on the streets. No APCs.

Why did she let Jamal drive them?

It's now 2.00 a.m. Three hours left to sleep.

Shit.

Only a drink will do. Why fight it?

She swings out her legs, wraps the thin bathrobe around her, and walks on swollen ankles down the tile stairs.

Brandy is what her grandmother taught her to drink to calm her nerves. She prefers Torres from Spain. She pours a stiff one.

There is a sound behind her. She turns, and sees Herb standing, without a shirt on. It is a wonder how some middle-aged men do it — look that solid.

'Why are you up?' she asks him.

'A text message. There's going to be an offensive tomorrow. The explosion on the road left nine dead, including four police. And the gunfire that followed killed eleven more. The security forces are very, very angry about it, and they have some new weapons from the US they want to try out. I don't know where they're going, but it's in Ninawa province and it's going to be aggressive.'

'How do you know this?'

'The UN Department for Safety and Security just raised the security level to five. Non-essential staff are going to be evacuated tomorrow. ICRC is moving staff from Dohuk and Domiz to Erbil. I checked with some people in Baghdad.'

'What about sleep?' she asks.

'Sleep would be good,' Herb says.

The windows are open, and there is a cool breeze blowing through the security bars. The sound of wind through palm trees has always reminded Märta of rain.

'I've been thinking, Herbert. I've decided that I'm not going to use you as our communicator with the hostage-takers, assuming there are any. I want to use someone local.'

Herb, normally hard to read, looks crestfallen.

'They'll find you out, Herb. I need a communicator between us and the hostage-takers who can remain totally anonymous. I have no doubt that someone here is reporting to the Iraqi authorities or the opposition. You're a big, black American baritone. And you're the only one here. Your accent, your tone of voice — you're too easy to find. And I don't know what'll need to be said, and I can't put you at risk by asking you to say it.'

'Märta—'

'Also, I need you in the crisis-management team. You, me, Tigger, Clip. I don't like mixing the communicator role with the decision-makers. It's standard ICRC practice, and I've taken it on with IRSG, too.'

'Märta—'

'Plus, you now have that insipid US Supreme Court ruling that makes it illegal for an American citizen to be in contact with terrorist organisations—the "material support law". You could be breaking the law by talking to them, because it could be viewed as providing material support to the terrorists.'

'We're denying material support to ourselves by not talking with the enemy. It's a stupidly written law.'

'Not my country. Not my law. But it's my problem if it exposes you to unnecessary risk.'

'I'm going back to the sofa now,' Herb says.

Märta takes the brandy to bed.

Benton chews, and Arwood talks. The night is deep, and their prison is black. The bloody dress remains where it was thrown. There's nowhere else to put it.

Benton chews on Arwood's restraints, and Arwood talks to fill in the time.

'When I got back, it was midsummer, 1991. There was this huge parade for returning troops in DC. I was *persona non grata*, obviously, not that I would have gone anyway. So I did what every American man does who returns fucked up from a war. I bought a motorcycle.

'I didn't go so much Hunter Thompson as I went Bob Seger. The hair, the goatee, the swagger, the classic-rock-only mentality, disco sucks, feel uncomfortable in roadhouse bars—that sort of thing. Got an open-faced helmet so I could be slapped in the face by the future. I called my bike the Sopwith Camel. You know, because of Snoopy. Didn't learn until 1996 that it was actually an aeroplane from World War I. How are you supposed to know things like that? Thought the guy who told me was pulling my leg. He swore he wasn't. Told me not to feel bad. Told me that whenever he heard "Woodstock" he immediately thought of the cartoon, not the concert. You meet people like that on the road. It occurred to me after a while that maybe I needed a girl.'

Benton isn't listening. He continues with his degrading work. For the first hour, while Arwood was talking, Benton wasn't sure whether he was making any progress at all. The plastic became warm and pliant, but didn't shear. It seemed to be made of fibres, rather than plastic. His lower incisor became instrumental. He thought he could hear tiny fibres breaking every few minutes, but maybe they were only saliva bubbles. All this chewing and salivating meant a loss of liquid, and he started to get thirsty, which made him impatient and frustrated. The only reason he was able to continue like this was that it was better than being terrified.

Arwood is digressing from his previous tangent to discuss classic rock-and-roll and the merits of a band called Kansas, which is easy for Benton to ignore. At some point, when the frustration reaches a peak, he says, 'Arwood, you need to try twisting and moving it around. It might respond to some shearing force.'

Arwood tries this, and finds that it does not prevent him from talking.

'I stayed in Bozeman, Montana, for a while,' he says, returning to the earlier topic. 'It's a little desolate, but I like it there. Nice people, good air. Food was better than you'd expect. Eventually, they invented the mobile phone, and I became the Once-ler. You know *The Lorax*? Well, anyway … oh, baby, oh, how my business did grow. I went on the road for years. I left America. I was gone when the Trade Center went down. Saw it on TV in Italy. I remember the first line in the Italian paper. It said, "Today we are all Americans." No shit. It really said that. I cried my eyes out. It said that sort of thing everywhere in Europe. *Le Monde*, *El País*. Every major paper. But America didn't thank them. You know who doesn't say thank you to a person who extends a hand when the going gets tough? I'll tell you who: an alcoholic. And not just any alcoholic: one who thinks he's better than other alcoholics, because he's found God and stopped drinking and became president after a five-to-four split vote in the Supreme Court. The kind that knows how best to drive a wedge between people. So … mission accomplished.'

Benton stands up and turns. His shoulder hurts. His knees hurt. His jaw is so sore he is forced to whisper: 'I think I softened it in a spot. It might give if you rock back and forth for a while. You understand that once we break these, they'll know? You can't put them back on. And there may be consequences.'

Though the room is exquisitely dark, Benton feels as though he can see the expression of bewilderment on Arwood's face. Through that darkness, Arwood says, 'What are they gonna do, put us on double secret probation? I sort of feel like we're on the last rung of the consequence ladder. After this, we're headed for the mystery bag, if you catch my meaning.'

'Right, then. On with it,' Benton says.

Benton sits back against the wall and rests his muscles. He watches Arwood contort himself, trying to weaken and snap the restraints.

'Were you listening to me?' Arwood asks.

'Were you saying something?'

'I was pouring my heart out.'

'Can you break it loose?'

'I'm trying,' Arwood says as he twists his wrists. 'It doesn't feel looser.'

'I don't think it will. I think it'll snap or not snap. It isn't a knot.'

'So anyway, I drank and drank and drank, and I found a calling.'

'Good for you.'

'You asked what I was doing. I'm trying to tell you. So listen. After my parents kicked me out of the house for not killing Arabs, I started working at flea markets and gun shows—'

Arwood's twisting around isn't breaking the restraint. But maybe twisting or cutting isn't the answer. Maybe the plastic is loose enough already, and all it needs is enough force to pull the ends apart. But the two of them pulling against one another won't do it. Their wrists are too pliant. The plastic fibreglass will cut into the flesh, and the pain is too great.

What would Leonardo da Vinci do? 'He wouldn't be in this bloody mess, that's for sure,' Benton mutters to himself.

'What?' asks Arwood.

'Nothing. Go on. Gun shows.'

'I started brokering weapons. I'm an arms broker. I got around. That's why I was able to get your ticket using frequent-flier points.'

'I think we might be able to loop your cuffs around the handle of the door, then I can stand to the other side and pull you. If it's weak enough now, it might give.'

'That's not a bad idea. But you were so interested in what I did for a living, and now I've told you, and ... nothing.'

'I've been chewing fibreglass for an hour after the possible murder of our colleagues. I don't have what it takes to negotiate your stories now, Arwood. In some deep sense, and for some reason, I still trust you. But I also don't believe a word you say. So that's all going to have to wait. Let's try to break these,' Benton says, stepping toward the inner door where the Stooges took Adar and Jamal.

Arwood follows Benton to the door and finds the handle. Turning around, he wedges the metal cylinder in the space by his wrist near the watch.

It is a tight fit.

'No way you can get your fingers in there, too. You'll never reach, anyway. Your shoulders are too wide. I'm going to lean forward as hard as I can, and I want you to grab my belt and pull me even harder. That's both of our bodies and our strength versus the spot you've been chewing on.'

'OK. Try rocking a bit, too. Put as many kinds of stresses on that weak point as possible.'

Together, Arwood and Benton lean forward, putting all their weight against Arwood's wrists, the cuffs, and the door handle. Benton knows he is facing the outside door and, in pulling, tries to will himself through it.

And, without a sound, Arwood's cuffs snap.

Together still, they fall to the floor. Benton lands on his face, breaking his nose. Arwood can feel blood around his wrists, where the plastic has dug into the flesh.

'I think ... I think I've really hurt myself,' Benton says, but Arwood isn't listening. He's off to the mattress and recovering the iPhone. He turns it on, and muffles the sound by placing it beneath his armpit. The room glows a pale blue, and Benton whispers

'The light.' Arwood covers the screen until he can hide it beneath a mattress and adjust the brightness. Opening 'Messages', he types one with the coordinates and a brief note.

'We don't have a signal,' Benton says.

'No,' Arwood whispers. 'But we're not going to miraculously get one, either. It's like this, Thomas: either there's a signal a few metres outside that window, or there isn't. You know what a Hail Mary pass is?'

Spitting blood from his lips, Benton mutters, 'I can guess.'

'Football. American football. You can either get tackled and lose the game, or hurl the ball into the unknown and hope for the best. You might still lose the game, but the thing about a Hail Mary is that you also just might win.'

'I see where this is going.'

'After you hit "send" on an SMS, it usually says "sending" for a second or two as it looks for a signal and catches the wave. My hunch is that if I hit the button and I hurl it out the slit in the roof, maybe it can catch a signal and send the message before it smashes to bits and it's game over.'

'It's not much of a plan, is it?'

'Not really, but my thinking is that the odds are better than zero, which is what they absolutely are right now if we don't do it. And, like you said, my restraints are off. This is the window of opportunity, no pun intended. So, what do you say?'

'Who are you writing to?'

'Märta. And a local friend.'

'Can you do that?'

'Yeah. You click the little plus thing, and you can add recipients. See?'

'You really think Märta would move the world to come and get us? It wouldn't be a rational choice. That would be a lot of chips to cash in for two people who did this to themselves.'

'Yes, I do. And I'll tell you why. Because people aren't rational actors, Benton. People are *themselves*. If you want to know what's going to happen next, you don't look at the choice, you look at who's making it. That's what I learned as an arms broker. In this case, it's Märta. I think Märta wants to see you rescued, because she either loves you or close enough to it. And I think she wants to help the underdog, and that means Adar. And I think she wants to protect her own staff, and that means Jamal. And I think she doesn't ask for a lot of favours from other people, so whoever she is going to ask for help is going to say yes. She doesn't care about me, but there should be enough seats on the bus if it comes along.'

'That's quite an analysis.'

'I'd bet your life on it.'

'All right. Get on with it,' Benton says.

'You need to kneel by the window so I can stand on you. I can't reach otherwise.'

'Of course you do.'

Benton moves on his hands and knees toward the wall across from the mattresses and between the two doors. There are three slits near the ceiling, each a metre long, separated by small supporting columns. They are too small for a man or a child to slip through, but wide enough for binoculars, a rifle, or an arm to hurl an object the size of a grenade or a mobile telephone.

The room has all the qualities of a crypt. It smells like a construction site mixed with cooking spices and bare feet. In the dirt and the dust that coats everything, as Arwood places his right foot in the small of Benton's back, an unexpected thought comes to him, and not one he's entertained before.

'I want to die outside,' Benton says.

'Me, too,' says Arwood, and he now shifts all his weight onto Benton's back. The skin over his old bones slips around like a plucked chicken's. 'I want to get out of here and have a nice long life selling weapons to oppressed people with cash.'

'I don't mean outside this room. I mean outside all rooms. I want my last breath of life to be taken outdoors. A clear shot, so to speak.'

'This window opens to the outside,' Arwood says. 'We seem to be in a small valley, or a canyon, or something. I can't fit my head through. I can see stars above us, but there are rocks or — well, something that blocks out the stars — maybe ten or fifteen metres away. There's no artificial light anywhere. I can't see any buildings. Wherever we are is blacked out.'

There is blood dripping from Benton's nose, and he cannot move his hand to wipe it away. All he can do is stare into the floor and listen as Arwood narrates his own movements: 'I'm reaching my hand out to see what's there. The outside wall is smooth, more or less. I can't reach the ground. I can't tell how high up we are. The light is too strange. A metre or two? It doesn't feel like the ground in our room is the same level as the ground outside. I think we're dug in. That's why the slats on the wall are so high.'

'If you have a clear throw, then get on with it. My back—'

Arwood falls silent above him. His feet become still. There is a moment when their absurd pose becomes statuesque — a new member in the Garden of the Fugitives, those human statues at Pompeii. Then, without a sound, Arwood's weight shifts to Benton's lower back, rests there a moment, and then shifts forward to his upper back as he hurls the phone with all his might.

A silence follows — as complete and warm as a ceasefire — to be replaced by the sound of plastic and metal crashing into an ancient crevasse, echoing outward from the Sinjar Mountains to al-Anbar in the south and Ninawa province to the north, with a message for anyone with the ability to hear it.

PART III

OTHER THAN HONOURABLE

THE NEXT MORNING

28

Märta Ström wakes to the sound of her phone. She checks her watch to confirm the time. She can barely make out the faintly luminous green glow of the watch hands. It doesn't appear to be 5.00 a.m. yet. Which is nice. There is more time for sleep.

Her grandmother used to call sleep 'delicious', as though it had a flavour. Her grandmother died almost twenty years ago. Märta would lie in bed with her as a child, after her grandfather had gone off to wherever men went at six in the morning. The bed was still warm. The blanket smelled of wool. The wooden walls of their home, two hours from Stockholm, never entirely lost their smell. Everything in their home was simple. What they needed they had, and what they had they needed. Life was about the relationships between people, and the love that peace allows. She can still feel the knuckles of her grandmother's hand and the way her index finger would curl across all four of her own fingers while they lay in bed, toasty from the neck down, a thin layer of cold over her cheeks from the windows that were not thick enough — not really — to keep out the early-morning chill of a Swedish winter. She can taste it, just like her grandmother said. But it isn't the sleep she can taste. It is the memory.

More time to sleep. More time to hold her grandmother's hand and wonder what might be for breakfast. To enjoy this time alone with her. Her parents aren't here now. Or her older brother. They'll be able to talk this morning, just the two of them.

There would be nothing preventing them from sharing a stolen moment together this morning, were it not for a question forming off the bow like a storm front. She knows, instinctively, that if she allows the question to take a proper shape, it will disrupt her planned course. She needs to ignore it. Maybe it will go away. She wants to have breakfast with her grandmother, because they love each other and this time is set aside for the two of them.

But it nags her. It irks her. It knows her too well. She is not one to avoid a good question. And so it comes: *If the sound on her phone wasn't the alarm, what was it?*

Märta unclenches her hand from her grandmother's, and the bond is broken. Her grandmother's spirit leaves her, and she is alone again. She is older.

She looks at her phone.

It is an SMS message:

N36º 23' 15.88", E41º47'32.87". Held hostage. Need help. In some kind of old building. Probably ISIL. Come get us now.

She's up. Phone in hand, she skips the formality of slippers and bathrobe, and pads down the tiled staircase with the agility of an eleven-year-old girl. In the living room, she flips on the light. Herb is lying on his side, fast asleep in his blue boxers, as peaceful as a baby giant. She says, 'Herb,' only once in a quiet tone, and his eyes pop open.

'We got a note. They're alive. Ten minutes. Make coffee. Where's Tigger?'

'In the guest room. He won the coin toss.'

Märta is up the stairs quicker than a sound. She opens the guest bedroom door and flicks on the light from the wall switch. Tigger is sleeping face down and naked, his feet toward the head of the bed.

'Tigger?'

No reply.

'*François Armand?*'

'*Je ne veux pas aller à l'école. C'est ennuyeux,*' he says.

'*Réveille-toi. Ils sont vivants.*'

Tigger raises his head. '*D'accord.*'

'Time to go to work.'

Märta showers quickly, dresses, and then goes downstairs to meet the two men, who are already dressed in field gear—no more than ten minutes after she woke them.

'What do we have?' Tigger asks her.

Märta reads off the coordinates from her cell phone. Herb writes them down, then copies them a second time and hands the second copy to Tigger, who puts them into his pocket without looking up.

Tigger spreads out a map of northern Iraq on the kitchen table while Herb fixes three cups of coffee with sugar and no milk. He uses the laptop to find the location of the GPS coordinates, and the program zooms in on the Sinjar Mountains.

'Well … shit,' Tigger says.

'Why?' Herb asks, back at the table in his blue Patagonia field shirt, the sleeves rolled over his forearms and fastened by buttons.

'They're in the mountains. West of Tal Afar. It's a bad place,' Tigger says, pulling out a chair and then sitting down on it.

'Who do we know in Tal Afar?' Herb asks.

'Some of the people we helped in '91 were resettled there,' Märta says.

'This isn't Tal Afar,' Tigger says. 'These are the Sinjar Mountains. They rise out of absolutely nothing. Geographically, they look like they shouldn't even be there, the way Monument Valley rises from nothing. Culturally, those mountains are not even Iraq. They are a different universe. They don't like foreigners. They don't like Shiites. They don't like the government. They won't like us. Mostly Yezidi.'

'I know some of the Yezidi,' Märta says. 'I'm not saying they like foreigners. I'm saying I think they'll answer the phone if I call.'

'The Yezidi worship the devil,' Herb says.

'They don't worship the devil,' Märta says, 'at least not the devil as Christians think of him.'

'How else should I be thinking about devil worshippers?'

'The Yezidi,' Märta says, trying to find out how to explain this even to herself, 'are a very, very old tribe. Older than the Jews. As old as the Zoroastrians. They see the world as being made of opposing forces—right and wrong, good and evil. The Yezidi recognise that they need to come to spiritual terms with them both, and so they engage in worship that somehow involves talking to the darker forces as well. I don't know much about them. No one knows much, because they don't speak of their religion or their identity with foreigners. They've been a brutally persecuted minority, and see themselves as put upon by both the Arabs and the Kurds, and they aren't wrong about that.'

'Arwood said he thinks it's ISIL, not Yezidi,' Tigger says.

'Makes sense,' Herb says. 'The Yezidi are weak, and the land is good for hiding in. It's close to the Syrian border, it's good for attacking farther south into the Sunni regions, and it's easy to defend. The government is using the Sunni tribes again against ISIL. This is high ground. Not a lot of that around.'

Märta says, 'The Yezidi are politically sensitive, and they're very attentive to what's happening in their land. It's how they survive.'

'You think they owe you a favour?' Herb says.

'I don't think anyone owes me anything but a paycheque at the end of each month. But some people are grateful nonetheless, and they remember things. Back in the nineties, when I was with UNHCR and then the Red Cross, I used to get out of the office more and actually meet people, rather than fill out funding proposals for junior government staff who have never been in the field. And since I'm considered pretty funny-looking in this part of the world, they tend to remember me. We still have reputation and access as strategic assets. Now would be the time to use them, don't you both think?' she asks.

'We need to make contact,' Tigger says. 'I will speak with Firefly immediately. Get started. Herb should work the government. See if we can negotiate their release.'

Herb is looking at the map and considering the location of the Sinjar Mountains in relation to the safe zones. 'Even if we do reach an agreement, we'll still need to get them out of there. If the military is hunting ISIL after that attack, then this zone is going to be very hot. No travelling by ground. That means we'll need a lift. And there are no airfields, so that means helicopters. And if we're flying at only eight hundred metres, we'll be very vulnerable, which means we need to be allowed to fly. Because there's no defence.'

'Tigger, you have thoughts on this?' Märta asks.

'I suggest we put the players on the board, learn what we need to learn, and then see what the world looks like after that. Herb, you do the government, yes? Tell our friend in Baghdad what we know. See what he says.'

'Yeah, all right.'

'Märta, you warm up Louise. We may need her, like you said last night. I'll talk to Clip Maxwell. *On y va?*'

'You two work from here,' Märta says. 'I need to see Louise in person.'

They sleep like the dead until dawn. It is Arwood who wakes first, to the feeling of a boot in his gut. It is Arwood's involuntary grunt, and then his wheezing attempt to inhale, that wake Benton.

Hands still cuffed behind him, he opens his eyes. There are two men with AK assault rifles by the door, and one standing above Arwood. Once Arwood has taken a full breath, the man kicks him in the solar plexus again, and again Arwood wheezes for air.

'Stop kicking him,' Benton says from a sitting position. He says it only so that it will have been said.

The man—Abu Larry—is wearing a dark tan shirt that falls to his knees over trousers of the same colour and fabric. He wears desert army boots the colour of sand, and has a leather ammunition belt around his thin waist. On his head is the black headscarf of ISIL. On his wrist there's a vintage gold Longines watch with a fine leather strap. He does not carry a gun.

Abu Larry crouches down by Benton and studies his face. After a long look, he says something in Arabic, and one of the men by the door quickly kneels on Arwood and binds his hands behind his back again. Then he hits him on the head with the rifle.

'What are you accomplishing? What does this serve?'

Larry says nothing. He checks Benton's restraints, sees they are secure, and then removes a rag from his pocket. He pushes Benton to the mattress, kneels on his head, and shoves the rag into Benton's mouth. He ties a bandana around his head to hold it in place.

The two other men pull Arwood to his feet. Dizzy and obviously in pain, Arwood is unable to walk by himself. Head bent, he says as loudly as he can, 'We're not alone, Benton. There's still hope. And if they kill us, we'll be avenged. Mark my words. The land remembers. That's the only truth of the Middle East.'

The two men drag Arwood from the room, and one of them kicks the door closed.

Larry remains crouching by Benton, studying him. His eyes are nothing like Märta's. Or Vanessa's. Or Charlotte's.

Benton's broken nose is making it hard for him to breathe. More than fear, he is starting to feel a sense of anxiety and claustrophobia. There isn't enough air. His breaths become more rapid, more shallow. To look at his abductor or to look away—have his options dwindled only to this?

Then the man stands and leaves. He does not kick Benton. He

does not say a word. He passes through the inner door into a room Benton has never seen. The sliding bolt is engaged, and then the padlock is replaced.

A moment later, there is a third gunshot.

Dawn again, and the Syrian refugee men in the Domiz refugee camp are already smoking. There is smoke everywhere—smoke from their cigarettes, smoke from the cooking fires, smoke from the makeshift chimneys in the more permanent structures. The drive from Märta's home to the IRSG office at the refugee camp is uneventful. The police only have one roadblock set up, and they're searching cars at random. They wave her through.

She pulls into the Red Cross parking space reserved for visitors. Her Land Cruiser is not as well equipped as those from the UN or the ICRC. She has her handset but no HF antenna, no black rod that stretches like a thin roll bar across her vehicle to fasten in the back. In Sierra Leone, when she was posted there, the locals called them 'white rhinos'. She always hoped they were referring to the vehicles.

In Pakistan, they laughed at her and said the 'internationals' never leave the Egg: an egg on wheels. It wasn't only the colour of the Land Cruisers that inspired the name: it suggested that Westerners were never really born into the world in which they now lived.

She gets out of the car and locks it. It is six-fifteen in the morning. Farrah isn't in yet; she comes in closer to seven. Louise, however, is there. Märta can hear the sound of the BBC streaming through tinny computer speakers.

Märta knocks, because people are supposed to knock, and then walks directly in because she wants to. She sits on Louise's sofa.

'Good morning,' Louise says.

'They're alive. I got a text message. They're being held by some ISIL cell in the Sinjar Mountains. I've heard that the security forces are planning some kind of offensive today, west of Mosul. So there's a clock on this.'

'I heard that, too. It's in the sitrep. We've all been told to evacuate the area. I've cleared my people, but the Iraqi Red Crescent is being a little stubborn.'

'Which means,' Märta says, 'this all needs to be over in a few hours. I'll send you a letter for the record, but I'm formally requesting that the ICRC extend its good offices to mediate release. And we're gonna need a ride.'

'Have you made contact yet?'

'No.'

'What's your play?'

'I'm afraid the military knows about this base in the mountains, and they plan to strike it. If they do, they'll kill my people. I also don't want them going underground. I was in that situation in Somalia. They captured our people, they didn't reach out to us for months, and when they did, our nerves were so frayed we agreed to anything. I also can't ask the military if they know about the base, because then they'll definitely bomb it. So all I can do is hurry.'

Louise says nothing.

'We have an arrangement with Firefly International. Tigger says he trusts them, and thinks they have systems we can use. Apparently, the IRSG keeps them on retainer. Have you used people like this before?' Märta asks.

'Officially,' Louise says, 'I can't confirm or deny that we've used specialised firms to set up the negotiating structures to secure the successful release of our people in Afghanistan, Pakistan, and Colombia in the last few years. And I can't confirm that I think it's a good idea to follow Tigger's advice. What I can do is tell Spaz that we'll help when the time comes—if all parties accept us, the government is informed, and we can secure a flight path. You realise, though, that to do this I'll have to pull air assets off the relief effort to help your people instead. You want to use my lift during an assault. That'll have consequences.'

Märta nods. 'I know.'

'How do you feel about that?'

'I'm going to put off feeling anything about it until it's over.'

'Are you in touch with Geneva on this?'

'I'm putting Miguel in charge of liaison work with headquarters. You know him? My kid from Spain? Big eyes, floppy hair, the voice, the whole thing? I find they're a little afraid to talk to him. The Swiss don't react to his verbal style very well, so they tend to leave me alone if the choice is Miguel or silence. Meanwhile, Herb is working the government to get approval for the pickup, without telling them exactly where it is.'

'That sounds tricky,' Louise says, turning off the radio.

Märta explains her gambit in Sinjar. How she needs to contact the kidnappers because of the time pressure, but how she fears surprising them and what the consequences might be. Better for them to reach out first. But she can't risk waiting for them. She has to make decisions without sufficient information or basis for judgement. Some call this 'leadership'. She considers it a failure of preparation, analysis, policy, and systems. You're only on your own once you've been abandoned.

So she has to improvise. She says she knows a family in Kursi. If ISIL has a facility there and it's staffed, she reasons, they'll need to shop for food and supplies periodically, just like everyone else does. And since there aren't many places to do that, people in town will know where they go each day. 'I'm going to write an email,' she explains, 'and send it to the family I know there. They'll give it to the son, and the son will drop it off at the market. It will be clearly marked for the hostage-takers. I don't think this will place the shop owner at risk, and if it does, he can say he was given the letter by the IRSG.'

Louise thinks it's too risky.

'I know a good man with the Iraqi Red Crescent in Mosul,' she says. 'He can deliver the letter to the shop. You don't have to put the family at risk.'

'I thought the ICRC and the Iraqi Red Crescent weren't getting along so well these days.'

'We're not, but I know who's who. His name is Sharo. He's Assyrian. He's a medic, and knows the area well. He can deliver the message. I think he'll say yes, too.'

'What makes you think so?'

'He loves his motorcycle.'

'I don't see the connection.'

'The road that winds from Route 47 into the mountains is one of the twistiest mountain passes in the world. His wife doesn't let him go riding there, because she says he takes enough risks with his job. This would make it his job.'

'How far is Mosul from the mountains?' Märta asks.

'About an hour and a half, if all goes well.'

'Assuming he leaves immediately,' says Märta, 'and gets there without incident, and they get the letter on arrival, which is a long shot, we're talking two hours from now. That's a lot of time with the clock running down.'

'It's your call, Märta. I think Sharo has the best chance. The Red Crescent can get through. We should use it. If you screw up the approach in a scenario like this, you screw up the entire operation. These things are very delicate. There's no room for heroics.'

'I'm not convinced the Red Crescent or anything that sounds remotely connected to the West has a reputation with ISIL.'

'Me neither. But better to use Sharo and a legitimate regional actor than some boy.'

'We'll be putting one person at risk to save another.'

'Märta,' Louise says, becoming visibly agitated, 'I'm spending time talking to you about your team rather than prepping my people for the influx of refugees from across the border. What we're doing here is diverting emergency resources from their sanctioned purpose to clean up a mess that shouldn't exist.'

'Yes,' Märta says. 'All right. Can I use your computer? I'll write the letter. I don't want to waste any time. You can send it to Sharo from here via email.'

Märta launches Word '98 and looks at the blinking black line on the simulated white paper.

'What do you think it should say?' she asks.

29

'François Armand?' says the voice on the phone.

'Yes, Clip, it's me. *Bonjour.*'

Clip is British and comes from London. He has a Sandhurst affectation and attitude and, like Tigger and Herb, is in his late forties. One quality that Tigger appreciates in Clip is that he listens.

'I received and reviewed all your briefings and notes,' Clip says. 'Correct me if I'm wrong about any of the following points. Looks to be ISIL, but we're not sure?'

'ISIL is what we are supposing. It could be al-Qaeda, and it could be that there is no difference between the two. It could also be someone else.'

'If we're lucky, this will be an express kidnapping. They'll ask for a reasonable sum that you can pay, then you pay it, and we call it a day and debate the ethics afterward. Have they contacted you?'

'No. No one has reached out to us at all. And this worries us,' Tigger says, adjusting the phone and putting the call on loudspeaker so Herb can listen. 'If they killed them right away, this would have made sense. Contacting us for money, that would have made sense, too. But the silence? The possibilities are endless. We've had to wait before, in the Philippines with Abu Sayyaf. They tested our nerves, and they won. I hate waiting.'

'The Arab boy, Jamal. He's yours?'

'Herb and Märta are especially protective of him. Märta knows his family well. There was an incident when she saw his brother die.

We are supposed to keep a distance, but sometimes our humanity interferes with our humanitarianism. It is a failing that is our most redeeming quality.'

'And among the hostages is a Brit and an American. Have you notified the embassies yet?'

'In writing, yes, but it's before office hours here, and I don't expect a reply until after 8.00 a.m. So, Clip … what do we do?'

'We establish the crisis-management team.'

'Yes. It is me, Herb, Märta, and you. Märta is the decision-maker.'

'Good. Next we need a communicator. The decision-maker does not talk to the hostage-takers. Only the communicator does. We don't know what language the kidnappers speak. We're assuming Arabic?'

'We're assuming Arabic. That, and perhaps English. It is the *lingua franca* these days.'

'You have someone?'

'No,' Tigger says. 'Herb wanted to do it, but Märta said no. She thinks my accent and his will give us both away.'

'She's right. I suggest a village elder. Also, accents are a problem with the Arabs. They have a remarkable understanding of where people come from and what it implies. You mustn't get that wrong here. Once you choose someone, you let me know. Just remember that the purpose of the communicator is to isolate the decision-making team. It is essential that no one be put in a position to have to make decisions while talking to the hostage-takers. He's merely to pass along messages from one party to the other. This leaves us plenty of time for deliberation and strategic decision-making.'

'I understand.'

'Just to be sure, you three want to take point on this? Because we can take over if you want.'

'No. We'll do it. We know the environment. We can better sense the actors.'

'Then our role at Firefly will be to serve as your backup team on decision-making. We'll question you. Probe you. Second-guess your judgements. Test you. Make sure your decisions are reasonable, even if we can't prove they'll work. You follow?'

'Yes.'

'We need an open channel at all times, and that means redundancies. I'm emailing you all' — Tigger and Herb can hear Clip shuffle some papers and click some keys — 'a set of solutions on email, SMS, phone, Skype, and Thuraya satellite phones. There's no reason we should lose contact.'

'Understood.'

'The Iraqi government?' Clip asks.

'We're afraid to tell them where our people are,' Tigger says. 'They might be more interested in where the insurgents are, which would be unhelpful.'

'What about external communications?'

'Nothing. We are keeping this quiet. We figure that if the hostage-takers know they have an audience, it will empower them.'

'Good. You should still have some statements in the works, though, for different contingencies. I recommend the crisis team not direct that. Farm it back to Geneva,' Clip says. 'Let me know when the communicator is selected.'

Sharo is a motorcycle medic for the Iraqi Red Crescent. His facial hair is so extreme, so unruly, so expansive, that his wife likes to tell her friends that she hasn't seen him in years.

He has slender shoulders and long arms. He imagines his legs as the physical extension of the Yamaha XT's 41mm telescopic, oil-damped forks, soaking up each bump in the road and each bump in life.

The 600cc motorcycle is Sharo's one joy beyond his three remaining children. It's a '93 model, and when he rides it — high off the ground, with a view over traffic, and further into the future than other people can see—he feels the way he is supposed to feel when he prays. Sharo does not lack faith, and he puts his trust in the words of the Prophet, but he does not feel the euphoria that others seem to feel. He lost his eldest son to a killer who was robbing him. Sharo stood and prayed as the corpse-washer prepared his son's body. He did not believe, when he closed his son's eyes, that God was great. He only felt that God was big.

But riding a motorcycle is great. When he wears his open-face helmet and sunglasses, he hears only the sound of the wind and the rumble of the single-cylinder engine. He floats with the birds, which do not feign to understand the ways of man below them. The air tickles his face as the breeze tickles his whiskers. To turn into a hairpin on a mountain pass is to forget the loss of his boy, to forget the state of his country, to forget his fears for his daughter's future and the impossible sadness of his kinsmen.

To ride is to focus the mind. It is to be present and feel that—briefly, if for the moment, and maybe never again—a man can control the speed at which the future will meet him.

Carry a letter to Sinjar?

Yes.

You'll need to hurry.

Good.

Be discreet. Take it to the market. Talk to the grocer. Ask how the foreigners get their food. Have it delivered with the food. Come back.

Yes. Good. Right away.

I emailed it to you. You printed it? It reads legibly in both Arabic and English?

I did not read it. I don't want to know what it says. But I see the text is black and clear through the paper.

Ride carefully.

Always. Yes. Thank you, Ms Louise.

Don't thank me, and don't make me tell your wife where you went. I have enough problems.

Yes, Ms Louise. Thank you.

The military may take action today. She told him this.

Sharo fuels the bike, wipes the drops of the clear petrol from the cap onto his soiled trousers, and lets the bike warm. Then he's off.

He rides west, chasing yesterday, like an old man who is not ready to let another day slip by. The sun warms his back. He could almost be happy again if only he could close his eyes long enough to disappear entirely, but alas, he must open them again too quickly so that he can see the road, and this is what keeps him bound to life.

There is only one turn off Route 47 into the town of Sinjar at the base of the mountains. And now, there before him, is one of the most majestic roads on the planet. He knows, as he takes the turn, that he is one of only a few men in the history of this new earth to ride this road by motorcycle. And of those, no other man has ever appreciated it more.

He has never left Iraq. He has never seen the Stelvio Pass in Italy, with forty-eight hairpin turns up the Alps, or the Trollstigen serpentine in Norway, with its eleven famous bends at an incline of almost ten degrees up the mountain. He knows of these only from books. He dreams of these Occidental legends the way Westerners dream of magic carpets from the East. What he does know, in front of him, by the grace of God, are ninety-four hairpin turns from Sinjar to Gune Ezidiya in only twenty kilometres.

This is one of the greatest and most exciting rides on earth.

Pity about the politics.

But take it slowly. There is no rush. There is work to be done. And every turn, every straightway, is a breath of life to be cherished.

For an hour, there is no death.

For an hour, there is joy in the hearts of all children.

For an hour, his body becomes one, uniting the physical world with the spiritual. For an hour, he is alone with his memories and with the spirits of those who have passed before him, and they ride with him, and they sing together about the love that once was and will continue, so long as there is a person left alive to remember it.

For an hour, Sharo rides.

Sharo stops riding at a town that is unmarked on the map and has no signpost before it. The hard-cased panniers of his bike are holy white, marked with a red crescent. It is quiet when the engine stops. There are no cars moving through the town now. People seem to have disappeared. He does not blame them, given the way the Yezidi have been treated by Saddam and by the Sunnis in Mosul, and the pressure put on them by the Kurds. They are alone in this world, having only themselves as comfort. Why greet a stranger?

There is a dirty blue-and-white awning extending from a square building. In front, there are fruits in crates. The thin steel door to the shop is open. Sharo removes his helmet, which is also marked with the crescent. He sees the shopkeeper, standing, behind the counter.

'*Salaam alaikum,*' he says to the man.

'*Alaikim as salaam,*' the man replies, without warmth. His accent is unfamiliar to Sharo. He knows that these people speak a language other than Arabic, but he does not know it.

In Arabic, he says to the man, 'Your shop is quiet now.'

The man nods. 'It is quiet.'

'Other times, I imagine, it is busier.'

'At other times.'

'Perhaps there are strangers who enjoy the hospitality of your shop.'

'We have many visitors. Sometimes we visit them.'

'I see,' Sharo says. 'Perhaps the women or the children carry food on these visits. Perhaps in those baskets by the door?'

The man looks at the baskets that people use as they shop. They are handwoven and worn. 'It is a practical and expected way to bring what needs to be brought,' he says.

'If a letter were placed in such a basket,' Sharo says, 'a letter that never touched the hands of the basket-carrier, and that letter fixed more problems than it caused, might it be carried?'

The man does not speak. Sharo looks behind the man at the shelves, and asks for a packet of Western cigarettes.

The shopkeeper takes the cigarettes down. He says, 'Two boys from a nearby village were murdered in Mosul for smoking in front of Muslim men.'

Sharo takes a cigarette from the packet, puts one in his mouth, and hands one to the shopkeeper. He lights them both with one match.

'Then it was a black shame on them for not welcoming and protecting those boys who were guests and should have been treated with all the honour, the understanding, and forgiveness and mercy that God demands. I would never forgive such a thing. But I would try not to misplace my anger. These are the times we live in. Which is why we help each other when we can. That way, decent people can enjoy honest pleasures, and the wicked can go their way.'

The shopkeeper blows out the smoke and looks at the basket. He gives the most subtle of nods.

Sharo places the letter in the basket. The man immediately fills it with supplies, and then calls a woman from the back room. He says something in a language that Sharo does not understand.

A woman appears. Sharo nods to her, but she does not acknowledge him. He does not take offence. He does not know their ways.

Sharo pays twenty times what the cigarettes are worth, and then leaves. If his front wheel does not slip on sand on the way down the mountain, if the bombs do not fall around him as he commands the turns, if a car does not run him off the road on his way down, and if he has luck and the will of God on his side, then for one hour more he can ride and be free.

The woman who collects the basket is dressed as a Yezidi woman, not a Muslim one. Concessions are made to the existence of the foreigners, but the Yezidi are too proud and too formal in their ways to concede everything. They have been here for millennia before the Muslims. Perhaps, with the aid of the god Melek Taus, they will remain here — in peace — after the Muslims have gone.

She walks down stairs carved into the rock. She walks beyond the edge of the village to where the valley stone rises, and where the waters run fast and unhindered in the winter beneath the thin ice that collects here. She walks to an old, long-forgotten building. An Ottoman fortification from World War I, it is made of stone and concrete. It is a garrison building. She does not want to know what happens here. She prays it will someday be gone, but she has no expectations that her prayers will be answered.

Without uttering a name, without making a sound, she knocks three times on the steel door and then turns to leave before it is opened. There is no need to wait. She knows she was being watched the moment she entered the small pass that leads to the only two outer doors — one to the left and into the main building, and one to the right into the dungeon.

If they did not want her to come this far, she would be dead already.

She walks back the way she came. She has two kilometres to go. She is old now, and tired, but this is what her body has learned to do. Before the building vanishes into the mountain behind her, she hears a door open, and the sound of the basket scraping against the earth before it is taken into what she imagines is Hell. And why wouldn't she? Where else would the devil live?

30

Thomas Benton is alone, his shoulder causing him so much pain that it dominates his attention and infuses itself into his hallucinations. The only question that holds his mind together is *Why am I here?* If he can answer this, before the end, he will have achieved something and given himself permission to die.

But the pain and the fear and the thirst disrupt the continuity of his thoughts. And his capacity to imagine.

He tries to fight this domination by using techniques he imagines a Buddhist might use to meditate: the image of a flickering flame against a mahogany wall; walking along the undulating green hills of the upper coastal path by Dorset; tracking the slow descent of a single drop of condensation on a pint glass on a hot summer's day.

Well, a British Buddhist, anyway.

When his phone rang in Cornwall and it was Arwood Hobbes on the other end, it did feel — if he allows himself to admit this — as though the cosmos were intervening for the first time on his behalf. Everything he was, and had failed to correct in himself, had finally reached its natural conclusion, and his family had fallen apart. And then Arwood's disembodied voice asked him to come back to Iraq with him. To look for something. To make the dead live again. To make the world complete. And he said yes.

Why?

A coincidence. An echo. A midday moon in a blue sky.

There really was no explaining it.

Benton hears a door open to the adjacent room. There is a shuffling sound as something is pulled inside. The door is closed again and bolted. Then the uneasy silence returns.

He can see the green dress more clearly now that the sun has risen and the room is illuminated. A warm, yellow light spreads across the ceiling. It will not touch him, but it is good to look at something connected to life.

Benton is thirsty. He has tried to convince himself he's not, but to no effect. Whatever the body wants, it does not stop wanting until it gets.

He used to want many things. He wanted the MG he once purchased with his brother, Edgar. He wanted Vanessa. It wasn't that her beauty was so overwhelming, or that her eyes glittered like the moon, or that her body was perfect beyond measure. That was for women in magazines. He always preferred three dimensions to two.

Vanessa was lovely. It is a term that has fallen from favour, but it still means something particular. Her face was kind and intelligent and inquisitive and warming. Her eyes were healthy and bright and commanding. Her body was the kind that most young women actually have. Vanessa probably saw in it a litany of imperfections when she was naked, but they all went entirely unseen by Benton, because she was naked.

What else had he wanted? He had wanted children. They had had Charlotte. They tried for more. After three miscarriages, they called it a day. It had been starting to affect their ability to be parents to the one they had.

What else did he want? He had wanted to take the girl in green to the American side of the ceasefire line twenty-two years ago. He failed in that, too. Which is when he stopped wanting things. When Charlotte stood in the doorway and he heard the pauses between her heartbeats, and he could have stepped through the silence between them as though it were an eternity, he knew he could not want her to live and love him the same way he had before. The reason was simple, really. He was too weak.

Was this what Vanessa was trying to accomplish—why he caught her in bed with another man? To make him want her again?

The door to their bedroom in Fowey was at the end of the carpeted hall. It was very late. He had planned to stay in London that night but came back instead, although not before stopping off at the pub for a pint. He had fallen into a conversation with Lester, and the hours had slipped by. It was a black and wet night under a low sky. Coming up the stairs, he was surprised to find his bedroom door framed in light. He turned the handle quietly so as not to startle her. She'd likely fallen asleep reading a book. He wondered what she was reading these days—John Irving, maybe?

The door didn't creak as he slowly waved it open. The table lamp on his side of the bed gave out a weak orange light. When the door was halfway open, he heard a muffled grunt that startled him. Instinctively, he flicked on the overhead light.

The inner door to his prison opens.

Benton doesn't move. He sees two men walk into the room. One takes a position by the door; the other brings in a folding chair, which he places a metre from Benton. He sits and crosses his legs, settling into a position thought effeminate by Western men.

He holds Benton's satchel.

Benton looks up into his face. It is Abu Larry again. The man reaches down and unties the bandana from Benton's head. He places his fingers between Benton's lips and pinches the remaining cloth, pulling it slowly from his mouth so it winds like a snake.

'Do you know who I am?' he says.

Benton shakes his head. 'No.'

Larry removes a pistol from the satchel. It is an ancient gun, a Webley.

'Who is the girl?'

His accent is Arabic, but with British intonations again. He sounds educated. His voice is calm. He sounds deliberate and in control of his actions. He looks pitiless and calculating.

Benton notices the present tense used in his question.

'We found her by the side of the road,' Benton says. 'I was taking her to Domiz. There is a refugee camp there.'

'Everyone is by the side of the road in Iraq. Why this girl?'

'She reminds me of my niece.'

'I think you're lying to me.'

'I don't feel a strong need to tell the truth to terrorists.'

'I'm not a terrorist.'

'Well,' Benton says, 'you're not a duck.'

Larry shoots Benton in the leg.

The bullet tears through the muscle of his upper right thigh, missing the femur. His body cannot decide whether to inhale for life or exhale to scream. Then, from deep in his diaphragm, the initial shudder of exquisite pain finds its voice, and he wails. The smell of his own urine fills his nostrils, and tears, from a well of moisture he didn't know was there, burst from his eyes.

Of course. Of course this.

The shooter sits calmly, resting the warm pistol in his now limp hand. He is speaking softly, saying something. Benton can see his lips move. It is not loud enough to rise above the ringing in Benton's ears.

And his accent is too thick. Benton would only understand his own mother's loving voice now. It was always the only voice that could reach him when he was in distress.

'Listen to me. Can you hear me?' Abu Larry claps his hands together. The other man by the door, the man with the Chinese assault rifle, stands motionless. Abu Larry's voice remains calm. 'Look at me.' He uncrosses his legs and rests his boots on the floor.

He leans forward, trying to get Benton's attention. 'I said, look at me.'

Benton looks.

'See if the bullet went through, Mr Bueller.'

'Can't move. Can't look. Can't feel.'

Larry makes a gesture to the man by the door, who then takes out a knife and, standing behind Benton, cuts off his plastic binders.

The feeling should be one of relief, but in fact there is even more pain. His arms have not moved in twelve hours. The first repositioning is excruciating.

He wants to touch the back of his leg, but his hands do not obey him.

'See if the bullet went through, Mr Bueller.'

He looks at the back of his leg.

'Did it go through?'

'You sonofabitch.'

'Good.' He throws Benton a cloth. 'I suggest you tie this around your leg.'

Benton ignores the offered cloth, and instead removes a faded red bandana from his jacket pocket and presses it against the exit wound, which is larger than the entry one. He would tie it, but the pain is too great.

'You're a Jew, Mr Bueller. An assassin?'

'No.' Benton's voice is low and weak. The throbbing has started. He needs his strength to hold his leg. Talking drains him. He is forced to listen.

'Does it hurt?'

'Yes.'

'I've never been shot. I have no idea what it feels like.'

'Don't lose hope.'

'Are you thirsty?' Larry asks. 'Thirst is a horrible thing. That is something I have experienced.'

'I'm thirsty,' Benton says.

'Would you like some water?'

'Yes.'

'Me, too. It gets hot in here. Maybe we can find some later. The Jews want to support the Kurds and Druze, and take Arab land away from us. You are here for them?'

'I'm British.'

Benton tries to elevate his leg. There is a lot of blood, but none of it is pulsing. He does not know how much blood he can lose before passing out or dying, and he has no way to measure this, in any case.

'I'm losing my blood. Can I have some blood? Or water? Yes, I'd like some water. I'll make my own blood. The Catholics say the wine becomes blood. It's true. Only it's our own blood, not that of Christ.'

He looks up at the ceiling of cheap cement and cracked white paint. 'I have a wife named Vanessa,' he says, for no other reason than to be sure it is said. 'She loved me. I was mad for her. We were happy for a long time. Then I faded away from her. My daughter, too. I used to pick out her clothes with her when she was seven years old. Before she went to school. You wouldn't believe how complicated it was.'

Then he jerks his head to the left and vomits on the mattress. He moves his head away from it, only to vomit again. He pushes himself away from that as well, and his eyes tear again. He lets them roll down his cheeks without shame.

Benton says, 'You killed all those people. All those people in the breadline with the mortar. The people in the traffic jam. The police. They were little more than boys. So many. So very many. I've seen so many die. They say there are sixteen hundred factions in Libya now. Hundreds in Syria. You want a caliphate? Have you no perspective?'

Abu Larry taps the Webley against his knee.

'Do you speak Arabic?' he asks in a quiet voice. 'You don't. I can tell. Have you ever noticed how many Arab men speak English when

interviewed on CNN or BBC? Barbers. Taxi drivers. All these regular
people you care about so much. And yet, when was the last time you
saw a European or American ask someone a question in Arabic? You
don't speak the language of the people you are speaking for.'

'I want some water.'

'You think you're superior to us. To what goes on here. You
kill whoever you need to kill. Men, women, children. You became
mighty powers on the bones of your enemies. There is no difference.'

The sharpness of the pain is giving way to a debilitating throb
and tenderness. He fears the coming of the next wave more than the
experience of the pain itself — like stepping on a tack and waiting for
the mind to register what the eyes have already understood.

'We're different, all right,' Benton says, catching his breath and
regaining himself as he puts pressure on the wound. 'We have done
terrible things. But we've responded by trying to make a more
humane world. And we see our failures in the light of what we're
trying to achieve. To make a better way of life.'

'The only way of life,' Abu Larry says, 'is the Koran.'

Herb Reston is on the phone, speaking with the Iraqi government.
Herb has historically been diplomatic and has a reputation for having
a steady temperament, but reason has its limits. Herb's personal
philosophy for getting things done has always been a linear one that
starts from the head and works its way down. First, use your brain.
Then, trust your heart. If that doesn't work, trust your gut. And
when all else fails, it's time to use your balls.

The primary reason for his current sinking feeling is that, though
well educated in the tenets of Christian charity by his mother,
Herbert Reston does not suffer fools lightly.

And he is talking to an idiot.

'Kasim, if you tell me where you're going to attack, I'll know if
my people will be safe when you do, because I know their location.

All I need to know is the time and location of the planned assault. I know it's classified, so give me a window and a zone. That's all I need. I need to see if my people are inside it or outside it, and then I can devise a strategy.'

'Yes, yes, Mr Herbert, but if you tell me where they are exactly, I will be able to tell you if they will be safe.'

'I don't want to tell you where they are, because someone in your military might choose to bomb them, since they are probably located in a terrorist safe haven, and the whole purpose of your operation is to strike them. So how about you tell me where you're planning to attack?'

'Unfortunately, Mr Herbert, it is a military operation, and I cannot share the specifics of the operation, as these are very secret. Very, very secret. So it is better if you tell me where they are. I will tell people the coordinates.'

'Well, the thing is, Kasim, I've seen the Iraqi military in action, and I know a thing or two about how you share information and coordinate. I also know you're mostly staffed by Shiites, and my people are probably being held by Sunnis who used to run this country under Saddam, and they slaughtered the Shiites. So forgive me if I err on the side of caution here—'

Kasim turns it around again as though they are bartering over pirated CDs at the market. After five minutes of this, Herb gives up on specifics and tries for generalities.

'Are you attacking into Ninawa?'

'Oh yes, definitely.'

'South of that?'

'Hard to say.'

'North of that?'

'I'm not sure.'

'In the mountains?'

'Maybe in the mountains. Maybe not.'

'Will you be using helicopters?'

'Helicopters are very effective.'

'So are friends,' Herb says, and hangs up.

Tigger asks Herb what Kasim said, and Herb gives Tigger a look that means Kasim will not be receiving a Christmas card from the IRSG this year.

'This Iraqi government is useless,' Herb says.

'Would you rather have the last government, this one, or the next one?' Tigger asks.

'The last one was hanged by its neck and deserved it; this one is corrupt, tribal, and hapless; and the next one will make Iraq the world's first terrorist caliphate. Personally? I think we should bring the troops back in, stop worrying about what the liberals say, and recognise we're at war with jihadist Islam and that we need to win like we won against the Communists,' Herb says.

'You want to fight more wars?'

'America will do what it has to do. Because that's the American way.'

'Let me tell you a story, my friend. In the thirteenth century, a Spanish scholar named Don Juan Manuel referred to his country's occupation by the Muslim Moors since 711 AD as the *guerra fría*. The cold war. It was not a war of swords, but a war of ideas. We are still in this war. But we are winning it, no matter the momentary gains of these ISIL people. You know why? Because they are surrounded by ideas they cannot fight, because they are ideas they cannot answer. On one side are the real teachings of the Prophet — love, kindness, tolerance. And on the other are Western ideas so deep, so significant, we don't even notice them. They are the air we now breathe. And the most significant of these ideas? Romantic love. It is the most disruptive and transformative power in the history of the world. Terrorists are powerless against it. We support love, and they will lose.'

'That is dreamy bullshit.'

'No, no. Consider it. Think of Romeo and Juliet. "Two houses, both alike in dignity," we are first told. Why? Because the houses are the power, and dignity is the currency of that realm. We need to know this so we can understand that what keeps the lovers apart is not a higher justice, but a higher power. And then, here come these two children who defy and disrupt the underlying social order, and who die for their efforts because their humanity cannot survive in concert with that world. The moment Shakespeare makes our sympathies go to them, the system is overturned. Personal love is very disruptive to tribal thinking. And what of Juliet? A young woman? Romantic love empowered her to be equal to a man, to choose her own destiny, to make her own choices, to be in absolute control over her own body and her own heart. It is the first truly feminist story. It validated love, and fuelled a revolution.

'These people, this ISIL, we should fight them, yes. We can bomb them, yes. But that's not a strategy for victory. This is a *guerra fría*. Victory lies in replacing their social order, which is why they are afraid, and they should be. And our secret weapon? It is not drones. Quite the opposite. It is women. We should free them, educate them, give them power — put a Juliet in every village. They will change the world. This is why Boko Haram is so afraid of the girls and abducts them, why the Taliban will not educate them, why ISIL murders those in Western clothes and who think freely. Women. They are how the West will win. They are how love will prevail.'

'You are so relentlessly French.'

'Thank you.'

'I hate this waiting.'

'I feel the same. But the silence upsets me more. I would rather argue with you.'

'What do we know from Sharo?' Herb asks.

'He made the drop, and got back safely. Beyond that, we're in the dark.'

'What do we know from Clip?' Herb asks.

'I gave them some names, and after doing some checking they've agreed with my recommendation for a communicator. He's a professor of dentistry at Hawler Medical University in Erbil. He's from a village not far from the Sinjar Mountains. He's Sunni, and his wife is a Kurd. Clip said that if we protect his identity, his voice will not implicate him. Apparently, his accent is so hypnotically generic that some of his patients pass out without anaesthesia.'

'Why did he agree to do it?'

'He hates the jihadists, and Firefly is going to pay him. It's a win-win for him.'

'We trust him?'

'We trust him to convey information responsibly, yes.'

'When are we supposed to hear from him?'

'As soon as he hears from the hostage-takers.'

'Any other news?'

'I learned recently that the can opener was not invented for a full eighty years after the invention of the can.'

'What's your point? That nothing is inevitable?' Herb asks.

'Maybe. Or that even the inevitable takes time.'

31

Märta has returned to the house. She is sitting on the red thinking chair, hoping it'll live up to its name. Herb is leaning against the countertop where Märta stood last night, and Tigger is sacked out on the sofa. Clip is on the speakerphone.

Tigger has heard from the dentist. There are decisions to be made.

'What did he say?' Märta asks Tigger.

'He said he'd been contacted. He said the man on the other end of the phone did not sound Iraqi. He sounded foreign, perhaps Yemeni. He wasn't sure. The dentist said the man was calm and professional, and therefore very scary. The dentist explained to this man—who has no name—that he is only our communicator. He said he does not work for any party, is doing this as a favour, and he has no power to make decisions. After he said this, the man on the other end said that he will not speak with a go-between and will speak only to the decision-maker himself. Our dentist explained that this is not a better solution, because the organisation forbids such direct contact. It is beyond his control. This way, with his own involvement, the path is more clear for a settlement. Then he asked if the hostage-takers had any requests or demands they wanted him to pass on. The kidnapper said yes, that he is to explain that if the decision-maker does not meet him face-to-face, he will kill everyone to help fill his quota. The dentist asked for proof that our people are alive. The man ignored him, and said that we are to come to the village on Sinjar. The market we used for the letter drop, he explained, also serves tea. We should come there, and then they will talk further. That was all. He gave us the day to make a choice.'

'What does that mean,' Märta asks, 'about making a quota?'

'ISIL,' says Herb, 'have apparently become Terrorism, Inc. They actually put out reports of the number of people they've killed, how, and when. In August, they published one detailing their attack metrics. I don't even remember the categories, but they're keeping numbers on their assassinations, bombings, suicide-vest attacks, cities taken over, IEDs, houses burned — you name it. That was from the 2011–2012 period, when most of us had barely heard of these guys. And there's PR material now in English, profiling suicide bombers, giving bomb-making instructions, explaining the best places to kill the most civilians, and quotes from the Koran explaining why all this is a grand idea. It's never been easier to step into their minds and lose your own.'

'What are we going to do?' Tigger asks, his leg bouncing slightly on his knee. 'We go to the meet, we probably die. We don't go, our people almost certainly die.'

'If we show up,' Herb says, 'we are giving them more hostages or more bodies. Going there is out of the question. Clip, you still on the line?'

'I'm here, Herb,' a voice confirms from the loudspeaker on the computer. 'You're right. You can't go. Maybe we can offer them money.'

'We don't negotiate with terrorists,' Herb says to Clip. 'And that's not just my opinion. UN resolution 1373 was passed after September 11, and we're supposed to comply with it. It explicitly prevents the financing of terrorist organisations. We're not supposed to pay them off. We're not supposed to negotiate with them.'

'Everyone is paying these people off,' Märta says.

'You used to be Red Cross,' Herb says. 'They have never once paid to get someone back. And their people are safer for it.'

Tigger makes a wildly exaggerated arm movement and blows a raspberry through his lips that could have filled a balloon. 'We are negotiating with terrorists! We're aggressively doing our very best as a team to negotiate with terrorists. No, we don't want to give them money or more hostages, that much is true, but please, spare me the high-level legal rhetoric. This is the real world. Here in the dirt. *Merde.*'

'I'm meeting with them,' Märta says.

At which point, the three men fall silent.

'That is out of the question,' Herb says.

'That's right. You can't possibly,' Tigger says. 'And you are a blonde woman. They would love to kill a blonde woman after raping you to death.'

'I just sent a motorcycle medic into the lion's den, and he's home again,' Märta says. 'The Kurds will not deliberately fire on us. Neither will the military. That leaves Sunni tribesmen, who might, and ISIL. If ISIL are extending the invitation and think they might get something out of it, it makes sense to conclude that we have negotiated access to them. The best protection would be to use a marked vehicle and to let everyone know who we are and why we're there, and make sure they're OK with it. You boys are missing the big move here. We have negotiated access.'

'If the ICRC has better access,' Tigger says, 'why not use them?'

'Louise won't let us in one of her vehicles until we have an agreement with the kidnappers. We have an invitation, not an agreement. This step belongs to us. It's only one step away.'

'I'll go,' Herb says.

'No, I'll go,' Tigger says. 'It makes more sense.'

'It makes no kind of sense,' Herb says to Tigger, 'because you're about as scary as Linus and his blanket. Also, and I'm sorry to have to say this, man, but your accent in English is not intimidating. Mine is.

When people hear me, they think of Samuel L. Jackson at his most unholy. When they hear you, they think of Pepé Le Pew smoking weed.'

'Herbert,' Tigger says, 'you are not scary. These people have never heard of Samuel L. Jackson, who is also an actor and not an assassin, by the way. So he is not scary either. And I happen to know that you are in fact a giant teddy bear. You may think that having dark-brown skin makes you scary, but it does not. It makes you a very popular colour for a teddy bear.'

'I'm scary.'

'Uh-huh. I was in the movie theatre with you and your son, where you cried when little Nemo heard his father's voice for the first time after their journey apart.'

'My biceps are bigger than your thighs.'

'Your son, incidentally, did not cry.'

'OK, you two, knock it off. I'm going,' Märta says. 'The only question is whether I'm going alone or not.'

'Oh, Märta, please,' Tigger says. 'Your very presence would be an insult to these people. I hate this Scandinavian quality you all have, especially that face you all make when confronted with your own naïveté.'

'What face?'

'That face — the face of fake confusion you hide behind to pretend you don't even understand me, so that your Scandinavian identity of moral purity is not threatened.

'The Finns are different,' Herb says.

'They never speak,' Tigger says.

'That's the old ones. Young ones never shut up. Something's going on up there.'

'I feel as though we're getting off track,' Clip says through the speakerphone.

'Yes, we are,' Märta says. 'It doesn't matter that I'm a blonde woman, or that my hair is exposed, or anything else, for that matter. I'm the decision-maker. I'm the one they want to meet. And the Finns aren't Scandinavian. They're Nordic, but Finnish is from a completey different language group.'

'Let's just suppose,' Tigger says, 'that you go. You meet. You sit across from one another. You and the killer — the one who just bombed the security forces, and murdered civilians with a rifle to make a quota, and left their bodies to rot. You order tea. It comes. Describe this conversation to me. I'm having trouble imagining it. I'm having trouble imagining any scenario, except for you being thrown into an *oubliette* or worse.'

'I have an idea of how to make the best use of that conversation,' she says.

'What kind of idea?'

'A bold one.'

'What does that mean?' Herb asks.

'Do you remember when we met?' Märta asks him.

'Yes, yes. Chicken Little had it backward — so what?'

'I made Herb open the door by going over his head.'

'I don't see the relevance,' Tigger says.

'I don't think our people are dead,' Märta says. 'I think our people would have been killed right away and left there, like the others, if that was the goal. But it wasn't. So that means they decided to make use of them. I think these people want to gain from that somehow, and right now they're testing the waters to see what use they have. But they need to stay in control. I think the right move is to get close, like they want us to, and then take that control away. When they're off balance, we'll have the advantage, and then we can solve this. At some cost, but we can solve it. That's my strategy.'

'What does this plan have to do with having gone over my head twenty years ago?' Herb asks.

'That's where the boldness comes in.'

32

Märta is emphatic about Herb not coming. She tries to argue against Tigger coming, too, but the men shut her down so completely she knows that her authority ends there.

The security guard, for reasons of his own, breaks from his sleeping regimen and washes the Land Cruiser, leaving the emblem of the IRSG shining brightly. If anyone wants to shoot at it, the rounds will easily penetrate the factory-standard sheetmetal of the Japanese consumer product, and the logo—glittering—will make an excellent target. But, of course, it always has done.

The vehicle is packed up for the seven-hour round-trip journey. Märta oversees the communications equipment, insignia vests, and provisions, while Tigger calls Ahmed in the radio room.

When Tigger calls to report their trip and explain their route, Ahmed tries to be as helpful as possible while nibbling his beloved sour -cream-and-onion potato chips. Hosni, in management, has tried to explain to Ahmed the inappropriateness of a radio operator eating potato chips—which he tried to prove by eating potato chips during the conversation to illustrate the point—but Ahmed likes them, and Hosni isn't around very much, and everyone likes Ahmed because he is both friendly and trying to save their lives.

And because Ahmed cares about the people in his charge, he tries to be as honest and delicate with Tigger as possible. He does this by yelling at him: 'You are a crazy man! There will be a big attack today.

No one knows where, no one knows when. Top of Sinjar Mountains and back is eight hours. That's eight hours on the road in the middle of a battlefield.'

'It's seven hours.'

'Those are seven Iraqi hours. Iraqi hours are different from Western hours. Not all Iraqi hours are the same length. And not all Iraqi hours are consecutive hours. It could take days to go seven hours. You don't want to be out in the field for seven Iraqi hours.'

'I think—' Tigger says.

'No, no, no. I think. I think for you. Here is what I think for you. There is one road up the Sinjar Mountains to your location. You get stuck behind a big truck? What then? You could be on the mountain all day. All night. What if your truck breaks? Flat tyre? You think the tow truck will come get you? What if you come down the mountain too fast and go off the road? Or one of the big trucks is overloaded? They are all overloaded. No brakes, no shock absorbers. What if it takes a turn too widely and can't back up? Or the transmission fails? Or there is an IED. Or ten IEDs? And, by the way, they are not so improvised anymore. People really know what they're doing. They are just EDs. This is what it is to take a drive in Iraq. Why you think people say *inshallah* after everything? You think everyone is a jihadist? You think everyone is even religious? You think everyone is even Muslim? No. Shiite, Sunni, Christian, Jew — everyone says *inshallah*, even if to different gods. You know why? Same road!'

'We need to go.'

'You make me nervous in my stomach, Mr Tiger.'

'Tigger.'

'That's what I said — Mr Tiger.'

'It is pronounced "Tigger."'

'It is not pronounced "tiger"?'

'"Tiger" is pronounced "tiger". But "Tigger" is pronounced "Tigger,"' Tigger says.

'Whoever you are, don't go. Too many of my friends are dead. My soul cannot stand any more sadness. And I have to stop eating so much. This will not help me.'

'Smoking helps.'

'You make jokes, but please, Mr Tigger, today will be a heavy day for many people.'

'We will be careful.'

'And be safe. And Ms Märta. She is very respected. Very loved here. You keep her safe, too.'

'*Inshallah*, Ahmed. *Inshallah*.'

It is a three-hour drive to Sinjar, through Tal Afar, and at least another hour or more up the mountain, which is longer than planned but still early for the meeting. Märta contacts the dentist from the car and tells him to let their interlocutor on the other side know that she's on her way with a driver because she doesn't drive, which is a lie that will have to do. He is to inform his people not to obstruct or otherwise delay the vehicle, which the dentist is to describe carefully.

Beyond that, there isn't much to do, and listening to music is too incongruous.

Tigger communicates with Ahmed in the radio room with the precision of a former military officer. She finds it soothing. Too many young NGO staff scoff at formal systems and procedures, or else giggle, and don't understand the importance of them. She's met young project-officer teams in far-flung locations around the world who haven't even registered their presence in the country with their own embassies, let alone become certified in basic security in the field or advanced security in the field through the UN's free and online training courses.

Not with Tigger and Herb. The giggling ends when you watch someone die who didn't need to if they'd followed procedure. They both have.

Of course, all this faith and respect for procedure is quite rich, given that she's currently breaking every rule in the book by putting the decision-maker in touch with the hostage-takers.

They drive past the Mosul Dam, built by a German-Italian outfit, with its four massive towers rising from the turbine generators. It stands over one hundred metres tall and is the fourth largest in the Middle East. Märta and her NGO have been watching it since 2007, because of a report from the US Army Corps of Engineers concluding that it has an exceptionally high probability of failure. If it breaks—or someone blows it up—it will kill half a million people.

They leave it behind, and drive through Tal Afar. It is different, which is not to say better, with the Americans gone. There has not been a moment of peace here in over a decade, though the level of violence has gone up and down. It all feels dangerous: driving is dangerous; stopping is dangerous. There is no way to know whether the dentist's message will produce the hoped-for effect, or how far ISIL's reach extends. Someone might jump out at any moment and capture her and Tigger, just as they captured Benton and his party. Safe passage will be the result of either careful planning or dumb luck. She'll never really know which it was.

Märta is feeling nervous. She's in control, but she's nervous. She has too much information and knowledge, and too vivid an imagination not to be nervous. There are also not enough distractions. Without something to do, her mind is building highly imaginative scenarios of death and destruction—the kind that never announce themselves, are never predictable, and that happen in a sudden burst or explosion of hyperactivity from out of nowhere, followed by nothing. The kind of events that happen in fits and spurts. That's why more PTSD is being produced by this war than others. The danger is permanent, but it only happens in fits and spurts.

Fits and spurts.

It sounds funny, doesn't it?

Fits and spurts.

She says it aloud. She hasn't spoken in an hour.

'Fits and spurts.'

'What?' Tigger asks.

'It's an American expression. "Fits and spurts." It means something that happens in a sudden or jumpy manner. That's how violence happens here. In fits and spurts. They're funny words, aren't they? Try and say it fast: "fits and spurts". Sounds like a law office for the porn industry. "Good morning, you've reached the law offices of Fits and Spurts, how may I direct your call?"'

'Are you OK?'

'It's funny, right? I'm not losing my mind, am I?'

'I was thinking about something else. Besides, the phrase is "fits and starts," not "spurts". But who am I to judge whether you've lost your mind? I'm right here with you,' Tigger says.

'You were thinking about something else? You weren't thinking about how funny the words "fits" and "spurts" are, and how much funnier they are when you say them together?'

'No.'

'What else is there to think about?'

'You always get like this before something difficult.'

'I'm sorry. It's … after all this time, I still can't believe people act like this.'

'Like I said, you are Swedish. You cannot stop being yourself.'

'I've been gone from Sweden for so long.'

'Doesn't matter. After the age of twenty, we don't change.'

'You believe that?'

'We do not change. We make better choices, perhaps. Get smart. Wiser. More experienced, certainly. But I will always be French. You will always be a Swede. There are worse places to come from. You can see some of them if you look out your window.'

'I think about these orphans. No parents. Refugee camps. What will they become?'

'The answer is in the question,' says Tigger. 'They will be orphans and refugees. It will go into their hearts. It will become what they are. It is a neglected fact that, in thirty years, Iraq and Syria and Afghanistan, and Congo and Somalia, they will all be run by orphans. By people who never knew a real home. They will be the people who will form the governments. One can only imagine such a world, because such a thing has never been.'

'That's a dark answer.'

'I didn't create the answer. It's true, whether I say it or not.'

Märta's giggles have passed, and she becomes nervous again as they leave Tal Afar and make toward Sinjar and then the steep climb up the mountain.

She hates twisty roads. Such uncertainty. Crazies coming the other way. The Iraqis are terrible drivers, whatever the men think of themselves. The Swedes can drive in the pitch-black of a December night on ice, but these people can't follow the lines in the sand. It's as though they have to argue with everything.

At the outskirts of Tal Afar, Tigger radios in their location to Ahmed again. It is a public channel. Ahmed's relief and nervousness are broadcast to the skies and the clouds, and the rocks and the sand.

'You're quiet,' Märta says, lighting a cigarette and opening the window more.

'There's no smoking in the vehicle. It's IRSG policy.'

'There's an exception, subparagraph 2B, which says that when programme managers are meeting with people who cut off other people's heads, they're allowed to light up and use the ashtray for its God-given purpose. Besides, the Geneva Conventions say POWs have a right to cigarettes. I figure that applies to us.'

'We're prisoners of peace. *Pas la même chose.*'

'I can't tell the difference anymore.'

'*Oh là là.* A Scandinavian becomes cynical. A milestone. Perhaps now you are ready to know the truth about Santa Claus?'

'Why are you so quiet?' she asks, blowing the smoke out the window. 'You usually start waxing on about philosophy when you're anxious.'

Tigger does not turn to Märta, and continues to take one steep turn after another without comment or expression. 'I am married with two daughters,' he says. 'When I was young, I wanted a life filled with travel and girls. Now, as fate would have it, I have achieved exactly that. But my needs have changed. What we are doing today is very risky. I think it is too risky, though I do not think it is wrong. What we are doing is too much like heroics. And I don't like heroics. I like systems, and structures, and policies, and procedures. Heroics are not for me.'

'What about Herb? He has a son. He wanted to be here more than you did.'

'Herbert believes that one man can change the world.'

'You don't?'

'Herbert is another kind of creature. He is a righteous man. I am not. His righteousness has a fire. He would prefer justice. He would be the hand of God, if only God would ask. He lives as an example to his son. Me? I want to be a father to my daughters, not an example. I love him like a brother, but I am glad he is not here now.'

Hours earlier, immediately after Tigger and Märta had left, the security guard closed the gate, and Herbert Reston retired to Märta's living room to make a call he didn't want his colleagues to hear.

'Are we ready for this conversation?' Herb asked Clip when he was sure they were alone.

'I'm here,' Clip said.

'Tigger and Märta are gone. So it's like this: this is a stupid plan. I don't have the faith in it they do, and I have no faith in the rationality of the people they're about to meet. I think there's every reason to believe they're walking into a trap. And right now ... we're blind.'

'You want eyes on,' Clip said.

'Damn straight I want eyes on. They vanish up there, they are gone. These terrorists take our people someplace else, they are as good as dead. We are never going to get as lucky as we are right now with accurate GPS coordinates of our people. Arwood Hobbes must have done some pretty fancy footwork to get us those numbers. I don't want to waste the small tactical edge we have right now. Here's my question. With your resources, is there even a scenario where we can get them followed at this late date?'

'We might be able to watch them,' Clip said.

'How?'

'We know some people in Tal Afar. One of them is a blogger, and he's very good. He goes by the name of Yusuf — no other name. He posts updates in Arabic and English about the state of affairs there. I think he's in his late twenties, a rebellious young man with a good heart. We follow his feeds to get updates on the Arab street, and we pay him six thousand dollars a year to help him continue the work. That's a fortune around here. The international media doesn't have the same access, and they don't pay consistent attention like he does. We pay people in about a dozen cities, and Tal Afar is one of our target cities. Usually we just leave Yusuf alone and let him do his thing, but sometimes he'll follow up a question we have to make us happy. He's a bit of a daredevil, and I think we could get him to tail your people.'

'Fine, do it. But it's your idea and not ours. I can't implicate the IRSG in this. Got it?'

'We understand. It would simply be a blogger following a story. There's no connection to you.'

'And this is between us. I know you're close with Tigger, but he can't know.'

'I understand that too,' Clip said.

'How fast can you make this happen?'

'Very fast. We need to move quickly, or there will be a gap period when your team arrives. And that would be suboptimal.'

Herb is silent for a moment. It is deceptively peaceful in Märta's living room, especially when it's empty. It feels like a sanctuary rather than an operations centre. The tranquility of the room is contrary to the moment's urgency and the need for decisiveness, and the distance between his perceptions and his knowledge makes him sit in the thinking chair and pause for a moment.

'Tigger says you were in logistics in the navy.'

'Yes, I was.'

'How'd you get your name?'

'Clip? I used to carry a clipboard around. Sailors can be pretty literal-minded.'

'I was infantry,' Herb says quietly. 'When it came to logistics, we didn't think you guys really understood it. See, from our point of view, if you sailors want six thousand people to move a mile to the east, the captain shouts an instruction, a guy turns a big steering wheel, and six thousand people on an aircraft carrier move a mile to the east. In the army? We've got to mobilise six thousand independent minds, bodies, and souls who have twelve thousand feet among them. And those feet have twelve thousand socks and twelve thousand shoes that have to be found and put on before they can start walking. The navy does not impress me with its logistics. So I need you to take this opportunity to win my confidence about this. Got it?'

33

The longer they ride up the mountain, the more nauseous Märta becomes. The Land Cruiser rides high on the road. It prefers straight lines, dips, and rises. It does not perform well in turns, and its body rolls, turning the trip nautical. Tigger has engaged the optional four-wheel-drive system, and stays in second gear as a compromise in having to choose between speed, power, and torque.

Tigger knows little about the Yezidi who live on Mount Sinjar. All he knows for sure is that they have been there since the time there were gardens hanging here. As he finally rounds the bend at the top and comes into what passes as a village, he is a bit ashamed to wonder what they've been doing all that time, seeing as they don't appear to have made tremendous progress in their standard of living. But, of course, their lives and history are a mystery. Like the Druze, they do not speak to outsiders about themselves. This strategy, unfortunately, has never worked in their favour. Their mysterious ways have only engendered mistrust and hostility.

As they roll slowly into the village, Märta feels as though she is being watched. The ride, at least, is over, and that is good, because the randomness of an accident has passed. Now, at least, comes a deliberate and social risk that can be managed. That is the kind she prefers — the kind where experience, relationships, and judgement have a chance to shape the outcome. Physics and engineering alone — the removal of the human element — that's a nightmare for her.

The village seems abandoned, though she knows it is not. She should have called around and secured an invitation from the village elders. That way, at least, they would be welcomed here. As it is, she is intruding.

And, as intruders, she and Tigger will be viewed with suspicion, which only invites challenges she doesn't need now. It is always best to be invited when entering a dangerous place.

However, there might still be a way to shut that down before the meeting.

'Pull in over there,' Märta says to Tigger, pointing at a small market with fruit outside the door.

'You're going in?'

'I want to introduce myself.'

'The meet is close by. Around the corner,' Tigger says. 'We don't have time for long Arab chitchat sessions.'

'A little respect can go a long way if people haven't made up their minds yet. Go park the car. And Tigger … they aren't Arab.'

Märta opens the door and steps into the warm day. The air is dry. There is a breeze through the hills. The terrain is rocky.

Märta steps into the market, and finds it empty of patrons. There is a man behind the counter. There is a subtle smell of cigarette smoke that grows more intense the deeper she walks into the dark shop. The shelves are half empty. There are canned goods from Lebanon, Egypt, and India. Lazy bags of lentils and rice droop from the edges of wooden shelves.

She greets him in Arabic, and he responds in kind. His voice is flat and weak. She asks if he speaks English, and he shakes his head. She explains, in simple Arabic, who she is.

He nods. She is certain word has travelled here. He knows more than she does at this point, but the most valuable relationships in war zones are among those who share information across party lines. She tried explaining this to the Americans during their civil-military cooperation meetings. They offered money and roads to win hearts and minds, and kept information to themselves. But who needs a road in a year's time, when the danger is now?

'Time,' she had said at the CIMIC meetings, 'does not mean the same thing to you as it does to them. It literally does not work the same way. Until you understand time, you cannot understand any concept of development.'

They said her comments were academic and intellectual, so they ignored her and continued the planning process.

What she says next she has never said in Arabic before, so her grammar is awkward. What she intends to say is, *My people are here. They want to leave. I am meeting those who have them. I will go as soon as I can.*

What he understands her to be saying is anyone's guess.

The man nods. She wishes him peace, and leaves.

When she walks out of the shop, she is back on the only main road through the town, which is a narrow road. The town grows larger and more populated the farther they travel west, but here, at the eastern edge, there is almost nothing. Across from the shop is a steep and rocky outcrop that rises to a higher summit. Built from boulders and stones, it may be the ruins of an ancient civilisation, or the raw material for the next.

There is not a soul on the streets. To her right, she can see the back of the white Land Cruiser. Tigger is standing behind it, opening the glass section of the back and removing their bags. Otherwise, nothing.

She feels, though, more strongly than ever, that she is being watched. The empty hills feel alive. They feel dangerous. Orcs and trolls and other creatures from Middle-earth threaten to spring from their hiding places and descend on her, tearing her limb from limb, and dining on her entrails.

As she starts to walk toward Tigger — who glances up and sees her — she catches a glimpse of a figure in the hills to her left. She is afraid to turn, and yet she does. There, only twenty metres away, stands a man in a hooded cloak. The sunlight illuminates half his face. A living statue, he looks about thirty years old, with dark and brooding eyes. He has no beard. There is a scar that runs down his face from his left eye, all the way to his chin.

Too shocked to speak, she stands still and exposed. The man smiles at her, and steps backward into the rocky wilderness to disappear like dust passing out of a sunbeam.

She stares at the space in which he once stood. He does not reappear.

'Märta?' Tigger calls out.

'What?'

'Ça va?'

'Yeah, I'm fine.'

Märta walks backward, and turns to Tigger when she draws close to him. 'Did you see that man?' she asks.

Tigger looks to where she points. 'No. You think it was our contact?'

'He smiled at me.'

'In that case, I doubt it.'

'He did. I'm sure of it.'

'The shop with the tables is over there,' he says. 'It is time to go.'

The street runs south to north, and the Land Cruiser sits on it like a magnetic needle. The high hills cast a thick shadow over the road, but there is a gap in the rocks above, and that sliver of light makes the café glow in the midst of shadows all around.

Märta and Tigger sit down together on the same side of a small, plastic, rectangular table. There are small squares on the table that feel like plastic, but claim to be napkins. There is a plastic ashtray with slots for four cigarettes. There are three tables in all. A bright-blue door opens into a black and unlit room of an adjoining concrete building. Thus far, no one has come out of it.

Tigger radios in their location to Ahmed. He deliberately turns the volume up so the crackle and hiss of the handset unmistakably echoes and travels down the street. He shares his call signs and Märta's. He notes their arrival time at this new site — now dubbed Romeo 5 — that Ahmed has added to the maps. No one from the UN ever comes here. No NGOs have passed through here, according to the records. It is *terra incognita*.

'We didn't set a time,' Märta says. 'How will they know we're here?'

'They already know.'

'I suppose you're right.'

'Maybe you should make sure your phone works. Phones are all different. What's true for one—'

'I have a damn signal, Tigger, OK?'

'I'm sorry.' He reaches into his bag to remove a cigarette, but thinks better of it, so returns the pack. 'There really is nothing to do now but sit here and hope we don't get shot. Should we do that in silence, or would you like to chat?'

'Herb would have said something reassuring,' Märta says.

'I suspect that's true.'

That is when they hear the first helicopters. They are distant. There are several of them, from the sound of the rotors, but their sound is impossible to track in the rock and concrete surrounding them. Wherever they are going, they will be carrying ordnance and orders.

A man steps out of the dark doorway of the market in a dirty robe that hangs to his feet. He wears a blue Western-style blazer that is fitted for a stranger. He does not look at his two patrons. Without acknowledging them, he unfurls the awning so it extends well beyond the three tables and blocks them from the view of whoever might pass or linger above. He walks to their table, and wordlessly takes a wet and filthy rag from his pocket and rubs it across the surface of the table, leaving a grey streak of droplets behind that immediately evaporate into the hot day, leaving the table identical to the way he found it. He then leaves.

Tigger, ignoring the man, has turned his closed eyes to the sun, and washes his face in the light. Märta envies how much it refreshes him.

The man returns to them with tea for three. He retreats into the building quickly, and closes the blue sheet-metal door behind him.

'Three cups. Here we go,' Tigger says.

Tigger folds his fingers together. He has walked into many different conversations and spoken to many hostile leaders—youth leaders, elders, tribesmen, angry military staff. Like stage fright, it can be managed. This feels untamed, though. Colder.

'I'm having some tea. You want some?' he says to Märta.

'It's a diuretic. It makes no sense to drink tea in this circumstance.'

'It's calming. And it is a diuretic only if you consume three hundred milligrams of caffeine in the same sitting. An average cup has fifty milligrams. That means it produces a diuretic effect only if you drink six cups. Personally, I think it's the six cups of water doing it, not the caffeine, but I am no doctor.'

They come—three men, two of them armed with eastern-bloc assault rifles that Russia has been pumping into the region since 1955. The third one carries no weapon. They approach from the main road, and walk toward them with the sun at their backs.

'Game on,' Tigger says, sipping his tea.

And then, behind those three men, come three others. Two of them, with weapons, are pulling along a third man in the middle. His head is covered in a black hood. There is a halo of sunlight behind him, turning the hood blacker.

The unarmed leader takes the seat across from Märta and Tigger. His eyes are set. Märta senses that what passes before those eyes will not affect their vision of the world.

Märta pours tea into the man's cup. He does not pick it up.

The leader is the first one to speak.

'You know this man?'

One of the hostage-takers yanks the hood from the captive's head. He is a young man in his twenties, has a ponytail, and is clean shaven. He has been badly beaten. His stylish clothes are dirty.

Tigger and Märta look carefully at him, and turn to each other. Neither has seen him before.

'I came here for four people,' Märta says. 'Three men and a girl. This man makes me think you don't have my people, and that we should leave. You obviously have other business.'

Märta makes to stand, and Tigger stands as well, without saying a word.

The man across from them raises a hand and signals them to sit. Then he nods to one of his men, who withdraws an automatic pistol and places it against the man's temple. The captive's shoulders rise and he whimpers, but he says nothing.

'So if I kill him, it means nothing to you?' the man says. 'He says he is a journalist. Writes stories for the Internet. You say he is not with you?'

'It means everything to me if you kill him,' Märta says. 'Our work is committed to saving human lives. All lives. The purpose of this conversation is for me to recover my people. If your first move in this conversation is to insult us, to harm someone else, and change the purpose of our meeting, then nothing will be able to continue. I'm not here to be intimidated. I'm here to talk. And since he is not one of my people, I'd like some proof you have them. I assume you have their names. At least give me those so we can proceed.'

The leader nods to the man with the pistol. Immediately, the man shoots his captive in the temple. Blood arcs from the wound, and he is dead before the sound of the gun reaches his ear.

His limp body is collected by his executioners and dragged back the way they came.

Märta's heart races, but she does not stand and does not move. Though her voice is weak, she says, 'Do you have what I want, or don't you?'

'They aren't here.'

'You could have anyone. I don't know you.'

He nods. He reaches into his pocket and withdraws a piece of white paper taken from the pages of a child's school notebook. He reads the names aloud.

'Adar al-Kaysi. Jamal al-Khedairy. Ferris Bueller. And'— he checks his note again — 'Inigo Montoya.'

Tigger shakes his head.

'These are not your people?' the man asks.

'Those are our people,' Tigger says.

34

When Arwood was stuck in the cell with Benton, he'd wondered what was behind the inner door, if only because, after so many years of game shows, he had no choice but to wonder what was behind curtain number two.

It turned out that when they finally dragged him through that door, there was nothing behind the proverbial curtain, because it led first into a small antechamber or guardroom, and then outside to a courtyard that could once have garrisoned a company of men and their horses. Outside, in that courtyard, Larry shot into the air as a signal or warning — a message in a language Arwood did not speak. Maybe it was a signal to someone. Maybe it was to make Benton think Arwood had been killed.

'I'm not sure there's been anyone to tell you guys, as you live in kind of a closed-off world that only reads its own press,' Arwood says as he is pulled across the courtyard, 'so just in case you don't know this, you are in fact a bunch of complete fucking arseholes.'

What this journey behind the curtain has taught him is that the room where he was kept with Benton is but one corner of an old military fortification. Of the four square towers, only his holding cell and the one directly across from it look intact. The others were bombed out and ruined long ago. Connecting these four corners are castle walls. Arwood looks up as he walks, and views the mountains to the west. Ahead of him is only the wall. Beyond that is a clear view north into the plains in Ninawa that he cannot see.

Long ago, this fortification provided a high-terrain advantage
— an Arab Masada. Later, when man took to the skies to kill from
above, and war was fought from the wings of eagles, the advantage
was lost.

As Arwood walks, he imagines the view of this fortress from
inside the cockpit of an A-10 Thunderbolt—a plane that many
call ugly, but one that Arwood has found stunningly beautiful since
he was a boy. He made one with his uncle. He studied the specs.
What might it be like to hear the 1,100 rounds of 11-inch-long
30mm tank-killer bullets ripping into these walls at four thousand
rounds a minute? He smiles at his captors as he imagines those aerial
gunfighters lingering over the fortress, giving close air support to
onrushing infantry—flying low and slow, distinguishing friend from
foe, getting their chins into the fight, and blowing these people to
hell.

Inside the next room, he is tossed onto the floor. Half an hour
later, Abu Larry comes in for a chat: he wants to know Arwood's name
and who he works for. Arwood explains that he is on assignment
for *Wallpaper Magazine* to write an exposé on the interior design of
terrorist holding cells.

'And I've got to say,' Arwood adds, 'I love what you've done with
the place.'

Abu Larry shoots him in the leg.

The bullet rips through his quadriceps. Arwood is then uncuffed,
and allowed to tend to the wound. He is left alone, and there he sits
for hours, thirsty beyond belief. Later, in the blackness of that night,
the door opens, and Adar is pushed at him.

He rushes to her as best he can, and holds her face in his hands.
She starts to cry when she sees him. He turns her head, and examines
her scalp, neck, and shoulders. Though it is against every local code
of behaviour, he turns her around and lifts up her garments, to reveal
her bruised but unpunctured back and then belly. She does not resist

him. When he is convinced she isn't injured or bleeding, he again sits on the floor, and rests his body against the wall.

She sits by him, as she did on the Ural.

'I'm sorry about this,' he says.

Adar does not speak.

'Did they touch you?'

Adar still does not speak.

Later, they toss in Jamal, too. He has the same gunshot wound as Arwood.

'You OK?' Arwood asks.

'Of course I am not OK. They shot me.'

'Have you seen Benton?' Arwood asks.

'No.'

Jamal explains that they gave him Adar's dress to stop the bleeding of his wounds. They had told him that his companions were dead. Jamal said he was happy to see them, but he does not look happy.

'Did they ask you any questions?' Arwood asks.

'My name. Who I worked for. If I was sent to spy on them.'

'Uh-huh,' Arwood says.

'Do you think they are going to kill us, Mr Arwood?' Jamal asks.

'I think that whatever is about to happen is going to happen soon.'

He calls himself Abu Saleh. He talks at Märta and Tigger for twenty minutes about the imperialist West, about the treatment of the Palestinians, about the will of God, about the suffering of his people, about the meaning of jihad, about how Muslims must live by the word of the Koran, and how no power on earth will ever stop that from happening again, and how Märta and Tigger are now his hostages.

He explains how ISIL in Syria has new needs that separate it from al-Qaeda in Afghanistan and Pakistan. He says there will be a caliphate again. And the West will shudder.

Märta has never seen a man shot before. She does not know whether Tigger has, but she is glad he is the one to talk. 'Time is wasting,' Tigger says, sounding unimpressed and uninterested. 'I suggest you tell us what you want, because we have a call scheduled at eight-thirty. And if we do not make that call at eight-thirty, then this conversation is over, and there will be consequences for everyone involved.'

'You will give me your telephones now.'

Tigger, conscious of the time now and the window that is about to close on their chances, looks at Märta and tells her to place the call.

Abu Saleh raises his hand to signal his men to come.

Märta dials.

Tigger looks up, expecting to see two assault rifles in his face, but is surprised to see only the calm street.

The two henchmen are no longer at their posts. They no longer seem to be anywhere.

Abu Saleh looks at Tigger, and registers the look of confusion. He turns to look for his men, and finds them gone.

He shouts in Arabic for them to come.

Märta has dialled, and the phone rings.

'Put it on the speaker and turn up the volume,' Tigger says.

Abu Saleh, irritated for the first time with his new loss of control, shouts again for his men.

'No one's answering,' Märta says.

'There is no Plan B,' Tigger says.

It is 8.32 a.m.

Yelling something in Arabic, Abu Saleh, certain his men are not coming, bursts to his feet and yanks a hidden pistol from his belt, and makes the mistake of leaning across the table to place the barrel of his gun against Märta's heart.

Tigger is no longer in the military. When he was, he served in intelligence. He had no interest in joining the special forces, no compulsion to prove his manhood through brute force and sustained discomfort, and he did not believe that most conflicts could be solved by violence. He was a thinking soldier, and liked reasoning his way to victory.

Abu Saleh, sensing that Tigger is a man of talk, has made the error of equating that with weakness.

Abu Saleh is a tall man. Like Osama bin Laden was, he is spindly — not unlike Tigger himself. So when his Webley is extended across the table, and the edge of that table meets Saleh's legs at mid-thigh, Tigger has little trouble using his own left hand to grab Saleh's gun wrist and — rather than pushing against him — twist the man's body, using inertia to pull him over the tabletop and flat onto his stomach, in a motion as smooth as dance.

With Abu Saleh prone, Tigger immediately twists his wrist to the breaking point while tucking Saleh's arm into the pit of his own. With Saleh's elbow and wrist painfully locked, and the weapon pointing harmlessly into the distance, Tigger bends his hand back until the gun comes loose.

Holding it in his right hand, he presses the barrel of the pistol into Abu Saleh's temple without changing his own body position.

'Oh, this is just swell,' Märta says.

'How's that call coming?'

'He hasn't answered yet. When I said earlier I wanted them off-balance, this isn't what I had in mind.'

'Well, this is all very awkward for everyone,' Tigger says.

'Who are you?' Abu Saleh asks.

'Believe it or not,' Tigger says, 'we really are who we say we are. Only, we are not feeling ourselves today, because you have made us very nervous.'

Märta holds up her finger to silence them. The call is connecting.

She says, 'Yes.' There is silence while the voice on the phone speaks. 'His name is Abu Saleh,' Märta says next. 'You know him?' Märta nods to Tigger. 'You'll do this?' she asks the voice on the phone.

Moving the phone away from her ear, she presses the speaker button and places it on the centre of the table beside Abu Saleh's undignified and prone body.

'It's for you,' she says.

35

Herbert Reston was born at the back-end of the 1960s, making him old enough to feel that, somewhere along the line, science had promised him a jetpack.

His would be silver and would look like dual scuba tanks. It would have a bright-red button on the grip, and it would be on his back with thick leather straps right now, allowing even a big man like himself to lift off from Märta's upstairs balcony and scare the crows from the sky as he jetted toward Louise's subdelegation office. He would use the red tail-lights on the highway below to direct his flight path.

But he isn't in the air like an Avenger. Instead, he's stuck in traffic. And if that isn't bad enough, he's had to listen to Clip Maxwell apologise. Because his blogger is out of contact, and they fear the worst.

'So you have nothing useful to tell me,' Herb says, calculating the time to the office with traffic, and hating the results.

'The Iraqi air force,' Clip says, 'is going to start a ground assault on ISIL positions and weapons depots at nine o'clock tonight. That is in ... about fifteen minutes.'

'You know this how?' Herb asks.

'We paid for it from someone inside the ministry. There's no way to get them back here tonight, assuming they can even come. I'm sorry.'

'We need a helicopter,' Herb says.

'The area's too hot, Herb. No one would be crazy enough to even think about taking off. No one can get to the mountain in this sort of maelstrom. I know six private security companies in Iraq, all with lift, and they're all grounding their people during this. Everyone's grounded until the assault is over. It would be madness to fly in Ninawa today. Everyone is sitting this one out.'

'Not everyone,' Herb says, and hangs up.

He honks the horn.

Horns honk back.

When his phone rings again, he answers it, hoping it is Märta or Tigger. But it is, instead, Farrah, Louise's assistant.

'Mr Herbert, I have Louise here for you. You were trying to reach her?'

'How are you hanging in there, Farrah?'

For the first time since he's known her, he hears a faint tremble in her throat as she speaks.

'It is very hard for us, Mr Herbert. Our families—' She does not finish whatever she was planning to say.

'It's not over, Farrah. There's hope yet.'

'I don't know, Mr Herbert. We thought that maybe Iraq could be a democracy. The national staff here … with the NGOs. What's wrong with us? Why can we not find peace among ourselves? Why do we always fail?'

'There's nothing wrong with you, Farrah.'

'Maybe we are being punished.'

'You're not.'

'We are so very tired, Mr Herbert. It feels like the world is caving in around us, and no one will dig us out or know we were ever here.'

'Farrah, let me just say this. Iraq has been here since the dawn of history. And things are bad. And you're right, they're gonna be bad for a long time. But someday people will need to look back and know there have always been people like you trying to fight the good fight and in the right way. I learned that from my civil rights movement.

Yours is the real jihad, Farrah. So keep struggling, keep your faith, and, if you can, keep your sense of humor.'

Herb cannot know what Farrah is thinking or doing in the silence that follows. She is too composed. He does not, however, interrupt her. When she does speak, she says, 'It was nice talking with you, Mr Herbert. I'll pass you over to Louise now.'

He hears a click, followed by Louise's voice.

'What's happening?' she asks directly.

'I don't know,' Herb says. 'It's eight-forty in the morning. I should be getting a call, and no one's calling. No messages—nothing. I can't reach Tigger. I can't reach Märta.'

'Tigger probably has his hands full,' Louise says, 'and it's likely that Märta is still on the phone. Do you have any reason to think something might have gone wrong?'

The traffic moves. Unconcerned with obeying protocol any longer, he angles his 4×4 onto the shoulder of the road, forcing half his vehicle into the desert itself. It is bumpy at fifty kilometres an hour. Still, it is faster than before.

'I don't know anything,' Herb says, not mentioning the missing blogger. 'Either way, we need to prep the helicopter, and we should prepare to pick them up.'

'We've heard rumours of a possible offensive today,' Louise says. 'If it's true, there will be mass casualties. I need that helicopter for non-combatants.'

She knows this will irritate Herb, but there are reasons that the ICRC is here. She wants to be helpful, but the rules were explained to Märta in clear terms, and Louise will not rush in where there is no agreement between the parties. 'We're not a hostage-rescue outfit, Herb. I will make AirOps available to you, but only once you've secured an agreement and we can contact the different parties. And I hate to ask the obvious, but if they drove there, why not drive back?'

'There's no time,' he says.

'Why not?'

'Because it's not a rumour. The military is going to start striking targets in twenty minutes. And seeing as ISIL is entrenching in Kurdistan to solidify their positions in Syria, I strongly suspect that they are going to hide in highly populated civilian areas to neutralise government air superiority. And there is no route back that doesn't pass through a city. Which means Tal Afar, at the very least. That town is cursed.'

'What if they sheltered in place?'

'In a terrorist holding cell, among devil worshippers?'

'It's not ideal, I admit,' Louise says, 'but it might be better than being on the open road. And I don't think they're devil worshippers. I think people keep calling them that because it's fun to say—'

'Louise,' he interrupts, 'I understand you have your policies and your laws and your rules, and I like policies and laws and rules, but please be prepared to get off the ground the second that confirmation comes through. Promise me that?'

'If they left at five in the morning for a run that takes eight hours, and you knew there'd be an assault, it sounds like you deliberately put me in an impossible situation, Herb.'

'We didn't know about the offensive until after we'd made contact. It's all unfolding, Louise. All I can do is try and get my people out safely. That is my job.'

'I'll have it fuelled,' says Louise unenthusiastically, 'and I'll make sure Spaz is ready. I'll even bend the rules and let you fly along, but only because we have a signed memorandum of understanding with the IRSG, not because it's a special favour. You give me confirmation, and you can go get them. But do not put the International Committee of the Red Cross in a political pinch, Herb. I don't want us kicked out of Iraq.'

'I don't know what kind of condition they'll all be in.'

'The helicopter has a team. I have a woman who's a top-notch emergency medic from Colombia. Go make the deal, Herb. Until then, there's nothing we can do.'

Benton can hear his captors talking outside the door, but he does not understand what they are saying. They are arguing. The argument sounds heated, but it is hard to tell with Arabs. He has found it too easy to misunderstand them in the past. He was in a minor car accident in Cairo off Tahrir Square in a taxi once. They pulled over, and he thought the other driver was going to murder his own. 'No, no,' explained the taxi driver after their altercation ended and both had pulled away. 'He was being honest with me. He was sharing his emotions. It was OK. It was respectful. You cannot trust people who do not share their emotions.'

More voices are added to the drama beyond the door. All the voices are male. Some mumble; others shout.

On his back, gripping his wound, he gazes at the yellow sea of light spread over the ceiling by the slats on the wall. It is the same mustard-yellow light that comes to his bedroom in Fowey through the window that faces south toward the English Channel and northern France.

The door opens. It is Abu Moe, who sat behind him in the Land Cruiser on the way here. For no helpful reason, he delivers a half-hearted kick to Benton's foot, and the pain from the gunshot is renewed.

'We go,' says the man, with the diction of a Neanderthal. Knowing what is next, Benton is not quite ready to go.

'My grandfather,' Benton says for no good reason, 'died at the battle of the Canal du Nord, 28 September 1918, springing out of a trench to charge a machine gun. Part of the Hundred Days' Offensive, they called it. Thirty thousand dead in that battle. You bastards think the West doesn't have the resolve to outlast you? Only one utterly ignorant of history could think that. You know nothing about us.

You think we're soft? If anything, we're too hard,' he says, his face barely off the mattress, his hands locked around his wound, trying to keep the bleeding under control. 'And the reason you're ignorant is that you don't translate books. You starve your own minds. That's why you're eating yourselves alive.'

Thomas Benton is pulled up and pushed out of the same door that Adar, Jamal, and Arwood were all led through earlier. Beyond that door is a second and smaller room, and then he is led outside into a wide-open courtyard of some kind. The sunlight is a poison, and his chest constricts. He is drowning in the light. Even the dry air gives no quarter. Like thousands before him, to be sure, Benton knows he is being brought to his execution.

It feels medieval here, but the structure must be more recent than that. They're too far east, and the architecture is wrong. Byzantine? Ottoman maybe? Not British, anyway. Not recent enough for that.

Benton raises his eyes and looks at the fortress: one empire washing over another, taking over what it's abandoned, repeating its errors, learning nothing.

Fort Sinister.

He is pushed onto the ground, and blood flows again from his nose: proof there's even more to lose.

Instinctively, he curls into a foetal position, like an animal waiting for recovery or death. Neither comes quickly, though, and he is instead pulled to his feet by another man and punched in the kidney.

Benton vomits. He is sixty-three years old. He is overweight. He is without strength or will or water.

There is the door — the one that leads inside the approaching tower. It will be a dark place. He will be placed on a chair. A machete will be placed against the back of his neck. His captors will spout politico-religious garbage, and then they will hack his head off. He will not die on the first stroke. He knows. He has seen it before.

That soldier as beautiful as a Greek statue — was he a sniper who had shot pregnant women? Or was he only a twenty-two-year-old boy of the most gentle disposition, scared and sad and lonely? He, too, was blindfolded. He, too, had only been in a world of sound and feeling.

They hacked him to death. He screamed while he could. He died in terrible pain, to the sounds of others' joy. It was the worst kind of death. Benton watched it all. There was no stopping it.

He wrote a report. It was edited down. It wasn't really *new* anymore, his editor said, so it wasn't really *news*, was it?

The surge of fear reawakens him. 'No!' he yells, and tries to resist. He tries to pull back and not go through the door. This isn't what it was like in the car with the hood on his head. They weren't going to shoot him in the car, but they will kill him here. And his companions have been shot. He is the last one left alive, and it makes sense. A journalist for a Western newspaper, a British newspaper, he has the highest status of the four of them. They will kill him slowest. He — not any of the others — is a political trophy. It is his head that will be hacked from his body and placed on a stick.

If he is lucky, they will shoot him right now. In the chest. He'll know he's been shot; the bullet will enter through the front of his chest, and his eyes will see the flash. Maybe his body will register the pain, so there will be time to acknowledge the end.

That is the best death he can hope for now, the one he wants. There is nothing else to want.

'I'm not going in there! Outside. Right here! I want to die here!'

But in he goes. There is no resisting it — in through the outer door into a room much like the antechamber he left moments ago, and toward another steel door. This one is opened by two Stooges with rifles, who take him from the first guards and chuck him inside the room where they'll kill him soon.

Benton's fails to notice the step leading down, and, missing it, falls forward. He thrusts out his hands to cushion the fall, but he is weak, and his arms fail him.

On his chest, cloaked in the last light he'll know, he stares into the dirt.

That is when he feels hands touching him. He is powerless against them. There is no protest left to lodge.

The sounds that come from above, however, are not guttural and foreign. They are familiar and soft.

He has heard those sounds before.

'Thomas Reginald Benton,' a voice says. 'Open your eyes.'

Benton turns his head and rests his cheek in the dust. The face of Arwood Hobbes is smiling warmly at him. It is the smile Arwood gave to the boy in the minefield. It is the smile he gave to Adar in the truck. It is the smile he gave to the girl in the green dress who died in his arms. And it is only now that Benton understands why they responded to Arwood as they did, because that is precisely how he feels now.

'Arwood.'

'Hey, buddy,' he says. 'You look like you could use some good news.'

Benton turns his eyes in the direction that Arwood's pointing. There are two figures there—both Arab. One of them is still very much a child; the other, a young man with an injured leg.

'They're alive, too?'

'Like I said, we're the luckiest.'

36

The man on the other end of Märta's phone is one of the worst people she has ever had the misfortune of dealing with. He is cut from the same cloth as the man Tigger is threatening with a pistol. He is the man Märta saved on the Syrian border yesterday morning.

He is a character assembled from the stuff of human misery — Abu Malik al-Almani. At the border, he had been shot in the gut after he and his group killed one hundred women in front of their families for dressing inappropriately. He was suffering a bleed from his femoral artery. How his men got him to the unit before he bled out was some kind of satanic miracle. His people had occupied a Syrian town near al-Maabadah after their murder spree, and were rounding up more women and starting public executions when the Kurds, on the outskirts of the city, started giving them hell.

The Kurds were no longer respecting international borders, and they considered the invasion of ISIL into Kurdistan to be a threat to their autonomy. Abu Malik joined his forces for a counteroffensive and, one way or another, was wounded. As the Syrian government was assassinating doctors and nurses who helped the people he was trying to kill, Abu Malik's only chance was to make the journey through Kurdish-held land, past the border, and into Märta's tent. Which is what he did.

On the stretcher, before the surgery, he reached up and held her shirt in his bloody hand.

'You know who I am?'

'Yes, I do,' she said.

'And you will still help me?'

'I've taken an oath,' she said.

'To help me is to help my cause. You are with us?'

'To help any person is to ensure that all people will be helped. That is my cause,' she had said. And — unlike now — she was not scared. Because then, at least, she knew what she was doing and was prepared for it, and she knew it was right. Helping him was not in itself a good thing; obviously, poisoning him on the table would have been the right thing to do. But it was right, because after he was patched up he allowed her team access to the refugees. Whether, in doing this, she would be helping more people live in the long run, or whether she was instead killing even more people by having saved this mass murderer, she could not know. Sleeping with Benton last night had been a helpful, if temporary, way to stop asking herself these questions.

All she could do to make it worthwhile was approach him after the surgery. 'I need something,' she had said to him. 'We need access to people on land you control. That means I need to be in contact with those who can grant it. I want your phone number.'

'So the Americans can send a drone after me? Send a Tomahawk missile to my encampment? I don't think so.'

'Something, then. An email address. A solution.'

So he left her something. Someone else's number. And this morning she called it and made an appointment to speak to him personally at 8.30 a.m. It was, as she said, a bold move.

Abu Malik speaks in a low and quiet voice through the speakerphone as Abu Saleh listens. Once Abu Saleh realises who it is on the phone, he shrugs Tigger off his arm and sits down. A pistol trained on his heart, he lifts the tea and sips it as Abu Malik speaks.

Märta's Arabic is not good enough to understand the details of what is being said, but she can follow the sequence of topics. A word here, a word there. She connects the dots.

Abu Malik greets his comrade, who evidently knows who he is. Then he speaks about Märta. And jihad. And Iraq and Syria. He speaks of the umma and the community of Muslims. He speaks of *dar al-Islam* and *dar al-Harb*, the realms of submission, and of war.

As Abu Malik speaks, and lectures, Tigger realises he has no idea what is happening, his attention isn't required, and that it would be a good time to check in with Herb.

He hands his own phone to Märta and asks her to dial and press it to his ear. He is not an amateur, and is not going to take his eyes off his mark.

The phone rings only twice, and Herb answers it. 'Where the hell have you been?'

'It has been a busy day at the office,' Tigger says, aiming the Webley at Saleh.

Märta watches Tigger's expression grow grave as he listens to Herb. He glances once at her, and she knows their plans have changed even further. And yet he says nothing, because it is information Tigger does not want Abu Saleh to know.

'I'm done,' Tigger says to her. She takes the phone away.

Soon, Abu Malik is done, too. He stops talking, and, as befits custom, it is Abu Saleh's turn to speak. He greets Abu Malik in the traditional way, but after uttering abbreviated pleasantries, his tone turns argumentative and insulting. Märta hears him talk about power and money and corruption. He mentions Abu Musab al-Zarqawi. He talks about Tal Afar. He talks about al-Qaeda, and spits on the ground. He, too, talks about the caliphate. He rages.

Tigger, for no reason she can understand, smells the Webley. She has never seen him hold a gun before. She has never imagined him capable of harming someone. Now she is certain he can, and that he absolutely will if called upon.

When Abu Saleh has finished, Abu Malik speaks again. When he does, it is in English, so Märta can understand. He sounds tired, as though talking to such people has worn him down over the years. Inter-terrorist politics, Märta concedes, must be exhausting.

'You are going to release them,' he says in a quiet voice. 'And if you do not, Abu Saleh, I will raze your home village in Tunis and kill your children, who attend not a madrassa, but the British International School on rue du Parc. I know your wife's favourite flower is the lily. I will kill not only them, but all your extended family, so that your line does not continue. I am tired of disobedience. I am healing from a bullet wound, and my energy is elsewhere. If I learn by sundown tonight that you have not done as I say, your family will die. And if you call them to warn them, and my people see their routine change, they will die. And when I find you myself, I will strap a bomb to you and use you in my war. These people you have captured, Saleh, are not our enemy. Even our correct reading of the Koran does not direct us to jihad against everyone. And if you are such a fool that you cannot understand this, then I will think for you. Ms Märta? You and your people will be released. What happens to these people after you go is no concern of mine. They are petty thieves and not Muslims. Can you hear me?'

'I hear you.'

'Peace be unto you.'

Then, in a small mercy, he does not wait for Märta to say the same, and instead hangs up.

'I suggest,' Tigger says to Abu Saleh, who has been left holding the phone at the other end of the line, 'you accept that we have an agreement, and that we now go to collect my people before you start thinking better of the idea. It is also very clear to me now that if I kill you, with your own gun, no one will avenge you. So call your men on this phone and let them know we're coming. I prefer to show up invited.'

37

Charlotte slept after her walk with Miguel, and woke early, determined to see her mother. It is a three-hour drive from Bristol to Fowey on the M5. Charlotte drove it with a bag of yogurt-covered peanuts between her legs until the peanuts were gone. She has always liked to split the yogurt with her molars and break it off from the peanut evenly to save the crunch for last. It is more than a preference; it is a skilled compulsion.

Thirty minutes from Fowey now, she calls her mother from the road, with the Saab in overdrive.

Vanessa answers and says she is in a teahouse down by the water. She is reading a book. She is marking it with pens and pencils and highlighters. 'I don't know why everyone is so respectful of books,' she says to Charlotte. 'They are meant to be engaged with, not preserved. There's a woman,' she whispers, 'looking at me from across the room as I mark up the novel. I wonder if she thinks I'm a critic. Every so often, I shudder and make a disapproving face. I think she's a tourist.'

'I can't reach Dad,' Charlotte says.

'Your father has been unreachable for ages. That's how all this started.'

'No. I mean, he's in Iraq. He's properly missing. I'll be with you by nine or so. That's eleven in the morning in Baghdad. I've been speaking with someone at a refugee camp in the north. His name is Miguel. He's helping me find Dad.'

'What's he doing there?'

'There's a girl who is missing. He went to find her.'

'What on earth for?'

'It's a long story. I only have a guess at it.'

'Is this why you're driving all the way down here?'

'I'm driving down because he's missing and I want to be with you when we place the next call, because we are in fact a family.'

'Maybe I want him missing,' her mother says.

It is starting to rain. A slick sheet of oil floats over the new and fresh water reflecting the red taillights that glimmer before Charlotte under an iron sky.

'Just be home, OK? I'm to check in with Miguel when I get there. Hopefully, there will be news by then. He's making a lot of time for me, considering how busy his own job is.'

'Drive safely.'

'Is it raining there?' Charlotte asks.

'Yes,' Vanessa says. 'It is beginning to.'

Spaz does not smoke. He does not chew gum. He does not smile. He seldom speaks. What he does is fly helicopters. He is of medium build, medium height, and speaks English with an unapologetic Russian accent he has no interest in improving. He does not allow music in the aircraft. He prefers the sound of the wind, the whirr of the rotors, and the opportunity to explore the airspace around him.

He is conducting the pre-flight check. He is meticulous from habit. Beside him is a small, dark-haired woman with exquisite skin. They don't talk to each other.

The helicopter pad is little more than paint on dirt at the edge of the refugee camp. It is surrounded by a thin fence to fend off the curious: usually children who seem attracted by nature to anything that spins.

Louise, his boss, walks out to meet him. Following her is a large black man in blue trousers and a T-shirt white enough for an imam.

'Good morning,' she says.

'OK.'

'You are going to be sharing airspace today with the Iraqi air force and probably a lot of bullets and missiles. Also an American named Herb Reston.'

Spaz looks at Herb. He can tell that Herb was once military from the way he stands.

'OK,' he says again.

'Where did you learn to fly?' Herb asks Spaz as he opens the door and climbs inside the EC155.

'Chechnya,' Spaz says, handing the completed paperwork to Louise and opening the cockpit door.

'Repenting?' Herb asks, climbing in.

'Depressed economy,' he answers. Turning to Louise, he asks, 'We have a flight plan?'

'No.'

'When does shooting start?' he asks, about to put on his headset.

'It's started,' Louise says, ducking her head as the rotors spin up. 'I have to go—my hair can't take this. Herb Reston, meet Elise Garcia,' she says, nodding to the woman in the medical vest. 'She's a former combat medic from the Colombian army. She's been on the frontline against FARC. Whatever might come into the back here, she'll deal with.'

'If you don't secure us a flight path, we'll be shot down by everyone,' Herb yells to her as the rotors reach full speed.

'That's right,' she says, as she turns away and jogs off the helipad toward her Land Rover Defender.

Louise starts the diesel engine and radios back to Farrah at her desk as she watches the helicopter prepare to depart.

'Farrah, can you hear me?'

'I'm here, Ms Louise.'

'Get me flight-safety assurances. It's all on you and the national staff now. I won't be back in time. It's begun.'

Farrah takes tea in the morning. She brings it in a thermos from home, because people from outside Iraq, though they try, don't understand the making of a proper cup of tea. Hers is perfectly sweetened and, so as not to insult her employers, she drinks it when alone, and leaves two fine glasses in her drawer for the purpose.

Farrah rises from her desk, thermos in hand, and removes one of the small glasses from the top drawer of her steel desk. She is fastidious; Ms Louise has teased her about this quality by deliberately rearranging objects in those drawers in the most incongruous ways.

She enjoys working with Ms Louise. She finds her boss sociable and kind, and she knows that Louise respects her team and trusts them. This has not always been the case with foreign managers. Some people — usually men — treat her and the other local staff as though they have not been working this job longer than they themselves have. They ask no questions, and so grow no smarter. They leave in two years, and tell war stories about 'the field', and become promoted for the jobs they had, not the jobs they did. For Farrah and her colleagues, this is not 'the field'. This is home. The jobs they do are all that matters.

Farrah wants to make Louise proud. She wants to make her own family proud. She discussed her job only months ago with her father and her imam. They entertained long discussions about humanitarian action in light of the fatwa issued by Tahir-ul-Qadri condemning suicide, suicide bombing, terrorism, and violence — six hundred pages of legal interpretation and analysis shared throughout the Muslim community. Her father and her imam agreed that her work is indeed Allah's work, and that her concern for others is the correct performance of God's will. 'It is actually quite simple,' said her imam. 'The Prophet, peace be unto him, clearly said that, "none of you believes until he wants for his brother what he would want for himself."'

Farrah has always backed away from praise, and insisted there was nothing divine in her efforts. Surely kindness and decency were too simple and obvious to be the product of the One who made the entire universe.

Her father shrugged when she said this. He would be proud of her either way, he explained, whether the will was hers or Allah's.

Her imam, meanwhile, raised his eyebrows in surprise at her declaration of modesty and her theological analysis, and she laughed at him.

'You always raise your eyebrows in wonder,' Farrah said.

'It is true,' said her father, 'that they go up. But is it his own will, or does Allah pull them up from above?' And they all laughed.

Her father makes excellent tea. He taught her how to make her own. She still leaves a glass for him in her drawer to remember him.

For now, though, time is pressing, and there is work to be done.

She walks past Louise's empty office, past the broken colour printer no one knows how to fix, past the poor excuse for a coffee maker that the Europeans and Americans use, and into a room with six cubicles. There are four men and two women, all Iraqis like herself, and from different backgrounds—Shiite, Sunni, Kurd, Assyrian Christian, Marsh Arab, Turkoman. They look up when she comes in. She bids them a good morning, in Arabic, and they mumble the same in response. They are tense. They know what is happening.

'We have an emergency flight from here to the Sinjar Mountains,' she says to them in a voice soft enough for poetry. 'I am placing the coordinates on the board.' She walks to the whiteboard and raises a green marker to write down the numbers. 'It is a helicopter flight with a ceiling of eight hundred metres, and therefore subject to small-arms fire. We therefore need flight-safety assurances from all parties. Muhammad, you liaise with the government and military. Alim, you have the Kurds. Atef, you have the Sunni tribes and, through them, those who do not yet speak to us. Abdullah, you have the Shiites near Tal Afar. Akeem, please talk to the police in Sinjar. And Nasira, you will remain in contact with Spaz throughout the flight so he may adjust his approach according to circumstance. I will negotiate any disagreements between parties. You all have the numbers and group-messaging established. Start now.'

At her command, and inaudible to the wider world, six voices, with six accents, with six inflections, call to their tribesmen, their kinsmen, their allies, and their enemies, and speak with humility and directness to make possible what is impossible: *Assalamu'alaikum wa rahmatullahi wa barakatuh* … 'Peace and mercy and blessings of God be upon you. I call from the International Committee of the Red Cross and Red Crescent, and recall our obligations under both the laws of God and the laws of man …'

Märta and Tigger hear distant artillery fire as they follow Abu Saleh up the street, past their Land Cruiser, farther west half a kilometre, and down a rocky and ancient stone path with boulders rising high on either side, shielding them from view. Tigger points the Webley at Abu Saleh's back. He does not walk too close. Bullets can close the distance as needed.

'Is that necessary?' Märta asks him. 'We have an agreement.'

Tigger blows a characteristically French noise through his lips.

'How old is that gun, anyway?'

'It was used recently. I can smell it.'

They hear three consecutive and evenly timed bursts far off to the north, but close enough for the sound to carry and echo through the canyon.

'That's artillery fire,' Märta says.

'I heard helicopters, too. And some jets,' Tigger says.

'Herb didn't tell them about this place, right?' Märta asks.

'No. Of course, who is to say whether it might be on their list of targets anyway. Either way, a drive home is now impossible. I think Farrah is going to play it close to the chest as well. One trick she sometimes uses to confuse the government is to create a flight path that exceeds the actual destination so they don't know where we're going to set down. It is clever and has worked before.'

'The faster we get out of here, the better,' Märta says, walking behind Tigger, who follows their guide.

'I feel as though we are being watched. Do you feel that way?' Tigger says.

'I've been saying it for an hour.'

'It is too quiet here,' Tigger adds.

The path widens again. Into view comes the hidden entrance to a daunting fortress. There is a vehicle beside a steel door set into sandstone. There are no guards.

'Where are your friends?' Tigger asks Abu Saleh. 'Why's no one guarding the door?'

Abu Saleh says nothing. Once down the hill and at the fortress door, he bangs on it with his palm. The sound it makes is dead and empty. He announces himself, and no one responds. Eventually, he calls on his phone, and a man unlocks the door from the inside. Abu Saleh says something, and the two men disappear inside. Märta makes to follow, but Tigger holds his ground.

'Not coming?'

'Something is wrong.'

'They shot a man in front of us. We watched him die minutes ago. Our nerves are frayed. I can't read the situation. All I know is that if they wanted us dead, we'd be dead by now, and that little gun of yours wouldn't matter. I'm betting Abu Malik was convincing,' Märta says.

'That's not it. This whole event here is not playing out as I'd expect. I would have thought there'd be guards, and they'd take my gun, and they'd try to intimidate us until the moment they let us all go.'

'I'm happier like this,' Märta says.

'I prefer predictable to unpredictable,' Tigger says.

'I'm going in,' she says, and steps inside without him.

Tigger lowers his pistol to his side, having nothing to point at.

This is not the land in Provence. There, he knows all the sounds of the earth in each season: the hum of the insects in the lavender fields; the cicadas basking in the warmth of a summer day, and their startling and even comedic silence when the clouds pass overhead. He knows how, for the duration of a breath, all the sounds of all the creatures under the sun north of Vence will sing in unison as when a symphony stops warming up and strikes that first deliberate chord together to become the voice of God.

Not here, though. Here he is an alien. He does not know what it is supposed to sound like. He cannot measure the distance from the expected. He does not know the proper proportions of light to sound. But surely, even here, it is supposed to sound like *something*? Something must live. If it does, though, it does not breathe at all.

Tigger scans the mountains and hills and nearby boulders.

Alone, he exhales.

As he turns back toward the door to join Märta and the hostage-takers, he is only half surprised to find himself looking down the barrel of a rifle.

Charlotte pulls into the driveway of her family home. The door to their house has been drained of colour in the downpour, but it still manages to beckon. The brass knocker is shaped like a fish. As she turns the key, it occurs to her that the knocker is a cod. Strange not to have noticed this before.

Her mother is in the kitchen, preparing PG Tips with sugar and lemon.

'You're wet,' says Vanessa, who is dressed in grey slacks and a black-buttoned top, and is barefoot.

'It's on account of the rain,' Charlotte says, taking off her shoes and jacket, shaking out her shaggy hair, and immediately setting up the laptop.

'Are you really planning to put that on the coffee table first thing?' Vanessa asks.

'The congestion was awful. I don't understand why the rain is always a shock to drivers. We're scheduled to hear from Miguel any time.'

Charlotte launches the software and sees his name. It is marked not green, but yellow. He is away, but has sent a message: 'Must delay meeting. A helicopter has been deployed to collect your father. There have been complications on his journey. I will inform you when the helicopter lands. I will take you to the helipad to greet him. Stay close to the computer and send me your telephone number. They say we are not to use this software for emergency calls. I wonder if this is what they mean.'

Charlotte stares at the message.

'Tea?'

'No, thank you,' she says.

38

There is a pause between the instant Tigger sees the bore of the rifle
and the moment he overcomes his shock enough to speak. When
that moment does arrive — whether it was a second or a full cycle
of the moon, he cannot be certain — he is able to utter a few words:
'Please don't shoot. We have an agreement with your commander.'

The rifle is lowered, but only to Tigger's chest. It does not make
him feel safer, but it brings the rifle-holder's face into view. The man
has a scar along the left side of his face, from his eye down to his chin.

'Not my commander,' the man says, in an accent that is from
here but is not the accent of Abu Saleh.

It is a face with blue eyes, and not brown ones. It is a voice that
seems present and prepared for conversation. It occurs to Tigger
that, perhaps, he was not about to be shot a moment ago.

'Abu Saleh,' Tigger says, 'has commanded his people to allow
us access to our own and to take them away. He called ahead. You
should check.'

'Abu Saleh is inside? That is excellent news,' the man says. 'And
you have arranged transportation to get your people away?'

'I expect a helicopter. Soon, I hope.'

'You are here for Mr Arwood?'

'I beg your pardon?' Tigger says.

'Mr Arwood. You are here to save him?'

'Yes. Not only him, but yes. He is one of ours. How do you know
his name?'

The man lowers his rifle now and extends his hand. At first, Tigger thinks he may want to shake, but then he sees him wiggle his fingers, and Tigger understands he's to surrender the pistol he forgot he was holding. The man with the scar takes it and puts it into his own belt, alongside a military-issue Beretta 9mm that is as polished as the day it was made. 'You won't be needing that,' he says. 'You are no longer in any danger. You are under our protection now.'

There is something familiar about him. Not his voice or his countenance, per se, but his blue eyes; something about the shape of his face; the scar, too. Try as he might, though, Tigger cannot place him. On a whim, he asks, 'Have we met before?'

The man smiles and nods. 'Twenty-two years ago. I was a boy. We met in a minefield. Mr Arwood carried me to safety. You were there. I remember you. And so now we have two things in common.'

'I don't understand,' Tigger says.

'We have a common past. And we have Mr Arwood. You said he is one of yours. He is also one of ours.'

'I see. You are planning to rescue him?'

'We were. But I like your plan better. Now you will rescue him. And when you are done, and your people are safe, we — the Peshmerga — will stop walking before death, and allow death to lead the way.'

'We?'

The man taps his finger ring twice against his rifle. When he does, more than eighty men rise from hidden positions in the rocks, and stand silently at attention.

Tigger looks around him, less surprised than angry at himself for being so unobservant.

'Did you remove those guards? Near the café?'

'They have been removed from this life.'

'It is said,' Tigger answers, 'that the Kurds have no allies but the mountains.'

'This is true. But we do have friends. And we like to pay back our debts.'

'Where the hell have you been?' Märta says as Tigger finally catches up to her halfway across a wide-open space in the middle of the fortress. 'What were you doing out there?'

The explosions they had heard earlier are growing frequent. There is machine-gun fire from helicopters, and return fire from the ground. Jets pass overhead in formation, unaware of the drama being played out below their bellies.

'You know when you said you thought we were being watched?' Tigger whispers. 'Well, as it happens, you were right.'

'What does that mean?' Märta says as they walk toward another corner of the fortress.

Tigger is walking next to her. He becomes aware of his own sweat.

Two of Abu Saleh's men emerge from a tower in the north-east corner, across from the one they exited.

'Where are they going to land the helicopter?' Märta says. 'It's nothing but rock outside.'

'Right here,' Tigger says in a quiet voice. 'In this bailey.'

'In this what?'

'The castle courtyard. It's called a bailey. Sweden is a kingdom. Don't you know your castles?'

'It's not a very big place to land a helicopter.'

'We must hope Spaz's name is ironic.'

Abu Saleh turns and stops. He looks at Tigger and his empty hands.

'Where is my gun?'

'I suspect you'll see it again soon.'

'Why are we stopping?' Märta asks. Two more Iraqi jets pass overhead. They are F-16s.

Saleh does not answer, leaving them exposed in the fortress under a warming sun.

'It's going to be like Ramadi and Fallujah,' Märta whispers to Tigger as they stand in the courtyard watching the jets advance in formation toward a target somewhere beyond the wall that obstructs their view. 'The people are going to start streaming out of the cities again. We should be back there, preparing to receive them. This is all my fault.'

'Right now, we're doing this. Can you focus, please? Stop planning?'

'I can plan or I can scream,' she says. 'Why are we watching that door there?'

'That is where our people will soon emerge, or else men will come out to kill us.'

There are more explosions below.

Over the years, Märta has become a connoisseur of explosions. Car bombs. Suicide bombers with vests. RPGs being launched; RPGs landing. Hellfires hitting the ground. C4 blowing up markets. Scuds taking off; Scuds landing. Patriot missile batteries launching rockets; Patriot missiles missing their targets and landing somewhere else. It is hard to keep all the sounds straight, and perhaps useless, but the mind strives for order, and cannot help but seek patterns.

Once, at the base of the Zagros Mountains, she heard a strange and distant explosion. It was low and rolling. It lasted too long. It gained and lost intensity, like an arhythmic barrage of low-calibre mortars falling into a well, miles off.

'What is that?' she asked an old man who stood beside her, also listening.

'Thunder,' he said.

'Märta, look,' Tigger says.

A small figure emerges from the void of the open door at the base of the tower ahead. It is a girl in a shapeless orange dress that is

too big for her. She is very young—a teenager. She holds much of
the dress bunched at her waist, and pulls what remains behind her
through the sand and dust. She has the demeanour of one shivering
through rain.

Märta ignores the instructions from the terrorists, and runs to
the girl. She closes the distance quickly and wraps her arms around
the child, walking her back toward Tigger in a direction that feels
like an exit.

The girl is not safe, Märta knows, but she is no longer alone.

The girl, shaking, submits to the embrace of this new stranger.

Another figure emerges, limping, through the door. It is a young
man, short and clearly in pain. This time it is Tigger who runs
forward. He catches the boy and wraps his arms around him, kissing
the top of his head. He has been shot in the leg. He, too, is shaking.
Taking Jamal's face in his hands, Tigger sees he is dehydrated and
cold. Tigger can't tell how much blood he's lost.

'There's a helicopter coming,' Tigger says.

'Are you sure?'

'I'm rather counting on it.'

'What if it doesn't?'

'We'll find a nice hotel.'

'There are no hotels here.'

'I was pulling your leg.'

'Why would you pull my leg? I'm in terrible pain.'

Märta's phone rings. She answers it, freeing one hand from
around Adar's shoulders.

'Hello?' she says.

'It's me,' says Herb. 'We're inbound.'

'We have Jamal and the girl. I'm waiting on Arwood and Benton.'

'Where do you want us to land?'

'In the bailey.'

'What's a bailey?'

'It's the courtyard to the castle.'

'There's a castle?'

'You can't miss it.'

39

Herb sits in the copilot's chair of the EC155. There is a wall of instrumentation, buttons, and a joystick in front of him. He understands the altimeter, the rotor RPMs, the horizon ball, the clock, the fuel gauge. However, the only instrument he could control is the Maglite flashlight mounted on two rings to his right; the rest of the black panel is beyond him. He stares at it, though, because outside the window his helplessness is even deeper.

The flight path is 150 kilometres. Spaz has mapped a route over Simele and the northern stretch over the Mosul Dam lake. 'ISIL has no navy — yet,' the Russian says. 'But when they do, you remember you heard it here first, OK? The next war, it will be for that water. Assuming the dam doesn't break and kill everybody first. Mark my words. Everything I say comes true.'

'Maybe you shouldn't talk so much,' Herb says. And for the first time, he hears Spaz laugh. It is not comforting.

Herb turns to look for support from Elise in the back. She is not paying attention, and is instead immersed in a video game of Tetris.

Spaz changes direction to the south-west, taking them over the spot of the mortar attack and the remains of the Urals. They are avoiding the main roads with their mobile weapons and technicals, and circumnavigating Tal Afar, now being shelled by the military as the Sunni-aligned tribes attack the Shiite population.

How anything below coheres into a strategy is beyond him.

A call comes in that Herb answers. It is Märta. She has the Arab kids, she says. She gives him instructions on where to land.

Herb shouts to Spaz and Elise over the whirr of the blades. 'Apparently there's a castle. And we're to land in it.'

Spaz does not react, but Elise looks up and smiles. She points to her helmet and the headset system that transmitted the same call to her helmet, too. In a warm Spanish accent, she says, 'How's your stomach, Señor Macho Man?'

'Average. Why?'

'It is going to be a bumpy landing.'

'How do you know that?'

'If we are landing in a castle, we are landing in a box. The downward pressure of the air from the rotor cannot dissipate easily. So it will bounce off the walls and come back one way or another. It will be a tempest in a teapot.'

'I see.'

'Do you believe in God?'

'Yes, I do,' says Herb.

'I find that prayer helps,' she says.

'Really?'

'It gives me something else to think about, instead of throwing up. Focusses the mind.'

'Landed in many castles, have you?'

'Estates of drug lords. Physics are the same.'

'When this is over, I'm going to take a vacation.'

'You want some company?' Elise asks.

'I'm married with two kids.'

'Gets lonely out here among all the refugees and insurgents,' Elise says through the intercom.

'That's funny, because I feel like I can't get a minute to myself.'

Spaz interjects, 'Looks like the military has identified an arms depot. Down there. Look. They are bombarding them with mortars.

I'm taking us up to fifteen hundred metres. We will approach the mountains from the north.'

At a height of eight hundred metres, turning south, they fly into the shadow of the Sinjar Mountains. Rising to fifteen hundred metres, they align with their highest point. On approach, they meet the sun breaking over the castle walls, blinding them.

Herb's mobile phone is on, and he receives a text message. A moment later, both Spaz and Elise receive one as well. He and Elise look at one another.

Herb flips open the old Nokia. The signal, on the GSM system, has automatically switched over to MTN Syria, being the more powerful signal in their location. The message reads: *Ministry of Tourism welcomes you in Syria. Please call 137 for tourism information or complaints.*

'This place,' Herb mumbles.

'What?' Elise shouts.

'Nothing. How high can this thing go?' Herb asks through the headset.

'Two thousand metres,' Spaz says. 'That is the hover ceiling. But it depends on the barometric pressure.'

'That doesn't give us a lot of manoeuvring space if they don't respect the emblem, and things get hairy.'

Spaz and Elise both laugh at the same time.

'What's so funny?'

'If things get hairy,' Spaz says, 'we are going to die.'

'I'm glad we won the Cold War, you know that? You are a depressing, cynical, and mean-spirited group of people,' Herb says to Spaz.

'It's not over yet,' Spaz mumbles as they cross over the castle wall and look down into the bailey.

'How does it look?' Elise says from the back of the helicopter, putting away her video game and preparing her emergency kit.

'Busy,' says Spaz. 'I see three insurgents in the courtyard, a sharpshooter on one of the towers, maybe a machine gunner, and four of our people. But maybe many more inside. I think Jamal is wounded.'

Inside the tower, Arwood tries to pull Benton up, but is having little success. 'That's our ride outside. We can make it,' he says.

'I can't believe they got our message.'

'Please get up. I'm shot, too. I can't carry you.'

'I'm trying.'

'They're landing. It's a nice sound. I've hated the sound of rotors for a long time.'

'Me, too,' Benton says.

The doors to the antechamber and the outside are wide open. As the helicopter lands, the sheet metal slams repeatedly against the old stone walls.

'Come on, there's a war on the way,' Arwood says, 'and you don't want to be here for it.'

'You mean the military is coming?'

'Well … I think there's a lot of interest in this place right now.'

'Who did you write to?'

'I called in an old chip with the Peshmerga. We go way back.'

Arwood, his own leg also shot, uses his upper body to heave Benton to a semi-standing position. Together they have two good legs between them, and with cooperation they make that work for them.

'Why aren't you in as bad shape as me?' Benton asks as they hobble into the wind toward the courtyard. He can see a large black man, who must be Herb Reston. He is stepping down from the aircraft, wiping vomit from his shirt.

'I'm American,' Arwood says. 'We're upbeat by nature.'

'You're exhausting, is what you are.'

'All right, Ferris. Here we go.' And with that, Arwood walks them out, arms around one another, shoulder to shoulder.

Outside, three men stand around the helicopter. Abu Saleh, the one they call Larry, is holding his headscarf against the wind and is looking displeased. Benton does not look at Abu Saleh as they pass him, but Arwood does. With his arm still around Benton's waist, he jerks them both to a halt for a final word with his former captor and torturer.

'You're gonna lose,' Arwood taunts him. 'You know that, right? Maybe not today, maybe not tomorrow, but very soon and for the rest of your life. You know that, right?'

'No, we will prevail,' Abu Saleh says.

'No you won't. And I'll tell you why. Because groove is in the heart.'

A woman Arwood hasn't seen before hops out of the sliding back door of the aircraft, and helps Adar and Jamal inside. She has thick black hair and a great arse. It's a pity he's not planning to get on the chopper with her.

Benton waves half-heartedly to Märta and Tigger. Herb has lifted Jamal into his arms and is climbing into the helicopter with him. Tigger joins Benton and Arwood, immediately placing a pressure pad against Benton's leg, and raising him higher to further relieve the pressure. For such a skinny man, he is surprisingly strong.

'How did you convince them to let us go?' Benton yells to Tigger.

The fortress has never known wind of this kind. The people around Benton look blurred and shapeless through the fog of dust, unleashed and upended by the tumult from the rotors. It is as hard to see as to hear.

'Turns out they fear the devil,' Tigger yells above the wind. 'And, as it happens, Märta has his phone number.'

Tigger does not introduce Benton to Elise Garcia, and instead releases him into her care. She is small but steady, and sure on her feet. She smiles at him as her hands work expertly to strip off his trousers and reposition the pressure pad. She prepares an IV.

'Can I have some water?' he says, seated and grateful.

She opens a bottle and rubs his face wet before allowing him small sips. 'You are severely dehydrated. If you drink too fast, you'll vomit. The IV will help most.' She touches his forehead and says, 'You'll feel a little better in a moment.'

Out in the wind, Tigger braces to help Arwood over the steps into the cabin. But Arwood does not take his hand or step inside.

'Did you see them?' Arwood asks Tigger.

'Who?'

'Outside the walls. Did they come? Did you see them?' His eyes are pleading for an answer.

'Yes.'

'With the scar?'

'Yes.'

'He's close?'

'Yes. What's going to happen when we leave?'

'Thank Märta and Herb for me,' Arwood says. He does not shake Tigger's hand. He does not look at Herb, who is inside the helicopter, tending to the girl. He does not even meet Märta's gaze; she is trying to make sense of the conversation she can see but not hear.

Alone, he starts to limp across the courtyard to the first tower, which housed his first cell and leads beyond the walls to the Kurds.

As Arwood limps away, Tigger yells to him, 'You've lost your mind.'

'I said the girl was alive, and she was,' Arwood replies. 'I said we'd save the girl, and we did. I said everyone would be themselves at the moment of truth, and they were. I'm the sanest one here.'

'It's not the same girl, you know,' Tigger says, above the whirr of the blades.

Arwood Hobbes looks over his shoulder through the sandstorm

at Tigger. He can see the girl through the window of the helicopter. She is not looking at him.

'Oh yeah?' he yells. 'What's not the same about her?'

Tigger is the last inside, and he nods for Herb to close the sliding door of the EC155. He does, and climbs into the copilot's seat to strap himself in. Spaz looks at him, and Herb nods, to indicate they are as full up as they're going to be. Spaz looks back into the seating area, and watches the blood from the two injured men drip onto his floorboards.

Benton shouts, 'Wait a minute, wait a minute. Where's Arwood? We can't leave without Arwood.'

'He's not coming,' Tigger says, as Spaz increases the rotor speed, and they lift off the ground.

'If he's not coming, it means he's staying, and he's obviously not staying.'

'There are people outside the walls,' Tigger says. 'People waiting for him.'

'What people?' Märta asks, as the helicopter climbs to fifty metres, and then to seventy.

'Some kind of Kurdish assault force,' Tigger says. 'They took my gun. It's why I was late coming in. I thought it best to keep this to myself, given the company.'

Märta unhooks her seatbelt and rushes to the front between Spaz and Herb. She taps Spaz on the shoulder and yells, 'Take us south, past the tower and the walls over there. I want to see what's there.'

'North is safer. It's where we came from,' Spaz says. 'It is where we are going.'

'You can go north afterward. I want to see what's over those walls, and you're going to do it now,' she instructs. Her voice makes it clear this is not a request.

So Spaz, who has served under worse commanders, turns the

aircraft south, drifting over the castle walls to hover briefly over the rocky path that led to the door where Arwood and Benton and Jamal and Adar were first taken.

Still unable to see as well as she wants, Märta slips back into the body of the aircraft and slides open the window. She sticks her head out and looks down.

Standing, armed, are maybe one hundred men. There, before them all, is Arwood Hobbes and the man with the scar who smiled at her. She watches as the man hands Arwood a Beretta pistol, and Arwood caresses it and hugs the man, who hugs him back.

The helicopter is taking no one by surprise. It is clearly marked. Arwood, armed and with a new bandage on his leg, looks up and waves to Märta and the other passengers. Under the gaze of her disapproval, he motions the helicopter away and beyond harm as another man hands Arwood an M-16 assault rifle.

'We have to go, now,' Märta says. 'Spaz, signal to Louise that we've made the pickup and that we are officially on the way back. I don't want anything to implicate us in whatever happens next.

Quietly, seated and strapped in, she says, 'Shit.'

Spaz presses left on the cyclic, twists the throttle, and raises the collective to turn them northward as the Kurds take their position by the doors. The insurgents are still unaware of what is planned for them.

As they pass over the northern wall and out beyond the mountain into the vast flatland of Ninawa, two Mi-24 military gunships approach and, without pause, pass them by like dragons before a swallow, leaving the unarmed aircraft to continue on its scheduled route.

They fly with the sun out the starboard side and slightly behind them, and hear the first barrage of mortars land in the ancient fortress. They will be the last ones to see it; the last to have been held there. By tomorrow it will be a ruin.

Herb watches what he can, craning his neck through an open window. The last he sees is a dozen or more men emerging with Russian-made weapons and black headscarves from the bowels of the fortress. What he cannot see he can surmise, because military tactics are grounded in engineering. From their elevated position, the superior Kurdish force will weaken the terrorist defences with mortars and RPGs to upset the key strategic positions of ISIL fighters on the towers, who have sharpshooters and machine guns behind defensive positions. The battle mounts were not designed to withstand such firepower, and once the towers have been neutralised, the Kurds will swarm into the courtyard, where they will fight at close quarters to take up the tower positions and use them to lay down suppressing fire. A squad will remain at the entrance to ensure it can't be used as an exit. Having trapped their enemy, the Kurds will drop grenades into all the rooms their enemies are hiding in, and will work their way downward, forcing their quarry to ground—to be shot, burned, or hacked to pieces. They will take no prisoners and give no quarter. ISIL wants a world without mercy; they will not live in it for long.

Benton lies back on the soft upholstery of the aircraft. His head sinks into the forgiving cushion, and the cotton soothes his neck. Elise permits him to drink another quarter bottle of water. He tries to sip it slowly, but cannot. She places a cool compress on his head and smiles at him, and returns her attention to Jamal's leg.

Benton does not picture the battle or construct the events from the fading sounds behind them. He only imagines Arwood hunting down Abu Larry as he hunted down the colonel. He can see him raising the Beretta to the man's head, free and alone this time, to make the choice least likely to haunt him for the next twenty years. Benton wonders what Arwood might say as he trains the weapon on his enemy.

Perhaps, for the first time in his life, he will say nothing at all.

40

Adar watches the hands of Elise Garcia, which flow with the expertise and confidence of the baker from her village.

She sits behind Spaz and Herb. Adar does not wear a headset, and cannot hear Tigger and Märta's conversation. She rests, unattended to, by the sliding door on a stool secured to the airframe by heavy steel bolts — a place for a doctor or second medic to perch on and work from.

She has never been in the air before. She has never been a bird, or seen the world from above. Through the massive windows, she can see more of the world than she has ever known.

The helicopter flies north-east, and she looks north-west, toward Syria, where she used to live. In school, they showed her maps of the border. She looks for it: for the straight and wide purple line that cuts through the mountains, hills, and desert, turning the one land into two places. It is not there. She cannot see countries or colours or tribes, or families, or even cities. She can only see a vast and empty expanse of browns and the glowing sand of the desert that is hungry for more blood. There are white-capped mountains in the far distance, and small explosions across the wasteland that prove man is below and that he is angry.

It looked so different when she walked from her village toward Domiz. She had left with her mother, her older brother, and two cousins — both girls a little younger than her. Her brother wanted to stay and fight. He did not know who to fight with or even for, he

said. He only knew what to fight against. 'Then you've already lost,'
her mother said, and she would have no more of it, and she forced
him to pack his belongings, and instructed him to protect the family.
'The family is most important,' she'd told him. 'More than Syria,
more than the tribe.' He brought an old military knife with a handle
wrapped in leather. The knife smelled bad. It had grown mouldy.

The man who marched them to Iraq took all their money before
leaving. He did not even look into their eyes. He collected it and
shoved it into a bag with a large zipper. He took their passports, if
anyone had a passport. Adar did not. He walked them for kilometre
after kilometre. Babies were terrified and unable to sleep, because
their schedules were interrupted and there were no comfortable
positions to rest in. They were passed from tired arms to rested ones,
agitating them more. Eventually, they passed out from exhaustion.

They did not travel alone. There were other families. Some were
going north to Turkey—they would risk boats to Europe. Others
were going east to Iraq or Jordan. Some dreamed of Iran, but they
were Persian and spoke a foreign language. No one knew if they
would be welcome there.

Rumours formed and spread. They were going in the wrong
direction; the leader was a member of the government, and they
were going to be arrested or murdered; the children were going to be
stolen from the parents, and their livers cut out and sold to the rich
in the Emirates, and their bodies thrown into ditches in the desert.
Information and freedom of choice were their only possessions, and
to imagine not having either was to submit to powerlessness.

They walked for ten hours straight. Some didn't make it. No one
stopped for them. They had paid first. Down below, she could see
the river they were crossing by way of a narrow bridge when, nearby,
her brother was shot—by whom, or why, no one knew. Her mother
screamed and jumped into the water after him, and the people tried
to hurry away from the shooting, but there was no way to hurry

on such a narrow bridge, and so people fell into the water. Many could not swim. 'Run,' her mother instructed her from the river. And because the people pushed her with the force of water through a dam, she was lifted and taken to the other side.

There, down there — though the land all looks the same, and yet is called a thousand different names — was where the trucks were parked. Trucks had come to meet them, and they carried supplies. Those army trucks were travelling on a road while her people were crossing the dirt. There were fewer of them now, many wet and many weeping.

She waited for her mother and brother, but they did not come. She lost sight of her cousins. She was the eldest, and it was her job to care for them. The vehicles stopped, and people in white vests with foreign symbols on them ordered them into lines so they could receive food and water at the front. Where were her cousins? The little girls were gone, and it was all her fault. She was supposed to look out for them. They were so young, so helpless — only ten and twelve years old. She would find them at Domiz. That was what people said. The camp was safe. The camp was where everyone found each other. No one who said this had ever been there.

They had to be behind her. She had to wait for them. They would have to come this way.

She waited, thinking of the little girls and missing her mother. She did not know if her mother could swim. Can any mother swim? Where would she have learned to swim? There were no rivers in her village. The line moved on without her. She forgot to look ahead and close the gap.

Men in black outfits were carrying a tube across the desert. She did not know who they were, or what the tube was for. They were not dressed like the people giving food.

There was an explosion. She fell. When she lifted her head, she saw men killing people, shooting them as they sat on the sand. Many prayed. She did not. She hid inside a big truck, inside a big box, and curled into a ball smaller than a beetle.

Adar was alone. For one day, for two days, for three days, she was alone. The box had food of a type she had never seen before. It smelled awful. No one had cooked it recently. How could it still be edible? There were cups of water. She drank and slept.

And then a man found her — a man with kind eyes and clean hands.

And now she looks at the people in the helicopter. Who are they? She can only understand Jamal. His accent is foreign, and he uses words she doesn't know. He is like so many of the boys she knew in school. They are a little shy, but when they start talking, their bodies become full of stars, and they cannot contain the universes inside them. They must talk or risk exploding.

Outside, below, is her family — her mother, her brother, her two little cousins. She knows they are dead. They are in heaven, waiting there for her. Why should she remain here alone?

Below there are more explosions, as people she cannot see kill other people she cannot see.

This is not the real life, the Koran teaches. The real life is eternal. Maybe it is time for the false and lonely life to end, and for the true and eternal life with her family to begin. Maybe it is time to go.

Adar presses down on the handle of the aircraft's sliding door and pulls it.

A hand is placed gently on her shoulder. It is the large black man. She has never been touched by an African before. His hand is large, warm, and soft. Maybe it is warmer than other hands. He is smiling at her, and holding something. He hands it to her. It is a piece of chocolate.

The return trip is short. Märta and Tigger assist Elise in whatever she needs. Neither has any medical training beyond advanced first aid, but they are helpful in holding things, handing things, and passing stuff around as instructed by the medic.

The helicopter touches down as gently as rainfall. Around them, Domiz is no longer the quiet camp Benton first saw. It has become transformed, and now pulses with new life and new injured. People are streaming in to escape the combat, hoping the UN will keep them safe. An emergency surgical team is on the ground. They open the sliding door, take instructions from Elise Garcia, and remove Benton and Jamal.

Adar is taken in hand by a nurse, who speaks soothingly to her in Arabic. Benton watches her go. He is grateful she does not look back.

As Herb, Tigger, and Märta collect their personal effects, Spaz turns to them from the cockpit and says, 'Watch yourselves.'

'What do you mean?' Tigger asks.

'Louise. She will not be pleased to know what happened. ISIL only cuts off your head. But Louise—' and he makes a snipping motion with his fingers near his zipper.

'We didn't do anything wrong,' Märta says.

'I see,' Spaz says. 'So it is a coincidence that secret ISIL base is located and destroyed in pincer movement between government air force and Kurdish infantry, only moments after hostages are taken away in humanitarian aircraft?'

'Yes,' Tigger says.

'So,' Spaz says. 'Same like Russia.'

'I'm going to call my wife and let her know I'm all right,' Herb says, walking in the direction of the IRSG head office. 'I'll find you all later.'

'I'm coming with you,' Tigger says, as Märta walks off in another direction, toward the medical unit.

It is midday, and the sun is burning. Tigger and Herb walk in silence, side by side, past the UNHCR refugee tents, the giant water tanks, and the families gathered outside and under makeshift shade canopies.

There is a cafeteria used only by international staff, and Tigger asks Herb whether he can buy him a drink before they each call home.

'Sure,' Herb says.

They buy beers from a cold box and sit under the awning together. When they first arrived, the bar had no name. Märta called it Wonderland. Herb and Tigger followed suit, and later all the young people picked it up, which made it official.

There are few people there. Everyone else has a job.

'Your wife,' Tigger says, opening the beers and pushing one over to Herb. 'Does she know that you were in any danger?'

'I wasn't in danger — you were in danger. You and Märta took point.'

'You flew in an unarmed helicopter across a war zone, landed in a terrorist base, and carried wounded survivors to safety under armed elements of ISIL. Believe me, you were in danger.'

'I did something stupid, and I need to tell you about it.'

'Keep it to yourself,' Tigger says.

'I was worried about you two.'

'Keep it to yourself.'

'I sent someone to follow you, in case you disappeared. So there would be a fighting chance, in case they captured you—'

'Leave it be, my brother.'

'I committed the very sin I accused Märta of doing with Jamal.'

Tigger lays a hand on Herb's own. He pats it several times. 'You do not have to confess it to me. We are doing the best we can for each other in a world that is doing its worst.'

'I'm ashamed of myself,' Herb says.

Tigger raises his beer. 'To the best we can do.'

Herbert raises his beer bottle, too. 'Amen,' he says.

The surgical tent has six beds. Benton lies in one, hooked up to an IV. His clothes have been removed and discarded. He said that he didn't want to see them again.

'But not the shoes,' he said. 'Leave those right here.'

By early afternoon, the wounds on either side of his leg have been cleaned, stitched, and dressed. He is informed he's been fortunate, in that the wound has not become infected and, while he will likely suffer chronic pain and will need physical therapy back in England, he will be able to walk again if he follows the rehab regime properly.

'I'm a lucky man,' Benton tells the doctor.

The doctor is an Indian, from a town in Gujarat that Benton doesn't know.

'You are not lucky — you were shot. You're joking, right?' the doctor says.

'I'm honestly not sure.'

Benton sleeps. When he wakes, it is dusk. Märta is sitting beside him, reading a book. When she sees his eyes, she puts the book away.

'How are you?' she asks.

'I'm OK. How are the kids?'

'Jamal's mother and father came to collect him. She slapped him, hugged him so hard he couldn't breathe, and then slapped him again. His father started to cry. And when he saw that, Jamal started to cry. And then Herb started to tear up, which Tigger wouldn't allow to go unmentioned later. So, as expected there, I suppose.

'Jamal will be OK,' she continues. 'The bullet passed farther away from the bone than it did for you. He's in his early twenties. He'll recover. Apparently our administrative staff is now questioning whether he's covered for long-term medical care through our insurance policy.'

'What are you going to do?' Benton says.

'I'm going to tell Herb, obviously. I think it'll sort itself out quite nicely and quickly under the threat of an editorial to the *New York*

Times and a call to the mothers of every member of the board of directors.'

'And Adar?'

'In the short term, I'm going to let her stay with me for a little while. I don't usually cross that line, but this is a special case. The world media will be interested in her survival, given how much coverage they gave the original attack. It could turn her into an international celebrity, which would be uncomfortable, to say the least. The ICRC has excellent staff working on family reunification, so we'll start there. She must have people somewhere. We know her name and her village, so we'll put it together. But it's not certain she can go back. Or should.'

'My suggestion,' Benton says, propping himself up a little higher in bed, and then thinking better of it, and scooting back down, 'is don't tell anyone. There's more to the story than everyone knows, and it might affect her.'

'How do you mean?'

'My shoe. Give it to me — the left one.'

Märta hands him the boot, which she holds as though it were a rat. Benton digs out the sole and removes the SDHC chip. 'I took this from a video camera I found at the site of the mortar attack in the desert.'

'What's on it?'

'Proof that ISIL did it, and not the Kurds.'

'Which is good to know, but hardly surprising.'

'Well, yeah. But that's not what's interesting, is it? It proves they have a strategy for psychological warfare and public diplomacy. It proves they have the technical skills to stage, carry out, video, edit, and disseminate complex messages that can mislead the entire international news profession. It proves that their capacity for deception exceeds our ability to detect it. We can't simply stare at things anymore. We have to get to what they mean.'

'I don't work in intelligence, Benton. This doesn't affect us.'

'No, it does. It really does. If we come out with the facts, and ISIL finds out Adar survived, she could easily become a symbol of survival. They won't want a living symbol of resistance to their cause. They'll hunt her down. I feel like this girl's life is constantly in my hands and I don't know how to save her.'

'How long did the doctors say you need to remain in bed?'

'There's a flight the day after tomorrow. Farrah called the airline to say I need a wheelchair and assistance. I'm going to board that plane.'

'And that will be that,' she says.

'How do you feel?'

Märta isn't interested in explaining how she feels. She's done enough today. 'I think it's a wonderful and rare opportunity to learn that two people can still care for one another through it all. To learn that affection can linger,' she says. 'However, I feel that you belong back in Cornwall with your wife and daughter. Don't you?'

'I guess I do.'

'Here's what we're going to do. We're going to say, "Let's stay in touch," and leave it at that. I didn't know it when I was younger, but it turns out you can do that. I think we might even owe it to ourselves.'

'That sounds very nice,' Benton says. 'Let's do that.'

Märta then bends over and kisses him, long and gently on his unparted lips, before standing to leave.

'Märta?'

'What?'

'Thank you for saving my life.'

Benton sleeps as much as he can after Märta leaves. He does not sleep well. The drugs succeed in dulling the pain, but not in clearing his mind. The blessing, though, is that he is no longer thirsty. There is a cup beside him, always full. He often places his fingertips into the water to be sure it is really there.

When he does sleep, he does not suffer nightmares. He does not dream of the mattress soaked in his own blood, or of the light coming through the black hood. He does not dream of Abu Saleh's face — so that was his name — or his voice, or the gun that shot him.

What he does dream about is the other girl in green — the girl from 1991 who crouched with him by the truck as Samawah was assaulted. In these dreams, he talks to her, and she talks back to him. They sit together by the giant tyre, and chat as though she were a niece or the school-age daughter of an old friend unseen since a baby.

He asks her about school, and she shrugs in the way fifteen-year-old girls do.

'What subject do you like best?' he asks as the bombs fall around them, the shots resound, and the buildings burn.

'I'm good at maths,' she says. He is glad to hear her place the *s* properly at the end of the word — proof the British were there first.

'You like solving riddles?'

'I like it when there's a right answer and I can find it,' she says, drawing a picture in the dirt with a small stick. She isn't much for eye contact. She's shy.

'I like that, too,' Benton says to her. 'But I'm not so good at maths. I'm not so good at finding answers.'

'What are you good at?' she asks, not looking up.

'I'm better at finding the right questions,' he says. 'Are you in high school?'

She nods. She's a freshman. She started this year.

'Do you have a best friend?' he asks.

'Namira.'

'What do you like about her?'

'She's funny. She always makes everyone laugh. She's good at maths, too. She says she wants to be an astronaut when she grows up.'

'That sounds exciting,' Benton says. 'Do you want that, too?'

'No. I don't know what I want to be yet.'

'That's OK. There's a big world out there,' he says, as a tank shell explodes into the hospital, and a wall of black smoke approaches them.

'Can I be anything I want?' she says, looking up for the first time.

'No,' Benton says, as the sky grows thick with smoke. 'No, you can't.'

When he's awake, he watches television. He has no focus for reading. The pulsing in his leg and his head dissuade him from trying. The TV hangs in the corner of the tent. It is tuned to Al Jazeera, which is occasionally in English. What he watches is the war that is still not called a war.

The Iraqis have attacked, and continue to attack, ISIL positions in and around highly populated areas. They hide there, thinking they can use the population as human shields. Sometimes they are right. Usually they are not. The news says ISIL claims to speak for the Sunnis, and they want to establish a caliphate state in al-Anbar. They assassinate and murder the Shiites, some of whom have taken to changing their family names so they can better blend into Sunni society, and hide there, or at least signal their surrender. Other Sunnis are offended by the beheadings and the killings, and the arbitrary exercise of punishment that is claimed to be sharia law. It is a position these people can only maintain by willfully ignoring 1,400 years of Islamic scholarship, early interpretation, and legal rulings. And so that is what they do.

Benton watches a report about an attack in the northern city of Mosul. A suicide bomber has blown himself up in a market. The Iraqi Red Crescent was the first to arrive. It was a motorcycle medic, because they can navigate the crowds and debris. Once a critical mass of rescuers appeared around him — a hirsute man with delicate hands — an ambulance arrived packed with explosives. It detonated, killing the emergency rescuers and those who tried to help. There is footage of a mangled motorcycle, with its front wheel spinning in maudlin fashion. Later, after the dead were washed, the mourners were followed to the funerals, where they were met with another bomb.

Benton turns off the television when there is a knock at the door. 'Yes?'

A nurse opens it. 'Are you awake?'

'Yes.'

'You have a phone call.'

'Who is it?'

'Your daughter. She is insistent.'

'Yes. I'll take it, thank you.'

The nurse is Portuguese. She is reserved, and does not talk much. Benton suspects she has been here a long time. He takes the mobile phone from her.

'Charlotte.'

He has anticipated a long lecture and is braced for it, because he deserves it. Her voice, however, is not accusatory. She does not speak quickly.

'I've been trying to speak to you for so long,' she says, 'that I've forgotten what I wanted to say.'

'That's OK.'

'I was told you were shot.'

'In the leg. They say I'll make a full recovery.'

'And you have a broken nose, and severe dehydration, and bruising on your ribs, and abrasions on your knees—'

'I'll make a full recovery, and they are being very nice to me.'

'And yet,' she says, 'there's the story of how you got that way.'

'Yes, there is.'

'Mum's been staying with Vivian Bray.'

'Where are you now?'

'I told Mum it's time she moved back home. She says the choice isn't hers.'

'I'll talk to her. You're right.'

'What are you doing there, Dad? How could you have run off like that, when we're falling apart here?'

'I've been asked that many times by many people in the last few days. All I can say for now is that I feel as though I've passed out of a tunnel that I've been walking through for over twenty years, and while there's no bright light at the end, there is fresh air. And stars above.'

'I wish I knew what that means,' Charlotte says.

'What it means in effect is that I very much want to talk to you, too. Is that enough for now?'

'We'll meet you at the airport. I'm told you'll be home in two days.'

'I'll email the details. And Charlotte? Can you pass a message on to your mother, please?'

'OK.'

'Tell her that what I said over breakfast that day, it wasn't true.'

41

Thomas Benton married Vanessa when he was twenty-seven. She was twenty-five. It didn't seem young at the time. It started with a near run-in between her, in her late father's sports car, and him and his brother, Edgar, out for a ride in their new, co-owned 1973 MGB Mark III. It was 1978. They'd just bought the car from a friend of a friend of someone their father knew by chance in Launceston, in east Cornwall. They'd paid too much money for it, and they didn't care. They were splitting the cost, and each would have paid double for his share. The car was in British racing green, with beige leather. The chrome glistened. The exhaust note could have recited Yeats.

Edgar was older by three years. He couldn't drive on account of his gammy left leg. He had climbed a tree on holiday when he was nine and had fallen off it. The village doctor was incompetent, and had set the leg badly. It never healed properly, and, from then on, Edgar had chronic pain. He walked with a limp and was unable to work a clutch, but he could still feel the wind in his hair. Thomas drove; Edgar navigated, often too late. They weaved about the roads like madmen. The idea was to drive home south through Bodmin Moor and breathe fresh air, see the green countryside, and have a pint.

The early autumn of 1978 was mild. For years, Vanessa had had the idea of driving her late father's beloved Jensen Interceptor westwards, through the moor out to Penzance and then back to Exeter, where she'd grown up. Her dad had died eight years earlier, in 1970, when a hammer had fallen from a shelf and struck him at the base of his skull. It was a meaningless death that meant everything.

Year by year, the car rested under a tarp in the garage, where she would sit with a torch to read and try to remember what he smelled like.

Eventually, she and the car fitted one another, and she had the money to have it repaired, if not properly restored. The garage that towed it in was run by Phil Goddard. He was in his fifties then. The car needed a new battery, of course, but a near decade of inactivity had rotted most of what was rubber, and it needed work. A drive like the one she proposed was a good eight hundred kilometres if she took the most direct route—which she didn't plan to do, as that route was charmless.

Vanessa paid a crushing bill, donned her father's leather jacket, which she cinched at the waist, rolled down the windows, and fired up the distinctive V8.

It was to be an overnight trip. She carried an Italian leather duffel filled with clean clothes, a camera, two new paperbacks—one called *The Thorn Birds*, and the other *The Shining*—and a toothbrush.

She had driven through Dartmoor from Exeter, and decided on an indirect route that would skirt the scenic southern road on Bodmin Moor. She was looking forward to it, as that road was loved by bikers and drivers, who weaved and bobbed gently through its meandering turns trimmed by hedges and modest homes. People in other impractical cars waved to her, and she waved back. It was a road of flowers, and fences, and the occasional reminder to go SLOW, painted in tall, white letters on the road. Everything promised to be green and blue. But she never made it to the road.

As she travelled west into Upton Cross where the moor began, Thomas and Edgar were travelling south, planning to make the same turn. At that moment, Edgar was trying to prove—by way of demonstration — that Benton's aural cavity was precisely the same diameter as a steaming chip he had left over from lunch. Benton was complicating Edgar's proof by swiping wildly, which caused the car to swerve as they approached the intersection.

On reaching the primary school on the corner, it looked to Vanessa as though the driver of the green convertible was being terrorised by a swarm of hornets, and the other man was trying to pluck them out of the air, one by one. Watching these men, these gestures, this car — all of this was distracting. In that distraction, she failed to brake hard enough before the turn, and entered it with too much speed. She froze, and drove directly into a red public telephone box.

The impact was modest, breaking only a panel of glass on the phone box, ruining the grille of the car, and puncturing her front wheel. But it gave her a serious fright.

Vanessa was therefore in a very fragile state of mind when she turned to find the green MGB pulled up beside her, along with the two men who had caused her accident. The first thing she asked Thomas Benton was not the first thing she had expected to say.

'What's that in your ear?'

'It's a chip.'

'Why?'

'To see if it would fit.'

'Are you going to leave it there?' she asked him.

It was Edgar, though, who replied. 'I think it's an improvement, don't you?'

'Are you all right?' Benton had the wherewithal to ask, ignoring Edgar, and making his brother immediately wish he'd asked the same.

They bought her lunch, and called a garage to tow the Jensen, which — after they were married — they would keep for over a decade before relenting and buying a practical car. Edgar, who passed away in 2011 from colon cancer, never failed to remind his brother that Vanessa was a gift, and to not cherish her was to mock every decent man who would never have such an opportunity. Thomas knew that Edgar meant himself. With his leg and his feelings about it, he never managed to marry. He also never stopped loving Vanessa.

Vanessa and Charlotte collect Benton at the airport, and board the train that runs to Fowey every ninety minutes. The trip takes five hours, and Benton and his two women are silent most of the way. They talk of small matters. Charlotte keeps glancing at his leg.

When they arrive in Fowey, it is raining, in a persistent and steady drizzle. The school year has started. The kids don't mind the weather, having been raised in it.

You can drink it from the sky here, Benton thinks.

The house is empty and dark when they arrive. It is as he'd left it. Vanessa has been staying at her girlfriend's house down the road. He suggests to Charlotte they not come in immediately — he can see them later. Charlotte says she won't return to Bristol until they've talked. And she is going to stay with him. He can keep his preferences to himself.

He puts on music when they come home: *Well-Tempered Clavier* by Bach, played by a Korean woman named HyeKyung Lee. Hers is smoother, rounder, more affecting than Glenn Gould's, and more soulful than Daniel Barenboim's. There are others on the shelf — Maurizio Pollini and Sviatoslav Richter — but he hasn't listened to those. Vanessa went through a period a few years ago of buying numerous performances of the same pieces of music to try to understand better the relationship between composer, arranger, and interpreter. He never understood the theory. He only knew what he liked.

He bathes, with the music playing from the other room. He drinks a beer, and sits there until the water becomes cold.

The next morning is bright, and forecast to be clear. Benton and Charlotte eat in near silence. After breakfast, he puts the SDHC chip into his computer and watches the video from Iraq. Convinced by the quality, he copies the chip to his hard drive, compresses the footage, uploads it to a shared site for large files that the *Times* uses, and calls his editor.

'I'm back,' Benton says.

'Productive trip, I'm sure.'

'As it happens, I found out what happened at that mortar attack everyone's been going on about. The Kurds didn't do it. I have raw footage of ISIL setting the mortar. And this should matter, because if the Kurds, difficult though they are, don't have political support in the West, there will be no opposition against ISIL gains.'

'You have this in your possession?'

'I sent it before calling.'

'How?'

'I took it from the camera the terrorists abandoned at the site after taking the film and killing everyone. Clearly, before they sent it to the international media, they edited the version everyone is now watching, and we all took it as proof positive, because no one gives a damn anymore, as they'd rather be fast and wrong than slow and right. And at the risk of overstating the matter, it's because business depends on speed, and mere democracy depends on validity.'

'I take your point, but democracy doesn't pay the bills around here. And what about the girl? She's the story. What happened to her?'

'The girl?'

'In the green dress, Thomas. She's the human interest in the story. Surely you know that. If she's alive, there'll be a prize in it for you.'

'The girl is dead.'

By mid-afternoon, the sky has darkened, and the colours of the day have already shown their best. It offers a chance to wallow and withdraw, but Benton feels, for a change, he'll have none of it. He still isn't ready for the conversation, though. So he puts on his shoes, his parka, and his hat, puts his crutches under his arms, and takes a very small folding stool with him. Prepared, he goes out to face it all.

'Where are you going, Dad?' Charlotte asks.

'For a hobble. I'll be back soon.'

'We haven't spoken a word.'

'It's part of the process. It's going better than it looks.'

He takes a cab to Squires Field on Park Road, only a short ride up the hill. The driver lets him out, and Benton crosses the road north to where a few stout-hearted parents watch their boys playing football in the English rain on a plush pitch. The boys are fit and young and focussed. Their energy is boundless.

A man he's known for years, Albert Crowley, recognises him and comes over to shake his hand.

'Don't get up, for heaven's sake, man. What happened to you?'

'Bad luck.'

'That's the leading cause of death, I hear. Going to heal?'

'Better than most things.'

'They said it would be sunny today. It occurred to me recently that they get paid either way. I would say you made a mistake with all the war stuff. Weather was the smart money.'

'I rather like this weather.'

'You know the players?' Albert asks about the footballers.

'No. I wanted to watch the future of the Commonwealth run around a bit.'

'It's dire, isn't it? Little fuckers. Be getting drunk and ripping up bus stops before you know it.'

'I've seen worse.'

'We're going to get a pint when the clock runs down. Come along?'

'Safe Harbour?'

'Is there somewhere else?'

'Lester working today?'

'Hasn't missed a day since '78.'

'I'll meet you there.'

Benton watches the game for an hour before making his way by cab to the pub. Albert, with family obligations, hasn't arrived yet, so Benton seats himself at the bar. Lester places a coaster with a pint on top of it.

'Haven't seen you in a week,' Lester says. 'Staying in London these days?'

'No. An overseas assignment. Over now. Don't think I'll be going away for a while.'

'What happened to the leg?'

'Nothing permanent, I'm told.'

'Interesting job?'

'A little too interesting. Ask me again sometime.'

'Eat something?' Lester says.

'Not for now. Switch to the news for me?' Benton asks. 'These reality TV shows are unbearable.'

'So, Benton,' Lester says, leaning over the bar a bit. 'I don't want to step in anything, but Vanessa was in here looking for you a few days ago. Now that I know you were travelling, I'm a little surprised she didn't know. So ... how are you? Anything you want to talk about?'

'On second thought, bring me a prawn sandwich. And turn up the volume. I'm old.'

Benton checks the time. It is past 5.00 p.m., and so 7.00 p.m. in Dohuk. Märta is probably still at the office. She'll be busy as the camp swells. He could call them. Tigger and Herb and Märta can be right here in the pub with him if he presses the right combination of numbers on the phone that he can so easily dial with his fingers.

Still nothing from Arwood.

The trail is not completely cold, if he wants to follow it. The note he sent to Märta was also sent to Arwood's Kurdish friends, and Märta will have that number on her phone, too, having been copied into the message. He could ask her for it. Place the call. Maybe it would ring. Maybe the person on the other end speaks English, and survived the assault on the fortress. He may know what happened to Arwood: whether he survived, where he is now, where he's going next.

For now, though, Benton does not call Märta for the number. As Arwood correctly said, Benton is not hard to find. If he's alive and wants to contact him, he will. If he's dead, Benton would rather not know. It is better for now to believe he is alive, and simply obscured from view by the dirt and debris kicked up by all the mortars.

Benton takes a long pull on his beer, and dials the only number important to him right now. It is answered quickly.

He tells his wife that he is at the pub drying off — if not drying out. He was watching the local boys play some ball at Squires Field. It was somehow uplifting. He's ordered a sandwich. There is a long pause that Vanessa does not fill. Finally, he says, 'Would you like to come join me?'

'Do you want me to?'

'Very much.'

And then Vanessa starts to cry, and he tells her not to because there is no need to cry, and that he has been away but now he is back and will stay. And while he knew it all along, he appreciates even more how lucky they both are. Everything else seems childish or trite at this point.

She sniffles once, and suggests he finish his lunch and come back to the house. She's going to move back in. He needs the help.

He suggests that all of them rent *Ferris Bueller's Day Off* tonight. He doesn't say why. She laughs, thinking he's joking. He insists he's not. 'I need a laugh. And there are things I need to tell you both about the past.'

Benton watches the news, and drinks the remainder of his beer before ordering another. He had promised the Syrian with the footballer son that he would raise a toast to his dead wife and daughter. But it is too soon to fulfil that obligation. To rush would be to unburden himself of the promise, rather than to respect it. He will hold that for a moment when he is not alone. When he has friends near him. When he can find the courage to make death less of a private matter, and speak about it with the confidence of voice it requires. When he can find his inner Arwood Hobbes.

The sandwich comes. Benton places the napkin on his lap, and Lester glances at the TV, where a news presenter is showing the latest footage from Iraq about the mortar attack that happened a bit over a week ago. It shows men in black headscarves running from the launch point after the smoke clears. The commentators have opinions to share. They are the opposite opinions to the ones they voiced a week ago. This goes unmentioned.

'Here you go,' Lester says, putting the napkin and cutlery beside the sandwich. 'Front-row seats to the world's events.' He looks up at the TV on account of Benton's interest. 'The things going on out there — Shiites, Sunnis, all these ancient hatreds just playing themselves out, day after day. Good thing we're not there anymore, I can tell you. I wouldn't want our boys over in the middle of all that. What are you gonna do, right? It's all a damn shame, is what it is. A damn shame. Don't you think?'

'Yes, it is,' Benton says. 'It's a damn shame.'

ACKNOWLEDGEMENTS

My thanks to my agent, Rebecca Carter, at Janklow & Nesbit, for reading numerous versions of this manuscript and providing essential insight; to my wife, Camilla Waszink, who was my first reader, my second reader, and my third reader (...); to my friends in the International Red Cross and Red Crescent Movement and also at the United Nations; Mat Zeller at No One Left Behind (nooneleft.org) for his thoughts and figures on those national staff and translators and allies we in fact did leave behind; singer and songwriter Mike Doughty for saying I could use his song title 'Into the Un' as a possible title for this book, which I then didn't; to PJ Mark, Henry Rosenbloom, Angus Cargill, Lauren Wein, and all the unsung heroes with Janklow & Nesbit and with my publishers who helped turn a pile of loosely affiliated words into something called a 'book'.

This story drew heavily from my own PhD dissertation (2004), which became the book *Media Pressure on Foreign Policy: the evolving theoretical framework* (2007), in which I studied the Iraqi civil war of 1991 in depth. I was haunted by many of the stories I read, and I knew that, somehow, I needed to return to the subject matter through fiction in order to explore and share other truths.

Field-level history about Operation Provide Comfort drew facts, anecdotes, and timelines from Dr Gordon Rudd's excellent 1993 unpublished PhD dissertation from Duke University, accessed through UMI.

371

The setting of Checkpoint Zulu near Samawah was suggested by a 31 March 1991 article in *The Washington Post* written by Nora Boustany, called 'U.S. Troops Witness Iraqi Attack on Town in Horror, Frustration.'

The first draft of this book was completed on 30 January 2014 — before ISIL rose to international prominence; before the Yezidi were massacred on Mount Sinjar; before the Kurds fully joined the fight and became backed by the West ... sort of. This book, therefore, did not rush to press chasing headlines: it preceded them. In retrospect, my primary flaw of analysis was failing to anticipate just how bad it would all become.

The proof discussed by the Syrian father on the football pitch refers to photos from the Syrian defector called Caesar. I have changed the chronology slightly to allow for this conversation.

The working title of this book was 'Welcome to Checkpoint Zulu' because, in a way, we are all at Checkpoint Zulu now.

The phrase 'It's a Big Old Goofy World' was taken from John Prine's song of the same name (1991).

And, yes, the frozen-chicken thing really happened.